mbetoom Point

r-Yaas Pyramid

ungu's Village

of the
Lesser Pimbas

ort Beach

ttle Lyme Bay

10day journey.

MOUNT BAWWAAR-YAAS PYRAMID
a. summit b. meathole.

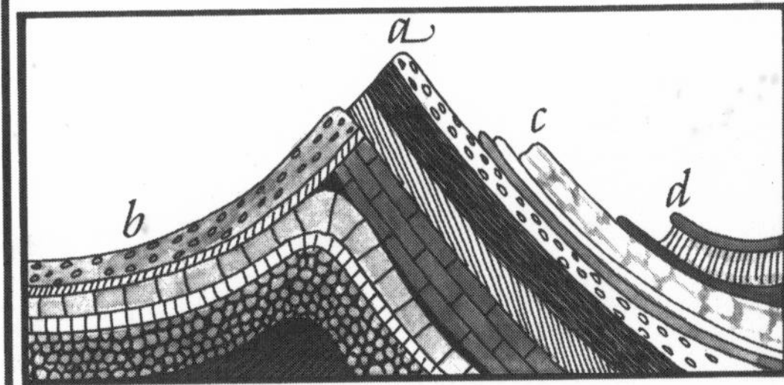

Stratification of Mount Bawwaar-Yaas.

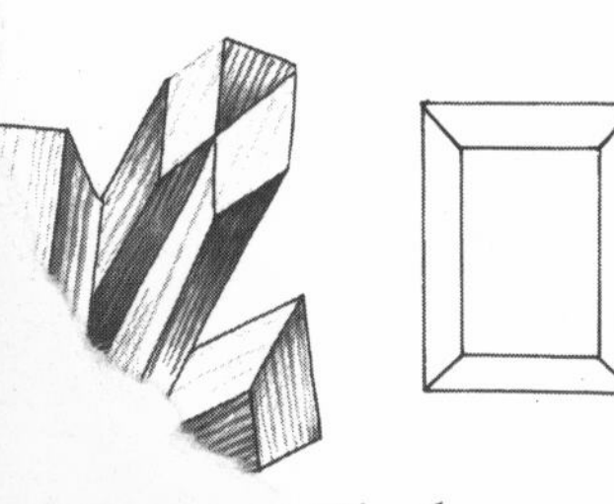

Fig 6

Fi

A
CANNIBAL
IN
MANHATTAN

BY TAMA JANOWITZ

American Dad

Slaves of New York

TAMA JANOWITZ

ILLUSTRATED BY TONY WRIGHT

CROWN PUBLISHERS INC. NEW YORK

With thanks to the National Endowment for the Arts
and the Alfred Hodder Council of the Humanities of Princeton University.

Publisher's Note: This is a work of fiction. The characters,
incidents, and dialogues are products of the author's imagination
and are not to be construed as real. Any resemblance to
actual events of persons, living or dead, is entirely coincidental.

Some of the products mentioned in this book are
trademarks of their respective companies.
Every effort has been made to
identify these trademarks by initial
capitalization. Should there be an omission
in this respect, we shall be pleased
to make the necessary corrections in future printings.

Published by Crown Publishers, Inc.
225 Park Avenue South, New York, New York, 10003,
and represented in Canada
by the Canadian MANDA Group
CROWN is a trademark of Crown Publishers, Inc.
Manufactured in the United States of America
Design by Dana Sloan
Library of Congress Cataloging-in-Publication Data
Janowitz, Tama.
A cannibal in Manhattan.

I. Title.

PS3560.A535C36 1987 813'.54 87-6694

ISBN 0-517-56624-9

10 9 8 7 6 5 4 3 2 1

First Edition

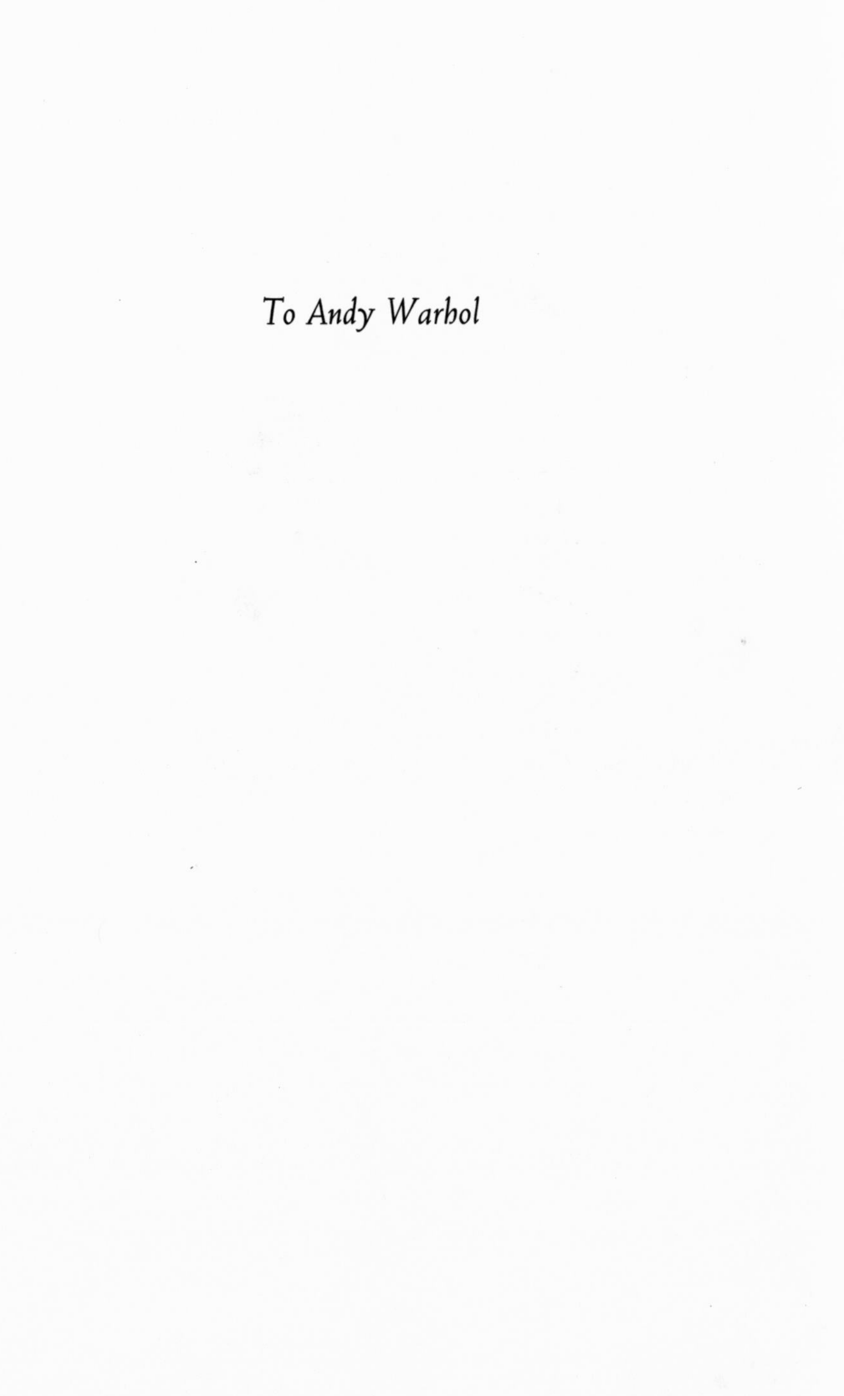

To Andy Warhol

"A loaf of bread," the Walrus said,
"Is what we chiefly need:
Pepper and vinegar besides
Are very good indeed—
Now, if you're ready, Oysters dear,
We can begin to feed."

"But not on us!" the Oysters cried,
Turning a little blue.
"After such kindness, that would be
A dismal thing to do!"
"The night is fine," the Walrus said,
"Do you admire the view? . . ."

"The Walrus and the Carpenter," by Lewis Carroll

Messrs. Publishers,

You request me to give you, as an introductory acquaintance to these incoherent writings, so much of the history of this strange being as I may have been able to collect. Although I consider his writings the best history, as every man's productions are of himself—and there is but little information concerning him in my possession—yet I cannot refuse to afford you the brief of what transpired between the old cannibal, his last companions, and himself, as it was detailed to me by him. I will tell you also, in a rapid manner, what I have heard of him in his native village.

He is represented, by those who knew him as a youth, to have been as gay and joyous as any of his companions; but that, at times, a seriousness would take hold upon him, which would last for days together, during which time he was indifferent to any act of those around him, and appeared to desire no communion of feeling on the part of his fellows. He seemed most to fancy occupations of a monotonous character, since they afforded him the best opportunity for indulging in constant, uninterrupted thought.

After a time, he determined to enter into society, but evidently without a taste for its insipid formalities and forced courtesies. He, like others, formed friendships amongst men. But a few, false to their trust, apparently disgusted him with mankind.

That he was ambitious—you will discover almost from the outset. That he loved—read his own account. He was careless of gain. He was heedless of fate. He never forgot a kindness, or remembered an injury. When he left society, he was forgotten by it.

The means by which I came into possession of this manuscript is, to me, very interesting; but thinking it may not interest others, I will not bother to relate the circumstances. Such is the history of one, which so beautifully interweaves itself with the history of another. Sacred! most sacred! if but for the cannibal's sake, is this manuscript; and I consider I am fulfilling a portion of my duty to him in having it published. It can, I judge, injure the feeling of no individual. His parents are both dead; and of his wives, some are indifferent and others have forgotten him; and association of every sort in regard to him, surely is buried now.

Tama Janowitz
Princeton University, 1987

A
CANNIBAL
IN
MANHATTAN

1

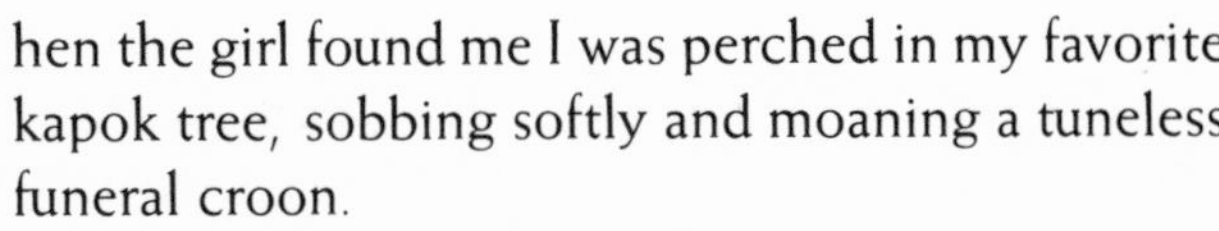

When the girl found me I was perched in my favorite kapok tree, sobbing softly and moaning a tuneless funeral croon.

It was nearly evening. The tops of the mountains, red, brittle, and porous, resembled ancient mushrooms. Below, the steam of the jungle rose hot and gray. From the branch where I sat the spines of dead banyan trees stuck out among the greener ones like sharks' fins, coated with a faint white ash.

At the moment the girl passed beneath, I dropped a yam skin, hitting her on the shoulder, and she let out a little scream. Understandable after all—it was not so many years ago there would have been nothing to prevent me from dropping out of the tree in a great leopard leap, to snatch her up for Yerba to cook for dinner. Then, trying to cover up her timid scream in a fit of coughing, she blurted, "Speak English?"

I did not say anything, but, peeling a banana, resumed my dull tune.

"Do you know where I'm supposed to go?" she said. When I remained silent, she placed herself on a rock at the edge of the precipice and looked out dramatically at the sunset and humid valley beyond. "I'm looking for a Mr. Mgungu," she said at last, in an uncertain voice. "I'm the new teacher from the Peace Corps. They said I should just look for Mr. Mgungu when I got here and he'd help me."

"That's me," I said.

At first I was not entirely certain whether she was in fact a boy or girl. Her eyes were crooked. One gazed up at me in the tree while the other remained looking out across the mountains, as if undecided where the most interesting view lay. "Would you like a cigarette?" she said, in a nervous voice.

"What kind?" I said. It was a Marlboro, and I was able to accept. "Come to where the flavor is," I said, jumping down from my tree. "Come to Marlboro country." The girl looked uncomfortable. "Well," I said, "we don't get many magazines up here. I treasure the ones I have. Shall we smoke?"

I sat down on the rock next to her at the edge of the cliff. "You say you're from the Peace Corps," I said, taking her lighter and lighting the cigarettes. "Explain, please."

"Where should I begin?" she said. "You see, I always wanted to join the Peace Corps. I'm a Fishburn."

"A fishburn?" I said.

"I'm Maria Fishburn," she said. "Really, I'm the only surviving Fishburn. This makes me heir to the Fishburn fortune."

"Excellent," I said.

"My grandmother was a champion tennis player, during the days when tennis was still played on the lawn. You know, they named a tennis championship after her, Fishburn Court, maybe you've heard of it. Grandmother Fishburn, of all the members of the Fishburn family, was the relative of whom I'm proudest."

"You admired this lady," I said. I rubbed my fingers along a scar that ran from my navel to my chest.

"Well, it's understandable, don't you think?" Maria said. "What women of any merit were there in my family, a family of moneymaking men, easy swindlers all of them from the first —that was Albany Phillips Fishburn, family founder, who made his money in the railroad industry. He invented the caboose. Compared to the men, the women were nothing. Most of them began as cleaning ladies and married into the family. As for the rest . . ."

"Go on," I said.

"Women poets. So you see, it's up to me in a sense to make good for the family, to pay back a small part of the debt we've incurred."

I coughed politely and inhaled on the remaining drag of the tasty Marlboro.

"Anyway," Maria said, finishing her cigarette and stubbing it out, "I'm absolutely exhausted, having been on the plane for thirty-six hours, then getting indoctrinated, taking the plane to the missionary center, then hiking for six hours. Oh, my god." She looked stricken. "What am I telling you all this for? Do you even speak English?"

"Oh, hither and yon," I said. "Hither and yon. Listen, would you mind stepping on your cigarette? Only you can prevent forest fires."

"I didn't mean to start going on like that. It really isn't like me. If you only knew how exhausted I am, you would understand." Here she stopped and recollected herself.

I noted her clothes had nothing to do—in a rather uncivilized way, I thought—with anything pertaining to the local weather situation. Her glasses, through which her eyes gazed askew, were tortoiseshell and steamed over. Despite the heat, the jungle an open oven below, she wore a heavy, drably colored garment with a skirt that extended below her knees, an important scarf, and a safari helmet from beneath which her hair hung silky and brown. "Tell me something," I said. "Who designs your clothes?"

"Oh, these things," she said. "They're just some stuff I found in an old trunk. Would you mind terribly—please don't be offended—if I set up my camera and had a picture of us taken together? It has a self-timer." She removed her glasses, and then, shortly, took off her helmet. Her silky hair was the color of some camouflaged bird, mottled brown, speckled with gold, and ruffled with dust. One hand reached up almost constantly to pluck at some hairs that grew from the top of her crown. I climbed back into my kapok tree, and thus was able to see, from above, how the hairs there were sparse and feathery spikes waving about as she worried at that one spot. Many Western people look alike to me anyway, and the only thing that made me realize she was female were her breasts jutting beneath her shirt. But there was something very attractive about her; my heart was deeply touched. Her two eyes, luminous and brown, appeared to take in everything at once. Though this may have been because she was slightly wall-eyed. And her lips were like those chiseled on some old stone statue, a highly sensual sight.

Still, I did not wish to let her know I felt some spiritual kinship. "No one told me we were to have a new Peace Corps worker," I said. With my toe I flicked a leaf onto her head.

"Oh, no, but that's impossible," she said. "I was led to understand that no one here would speak English. I guess you speak pidgin English though, hmmm?"

"Yeah, I do, actually," I said.

"Oh, I'm sorry. Mine's not terribly good at the moment. We only got a three-month training course in languages, though I do speak French. You don't speak French by any chance, do you? That's the lingua franca of New Burnt Norton, isn't it?"

"Aw, lady," I said. "I don't know how you ever got here in the first place." For I was irritated by this foolish thing. I sat, moody, legs swung over one branch, as I nibbled on the remains of a few bananas and a second cold yam I had carried with me. There were ropes of teeth around my waist and neck, my hair was stuffed New Burnt Norton–style with bright parrot feathers. My only clothing was a three-foot-long gourd, or calabash, a specialty of the village and used by any man past twelve years of age to cover the penis. This gourd, specially grown by Yerba, twisted and curled around several times into arcs and loops and then finally ended at my chest where it was tied with the aid of an orchid fiber around my neck. To show my boredom I drummed on it rapidly with my fingers.

"Well, umm," Maria said uncomfortably, "maybe you could show me where I'm going to stay?"

2

"I must apologize," I told Maria as we hiked up the path to the village, "for not introducing myself to you at once. But then, I am nothing more than a savage. I don't understand even the simplest theories of electricity."

"Oh, well," Maria said, wiping some perspiration from her forehead with a white cotton handkerchief, "I really don't think that makes you a savage."

"No, no, let me finish," I said. "Why is it that some electricians still go around believing the charge runs from plus to minus? This makes no sense to me. Either there is a scientific fact everyone agrees with, or there isn't."

"I don't know," Maria said. She looked puzzled. "I still don't think—"

"Oh, I am extremely savage," I said. "Once, long ago, in the capital city, someone attempted to give me the driving instructions. Immediately I ran the automobile into a petrol station pump, though at that time, luckily, there was a gasoline shortage and the pump was empty. In the United States of America, everyone drives the automobile, because they are a civilized people and I am not."

"But I really don't think that that—"

"One moment please. As final proof, my feelings toward my children are much less than the fond feelings I have for my pigs."

"That is somewhat savage," Maria said, after a pause.

"In fact," I said, stopping along the path to allow Maria time to catch up, "I am fonder of my pigs than I am of my children. Do you know why I was singing that funeral dirge in the tree back there? I was mourning the death of my most favorite piglet, the Princess Beatrice."

"I—I'm sorry to hear that," Maria said.

"Pigs are more affectionate, more intelligent than many people," I said, starting to walk again. "Each pig knows its own name and where it sleeps at night. The same cannot be said for my children. Each pig has a perceptive, amused eye, though some are meaner than others. There is nothing that can take the place of a certain pig I had—the Princess Beatrice, mentioned heretofore—for charm. Her flexible, pliant snout, constantly in motion! I ate her earlier this afternoon, and delicate and pink of flesh she was, too."

"You ate her?" Maria said.

"How unfortunate that you did not arrive earlier. Do you know, a pig is a grateful animal, besides being valuable. Even in her death throes, the Princess looked at me pleadingly, as if to apologize. 'I am glad to die by your hands,' she seemed to say as the last of her blood spurted hot from the knife wound to the jugular. Ah, Maria Fishburn, who could not be moved by such a spectacle? Only one as savage as me. And that is why I cry."

"I don't mean to be rude," Maria said, "but I think I'd feel better if you could tell me where it is that I'm going to be staying."

"Is that why you're following me?" I said. "I don't know. Nobody told me that you were coming, and the hut the other Peace Corps worker had—or was it that anthropologist from Columbia—has too many rats living in it now for you to move into. Also, I think the roof leaks. No, it may have been that journalist from *Life* magazine who stayed here last."

Maria's face flushed red and blotchy in the heat. Small fruit-like tears appeared in the corner of her eyes. "Well, don't cry," I said. "I hope you brought salt tablets with you to replace any salt loss you may experience. All right, all right, now quit it—something will be found for you, I'm sure."

The village was another hour's hike uphill from where we

now were. Occasionally Air New Burnt Norton flew Cessnas in to a landing strip a few hundred yards below the village, but unfortunately I had allowed this strip to fall into disrepair, and Maria had hiked from where the missionary was positioned, several hours down the mountainside. "Where are your belongings?" I said.

"I only brought my sleeping bag and a knapsack," she said. "Otherwise, I just thought I'd don whatever native garb is customary for women."

"I hope you don't mind if I take a look," I said. I peered into the knapsack. "Why, it appears that you've brought only contact lens solutions," I said.

"I'm not able to wear them right now," Maria said, "which is why I have on my glasses. They're Bausch and Lomb soft lenses, but for some reason my eyes have been irritated ever since I left the States."

"Oh," I said. "Best if you let me carry it. Too much difficulty for you in this heat and altitude, despite your stage of liberation as a female." I slung her knapsack over my shoulder.

"I arrived two days ago and I've just been meeting with government officials and Peace Corps people ever since," she said. "Down in—"

"Jaranekta?" I said. Jaranekta was the capital on the other side of the island, and a dirty, smog-filled place it was, too, stinking of rancid copra.

"Bless you. I'm so exhausted, I can't begin to tell you," she said. "Still suffering from jet lag."

But she was not too exhausted to carry on a running commentary about the history of the Fishburn family as we hiked up to the village, a walk I preferred to take in peace and silence. Still, it could not have been an easy task—talking, I mean—for one unused to the walk and the altitude, and this endeared her to me, in some curious way.

She had become interested in studying the natives of New Burnt Norton when a distant relative of hers had, during the mid 1960s, died in an expedition on the coast of New Burnt

Norton. This relative, one Oscar Fishburn, came to the island in the hopes of collecting primitive religious and erotic sculpture. Finding no specimens of any kind anywhere on New Burnt Norton, he had taken to collecting rare butterflies, one of the few items for which New Burnt Norton is especially famed. The story went that while attempting to climb a particularly tall causarina tree in pursuit of an elusive meat-eating butterfly (the butterfly dined off rotted carcasses or, less frequently, caught and ate other insects) the branch he had clambered onto broke and he plunged sixty feet to his death. However, the body was never recovered and several weeks later a Pygmy appeared on the west coast wearing a Rolex wristwatch bearing the emblem of a fish in a frying pan—the Fishburn family crest—and a T-shirt tied around his head that read, SAVE WATER, SHOWER WITH A FRIEND.

Maria grew up with the name of Oscar Fishburn never far from anyone's lips. At Vassar she majored in anthropology, but when she discovered that anthropological studies had been completed on New Burnt Norton for some time, she determined to join the Peace Corps. Though the New Burnt Norton government severely discouraged Peace Corps workers on the island, by pulling some strings her guardian was able to arrange for her to work in a remote village, where she was to teach algebra and English at the local adult education center under the auspices of the Peace Corps and the United States embassy to New Burnt Norton.

"Do you think we might be able to see the carnivorous lepidoptera?" she said, at last beginning to pant and huff a little from the exertion of climbing while talking. "Oh, look—what about that one? Is that it?" And just then over our heads a tremendous blue butterfly sailed, large as a small bird, with tattered, unfurled wings, some kind of omen or portent or sign. It was in some way damaged, and how it remained in the air I don't know.

"No, that's not it," I said. "The one you mean is very small. It is an ugly butterfly, as far as butterflies go, with a death's head on its wings. It used to be used in head-hunting ceremonies. I remember my grandfather would spend days out in the jungle looking for one before deciding whether or not it was safe to go out on a raid. When hurt it whimpers like a mouse."

The trail rose up steeply between the rocks, and though it was the dry season there was constantly the slow drip of water touching water, the *drip drip plink plink* of the glassy water that ran in a stream on one side of the path. The water here was very new and raw so close to the clouds, but by the time it reached the ocean it fed into, all the life had been beaten out of it from its icy passage between the boulders. Near the ocean it slugged out and the banks were filled with crabs. There the water was softer, less sharp. But up here there were few fishes, only steely tadpoles.

The sun had almost set now and glowed like one angry eye from behind the Mt. Bawwaar-Yaas pyramid, dusty red and jagged. Already the jungle below had plunged into gloom. Each leaf that dropped over the pathway was like a great dry porous sponge, and hidden under rocks and stones were grass-eating rats, leather-winged flying foxes that were delectable fried, the wings thin as parchment with a tender crust. Rarely one would stumble on a nonflying cassowary bird, leaning on a tree nonchalantly as a man against a street lamp, with feather whisks of brush jutting from skull and tail.

On either side of the trail hackled plants made passage off the path nearly impossible. Bougainvillea crept on every tree-trunk with flowers vermilion and magenta. Here the vegetable kingdom devoured all but the barest of mountaintops. I had a few small garden plots, but to keep the jungle back it was necessary to go out every day and slash down the new vegetation. In this part of the world, where every mosquito has a parasitic red flea perched on its back, it is understandable that even the candelabra trees are covered with a soft, fine fur or fungus, that the huge purple mushrooms that spring up everywhere would have blotches of eggplant- and yellow-colored lichens sprouting from their moist surface.

Then we rounded the corner—Ms. Fishburn asked if she could rest on a rock for a few minutes, but I said it would soon be dark, and besides, we were nearly there—and came onto the small clearing for the village. Actually, it could not accurately be called a village, though it was true I was the chief elected official. In the clearing were the six huts strung in a circular pattern, covered with silvery-green moss, which had grown down the walls like a fine ancient hair, making the houses almost indistinguishable from the trees behind. Clouds of smoke spilled from the middle of the roof of one of the houses—this was my wife Yerba's hut—and a smaller pool of black smoke rose from Nitsa's, who was not a good cook and frequently burned things. Behind the huts the sun sank small and red in the distance, and I let out a yell of "Yooow!" to let my wives know I was home.

When my pigs heard this they came running from the piggery, where they had already settled themselves in for the night, with little cries of joy and delight, that lovely grunting sound pigs make when they run and their bellies jiggle. There was the old boar, two hundred pounds, with his dignity keeping him at a pace behind the others, and his jowly tusk bobbing at a senile pace; the young castrated males with the stripe of black down their silver backs; the two sows with giggling pink teats dangling nearly to the ground and followed by their jelly piglets; and the young girl pigs, red and cream and dappled black. "Where is the Princess Beatrice?" I asked them as the herd approached me all at once, and then remembering what I had done that afternoon I turned to Maria Fishburn half-reproachfully—but she did not see me, being too nervous at the sight of this huge flock of pigs streaming around us with their delightful whiffles and gladnesses and shoving for banana peels or rotten yams or yam skins or bits of old meat, for I generally always had something with me to bring them. Maria Fishburn let loose little squeals herself as the pigs bumped around her bare legs, sniffling and driffling in the hope that this was the edible surprise I had brought them.

"This is a friend of mine I want you to meet," I said, addressing the pigs in the local jargon—the pigs did not speak English and though I wished Maria Fishburn was able to understand my introduction so that she would believe she was safe, it was more important that the pigs (who, when hungry, did have a mean streak) be instructed to leave her alone.

After their greeting the pigs returned through the doorway to the pigsty (though a few of them lived under Yerba's and Oola's houses) with only a little pushing and biting. They were an extremely well-behaved group of pigs. As usual, my older children were nowhere to be seen. Then, after the commotion died down, I gave my usual scream again, "Yoooow!" and this time my wives heard me and came lazily out of their huts—Nitsa with a baby clutching her breast and trying to nurse, despite the erratic motion she made climbing over the fence she had put up outside her door; Oola, half asleep, rubbing her eyes, large and mysterious as those of the jungle fox; and Yerba, who was still awake and cooking my yams, the two-year-old slung on one side of her hip and the baby on the other, her white teeth glinting in the dark. And all of them glad to see me, too, they were, until they caught sight of Maria Fishburn holding fearfully onto my arm.

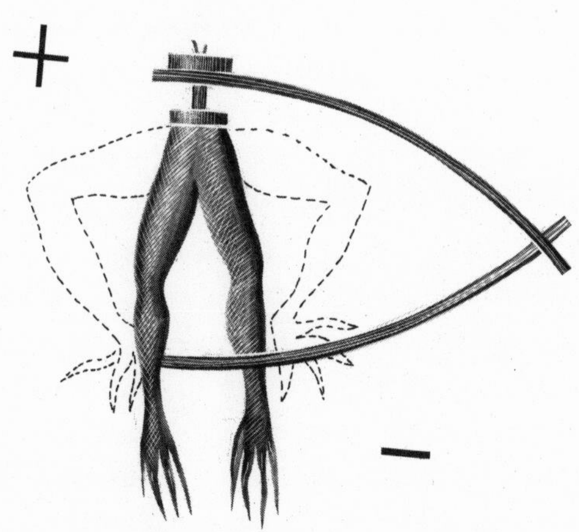

3

Though short in stature there is a certain commanding authority about me, and yet I do not have very much control over my wives. This is not due to personal faults but rather to the fact that men and women here don't have much to do with each other the way they do in civilized parts of the world. I have my house; they have theirs. When the boys get to be around twelve years of age they move in with me and then proceed to badger and harry me until I can manage to be rid of them. When the girls get to be that age or a little older, we sell them off. In a way I have outlived my time. I'm no longer needed for protection, not in the way I used to be, and as far as heavy work in the garden goes, my wives know better than to ask me.

Though they are contemptuous, they must, I assume, love me in their own peculiar, feminine way; once in a while one of them will invite me to step out to the woods with her and there she will seem to enjoy herself a good deal. But mostly they are friends of each other, and I am, as I say, an item of luxury.

This was not always the case. My first wife, Yerba, was bought for me by my father when I was only thirteen, to my shame and mortification. She was already twenty-one or twenty-two or so—a great homely girl whose husband had been sent to prison for allegedly taking part in a head-hunting raid and while in jail was beaten to death. What was I to do with this huge lummox who hung around the village skulking and weeping? Just as my father was about to give up on me and take her for use as his own wife, I came to my senses and set her up in a proper hut.

And so she picked at and bullied me for the next ten years, and I was very happy with her until my uncle died and I came into some pigs and property. Only a short time later I fell in love with Oola, who was at that time fifteen years old and extraordinarily beautiful, with mauve satin skin and an angry appearance.

So I was able to buy her and thought then that I would be genuinely happy at last, only the two wives did not get along. If I went out in the woods with Yerba, Oola followed and threw flaming brands at me. If I brought home a piece of cloth for Oola, Yerba screamed and carried on and tried to pull out Oola's hair. If I spent any time leaning against the fence and talking to Oola on a hot dusty afternoon, that night for dinner Yerba would serve me a rotten yam, swarming with grubs. If I played with one of Yerba's babies, later I would find Oola scratching that baby with a little pointed stick. And so it went. Thoroughly disgusted, I did not want to have anything more to do with either one of them.

"Forget it," I said to both of them. "I have had it with years of bickering. I am going to get myself a new wife, someone sweet and gentle, and then you will see how much you like that." So I traded some extra pigs and got Nitsa, very plain but of childbearing age and malleable. Whatever I told her to, she would do. And it worked, for Oola and Yerba became very close in order to gang up on Nitsa, and were always seen laughing and joking together.

Still, now Nitsa was very unhappy. Always they were torturing her in some way or other. At night one of them would creep into the hut where she was sleeping and move the fire over from the center of the room to right next to where Nitsa was lying, and she would roll over into it and burn herself. Also Yerba took her first child away from her and there was nothing I could do about it.

Then something happened, the details of which I will not go into here, and they all three became friends. However, you must remember this only took place after some ten or twelve years of suffering on my part. And when they all three became friends my position decreased to the status of that of a beloved dog. And they were each very strong and forceful, like wild chimpanzees or young crazy girls.

When they came out of their huts toward me, all but Oola had a smile on her face, and they were very glad. How they walked lazily: Nitsa, with a baby fondling her breast as it tried to nurse; Oola, half asleep and rubbing her tropical-cat eyes; and Yerba, who put down the kids and went back inside, emerging again this time carrying a fragrant pot of Joy Paul Guilford. This was our local hallucinogen, concocted from rare butterflies, primarily the death's-head.

I had been gone for about twenty days, down to Jaranekta for the first time in perhaps some five years, in order to find out how many pigs I must pay in taxes, and the women did not like it when I was not about them. There was no one for them to mock and make fun of when I was not there, and also they were fearful, I think, that I would bring back a fourth wife to take up space in the garden and eat yams and bear my children. So when they saw Maria Fishburn standing behind me, they grew very angry.

"Who the fuck's this, you great stinking baboon," Yerba said, charging out at me, a sexual pudding, my wife, the rolls of yam fat jiggling and weaving around her waist. Oola came up and quick as a whisk had unbuttoned Maria Fishburn's shirt and was trying to take it off while Nitsa was touching and pulling Ms. Fishburn's hair and the baby squalled. Yerba's two-year-old had snatched off Maria Fishburn's glasses—even the babies are strong up here in the mountains, if they live—but luckily they hadn't yet found her knapsack slung over my shoulder.

"Stop it, stop it," Maria Fishburn said.

"You didn't bring this slut up here to live, did you?" Yerba said, though of course Maria Fishburn couldn't understand her—I later learned that she had spent three months in the Peace Corps language training program learning the wrong language—and Oola, putting on the shirt that she had managed to partially pull from Maria, said, "There's not even enough food for all of us as it is; if you have brought her up here to live, don't expect us to help. Look how weak and flabby she is, she will not be able to live very long. What did you bring me from Jaranekta?"

"Get your hands off her," I said, but I did not dare make any move to protect her because my wives would have had no qualms about slugging or biting me either, and a blow to the groin can be decapitating for many days.

But still they plucked at her and tugged and pulled and Maria Fishburn began to weep. And I think they would have killed, or at least severely damaged her, had I not said, "Hey, cut it out! This isn't my wife! She's from the government! Leave her alone!" For they have all sorts of strange and primitive beliefs, my wives, and they think if they annoy somebody from the government they'll get into trouble. So they let go of Maria Fishburn, and the baby was so startled it stopped bawling.

Then I said, "She's come here to teach us some stuff. Where are we going to put her?"

"What did she come to teach us?" Oola said suspiciously.

"Algebra."

"Algebra?" All of them had been to school down at the Methodist mission below, and had never been able to put very much of what they had learned to use. "Algebra?" And they began to snort and chuckle.

"Yeah, well, just shut up and help me figure out where she's going to stay. We can't put her in the empty hut; there must be dozens of rats in it and fleas from the pigs. Let her stay with one of you until I can get something together."

"Well, she's not going to stay with me," Yerba said. "It's too crowded in there already, with five or six kids and a damn dog."

Both Oola and Nitsa looked equally reluctant.

"Well, what do you want? Do you want her to have to stay with me? Give me a break, will you?" The thing is, there's a sort of rule or law or something among us that no woman can come into the men's house—oh, once in a while an exception is made if she's under five, but it's like a sort of taboo, you see, that no woman is supposed to go into the men's quarters. It contaminates it, I guess, and while I don't necessarily believe in that, I always feel there is no point in taking unneeded risks. However, my wives looked indifferent as to whether or not she stayed in my house. Already Nitsa had found the knapsack and was trying to go through it, but I kept pushing her away with one of my hands while with the other I tried to recover Ms. Fishburn's shirt for her from Oola. "All right, I'll let her sleep downstairs in my house," I said. "God knows what will happen."

So I helped her to my hut, being careful to point out the pig turds for her to avoid, while all the while she clung to me apprehensively. "I don't think I'm going to like it here," she said, turning around to make sure my wives hadn't decided to attack again. "Where are my Valium? I hope your wife didn't take them out of my bag."

I could see the girl was hysterical. "Just relax," I said, as we entered the hut. In the gloom I could see my sons leaning over the edge of the sleeping platform, trying to figure out what was going on. "I'll see if I can get my wife to part with some of that Joy Paul Guilford. That should calm you down."

But I thought I would get her settled first. Inside the hut none of the boys had bothered to build up the fire to keep the mosquitoes away—I doubted they had bothered to since I had left three weeks before—and they leaned over the edge of the sleeping platform, six feet off the ground, and jeered at the sight of my leading her into the hut and handing her knapsack to her. "Shut up! Who gave you permission to say anything! Imbeciles!" I said to the three oldest of them who had pushed their way closest to the edge, all big, ungracious creatures fifteen years old or more at least, with their mothers always bringing them hot sweet potatoes, and them never lifting a finger to help in the gardens, completely useless for anything. Although I have to admit that with the constant practicing of bows and arrows and spears they would have made excellent warriors, had war not been made illegal, and one or two of them were very good at keeping the radio working until the batteries had run out and knew how to construct parts for the movie projector out of natural fibers.

"What's she doing in here," said Ugatame, the oldest, a big boy of eighteen years with his teeth stumps all blackened and rotting from the eating of sugar bars he would hike down to the Methodist mission to steal. "Did you bring me a wife at last?" and then, muttering under his breath, "you sorry excuse for a father."

"This girl is from the government and she is going to give you some lessons. I want it perfectly understood that you are to leave her alone or there will be serious repercussions. At least this will be a chance for you to learn something, if you are not too stupid, which I suspect you are." None of them could ever be induced to attend the school at the Methodist mission, claiming that there was no use in doing so, since even with a college diploma on New Burnt Norton they would only be hired as janitors or menial laborers and paid nothing per day.

I put Maria's knapsack and sleeping bag next to the fire. "You sleep here, lady," I said.

"But will I be safe?" she said, looking up anxiously at the leering faces.

"This is the *men's* hut," I said. "Of course you'll be safe." Then I turned to the boys. "Remember what I told you," I said. "Keep your hands off."

After this I went to find Oola. I peered in the doorway to her hut. "Hey," I said. "It's me, Mgungu." She was nearly asleep but gestured for me to come in. Very affectionate, my second wife was, and wrapped her little arms around me lovingly. And we would have enjoined as man and wife, in some kind of communal bliss, had she not violently and abruptly given me a quick punch in the solar plexus. "Ugh," I said, doubling over.

"I don't care whether she says she's from the government or not," Oola said. "I want her out of here. And I think you'll find that Nitsa and Yerba feel the same. Three wives around this dump is enough for a guy like you."

Now I felt like a man in a state of dejection, and I crept out to see if I could garner some of that Joy Paul Guilford from Yerba; but when I went and tapped her on the shoulder she rolled over, wielding a knife. "Keep your hands off me," she said. "And don't try and take any of that Joy Paul with you when you leave. Don't be surprised if you find yourself going breakfastless tomorrow: I want her out of here."

Had I worked hard all my life only to be met with this type of attitude? My heart was churning in rage, and also in a quandary, for I could see that until the girl left life would not be easy to live in these parts. So I sat on the stoop for many an hour, brooding, until it began to be morning and the sun rose up from behind Mt. Bawwaar-Yaas, turning it shades of gray and almond in the smoky morning light. Finally I went in to sleep.

4

now know I had never been satisfied with my life as a savage. Always there was with me the feeling: none of this has anything to do with you. As if all my life I had been experiencing a divorce, or at least a temporary separation, from my true self. During the days when cannibalism was still chic there had been a reason for me to live, a purpose in life, so to speak. Or at least there was something to do.

Provide, provide, was my motto, like the industrious ant, and this method of provision had granted me a modicum of respect among my fellows. Someone was always approaching to examine the arrow embedded behind my knee, or to admire old scars garnered in war. But now—nothing. And so it had come to me, after a while, after years of indifference and sleep in my hammock when the wars were made illegal—a new motto that went like this: *Don't trouble yourself.* And whether or not I was right did not make much of a difference, not yet, anyway.

In the morning the sun lightened up the interior of the men's house, although there were no windows, but the sun came in through the chipped and speckled walls—and Maria Fishburn was able to see how everywhere stuck in the roof thatch were little fetishes and bones and powerful things wrapped in leaves, some so old that even I didn't know what they contained. And the brittle smell of smoke was stronger by day and the whine of the mosquitoes quieter.

Even then, you understand, I was modern and paid no attention to such primitive things, a thousand tiny delicacies—eggs in the rafters that would be good for eating one hundred years hence; the crystallized bodies of bald baby birds that, if they had not been sacred, would have been devoured in one ginger crunch; patches of couscous fur sewn or knitted or stitched in the smoky walls and ceiling; ripening fruit on the rafters. And the dry husks of beetles and the death's-head butterflies nailed up in a line to protect the camp from intruders—still, though I was modern, there were certain things it was best not to toy with.

I could hear Maria scrabbling around the fire, rummaging through things in her knapsack and at last when I smelled something tasty I climbed out of bed, being careful not to disturb my sons, and went down to join her. "What's all this?" I said, looking at some yellow she had whisked up in a little folding pot and was holding over the low embers of the fire.

"Dehydrated scrambled eggs," she said. "Care to join me?"

"Say no more," I said, and sat cross-legged at her side after supplying her with a couple of old skulls she might use as bowls. The eggy-weggys made a pleasant change from old yams for breakfast. I decided not to mention the fact that she was unwelcome in the vicinity; perhaps when my wives found out she was willing to cook, they might let her stay.

"So, what is it with this stuff?" she said. "What you called, last night, Joy Paul Guilford."

I got up and fetched an ancient tome from which all the pages, save one, had been removed. " 'Guilford, Joy Paul,' " I read aloud. " 'Born March 7, 1897, Marquette, Neb., U.S. psychologist and practitioner of psychophysics, the quantitative measurement of subjective psychological phenomena. Guilford taught at the universities of Kansas (1927–1928) and Nebraska (1928–1929) before his mysterious disappearance in 1930. A leading U.S. exponent of factor-analysis testing for a comprehensive assessment of personality, Guilford constructed for this purpose batteries of tests, or factor inventories. His comprehensive, systematic theory of intellectual abilities, known as the structure of intellect, gave rise to what is known as informational-operational psychology.' "

"What happened after his mysterious disappearance?" Maria said.

"He came here," I said. "He was an unhappy man; it turned out his wife had slept with most of the student body at both Kansas and Nebraska. So he left her behind and set out for what was then one of the remotest places on earth. It was here that he studied the cannibal rituals with my father; at that time we men would hunt and track the death's-head butterfly and ingest this lowly insect in a precannibalistic rite. But the other insects were also of use to us—some were taken by the women, and some by children, and all produced varying results. Some were tranquilizing, some provided hallucinations. And, after years of experimentation, Joy Paul arrived at a mix of various herbs, grasses, beetles, and butterflies and fabricated what we have come to know as Joy Paul Guilford. There is another secret ingredient in the mixture which I cannot reveal. Unfortunately, he had a falling-out with my father, but you can see his sacred skull hanging someplace up there." I pointed ceiling.

"What happens when you take this stuff?" Maria said.

"Oh, well," I said, "it's not something you want to take every day. It's like this: taste becomes sight, sight becomes sound, sounds become taste. And you may feel like someone else. A man's wife's feelings become his, or two strangers may temporarily inhabit the same body. Of course, the drug is highly volatile and the same results do not commence each time."

"I've never even heard about this drug," Maria said, a strange expression on her face.

"Oh, it's just a local gizmo," I said. "My village only. There's not much use to it, really—we just take it for fun and spiritual recreation."

"I have friends back in the States who could take something like that and analyze it chemically," Maria said.

But I waved off this sentiment dismissively; for I had almost forgotten my aged aunt, nearly five and a half feet tall, and weighing close to three hundred pounds with face covered with a faint down of gristly black beard. She lived in the last of the huts.

"What do you mean to tell me is going on here?" she said, peering in the door of the hut. "Why, you good-for-nothing old shyster, bringing a woman in there! What's the matter with you, boy?"

"Don't come in!" I said. "Don't come in, Aunt DaBore! This is the men's hut, remember?" With one arm she was reaching in and grabbing hold of my arm from where I sat next to Maria Fishburn at the fire. "Would you excuse me for just a minute?" I said to Maria in English.

"What you mean, bringing this girl here, man?" Aunt DaBore said, twisting my arm up shortly, and her missing teeth causing her to speak in a sort of sticky spray.

"I brought you up a present from Jaranekta," I said. "Let me get it for you, Auntie."

"You got troubles enough of your own, man. You don't need this girl here! You can't even take care of your own wives! Shit, man, what the hell's wrong with you? You dumb as a Christian," she said. "You crazy for sure. All I hope is nobody don't think you any relation to me."

"Look, I didn't invite this girl here! She was sent here by the government! She wants to teach you something, help you become educated! You've heard of the Peace Corps!"

Inside the men's house my sons were spitting and hawking as they lit up their first cigarettes of the day, and from time to time a muffled chortle escaped one or another of them.

"Don't jive me, man," said Auntie. "You are not seeing the need to smash the source of national oppression, capitalism, for the proletarian alternative to bourgeois rule, which is revolution and socialism. Now, get this girl out of here or you may be forced to return to times more primitive! I wouldn't mind a nice meat stew anyway. She looks like a real well-fed gal." And she gave a severe blow to my rib cage and went off to tend the pigs, who had to be ushered out to the empty garden plots each day and watched over more carefully than if they were little babies.

I called the girl outside.

"Miss Fishburn!" I said, in my nervousness forgetting to call her "Ms." "Do you mind stepping out here for a minute?"

And she stepped out into the chilly sun, hugging her shoulders and blinking in the light. She looked happier this morning and her eyes appeared better able to focus in the same direction at once. She stared out as the clouds of mist lifted slowly in the morning light.

"Watch where you step," I said. "Ah, I wanted to tell you—did you bring any *Time* or *Newsweek* magazines with you?"

"Yes, I did bring one or two," she said. "I don't know if they're this week's or not, but—"

"That's okay," I said. "I wonder if I could borrow them?"

"Yeah, sure, I'll just get them. Is that what you wanted to tell me?"

"No," I said, and while she stepped back into the hut I began to say, "Look, I don't know if you were aware of what was being said outside just a few minutes ago, but there's been some kind of mistake made. That lady was my aunt, and she was upset they had sent you here, since all of us have already been educated. She was deeply hurt and insulted."

"Oh. I'm so sorry—I didn't know." A puzzled look came into her soft eyes.

"Well. You couldn't have known. How could you have possibly? But to be perfectly honest with you, this isn't much of a village. It's more of a family grouping, see. I think you would probably be happier and better off in a larger setting—a place where there's a few more people for you to teach, children and that sort of thing, maybe a lepers' colony. Lepers are always grateful. Not that we wouldn't love to have you here, of course. And we'll be sorry to see you leave us. But it wouldn't be right. It wouldn't be fair to the more needy natives of New Burnt Norton." This last had a sort of catchy ring to it and I repeated, "The neediest natives of New Burnt Norton need you more than we do. And so, though we appreciate your having come, I'm afraid at this time and place, it just wouldn't work out."

This is where I made my fatal mistake.

With this Maria Fishburn began to scream and yell, saying she had seen my picture on the cover of *National Geographic* years earlier and had fallen in love with me, not realizing I was only five feet tall (five feet two inches, actually), and how could I try to get rid of her after what I had done and said to her last night.

I was not quick enough to understand what was happening, and I thought, Oh, it is true perhaps someone could love me for my face on the cover of *National Geographic* alone, with my aquiline nose and karakul or poodle hair and my fierce, very clean, white eyes. "The Last of the Cannibal Kings," I believe this article was called, and in it I was asked such questions as "What is it like to eat human flesh?" "Very delicate and juicy," I remember as having answered, "rather like young tadpoles sautéed lightly for several minutes or deep fried," an interview for which I was not paid one red cent but instead was proudly presented with a steel ax. I invited the two journalists and the photographer to write to my children for fifteen dollars a month, which they did for only two months before forgetting the checks.

Also I now know Maria Fishburn was a little inconsistent and, though at first she seemed only like any other rich American on a search for a rare part of the world, she was in reality on a search for something else. And besides, her personality was not jelled and did not jibe with who she was supposed to be. In part she was very angry, due to her excessive wealth, and threatening me now as she was with jail or worse unless I agreed to let her stay and educate us was just the sort of thing she was likely to do. In a way she might have been called crazy, and in fact, I soon found out, she had spent several months one summer during college in a mental hospital for unsteady young adults, where her trust fund was used at a rate of nearly one thousand dollars per week to instruct her on the making of batik fabrics as part of a work-therapy program.

But gradually I induced her to leave, telling her she could return when her stint in the Peace Corps was over and then we would see what would happen if she still felt the same way. And she left her white blouse as a promise she would return and also because I asked her to leave it so we could use it as a cinema screen for our bicycle-operated movie projector at night, since due to this lack of movie screen we had not been able to watch our movie for several years.

I hiked down with her to the mission and left her there, only looking back to find her staring longingly at my skin, no doubt admiring how it shone so from the pig fat and coconut oils Nitsa rubbed on me every once in a while.

Though it always came to me as a shock and even a blow to the system that anyone could find me attractive, still, gazing at her eyes longing and slurpy, and her pale freckled skin, it was, I supposed, entirely possible.

At the same time I was relieved to think that was the last I would ever see of her and her skittery nature. Or so I thought. The sight of her standing there at the former mission could not but make me think of my own years at the school, which ended for me at age eleven, when my father, on a raid, killed the minister-teacher and we ate him that night for dinner.

I was very glad, as were all the children, for this minister used to kick us if we did something that displeased him, and his method of teaching consisted of having us sing endless rounds of well-loved American songs with words that went, variously, *"Oh, I'm a hayseed, my hair is seaweed. And my ears are made of leather and they flap in windy weather. Gosh-oh-hemlock, I'm tough as a pine-nut. We're the girls from, we're the boys from, we're the kids from Camp Louise,"* and, *"A horse and a flea and three blind mice, sat on a hilltop playing dice. Horsey slipped and fell on the flea. Whoops, said the flea, there's a horsey on me,"* and lastly another song that went, *"Who cut the sleeves out of dear old daddy's vest, why did they build the shore so near the ocean,"* and ended with the refrain *"a boy's best friend is his mother, his mother."*

As I say, I was not sorry to see this minister go the way of all flesh, though I still have his glasses somewhere in the house. A replacement for him was found after my father was caught and sent off to prison, but by then I was too old to go back to school, having already married my first wife.

5

wo years passed, while I slept in my hammock. I read the books from what had once been the missionary's library, talked to my piglets, made love to my wives, and all in all lived a peaceful if dull existence. Once in a while I did think of the girl Maria: but not all that much. Then one day there she was, as if no time had gone by at all.

This time she had a proper entourage of two or three natives, one of whom was my son Ugatame, who had run off the year before when I asked him to lend a hand in the garden. I wasn't surprised to learn Maria was paying him the standard fee of two boxes of matches a day, nor was I surprised to see her hair slicked back into a ponytail. Most signs of her former ravishments were gone; only she smoked cigarettes even faster than ever and her eyes still blinked behind her tortoiseshell glasses. "Still can't wear your contact lenses?" I said.

"I lost them," she said. "Crossing a rope bridge over a ravine during a ten-day survival course given for a group of us Americans, I slipped and fell and when they fished me out of the water they were gone. I was nearly killed." She looked around the village briefly, noting, I supposed, that the huts had fallen into a greater state of disrepair than ever and the pigs had rooted up the yard into a churning sea.

"No one to help me," I said, looking at my son Ugatame reproachfully. "And the little children quite hungry and tired of yams."

"I have some medicine if any of your kids need it," she said.

"That's all right," I said shortly. Almost every two weeks we had some do-gooder up there giving out acne medication or shots for typhoid. Another big favorite was giving tests all round, to even the smallest of the children, for venereal disease, or painting the gums and toes with a hideous-tasting substance called Gentian Violet.

"I've been thinking about you for a long time," she said. "I think you should come with me back to the States. I can't bear your having to stay up here, living out your life like this, unknown and unappreciated. I'll make sure you can get back, I'll take care of everything."

All this time, for nearly two years, I had been saying to myself, I am tired of being a savage, and in a dim portion of my head I half-remembered Maria Fishburn in the mission below. I was tired and disgusted of working out in the garden every day with a primitive digging tool and only having one or two movies to play over and over again at night using as a generator a wheelless bicycle Oola pedaled frantically for all she was worth, breasts flying in two directions at once, and this in order to keep burning in the dark the flickery picture of the Marx Brothers running in and out of the bedroom.

But I was careful not to say anything and instead invited Maria back into my hut, where I wound up the old wind-up Victrola and put a record on, scratchy and nearly tuneless from use. Django Reinhardt and Le Hot Jazz Club de Paris playing "Sweet Georgia Brown."

"Well, I don't know," I said craftily, humming along with the music.

"Oh, but you must," she said. "It will be wonderful. We'll go everywhere. You'll see the world. You'll be treated as a man, instead of as a savage looked at with contempt in a country that is supposed to be your own but where you have instead been humiliated and driven back in the same way the United States treated the American Indian."

"I don't know," I said. "It is true I would like to try a different life for a while, in a country with autobuses and the Concorde jet and television, as well as film for the Polaroid camera I once won in a magazine sweepstakes but so far have not been able to purchase film for. But I am a man now nearly in my forties," this last a small lie, for I did not want to frighten Maria Fishburn too severely and besides the mountain air was very preserving, "and I have grown accustomed to my life and feel that perhaps the world may be a corrupt and contaminated place. Who is to say I would not be happiest of all up here?"

Now she took a step forward and gently took my hands in her own; when she spoke I could smell her breath, which was as sweet as a rare scented clover we have up in this part of the world. And I was like a man befuddled, for she must have cast some kind of spell over me. "I haven't been able to stop thinking about you," she said. "If you come with me, I know you would never regret it. There are so many things I want to talk to you about! I know you are a wise man—and in New York, there would be others who would understand you; you and I would have an extraordinary life together, rich and imaginative." She released my hands but instead of moving away she leaned forward and performed some witchery in my ear.

What can I say? Gradually I allowed her to convince me to go with her, and then I said that perhaps I would, after all, but first I must consult old Aunt DaBore.

In two years Aunt DaBore had shriveled up considerably and was already an old lady, though only in her seventies, and the rolls of fat drooped sullenly around her midriff and from her goitery neck.

"Aunt DaBore, this girl wants me to go with her to New York and she will pay my way. I won't be gone long."

"Lord have mercy! Boy, I seventy-three. I older than Moses. And I know one thing at least: you a jive ass. Fool!" she said.

"Pardon, Auntie?"

"What you mean, going off and leaving your family this way, and Nitsa seven months pregnant and a whole garden full of yams killed last week by the blight!"

"Don't worry," said Maria Fishburn, who had by now learned to speak the native jargon in a timid and uneasy voice, "I'll make sure you're all taken care of up here. I'll have groceries flown in by helicopter."

Aunt DaBore snorted scornfully and between her teeth cracked a flea she found on her arm.

"What I came to ask you was: how will it turn out? Do one of your fortune-telling thingies and however it comes out, that will be the answer." And Maria looked at me with injured and worried eyes.

So Aunt DaBore was induced to grind up various hairs and nail parings and we cut off the ears and the tail from a living, screaming piglet and she burned them in a fire and the answer was: not good.

There were ominous things in store for me.

If I left, I would never come back.

But I passed this off as a lot of native superstition and pressed a coin into Aunt DaBore's palm, promising her my largest castrated pig if I were to happen to leave, and asked her to try again.

"Better you should go," she said. "I see here that if you do not leave there is a strong possibility the sun will never rise again over Mt. Bawwaar-Yaas, and this may bring about the end of the world."

So with her blessing—"Go! See if I care! Let the revolution come! Marxist-Leninists unite! Win the advance to Communism! Build a revolutionary party to smash capitalism and build socialism! Jive-ass turkey!"—and the knowledge that my wives were off in the mountains and not expected to return until late afternoon, I went to say good-bye to my pigs.

My favorite sow was dying of the stomach ailment, and I bent to kiss this aged one with tears in my eyes, knowing I would perhaps never see her again. Then I went back to the men's house to pack.

6

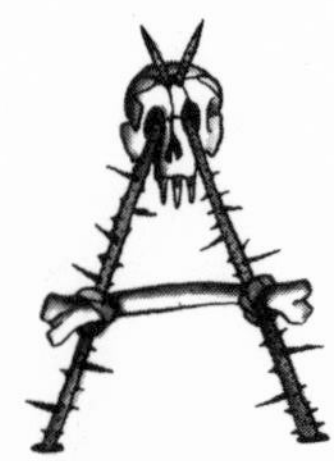

nd Maria waited in the yard, crooning at an infant playing in the mud, and Aunt DaBore stood scowling in the doorway of her house, shifting back and forth from one foot to the next and rocking the house as if waiting for something unsaid.

"Where is my life, Auntie?" I wanted to say, "The bowls of roast pork with prickly ginger, the puffy yams, the bottle of gin? Not here. Or else they are here but it's like this: they are no longer enough."

"Where are the dividends from the Feed the Infants Federation swindle?" she said.

Actually, trading on the commodities exchange with the money from the Feed the Infants Federation hadn't worked out so good for me in the past few years. In this last scam, each child of my tribe was put to work writing letters. "Please help me and my family with your contribution. To you, fifteen dollars may only be a little amount, but with your help my father can buy a franchise in the betel nut business. My brother will go to the hospital to be refitted with a new wooden leg, which he badly needs. My mother will be able to buy a dress. She hopes to buy a machine with which to sew. No longer will my small sister lie awake at night crying for food."

The money sent to us was then deposited in copra, coffee, and gold stocks in Switzerland.

I have done all this and more, but never with any malice intended. Of this I can assure you. And it was not easy, most of it, either. Once every two weeks the kids were lined up to have their "before and after" photographs taken. The "before" photographs showed them with dripping noses, smudges of dirt on their faces—"Stick out your stomachs, kids!" each time I shouted, hoping to portray them in the throes of kwashiorkor or beriberi—and then the "after" shots, in which the kids were shoved in the latest Sears clothing available, used only for this purpose: patent-leather mary janes for the girls, hair neatly plaited in pink ribboned cornrows, and some kind of zoot suit or little Levi's and cowboy boots for the boys—I'm not sure what kids are wearing anymore these days, but whatever it was, they wore it.

To be honest, after a while the Federation caught on to my scheme and refused to allow anyone to send my children more money. And I was pretty much wiped out when the recession came along. Copra and coffee crops had failed, and with the gold I had been advised to sell at the wrong time, losing everything I owned. This was because I had a lousy broker.

"First of all, it wasn't a swindle and I resent your calling it that," I told old Aunt DaBore, "and what happened to the dividends is one of the things I intend to find out when I am in the civilized world. I want to know what the hell happened to all that money, for sure. Does my broker know he has devastated the welfare of an entire village?" I ranted: "I have a feeling a lot of newspapers would like to hear about this."

Not that we had ever seen any of the interest from the commodities and stocks in the first place—it was all plowed back into a retirement fund and group pension plan. And that too, I had been informed, had failed.

Aunt DaBore did not look sympathetic. She nearly knocked me down with her radiant fragrance, her fine jungle or hothouse heat, and her bristling, shocking mustache, so irritating to the touch.

Meanwhile my heart was all churned by the fact that I was leaving and I swore to myself every other minute up and down that I would do good, that I would use this opportunity to make a contribution to my family and prove myself to them by becoming rich and powerful and transporting us all from our savage state and into the twentieth century.

I thought it would be best if I got Maria Fishburn out of there as soon as possible, for at a great distance away, on the peak of another mountain, I could see the brightly colored brassieres of my wives, who approached like elephantesses. But on the spur of the moment, knowing they were still many hours away, I asked her to hold on just for a little while longer, and I whipped up some native artifacts in case I was presented with the opportunity of selling them.

I made three tropical flutes from a discarded piece of hollow wood; this was an instrument no one from my tribe had ever seen or used, an instrument that in fact already was causing great bursts of laughter to emerge from the swarms of terrible infants, my children, who surrounded me. I put my two second oldest sons to work carving a statue with a huge phallus and pointed breasts, though they did drive a hard bargain, making me hand over all Maria Fishburn's most gaily striped stockings and knee socks. And from some straw I quickly knotted together I made a crude fetish to use as either a sexual aid or a votive to stop diarrhea, depending on which way the user held it. All rapidly constructed; they were shoddy goods.

Then I packed my suitcase, a net bag woven of orchid fibers by Nitsa and dyed in muted hues.

I was not able to bring as much as I would have liked to, since we were walking, but I strapped myself up like a donkey and leaned forward under the burden.

The hike to Jaranekta below was only a question of walking steadily for eight or ten days on a torturous mountain path over gulleys and ravines slippery from endless tropical rains.

In my woven bag I put a spider-web necklace, a delicate and complicated affair made for me by Yerba, who cultivated a grove of spiders specifically for the purpose of making my necklaces and ceremonial shirts; a ballpoint pen for use as a nose decoration, worn thrust through the hole in my nose I referred to as my deviated septum. This ballpoint pen belonged to Maria, which I had accidentally borrowed and forgotten to return. Also I had a plastic drinking straw for my pierced nose that I had once many years ago recovered or found in Jaranekta; the heads of five rhinocerous beetles I liked to stick on my nose when the mood struck me, attaching them by a sticky, gummy substance extruded from the dead beetles; and a nasal-septum bamboo tube; together with a cord strung with dogs' teeth; a hair extension or wiglet made of hemp and clay; a cowrie-shell necklace that had belonged to my grandfather, currently the most valuable thing I owned; a pigs'-teeth necklace and a girdle made of human skulls; an armlet made from pigs' testicles and tails; a bunch of cassowary feathers; and various parts of the human body including thigh bones, jawbones, etc. Lastly, three Fruit-of-the-Loom T-shirts.

Then we set off, the two of us weighted down under my worldly goods. I could see my wives' brassieres rapidly approaching but I knew they would not continue down below the village for fear of rapists, and I frequently turned to wave and blow my nose, for my eyes were filled; and the syrupy clouds of mist or steam rose from the jungle below as we descended, until finally we plunged into one, and my wives, and the little children, and the huts of my village disappeared at last from view.

And who was I, after all? I may even at that early time have begun to be confused. A man very small in stature, only five foot two—though that was cheating slightly, I must admit, for I was not standing perfectly flat on my feet when measured—and very muscular. A brutal and violently ignorant savage, though charming in a primitive way, who was fleeing his wives and thirteen children for the charms of a young American, possibly even the Hamptons and the New York Film Festival if everything went well and I played my cards right.

This was not the image I wanted to have of myself. So I tried to think of other things as we walked down the slippery clay path, the decline in altitude creating bubbling and popping in my head.

"Look, you're not going to mind if I take my shirt off, are you?" Maria Fishburn said, wiping her sweaty brow as she sat by the side of the path for a brief rest.

"No, no, perfectly understood. Go right ahead. Much too hot to stand on ceremony up here." For after all, none of my wives wore blouses and I thought nothing of it. You may think with constant exposure to such sights I would not be interested in these things—but all this was very interesting for a man to contemplate.

But seeing me glance at her, all Maria said was, "I don't want you to get the wrong idea, Mgungu; I'm not coming on to you —not yet—it's just that the temperature is so damn hot. You know I adore you. But I believe in friendship first."

So we descended, me sighing as I thought: This was not what I had expected but imagined instead velvet antlers and vanilla, flower-petal water and coconut cream, and was instead handed into custody of a woman no different from any of my wives.

But then even as a child I had never been satisfied with what I had always wanted—another wife, another pig, a new trip into unexplored mountain regions, or more rarely, the craving to go down into Jaranekta. And then upon receiving was always surprised to discover this was not what I had wanted at all.

For many days we did descend.

At night we had Maria Fishburn's clever tent to sleep in; it came in a case no larger than a pillbox and could be strung up in almost any direction. Though small in appearance from the outside, inside it was most roomy and spacious, with almost two bedrooms or sleeping quarters. It was of a bright orange fabric and inside the air remained quite stale and sometimes rose in temperature to above a hundred degrees—but it was well worth suffering the heat for sometimes at night there were torrential, unexpected rains, very chilling and impossible to dry off from. They could nearly wash a man away, they were so fierce. It was that time of year.

I had to be careful where I roped up this tent. Much of the

ground around us would be washed away in the morning; the tropical vegetation did little to hold together the clay-filled soil. And when it rained this tent inside began to look and feel like a sauna.

But I was deeply covetous of it and longed for American possessions and in particular this tent. Even though Maria was my mentor, I crafted ways in my head to steal it and nearly would have done her in had I not been a man fifty-five years old. But I can assure you any of my boys, Ugatame, Umii-tou, Gonzila, or even Radiocity would have killed for less had they not been such cowards, and it was a good thing Maria had me along for protection. And I was becoming more affectionate with her, at least in my heart.

Each evening when we stopped she whipped up the most extraordinary concoctions from little metallic packages she took from her sack. Not only did this save me from having to rummage for our food; by releasing these packages into pots of water she boiled, on the fire I made, the most wonderful meals were construed—things tasting of apple jelly and onion soup and granola-wheat cereal—these, too, she had gotten from a "sporting goods store." And there were macaronies and cheese and dehydrated scrabbled eggs.

A most astonishing girl, Maria Fishburn, with her breasts like porkers, refusing to wear a shirt or a brassiere until we got near the city, though she was not lacking in these objects of clothing. And daily we descended, and daily she refused to speak or allow me to touch her, although she looked at me with loving eyes and did say once, "When I decided to come back for you after two years, it was with a different feeling in my heart. For now to me you are the noble savage, and I am the first female Robinson Crusoe."

"What?" I said.

But she did not reply, and as we were due to cross the rain-swollen river, the Ijaaj, I did not pay her any attention but set to work chopping trees for the construction of a raft. And these logs I rolled somewhat before us down the path.

And as we got lower we came upon the river, and with the river were the crabs, whole banks of them basking and waving one distended foreclaw in what I imagined to be a scene resembling a cocktail party. And each was speckled orange and purple, though some were a brilliant blue. And these blue crabs, though smaller than the purple-and-orange ones, were very fierce. When another crab approached one of them, which was frequently, due to the overcrowded situation on the beach, the blue crabs would proceed to do battle, gesticulating wildly and with clattering and clacking of claws, and would sometimes even chase the bigger, more timid crabs and catch up to one. Then with a karate-chop blow the blue crab would snap off a weaker crab's large claw and devour it with huge appetite, leaving the crippled crab at the mercy of its companions.

And when I got off the raft I had built for us to ride on, to try and catch some of these crustaceans for our dinner, they all fled at once like a flock of birds, vanished under the sands. Only occasionally two eyes, extremely human, on the end of the two eyestalks, would appear above the pink sandstone sand and then the eyes would swivel and turn until they had caught sight of me. When they saw me a startled look came into these disembodied eyes and they would retract again in an instant with a puff of dust. Sometimes a blue hand or claw appeared above the sand, waving like a white flag of surrender. And the shell-bodies crunched under the sand beneath my feet.

The world has mostly been too strong a place for me. This is why in part I have never gotten ahead. Each day in the morning, throughout my life, I would wake with the feeling of being thrilled to be alive. So strong was this feeling that sometimes I did not dare to stir from my bed at all. As if each day could eat me up alive, so extreme was it. And on some mornings, in our descent into the civilized world, so shrill was the air that to draw too much of it into my lungs made me feel likely to burst. And the edible things around me: the tasty yams, of which we had brought nearly a dozen varieties—some sweet, some pulpous and veggy, some tough and chewy and good sprinkled with some banana-stalk ash Yerba had soaked in the salt pools, which I had neatly wrapped to carry.

And the crocodiles smiling with their clean white teeth and their hot mouths, cold-blooded satchels, their lascivious grins reminding me fondly of Aunt DaBore.

"Good-bye, good-bye!" I called with a terrible sinking and loneliness in my heart. For we were approaching Jaranekta.

7

We had arrived at last at the outskirts of the city. In the dirt yards and front walk-walks children stopped playing to stand and watch us pass, nibbling into one another's ears and giggling. The houses, low and cinnamon-colored, had egg-cup-shaped roofs and were made of a powdery clay-type material. Maria Fishburn was nearly brown from dirt; her knapsack weighed her down and her mirrored sunglasses with red frames turned her eyes into the two brilliant eyes of a beetle. Slung around my forehead was the drawstring of my orchid-fiber net bag, which was how they were generally carried. It was filled with the presents I had made and was so large it caused my back to resemble the back of some traveling hunchback. And my bare feet, from so many years of never having worn shoes in my life, were elongated and very broad and appeared even bigger on my short body than they were, as if I were rooted in two flat pods.

So I walked, followed by Maria, who was weighted down with the things she listed as most essential—Vidal Sassoon shampoo, a number of bottles of Clinique facial cleanser, and a certain kind of cracker she was very fond of called ESCORT CRACKER. These last being the Most Buttery Biscuit in the World. None of these products were easy to get hold of and now, after two years in the jungle, she was not sure she would be able to find them, even in a civilized country.

A white dog came out of one yard and rushed up to us, shaking his head and barking fiercely, darting in every so often to nip at Maria's ankles. So with one foot I shot out a kick at this animal and sent it spinning and yipping into the dust, and the streets through which we passed grew very quiet.

The yards of the houses, though poor and filled with dirt and rubble, were covered with plant life that had crept down from the jungle: clematis in shades of blue growing on the low walls; low fences made of tangled cactus limp and purple in the moist air like some exhausted sex; short and withered pomegranate trees. There were small goats long and black of hair nibbling absently at the dirt; and Norfolk pine trees spiky and of an effervescent green hue that resembled the newest of sprouted leaves; and lantana with flowers that crawled over the terra-cotta, lizard-spotted houses.

As we passed, the children froze up against the wall and stopped giggling, and faces appeared in the open windows, black and fearful, calling the children inside in hissing voices, for my cannibal breed still struck terror even twenty years after the fact. But Maria did not see what was going on as she snapped pictures left and right and said, "You see how these people cannot bear to be photographed for fear this camera is stealing some part of them away." At a public water pump an old woman with wrinkled brown skin stopped her pumping and scuttled off, leaving her bucket behind. Even the goats and small stunted pigs stopped their search for garbage to trot into the houses and stare at us from inside the door frames.

The afternoon was late and from where we stood on the outskirts of the city the sky was like a moldering basement of cement, and then turning to pink plaster, unfamiliar with pollution and grittily scented, nearly unbreathable. "I want to get a taxi," Maria said, although the streets were still paved only in dust and there were no cabs to be seen. She sat down heavily on the dirt, resting her backpack against the stone wall behind her. But when she went to pull out her wallet she found all her cash was gone, taken by my son no doubt, and she was left with nothing but a checkbook, which would do her little good in hiring a cab or even a man riding a bicycle who pulled behind him a little two-wheeled, two-seater cart, as we now saw occasionally, returning to his home in this dismal part of town at the end of the day.

We continued to walk and the streets became paved and then broadened out into the avenues very wide and ridged in the center with a row of jacaranda trees very feathery and wispy in the heat rising off the tar. On either side of the road were the low cement office buildings with smooth glass fronts and an importance about them. Still there were no hotels in sight and we continued to walk, sometimes turning off the main avenue down a smaller side street in hopes of bumping into a hotel, which I could have told Maria, had she asked, would not be found in this part of the city.

And the stars came out, twirling needles probing the heavenly ceiling, for the sun dropped quickly at this time of year, and then the moon rose luminous and miasmic, not friendly as it was on the mountains above, but toothsome and dangerous.

Maria's face had broken out in a sort of scowling, but at last we arrived at a large international hotel with an indoor swimming pool and an outdoor swimming pool and color televisions in every room that did no earthly good to anyone because, due to certain political problems, which I had read about on billboards plastered along the walls as we came, Jaranekta television was no longer broadcasting. Although even at best all it had ever transmitted were reruns of "The Munsters" and "Gilligan's Island."

"You sit down," Maria said. "I'll go get us registered."

I sat down on the elegant brown vinyl chair in the lobby, noting that there were very few tourists, probably because of the political situation. But the ones that were here were fat and mostly Dutch, and had skin as white and silky as if it had been preserved in a bottle, or there was now an Australian who passed me in a cowboy hat, from the back-out, with skin as boiled and red as if he had been stewing in a pot for not quite long enough. There were certainly no eggplant-colored people, which was perhaps understandable, as the only eggplant-colored people left in the world were those of my tribe, the Lesser Pimbas, and all twenty of them were still up in the mountains, except for myself and Ugatame, who had run away.

In a short time Maria returned and said, "Everything is fine. I've gotten us two rooms and you're supposed to go over there to sign in. Do you have an I.D. or a passport to leave with them? They want some form of identification."

When I got to the desk a young man with hardly a nose on his face took a look at me and said there had been a mistake, there were reservations on the list he had not seen before, and the rooms must go to those with reservations first.

And this appeared to be the case at every hotel we stopped at, until finally we found a dismal, run-down old building with a room the manager, grizzled and at a backgammon board, said he could let us have for two nights only, but we would have to share it.

The toilet was situated down a narrow hall with a lightbulb overhead that barely lit the toilet seat. The sheets of toilet paper were only slabs of brown paper. None of this bothered me, but Maria Fishburn, although just having returned from two years at the mission up in the jungle, was repulsed. And the double bed in the room, placed against one wall, had a noticeable slant to it in the direction away from the wall. But Maria said, "Well, it will have to do," and gazed at me with a surly expression as if I was somehow at fault, a look I was familiar with, having a number of children.

After she had half-showered in the small fishtank that was

part of the bedroom, or at least part of the alcove off the bedroom that also contained a sink, we set out to look for some dinner.

But no restaurant could apparently situate the two of us. So she managed to get cardboard boxes of take-out food from each restaurant, and at a little foreign gourmet shop, the only place open at this time of the evening, she found other food for us to take back to the room and eat. Because she had not eaten decent food for two years and because we were no longer speaking to each other she went berserk and bought vast quantities of edibles.

I spread them out on the bed, opening the white boxes onto tin plates Maria carried with her: a fleshy fish called the barrimundi made in a coconut cream sauce; various chutneys of mango and lime and tamarind; Indian breads flaky as thin buttered crusts of skin; slithering Chinese dishes; huge chunks of nearly raw pink steer from Argentina; a warm jar of Russian caviar plastered between two slices of bread to form a sandwich; bottles of brandied peaches from France; wines purple and green and amber. There were hot spicy magenta fish, each no larger than a man's little finger and so shrill and fiery as to bring tears to the eyes with their tiny fish eyes open and unblinking and unashamed.

And rubbery finger-eels writhing and jellied on a plate of glittering white pasta; and crisp water-vegetable shoots delicate and green; strange flowerets and buds and leaves growing on a plate dank with a sauce black and sticky and sweet and trembling with slabs of mushrooms resilient as mucus. And for dessert, fruit deep-fried in a crunchy, greasy gold batter, soggy and thick in a honey-nut syrup, and ice creams mostly melted in strange and unusual flavors such as a curry-flavored ice cream, a meat-flavored ice cream, and a walnut ice cream with hard bits of tutti-frutti fruit.

And after this the two of us were in the dark toilet and the sink off the bedroom, being sick in the heat of the un-air-conditioned cubicle.

8

The next morning after Maria woke she told me she was going out to get my visa, the airplane tickets, and an important package. "I may ask you to carry a few things for me," she said. "It may be that you'll be acting as a courier for me —I'm not certain I'll be able to get us tickets on the same flight, either, at such short notice. Now listen—don't go out while I'm gone. I wouldn't want anyone breaking in to the room."

After she left, I spent some time examining her possessions, Then, growing bored, I climbed on top of the massive, ornately carved armoire. The top was covered with dust and spider webs. A tremendous cockroach scuttled away. Then I froze myself into a feline, or strike position.

After some time Maria returned, humming softly to herself as she inserted over the sink the new set of contact lenses that had been waiting for her arrival at the American Express Office. She took off her newly purchased batik dress, which had no doubt grown sticky and dusty, and, still humming to herself, she began to wash. When she was fully undressed, I tried to leap down from the top of the armoire and stealthily come up behind her, but I was not as agile as I had thought, and I slipped from the top, landing on the floor with a crash. "Uuug," I said.

With that Maria whirled and from under the mattress whisked out a knife, which she held up to me effeminately, saying, "I know karate."

"Very good," I said.

"Although I still have every intention of taking you along

with me to the United States, I will kill you if you so much as try to touch me. The only reason we are sharing a hotel room is that there aren't any other rooms available."

"Don't worry," I said. I lay on my back on the floor near the bed, groaning softly. "I'm not offended. Believe me, I was only doing this to make you feel desirable. Having three wives keeps me pretty worn out, and although my appearance is that of a man a good twenty or thirty years younger than my age, my interest in sex with rich and thin American girls was never all that great in the first place."

Maria sat on the bed, clutching her head. "God, you scared me," she said.

"In fact," I said, "it was simply a gesture of politesse on my part anyway, for what I had thought was, What are you bringing me along for, if not for that." I tried to rise, but my back hurt too much.

"Let's get something straight," Maria said. "After two years in the woods, I think I've learned to live without men. I'd like to think of you as my Man Friday."

"You see," I said, "it is always better to bring these things out in the open. What I thought was, You poor thing, and how you must be starved after being up there in that neck of the woods for so long, no doubt hearing little else beside the great virility of Mgungu Yabba Mgungu, president and chief elect of the Lesser Pimbas. However, I now understand completely, and my feelings are only slightly wounded." I got up at last and preened in front of the mirror while Maria Fishburn dressed. I draped some spider webs over my head and glued a button I had picked up off the floor onto the end of my nose. "Here," Maria said, "I bought you this." She handed me a tie with a picture of a person called Andy Warhol printed on it.

Therefore I apologized, and we shook hands and gave each other an embrace. Then Maria attempted to teach me the waltz, which was a three-step dance she had learned as a child in some type of school, in order that I be prepared for the

International Dance Festival in Manhattan. It was a delight to smash thusly together back and forth across the room.

Now, as I have stated, it was very difficult for any native to acquire the passport, and even with the use of bribes Maria had to explain that I was wanted by the Museum of Primitive Cultures in New York and by attending this I would bring a modicum of pride to the island. And while we were waiting for the necessary paperwork, Maria decided we must go and get me a suit made; for although she liked my native garb of penis gourd and head feathers, she did not feel this was a look suitable for long-distance travel.

One afternoon we wandered down a back street and into a tiny shop where three Asian men—a father and two sons—held me up and had me measured and fitted for a suit. I protested very badly, I am afraid to say; but when the suit was made (a pink linen affair, complete with weskit and striped suspenders) I was most pleased indeed.

Yet when it was time for me to go to the airport and I tried to put this suit on, there appeared to be new holes in the articles of clothing that I could not remember ever having seen before, or what various limbs to stick into them. Maria was busy packing my things, and paid me no attention; I must have put the pants on backwards, for in my nervousness when I went down the hall to take a piss, I realized I must have done something wrong, for I was flyless.

When I came back to the room Maria took a look at me and started to laugh.

"Listen," she said as she struggled to pull my arms from the clothing holes and insert them in their proper locations, "I didn't tell you this before, because I didn't want to make you more nervous; but I could only get one plane ticket on a direct flight to Manhattan. So you'll go first; I'll stay over an extra day and fly to Paris. Which is okay—I have some business to conduct there anyway, and if you came with me you'd only be in the way."

"I am to travel alone?" I said, while she rebuttoned the weskit in the correct order. "To take my first plane trip to civilization with no assistance whatsoever?"

"Now, don't get yourself all stirred up," Maria said, for she could see my heart was fraught. "This is the telegram, which I'll give you to carry, from Parker Junius, formally inviting you to the dance festival and agreeing to pay your hotel and other expenses. You can show it to them at Passport Control if there's any problem. All you have to do is fly to Kennedy, get a taxi to the Holiday Inn and relax and enjoy yourself. I'll be there in a day or two, and if you get lonesome you can look up Parker Junius at the museum; he'll be glad to see you."

Though I assured her she could not possibly get away with such foul action, she finished packing my belongings, dragged me downstairs, and threw me into a taxi. "I can't come with you to the airport," she said, thrusting my ticket into my hand. "You'll be okay." She gave some money to me, and more to the driver, and with that the car took off. I pressed my face to the glass as the car began to move through heavy traffic, for I had grown quite fond of her and our leavetaking seemed rather abrupt. Then to my surprise, as we got to the end of the block, I saw Maria, who still had not gone inside, greet a man who came from around the corner, a man with an unusual resemblance to my son Ugatame. Of course this could not be; still, old memories returned, and I was sorry now I had not spent more time with my oldest son, teaching him baseball and so on and so forth, and forcing him to undergo some torturous initiation rite. He had never seemed like a very nice person to me, but maybe if I paid more attention to him he would have turned out better.

So, thinking these thoughts, I at last reached the airport. It was a short distance outside the capital, situated on a strip of land next to the ocean, a low cement building with a tin roof and a barely paved runway. The whole place smelled of burning engine oil and sour coconut milk.

Inside the building the heat was so intense I was nearly knocked flat. The place was almost empty, except for a couple of natives who tried to sell me a fake stone ax and a large bag of moldy sweet potatoes. These natives, of course, were not from my tribe, the proud Lesser Pimbas of the mountains—they were the Greater Pimbas, whose spirits had long since been broken, and now lived down here in various government housing projects. So I ignored these folk and went to the check-in desk: a sign proclaimed that there was only one flight leaving the island that day. Seeing me, the airline personnel person let out a little scream; perhaps she did not like my suit, which contrasted most horribly with my dull purple skin. But then she pulled herself together, and, taking my ticket, said, "Well, you better run—the plane is on the runway now, and they're preparing for departure. Do you have anything to declare? It's illegal to carry out foodstuffs or native artifacts."

"No, no," I said. Maria had packed my things for me back in the room, and while it was true I was carrying some *tchotchkes*, I did not think any of them could be considered an artifact.

I had taken the precaution of carrying only a few bags with me and a small one Maria Fishburn had given me the day before. It was filled with her cosmetics. Meanwhile many of my things she had insisted on carrying herself, including a fur coat she had decided spontaneously I should wear, which she had purchased. I was left to lug my steel ax, along with some forty boxes of matches I had earned working as a porter for an American expedition several months before to the red powdery stalactite top of the mountain, the Mt. Bawwaar-Yaas pyramid.

But when I stupidly walked through a little imaginary doorway, just for fun, I set off some kind of mysterious alarm system that I could have had no way of knowing about. A security guard raced to me with an evil grin: I knew at once he was a member of the Greater Pimbas, those old-time enemies, and would make sure somehow I would end up in the same prison that had finished off my dad.

And I was prepared to spend permanently the rest of my days

there on the island with no hope of escape, which frustrated me greatly, for I now felt very strongly that where Maria went I must go also. But to my good fortune just then a tour group appeared, led by a guide, who announced, as I was being rough-handled, "Take a good look at that fellow: a member of the nearly extinct cannibal tribe of Lesser Pimbas, whose ancestral village we're going to see later on in the trip." And this guide slipped some money to the security guard who was holding on to me, and asked if it was okay for the group to take my picture. Now, when the guard nodded that this would be fine, and released his grasp, I made my escape, for the loudspeakers were announcing the departure of my flight. One nice fellow, dressed in a colorful shirt stating his affiliation with the Banana Republic, pursued me out onto the runway and shouted at me to smile for the camera. He wanted to know where he might purchase some "ganja," and as I was curious to know what this was, because of this I nearly missed the plane.

By the time I got there they were already pulling the staircase away. The stewardess grabbed my ticket and looked at me suspiciously, since I was the only Lesser Pimba in first class and in fact on the entire plane. But there was nothing she could say.

Once on board I was most intrigued: I extended my nostrils and looked around. The air was very dead and dry, and the seats were blue and red cloth pocked and spotted with flecks of orange thread.

9

And the plane departed.

Flattened into my seat with fear, I could not bring myself to look out the window for more than a few seconds at a time, and above me the air-intake valve hissed in sympathy. My hand involuntarily went to my crotch, as if I had forgotten, although I hadn't, that I was no longer clad only in a gourd around my penis and a bunch of teeth around my waist.

I tried to look out the window, but in my nervousness I quickly had to avert my eyes. But what I saw, in brief flashes, was this: on the far side of the runway was the glassy sea, thick and viscous, heavy as corn syrup, and still in the heat. Then, as the plane got higher, I saw the over-all island, rising up from the ocean like an old coconut, the mountains covered with jungle until the very peaks, where they were old, bald, red rocks. And surrounding the island a rim of pink sand, with the water an extraordinary shade of blue.

Oh, how beautiful my island looked, ripe for tourist development, had it not been well known that no one could swim in the ocean, filled with sharks and stonefish which could kill a man in thirteen seconds, and stinging jellyfish as large as baby grand pianos. Nor could anyone bathe in the thin ribbonlike strips of river that crisscrossed this way and that, for they were filled with hippos, and fish with teeth, and eighteen-foot-long pink worms that liked to slither under a man's toenails. Nor would anyone want to stroll in the rain forests, where there were mosquitoes the size of cherry tomatoes, and leeches that hung undulant and dripping from the trees, and waited with a primordial knowledge until a person walked beneath their branch and then would drop onto the passerby and sink their teeth in.

Soon we had left the vicinity of the island and were deep over water. The man next to me touched me gently on the arm, at which I nearly bolted straight up from my seat; he apparently could sense my anxiety, for he gave me a set of headphones and placed them over my ears. Then commenced a terrible dirge: a voice moaned, *"Born free, as free as the wind blows, as free as the grass grows."* Now this noise, combined with the roar of the plane engines, seemed to be pouring directly into my spine, and like the lowliest and most pitiful of pigs I clung to my seat, wondering when this nightmare would be over.

At last the man sitting next to me yanked the headphones from my ears. "Feeling better now, mate?" he said. "Good. We're going to have to talk." And he picked up my limp hand and strangled it. He had electrocuted hair, badly hatcheted in appearance, and wore a leather jacket covered with effluvia. A highly excitable figure, for his nose quivered and his eyes gazed piercingly. "Kent Gable," he said.

"Mgungu Yabba Mgungu," I said. "Glad to meet you."

"I'm on my way to New York," he said. "I'm off to do a show."

"What kind of show?" I said.

"Radio and telly," he said.

"Oh," I said. I was quite interested. "Why is this?"

"Actually, I'm a musician," he said. "Just put out a record. But the reason I'm going on the TV is because three years ago I was taken from where I live by one of those machines, from outer space—"

"A UFO?"

"Yeah, right, I didn't think you'd know the term. Anyway, I was taken by this UFO into outer space." Kent Gable scowled abruptly. "What's the matter with you? You don't believe me? Listen, mate, you're a very limited person."

"No, no," I said. "I believe you."

"Okay, okay. So, when I returned, a short bit later, I wrote a lot of songs about my experiences—that's what's on the record. Allow me to show it to you." He began to rummage around in the bag at his feet, and at last produced a record with his picture on the cover. "Kent Gable, that's me," he said. And it was true he resembled the picture, with his phosphorescent eye and damaged spiked hair. I wished I could have read better, for I would have liked to have heard that record and what it contained. "Last week," Kent said, "the aliens returned. Once again they took me away: straight out of Catford, away from my family, my rock group, my manager, and my mates. Two years went by; but the startling thing was, when I was put back down on the face of the earth, not only was it only just a day later, but I was on some mingy island called New Burnt Norton."

"Fascinating," I said.

"Anyway, I called my manager straight away, and he's booked me on the 'Today' show. Actually, the timing has worked out beautifully with the album's release."

"And what will you say on the show of today?" I said.

"Oh, I have some important news," he said.

"What is it?"

"Oh, a little of this, a little of that," Kent said. He looked at me strongly, with a certain pleading expression in his eyes I could not interpret. "I have a few things I want to say. Very nice people, the aliens. No unemployment, lots of fresh fruit, that sort of thing."

Believe me, I knew very little about people, and I did not know whether joining civilization was going to help me. "You will not be staying in New York for long, then?" I said. For I had a momentary thought, in which I thought that at least in Kent I had a friend, and how pleasant it would be for me to have a dear friend upon my arrival in this new place.

"No," Kent said. "A couple of weeks, maybe less. But I'll give you my number, maybe we'll get together for a pint."

I was nearly overcome and took his hand in mine. "But how kind you are!" I said. "How dear! Now I know that in you I have a true brother."

His chalky blue eyes looked at me earnestly from beneath

his frizzled hair. "Where you come from, your island—it's a terrible, terrible place," he said. "I hope I don't offend you by mentioning this, mate. Yet I feel I have some information I must tell you. You've never left before?"

"No," I said. "I am an uncivilized man; but recently I met a young woman who agreed to civilize me. It's because of her I'm about to launch on this adventure: I am to go to Manhattan and participate in various cultural events."

Kent Gable seemed pained; he clasped his hands to his hot temples. "The ringing! The ringing! Can't you hear that sound?"

"No," I said, for there was only the roar of the engines.

"It's them, the people from the UFO." At last he took his hands from his head, from which the perspiration rolled. "This is what I have to say: I think it'll be better, if, as soon as you arrive in New York, you turn around and catch the next plane home. Will you do this?"

"I—"

"Listen to me!" he said. "You will do as I say! My voices are always correct, mate. And if you are not in serious trouble already, you will be shortly."

"Well," I said, not knowing what etiquette would dictate in a situation such as this. "Believe me when I say I consider you my true friend and brother. And I'll certainly keep your suggestion in mind."

"Bloody 'ell," Kent said in disgust. "You're effing impossible, mate! I can see my bloody words of wisdom will be of no use!" He stuffed his record back into his bag and leaned back into his seat before falling asleep. I thought he was no longer awake and stealthily leaned forward to find out what objects of desire he held in his valise, but just then he opened one blue cow-eye and gave me a sharp rap across the knucklebone.

Thus the hours did pass. Now, I was nervous of my surroundings, for the plane screamed and whined, and the clouds appeared strange and white, as substantial as the seat I was sitting on, a sight I found interesting though alarming. Already I was worrying about what was to come when I landed in Manhattan, though there was at least remaining eighteen hours of flying time. Also I had some fleas or bedbugs attached to my person, which must have joined up with me back at the hotel, for I found I was itching something fearful.

After a while I ventured out to the toilet. This was a marvelous place; into my handbag I deposited many charming little bars of soap and other toiletries such as premoistened towelettes. I found the toilet itself most fascinating, with the water in the bowl so blue I realized it was not water but liquid sky, piped in directly from the blue yonder. Several times I did flush and flush; I threw in some paper towels, imagining that if I flushed and ran back to my seat I might see these paper towels drifting past my window in the sky. Yet to my horror, the fourth time I flushed, the liquid sky did not go down but commenced an upward journey, filling the bowl and then, rising fast and angry, began to spill out onto the floor. It rose and rose and I could not stop the flow.

What was a person like me going to do? I rushed to the door, but the bolt appeared stuck, for I could not seem to break out. If the liquid sky continued to rush inward, soon the whole plane would be filled with the exterior and we would all be in big trouble. Yet I myself was reluctant to take the blame. I struggled and struggled with the door until at last the lock unhinged itself and I burst free and dashed back down the aisle to my seat.

There I sat trembling, for I knew how severely natives were punished, and at any minute I felt the stewardess and captain would approach and lead me struggling to the back of the plane, where they would push me out.

But all that happened was that after a time a stewardess appeared with a bucket and mop, and a while later another stewardess appeared with marvelous celebratory feast-trays, one of which was handed to each person. Oh, how delightful! For there was a little menu with each tray, and on my dish was something called the *hot pastrami sandwich*: this consisted of a very hard roll, soggy in the center and topped with tiny seeds like gnats, while within were some curious greasy strands of meat. And there was also a *salad:* which consisted of some pale-green slimy leaves and a tiny red rubber ball. Following Kent's directions, I squirted a yellowish substance onto my salad from a little plastic packet. There was also the *cake:* now this was a square brown object covered with a white hard surface. Each of these things I tasted eagerly, rolling the various textures and tastes around in my mouth to get the full flavor.

Accompanying this repast was an assortment of souvenirs, such as little packets marked PEPPER and SALT; a plastic fork, knife, and spoon neatly sealed in clear cellophane, suitable for wall-decoration if properly hung, or possibly for wearing in the hair; and a beautifully pristine white paper napkin. All these things I did place in my handbag, without doubts as to my action, for I saw many people who surrounded me doing likewise.

Thus sated, I leaned back in my seat. Kent had now roused himself, and began once more to speak. "When the aliens deposited me on New Burnt Norton, I found myself atop Mt. Bawwaar-Yaas. You know this place?"

"Why yes," I answered glibly. For the top of Mt. Bawwaar-Yaas was shaped like a pyramid, a natural formation apparently unique in all the world, and many were the white man's expeditions I had accompanied up to the top of it. "In fact, during my youth I served as lead bearer and guide on so many of these trips that I became quite excellent in English."

"This Mt. Bawwaar-Yaas is no natural formation," Kent said. "It is an alien construction built millenniums ago. What's the matter with you, mate? You don't believe me? You are a very mediocre person."

"No, no, I believe you," I said. "Do go on, pray tell." But apparently I had in some way offended him, for he would say nothing more. But the truth was that I *did* believe him. "It's like this, Mac," I said. "My dad, God bless him, always used to tell me when I was a boy that the top of Mt. Bawwaar-Yaas was created millions of years ago, a man-made phenomenon created by astronauts from another galaxy who needed a pyramid to preserve meat under."

Kent struck himself in the forehead. "Bloody 'ell," he said. "Forgive me, for I have underestimated you. But exactly!" And he firmly shook my hand. "Please go on."

"Very well," I said. "You see, as I mentioned, I used to be hired from time to time to assist various mountain-climbing expeditions to the peak. Of course, the knowledge of the fact that the pyramid itself was built by alien astronauts was a secret known only to my tribe; but when I had the opportunity I used to sneak away from the expedition in search of the so-called meat hole that my father had described to me—the hidden opening that led to an inner chamber inside the pyramid where bits of meat and old razor blades were allegedly stuffed by the ancients."

"My god, you are a wise man, for this is what the aliens themselves have told me," Kent said. "The aliens were in dire need of a place to abandon used razor blades, and the mysterious powers of the pyramid meant that when they returned the razor blades would be freshly sharpened."

"But allow me to continue," I said. "Usually four wealthy explorers would band together in determination to climb to the pyramid's peak. Then, of course, five or six newspaper reporters and cameramen would come along to record the endeavor. Now, food was needed for these men, and this took twenty porters carrying the Rice Krispies and Pop Tarts and chicken croquettes and dried pemmican that they needed. And also another ten men were needed for carrying the personal belongings of the group, and the photographic equipment and foul-weather gear. But this meant that there were thirty people still without food—the men who were carrying the food and equipment for the rest of the group. So another fifteen men had to come along to carry the food for these thirty men. But that still left these fifteen men without food. So another ten men were brought along to carry food for these. But of course these ten men were without food. Sir, for twenty-five points and a chance to enter the semifinals, can you answer the following question: What was the name of the man who led the expedition?"

"Uh—" Kent said, and his forehead broke out once again in beads of perspiration.

"Time's up!" I said gleefully. "I told you, it was me! Well, that is, I wasn't exactly the *leader* of the expedition—but in fact, without my presence, I can assure you, nobody would have gotten anywhere. I was the only one who spoke English! I always had an ear for languages."

The time did pass this way in happy conversation. I knew I would be sore to see Kent go and tried to induce him to stay with me for a few days, but he said that when we got to the airport we must surely part, at least for the time being. And he once more tried to convince me to return on the next flight to my native homeland, but though I knew he probably was correct, I said that each man had to follow his own path, and that mine led to reservations at the Holiday Inn.

As the plane began its descent over Manhattan, each of us wept and blew our noses, so close a kinship had we formed, though the hours spent together could only be measured in hours. But sometimes this is the kind of right hook Life throws in a person's way. Would I ever find such a friend again?

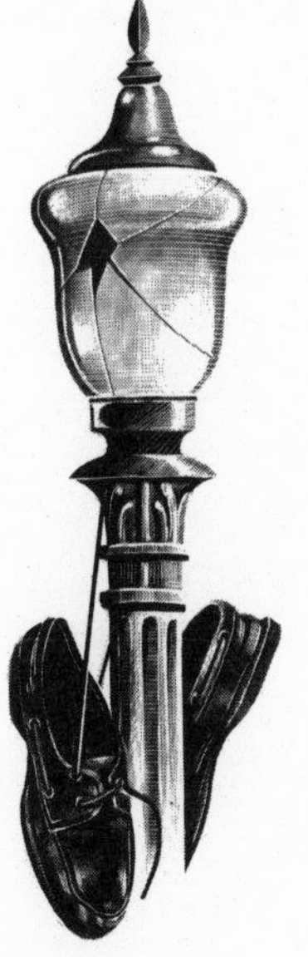

10

The plane landed at last at Mr. Kennedy's Airport. It was gray and dismal early morning, for the flight had taken overnight, and the place loomed large and deathly to me, dressed in my pink linen suit and shaking with cold.

At customs Kent and I were forced to separate, for a man showed a friendly interest in examining him and wanted to search through his belongings. How delightfully childlike, I thought, though Kent to my surprise did not seem to return the man's good humor. "Listen," Kent said, "I may be detained a while. I wish I could ride into the city with you, mate, but I can asssure you there's no need to wait. Now listen, here's the phone number of where I'm staying"—and he scrawled something on a scrap of paper and handed it to me—"and you just go ahead and call me if you have any problem at all. We'll see each other soon."

I tried to embrace, but the fellow in the uniform was joined by some of his friends, and Kent was led off. So I went on through, still clutching Kent's number in my hand.

On the other side the place was badly heated and drafty. Long trails of slush dragged across the floor and crowds of travelers rushed past me each with a destination of their own. There were men in suits, and women in suits, and people shouting at one another in foreign tongues and others kneeling in rituals of prayer. Then to my horror I was bumped into, quite accidentally I'm certain, by a man in a lime green suit who wielded a briefcase. The piece of paper Kent had given me fell from my hand and I scrabbled frantically for it on the ground, though it was kicked along by the crowds of various pedestrians who passed. When I finally retrieved it, the paper was now an indecipherable blot. And though I searched and searched for a sign of Kent, it seemed that he was gone. So, alas, was the suitcase Maria had given me to carry for her; I was filled with sorrow at my immediate failure.

I did not know where to go for a long time, and stood looking around timidly. I forgot the directions Maria had written down and felt sure I would never leave this place. Then two women—one in a delightful pink raincoat, one in a lively blue-checked dress—came up alongside me. "You want to grab our bags here?" the pink raincoat said. "We need a taxi."

"But of course," I said, and hefted the bags, though there were many. "Where do I go?"

The two women shook their heads. "Foreigner," the blue-check muttered. "I'm surprised he speaks English."

"I can explain why this is," I started to say, but the two ladies had commenced and I followed them outside, where I deposited their bags and bid them good-bye. One tried to impress on me a few bills, but I did not take them. "It's enough that you showed me how to get out of that place," I said.

Here there was a row of taxis and in front of them was an enormous lime green Cadillac automobile, in a vibrant and startling color. I paused briefly to admire this machine, a wonderful thing. Now in my pockets I scrambled for my directions and information, and I began to walk over to the first taxi in the row when I saw it was empty of driver. And a man approached, of whom I made careful note, for he was an interesting-looking person and my first New York taxi driver, a breed of which I had already heard. He had a little wizened beard and eyes that drooped at the corners suggestively, a romantic rat. Although not particularly overweight, his skin was rippled and sleek as a woman's, quite visible to me, for he was wearing only a short-sleeved shirt and the backs of his hands had blushed a delicate pink in the cold. He wiped his nose on the back of the right one, coughed and hawked a bit, then spit on the near side of my foot. "Need a cab?" he said.

"Yeah," I said, and I hurried forward. The lime green Cadillac pulled out as I passed it to get into the taxi and sprayed my trousers with a mucky liquid that covered the ground everywhere.

This brought to mind the time when, as a youngster in the Methodist missionary school my class and I had been taken on a field trip to the tiny zoo in Jaranekta. This zoo contained only local animals—man-like cassowaries and the pigs which all of us had seen before—but there was a balding lion in an iron cage with a sign over him that said, WARNING! STAND CLEAR OF THE LION WHEN HIS BACKSIDE IS TURNED OUTWARDS. This the missionary was reading for us and translating into Lesser Pimbanese as the group of us stood looking at the lion, when the animal had indeed done so, turned around that is, and pissed a stream of hot yellow urine fifteen feet out into the room, where it had landed exactly on me myself, to the delight and amusement of the missionary teacher and my classmates. However, it had only been a short time after that, in what was to prove to be one of the last native uprisings on New Burnt Norton to occur, when my father had come down into the mission school grounds one night and sliced the teacher up into a variety of pieces, which I, at that time renamed Mark Phillip by the missionary teacher, had dined on the next evening.

The taxi driver, before getting into the taxi, examined me suspiciously, his rat eyes scouring my body, looking at my suit and then the Bic pen and straw thrust through my nose like double propellers. My face, with its scars and deviated septum, was, I suppose, not appropriate to the rest of my body with its dapper suit. "Where you going?" he said. He lit a cigarette and then turned briefly to examine the rear end of a girl with a froggy face and thick gold shoes who passed. "Biffle," he said. "Kapow kapow kapow. What do you think of that chick, huh?"

"Oh, very fine indeed," I said. "I'm not sure where I'm going, however. I just have to find the paper. The Holiday Inn—you know where that is? I have directions someplace. I have a dear friend in this city, Ms. Maria Fishburn—no doubt you are old friends with her. But unfortunately her accommodations are not able to withstand me, so she has arranged for me to stay in a hotel."

"That's okay," my rat-eyed driver said. "I know where that is. Just wanted to make sure you didn't want to go to Brooklyn or something. Where are you from?"

"New Burnt Norton," I said. "Mgungu Yabba Mgungu, at your service."

The man picked up my bags, grunting, and placed them in the trunk of the auto. "Thank you," I said. "Delighted to make your acquaintance." For I had decided I rather liked this fellow. "I have always wanted to meet a real New York taxi driver."

"Yeah, sure," he said shortly. "Where's New Burnt Norton, anyway, huh?" I began to try and explain, but he was now driving in a very deranged fashion, so that I tossed from one side of the car to the other and my teeth nearly knocked loose from my head. "Is that all the clothes you have?" rat-eyes said. "Don't you have a coat?"

"Yes, I do," I said proudly. "Fur, but not with me at the moment."

"I don't know where you're coming from, but somebody should of told you it's cold here," he said. "Sometimes at this time of year it's already spring, but we've had twelve inches of snow in the past two weeks, ya don't look to me like you're dressed warm enough. The reason I don't have a coat, is because I get carsick if I'm too hot when I'm driving. But I don't know," he said, mashing out his cigarette and lighting another one. "Where ya coming from? You from out of town?"

"I'm from New Burnt Norton."

"Yeah? Where's that? Never heard of it." And so it went. The drive took hours and I nearly wanted to die, I was so nauseated, and a far worse sensation than any to be found on an airplane, I can assure you. How foolish to build the airport so far from the city! A real crazy idea, and much of what we passed began to look the same and even familiar. My first view of the city was not what I would have liked it to be, tossed and turned about like that in the ripped-up back seat. For though I had expected to be impressed, I was more filled with awe on a daily basis at the sight of the Mt. Bawwaar-Yaas pyramid than I was at the sight of these rugged buildings, colossal and foreboding. How terrible these scrapers were indeed, unsoftened by time and natural inclements!

In keeping with my mood the day outside was even more gloomy, and I was glad at any price not to have to walk. A gray dirt streamed down from the sky, and on examining my suit I found it was no longer pink but was covered with a fine filth. Gusts of exhaust blew in a crack at the top of the window through the journey, and I suddenly developed a miserable and hacking cough.

And then, too, I was shocked at the driver, when he deposited me at the Holiday Inn, where he told me the ride would cost one hundred and eighty-nine dollars. But considering the length of the trip I supposed it was an accurate fee. And I did have enough cash, only because luckily Maria had managed to cash a check and give me some on New Burnt Norton. What I would have done if this was not the case I don't know.

I might have been arrested or deported even, but as I say, I did have enough to pay the guy off. But I was sorely sick and wearily I unloaded my bags and dragged them into the hotel.

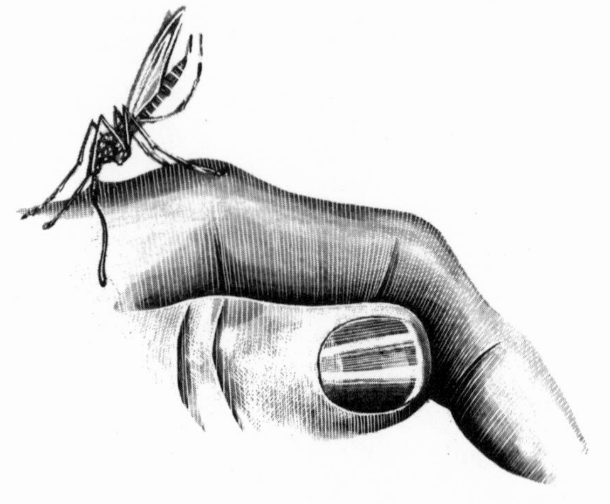

11

Upon awakening it was twilight and I had the momentary sensation of finding myself in unknown whereabouts. How could this be, I thought—for I was no fool. Luckily this feeling quickly dissipated, leaving me with a sensation of homesickness. I went to the window and looked out: I was on the fifteenth floor, and there were many tall buildings that faced mine.

How bleak and monumental it all looked, with the gray snow like pig-dandruff drifting down, and the various myriads of windows, behind each of which, no doubt, there lurked an occupant. A light grizzle fell, giving a powdery, glittery haze to the cement sidewalk below. There was a stain on my window in an uneven amoeba shape of white. It ran toward the bottom in a drippy pattern, as if some bird had driven itself to death against the glass. I could only look out the window for several seconds at a time before feeling dizzy and weak. In the first place I had not reconciled myself to the fact that it was possible to remain suspended so high above the ground in a man-made artifice—I was referring to the Holiday Inn—without falling. There was nothing to cling to in the hotel room. Across from me the wallpaper was a latticework of blue and white; the curtains were blue and red paisley, with an inner layer of blue. The light hung suspended from a wicker chain only inches above the floor. One wall was blue, another orange. There were two beds in the room; between them was a sort of bookshelf with several telephone directories and a Bible. The beds themselves were covered with a papery fabric splotched with a design of huge cabbages.

I knew then that I should probably enter that room known as the Elevator and descend to the lobby and find something to eat. Yet so lonesome did I feel at that moment I decided instead to indulge myself: I went to my suitcases and got my Baggies of beetles and herbs and butterflies and began the lengthy preparation required to manufacture some Joy Paul Guilford. Step one: cleaning the fingernails, for no unwanted substance must contaminate the rest. To my surprise, in my suitcase were additional little bags full of dessicated insects; the only person who could have placed them there was Maria Fishburn, and I saw now why she had made such a to-do about allowing her to pack my bags instead of letting me do it myself. For the generous girl must have acquired additional ingredients and sent them along with me, knowing that I would be here on an extended stay and would no doubt like to partake of my native hallucinogen on an occasional basis.

Now, the preparations for Joy Paul Guilford are elaborate and difficult, involving as they do ritual chanting and a small cookstove. Yet before I had much of an opportunity to commence, the telephone on the night table rang, and I went over to operate it. This I did by lifting the receiver and pressing one portion up against my ear, while speaking loudly into a flat disc dotted with little holes.

"Hello?" I said. "Who is it?"

It was Maria, and she was in the lobby, having just arrived from Paris via Concorde jet. "Come on," she said. "Are you dressed? We have to go to this cocktail party. And bring some of the Joy Paul."

"But I am not dressed," I said. "Nor have I commenced concoction of the Joy Paul. The preparations are lengthy."

"Get dressed, and let's get going," she said. She insisted I wear nothing more than my penis gourd and a chain of dogs' teeth around my waist and human jawbone jewelry at my neck, and though she told me to leave off the man-made artifacts, I wore the Bic pen through my nose and the peanut butter–jar lid earring anyway.

The party was in a townhouse on the East Side and it was decorated with large steel-and-leather appliances or furnishings that appeared to my untrained eye to be various parts of cars, though obviously this could not have been the case. Other furniture I could see at once was not at all new, particularly the shabby old Oriental rugs, and should have been replaced, though I never would have said this.

There was present, Maria Fishburn pointed out, a famous youthful Latin American playwright in a beret, a screenplay writer of violent movies, a clothing designer, an art critic, an investment banker, a man known for his invention of the Ziploc bag and his collection of antique instruments, a Texas oilman, and many others.

After telling me this she wandered off, and it was then that I made my terrible faux pas.

But the flowers looked so beautiful and tender in the center of the table, nestled next to a platter of rumaki and a bouquet of crude vegetables such as cauliflowers; pink, thin carrots; whitey-green scallions; and long silver radishes each carved into the shape of a rose or a gladiolus and on delicate stems. And when I overheard a man in a leather jacket and a mustache saying to another man, "I can't believe out of all the great florists in Manhattan Richard found someone to make up that hideous bunch of cattleyas! How incredibly tasteless," I found that I had to taste one for myself and so climbed up onto the table, reached across vegetables, plucked one from the center of the arrangement, and began to munch on it. And it was not tasteless but only delicate and with a slight waxy savor to it.

On the opposite side of the room was a man who stared at me with horror and bemused surprise. "You must be Mgungu," he said. "I'm Parker Junius, curator of the Museum of Primitive Cultures. Allow me to welcome you to New York. I'm looking forward to your participation in the International Dance Festival."

"It is a good thing to meet you," I said.

"Maybe you should get down from the table," Parker Junius said.

Then I realized I had made an error and my eyes focused on his eyebrows and I could not tear them away. These eyebrows, so firmly rooted on his head, were massive and untamed and grew far above the top of his glasses like a terrier dog, with stiff salt-and-pepper guard hairs springing into the air. Yet still I could not seem to get down from the table, and it was then that I sensed my penis gourd had dislodged itself, no doubt in my haste at removing my fur coat when we came in the door.

In my own sweet and stupid way I wanted to die. At last I got down and went to the bar. And so I began to drink steadily, knowing this thing I had done was a most terrible thing for a man, that I was ridiculous in my misfortune and alone. How could I have done what I had done? For now every way I turned there were voices laughing and fools giggling and no one would bring themselves to speak with me. In the center of the room I stood lighting one cigarette after the next, for I was dressed all wrong for the occasion, and I had eaten the centerpiece. To live like this, neither man nor animal, but only some wheeling and turning dumbo, was terrible beyond belief.

I got handed a drink at the bar, which I began to gulp, a clear brown liquid soothing and sugary on the throat yet burning with an acid and longing to it that reminded me of a mixture made by Yerba at home from a pomade of fermented bananas and coconuts that gave off a private white-hot heat and knocked you right down at a single sip.

But this liquid did not have the same effect on me, and I returned to the bartender, a little shriveled and sere person, stooped and crooked over himself in a most horrific way so that each time he picked up a bottle to pour a drink he nearly poured it on his own self and his hands trembled as if uncontrollable. And the liquor swirled thickly over the feathery ice, making rivulets where the one hit the other and I wanted to die.

Who had decked me out in this nonsensical garb and placed me in the group of civilized people like a short and muscular joke? I was nearly wet with exhaustion over this my first cocktail party, and the trails of sweat ran down my chest like hot tears and the ballpoint pen and yellow-white tusk shoved through my nose were not dashing and masculine but ludicrous.

If only they had had various sorts of pâté or chopped-liver mold in the shape of a fish or a lobster, then I might not have gotten so drunk. Now in one chair sat Maria Fishburn with her friends ignoring me and in another was the man who had remarked about the flowers, but nowhere was there anyone who would do more than leave me alone or chuckle furtively. So I went and tried to talk to the bartender but without much success, since his accent was so thick, due either to his condition, which appeared to be a facial palsy, or perhaps due to the fact that he was a New Yorker. "What? I'm sorry."

"I said, he drew these pictures of little bones and showed them to me. They're shaped like sesame seeds and called sescroidals, because they're like these little black seeded warts—plantar's warts they're called."

"I see," I said. He seemed to think I was some kind of a doctor attending the party. "What do you do during the day?" I asked him, feeling that here perhaps was a person who would permit me to speak to him and lead a life closer to something that I was used to.

"What do I do during the day? Find out where I'm going to work that night, see people, rest up from the day before. Have you ever heard of reflexology? A form of acupuncture. The theory is that the body is divided up into ten zones." He stopped speaking to mix up a drink. "Each terminates in the palms of the hands and the soles of the feet to work out the nervous system. A friend of mine had a crystalline deposit—a mucus-cell cyst. It was excruciating. Well, this friend of mine tried every which old way to get rid of it. She had it cauterized. Came back. A plastic surgeon cut it out. It came back in three days. But using reflexology I was able to eliminate it completely. Eventually all feeling did return to her tongue. What do you think of that?"

"You'll have to excuse me," I said, as my boss and inviter to the United States approached me. He seemed to be walking in a weaving pattern with a drink held loosely in one hand, his white hair tufted and giddy on his head like a balding bird.

"Ontogeny recapitulates phylogeny," Parker Junius, curator of the Museum of Primitive Cultures, said. His face was both gleeful and ponderous. "Know what that means?"

I did not respond but only looked at him in embarrassment, thinking of the flower I had eaten.

"Ever hear anybody say that?"

"No."

"Want to give a guess? Oh, I'm not advocating use of the doctrine. But I must give nature her claim. Take your behavior, Mgungu. It's certainly not instinct. A lot of things we do in a certain way are habits. A lot of morality comes from habit. We have a habit of doing this thing or that. But we don't have to go on doing these things."

"Mmm, sure."

"One of the great influences you are now being exposed to here in New York, Mgungu, is science. Herbert Spencer. Theory of development. He's not thought of highly today, mind you, although he was around long before Darwin ever thought of evolution. But he's too eclectic for today's taste. What does that mean, Mgungu? Eclectic." What his problem was I could not be sure, aside from the fact that he was rather drunker than I.

"Sticks things in here and there?" I said, trying to be helpful.

"Yes! That's one way of putting it. He's full of apologies—I mean analogies, of course. From a philosophical point of view it's distracting, but from another point of view it's very entertaining."

"I can imagine. But let me ask you a few questions. For I have been trying to read some literature and cannot fathom it." But Parker Junius was not interested in my questions and ambled off into the dusky twilight of the room.

Now for some years—ever since my father did away with the missionary and I did away with the missionary's library—I had read a great deal, as I can now see, in preparation for this cocktail party and life in general in New York, to try to educate myself and bring myself up to the level of the people I was meeting. But the volumes were very boring and for the life of me I could not plow through *Ulysses*. Every time I opened the book it was the same story: I fell asleep. Even the *Norton Anthology* held excerpts that were too lengthy for my untrained head, weakened by years of jungle sun and a bout with the tapeworm some time ago. So instead I began to study the Monarch Notes, yet still there were things I could not understand at all.

I felt this was my chance to find out. And yet, whenever I approached a group of people standing and sipping Perrier or wine in glasses so fragile they appeared to be living birds in the hand, with my questions such as "What is there to be enjoyed in Spenser's *Faerie Queene*?" (for I found it very tedious going) and "What was Thoreau talking about in *Walden* or was he perhaps crazy?" (for here I felt somewhat more confident, having been a man of nature, living among the mosquitoes and fearful ants for the majority of my life, and knew it must take a lunatic to willfully inflict this existence on himself), the looks the people at the party gave me were both puzzled and horrified, as if I had come up to them and begun to talk about how to stew a human head.

"You are making a fool of yourself," Maria came up alongside and hissed in my ear. "I've told everyone how marvelous you are and you keep going up to people with the most inane nonsense. If you can't think of anything interesting to say just lean against the wall and look savage."

So chastised, I just stood looking at a painting on the wall of some large squares of green, very soothing to the eye and exceedingly accurate in its squares, and tried to listen to what these people were talking about. Soon, however, a lady I had noticed somewhat earlier, a highly strung person with a lot of black hair and some kind of headdress made of feathers, approached my direction, and even with my back to her I could feel her glittery animal eyes traversing my naked body. And I was right, for I heard her say, loudly, "My God, will you look at the ass on that man! Not an ounce of fat. I didn't know there were so many muscles in the human rear end! I may go to New Burnt Norton myself if that's the way they're made there. Richard, why don't you take up ass exercises?" And I was very humiliated and my face turned the color of a crushed arkberry.

I don't know what I would have done had not at that moment Parker Junius reapproached me saying, "If you're going to live the right kind of life, Mgungu, there are certain things you're going to have to remember. When you break loose from a particular historical period we see it in an ugly light. And not only is the present always changing—and I think this is something George Eliot insisted on also—but so is the past."

"Yes, sir," I said with respect.

"Because so many things are in the air and so many people are saying very similar things," he continued, going over to the bar and getting another drink from my dear friend, the little deformed man in the white jacket. "It's a very tricky thing to say what influence somebody has on somebody else. But you are certainly capable of it, I realize that." I really could not fathom what he was talking about, but I found myself suddenly in the position of popularity, for the black-haired woman now approached us and took my arm. With a sweet scraping motion she said to Parker Junius, "Parker, darling, would you mind terribly excusing us for just a teensy while?"

Parker Junius waved his drink vituperatively in the air. "No, of course not," he said. "Do forgive me, Mgungu, if I've rambled on this evening. I'm accustomed to lecturing, at the university level. Graduate seminars. In any event, I'll see you shortly at the press conference, eh? We'll expect you there tomorrow. There should be a little map in your hotel room." And he wandered off.

Well, these cocktail parties were certainly very strange. For now this woman led me off down a long hallway to a sleek and mirrored bedroom, or so I presumed at least that it was a bedroom since it contained a bed, and she said to me, "Would you like to have sex?"

"Well," I said, "I guess so." Considering that I was a guest and this was perhaps an American custom.

"Why don't you take your clothes off then?" she said. A strange comment, for I had on no clothing except for a few decorative pieces and also my shoes and socks. So I thought it was this last that she was referring to, and I sat down on the bed done in pink and silver and I said, "I must apologize, for I'm afraid my feet smell very strong."

Now what can a person do? So my feet smell; I have apologized and removed my socks to be laundered. What should I do, keep my shoes on to not allow the fumes out? This would be very bad indeed—for the bed, I mean, and also for the feet. I was used to years in the jungle of walking without socks, or shoes for that matter, and over the years my feet had grown very hard and covered with a horny plate, like the feet of an iguana. And when they were put into shoes they cried and cried, carrying on about being imprisoned, and they swelled very much and very quickly. However I was not sorry, for this lady had been very glad to see a real savage at the cocktail party and even whispered to me that I was the most fun thing since she had gone out with the New York City Ballet. Therefore she would probably be most pleased at the odoriferous feet, I thought, and say, "How wonderfully original." But for myself I did apologize to prove that this difference was a superficial thing only.

But by the look on her face, and by her silence, I knew I was in error or that something had happened to make her very sick. And she would not come near me, which was I suspect a good time to leave, for just then Maria fetched me angrily as she would have retrieved a misbehaving child, saying, "I've been looking everywhere for you, can't you be trusted for a minute?"

At the door I had to put my shoes and socks back on, and my fur overcoat, as it was snowing outside, snow a gray or brown substance unlike the white stuff visible on the top of Mt. Bawwaar-Yaas, rather a stuff that turned to liquid on the ground, thus rendering it impossible for me to return to my hotel clad only in my native costume, however much Maria Fishburn would have liked me to.

Though it was she herself who had earlier insisted, back on New Burnt Norton, that she buy me a winter coat, saying it was only right or else I would freeze, and so I had a magnificent coat that came down to my ankles, of fur both red and tawny at the same time, with a long guard hair and streaks of blond and dapple flowing in a vertical direction, thus "giving the illusion of greater height than the gentleman has." So vast was this coat I must have appeared a sort of jungle cat or red polar bear.

I followed Maria Fishburn back to her apartment building, dutiful as a dog, all the time gazing at her tender backside and nape. I longed to be invited upstairs, if for no more than a cup of coffee and some proximity, but in the lobby she turned to me and said, "You better go back to the Holiday Inn as long as the Cultural Arts is paying for you to stay there." And she turned and went into her personal elevator.

"See you around then," I said, looking after her wistfully, though she might have been the age of my own daughter, had any of my daughters lived to reach maturity.

"I think we might as well get married," she called abruptly.

"What?" I said, stunned, but the doors had already closed. I stood there skulking about the lobby for several minutes without knowing what to do.

Up in my room, I thought I would continue making the Joy Paul Guilford—to have a smoke and contemplate the possibilities of what she had said. But to my surprise, though I searched and searched, the ingredients were truly gone.

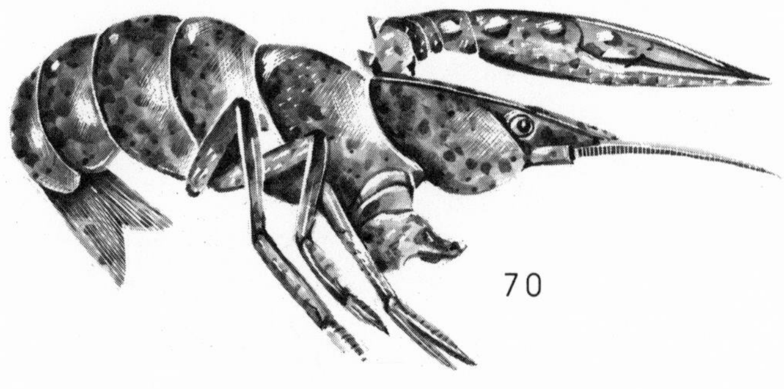

12

What a strange thing!

So, unfulfilled, I put my coat on again and went back out to the out-of-doors, what there was of it in this part of the world. Without the Joy Paul Guilford all I could hope was that I would come across my *moodla*—a highly spiritual item—which somehow I had felt to be absent since my arrival at Mr. Kennedy's airport. Though it was late at night, I was restless and lurking. I felt my body to be marching, though I was not with it.

A few blocks from the Holiday Inn I saw a little storefront, all lit up, with a sign that said JOE'S PIZZA. As the door was open I went in, for I thought this thing called pizza might hold some value for me and indeed might even be a different name for that which I was looking for.

Behind the counter was a man with knotted hair and thick princely arms, flipping a white ball into the air. His face was covered with dark stubble, a problem that I did not have, and one considered unsightly on New Burnt Norton. Only a few sparse hairs grew on my face, and these I plucked with a tweezers made from a piece of folded wood.

"We're closed," the man said.

"Oh, no," I said. "But let me ask you—are you the famous Joe?"

"Well, yeah," the man said. "I'm Joey. You from out of town?"

"I am here, and I am alone."

"Well, I tell you. I really was just about to lock up."

"You, Joey," I said. "You must have much wisdom, to have this place of pizza named after you."

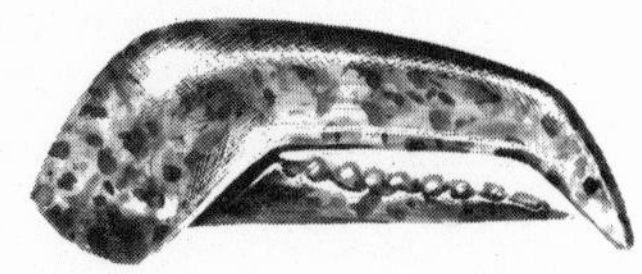

"Yeah?" Joey said, looking pleased. "Who're you, anyway?"

"Call me Mgungu," I said.

"I tell you what, Mgungu," Joey said. "I was just about to make a pizza for myself, before I went home. You stick around. I could use a little company while I eat." And he poured me a glass of blackish sweet liquid thick and syrupy, with a fizzy texture and consistency.

While the pizza was cooking Joey sponged the tables and I put the chairs up on top of them upside down and went to use the Gent's, a small urnlike urinal next to a rear exit that led into an alley. Looking out the little window that was covered with filth and a heavy metal grid, I peered into this back alley and there saw a man dressed in a green suit of some almost furry green substance, nearly luminous in the dark, like glowing phosphor settled around his body. He was beating with a small club another man who lay on the wet ground squealing in fear and rage or terror and saying, "Don' kill me man! Don' kill me! I've got it, I only borrowed it for a little while and you'll get it back! I'll get you some new stuff besides! Just don' kill me." With the little camera Maria had given me, I took a picture and went back into the kitchen to tell Joey what was going on.

"Just ignore it," he said. "This is New York."

But I was unable to leave well enough alone, and I went back to the toilet and threatened the man in the luminous green suit from the urinal haven. "Leave that man alone," I yelled out the window. "Leave him alone or I'll call the police." The man looked up briefly to see where the noise was coming from and then resumed his systematic striking of the smaller whimperer. Had this been the jungle of New Burnt Norton I would have ignored it, for during my younger days surprise attack and murder parties were all the custom. It was not safe for any person, man, woman, or child, to walk alone along a mountain path, or even for women to work alone in the gardens without the protection of several men standing around watching all day with bows and arrows.

Even if someone were alone in the village during the day,

some old grandfather or something, chances were in his favor that pretty soon two or three guys from an enemy tribe would come sneaking in and stab him in the gut or shoot a couple of arrows into him, then make off with the body. Pretty soon we'd see this group of enemy warriors standing on the opposite mountain, screaming something over to us. "Hey dumbbells! Quit picking your noses and look over here for a minute! We got something we want to tell you!"

"Yeah? What is it, you bunch of old sow's tits?"

"We just ate your Uncle Grabnetz!" And the enemy would be jumping up and down and shrieking with laughter, too far away to do anything about. "The old bugger was tougher than a rancid, randy old boar!" And sure enough, we'd all go back up to the village to look around for Uncle Grabnetz and he was nowhere to be found.

But this, on the other hand, this was supposed to be a civilized country, and I was trying to become a civilized man. So I yelled out the window again. "You better leave that guy alone or I'm going to have to come out and get you!" The luminous suit looked up again for a second, blew his nose into a long green handkerchief he drew from his lapel pocket, and spat onto the ground.

After some manipulation I managed to pull the grid from the window and climbed out into the back alleyway filled with trash cans and a dead Christmas tree and stacks of old *New York Times* and *New Yorkers* blowing around. As soon as I was safely down the side I let out a war yell my father had taught me when I first went to war, a yell that went something like "UUUURRRRRRGGGGGHHHHH-Ya." And I threw myself onto the back of this one guy beating the other and then put both my hands over this guy's eyes so he couldn't see and began to leave off his beating and crashed around through the trash cans, trying to shake me loose.

Then with my knees I practiced an old gouging custom, driving them, my knees, up into his armpits. "Get your hands off me, motherfucker!" this wild American said to me. And he was trying to throw me off with his hands and was moaning and turning his head this way and that as I parried and worried him like a dog, for I am afraid to say that I became uncivilized and would have really strangled him had it not been for the fact that I hadn't noticed another man standing guard at the entrance of the alleyway to the side street who was waiting next to a running car.

So I was hit suddenly with a very severe blow and fell to the ground with a grunt and lay there while the two men kicked me several times alongside my head and once I think in the side and then walked to the waiting car which was, I noticed dimly, long and lime green, the same color as the suit the man was wearing.

And while I lay on the ground with the world around me blackening and growing colder and the dirty snow under my back, the other man pulled himself up with a whimper and rummaged through my fur-coat pockets. He removed my wallet, from which he pulled my money and threw it then back to the ground, giving me at the same time another kick alongside my ear. And everything grew very dark.

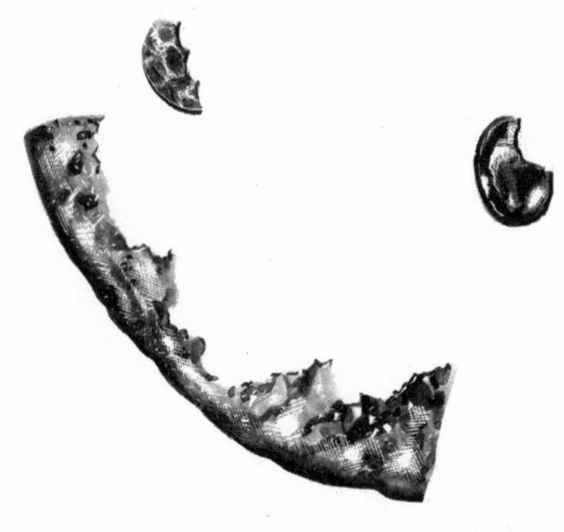

13

Oh my head! For when I awoke it seemed to be the next day and I was stretched out on a high platform indoors and everywhere was a hideous greasy smell that seemed somehow familiar, yet a smell I could not quite place.

My one eye was so swollen up I could barely open it, and each time I opened the other I was met with what appeared to be a sort of wavy black octopus and two swimming tubes of light.

Against one wall was a huge red blob that was indistinguishable as anything human, and some brown dots scurried up the wall. I was forced to shut my eye again, but then opened it to find the octopus waving its tentacles in my face. "Hey man, you all right? Hey, snap out of it! You want a piece of pizza?" The octopus wavered and then came into focus. It appeared to have a blue-black shadow on its face and wet black hair. I considered catching it to cook for a meal. Cooked octopus, when the suction cups on the arms were properly broken down and softened, made a delicious dish, I had learned from Yerba. "Mgungu?" A wet towel was wiped over my forehead and my eye cleared.

I was lying on the counter inside Joe's Pizza and the light that I had taken to mean implied it was the next day was in reality two tubular fluorescent lights that would not hold quite still overhead. Against one wall the red blob turned into a pizza that Joey now brought me a slice of. "Here, you want a piece of pizza? It's on me. It's good cold."

I shook my head.

"No? You want me to heat it up?"

"No, I'm all right."

"What the hell happened to you out there? I had to use a gun to chase that guy away from kicking you to death. Jeez, for a short guy you're not so light, either. I couldn't get you up, nearly had to drag you in here."

"Ambush," I said weakly.

"I told you to leave well enough alone. This is New York. You don't mess with anyone here. You just mind your own business in this city."

"Yeah, yeah. I've heard this is New York until I'm sick in the head."

"But you can get anything in New York if you want to. All you need is the dough," Joey said, bringing me a new cup of the warm black liquid. "Sorry that the Coke's warm. I turned off the machine a while ago. So tell me, what happened?"

I proceeded to relate briefly what had occurred in the alley.

"You said he was wearing a green suit?" Joey said. He had put some kind of ointment on my head and was sympathetically eating the pizza. "There's no point in taking you to the hospital. They'll only make you sit around while they ask you a lot of questions about your outfit." I had forgotten that under my fur coat I was wearing only my gourd and still had dangling around me the dogs' teeth belt and human-jawbone necklace. On my head, now bent and limp, were feathers of cassowary and lory parrot, and through my nose was a pen I had found on the hall table of my host earlier that evening. I had not been able to resist picking it up and taking it—a pen of the most marvelous gold color, with a retractable ball. For it I could not help but switch my Bic.

"You say this guy was wearing a green suit?" Joey said again.

"Yes, the most astonishing color. A sort of lime green, I think it was, a phosphorous green. It seemed to glow in the dark and I must say it fit him perfectly. Now, on the whole, the American designers are rather boring, and this suit seemed to me to be of a particularly European cut—"

Joey looked at me with interest. "European cut? You know,

Mgungu, you really are a strange guy in some ways." Thoughtfully he put another slab of pizza into his open mouth. The nauseating smell was beginning to make me hungry. "Anyway, what I think is you just happened to have a run-in with Reynard Lopato, a very well known common criminal. He's almost a celebrity criminal, you might say. The police haven't been able to touch him. And he happens, I know this for a fact, to have a thing about doing his own dirty work himself. He enjoys it, you know, one of those. Of course, I may be mistaken. There may be other well-known criminals in this city, who also wear lime green suits, with reputations for liking to do their own dirty work. For all I know, there may be thousands of guys in the city wearing lime green suits. I mean, there's sixteen million people in this city. How am I supposed to know how many of them are walking around in lime green suits with matching cars? . . . On the other hand, in all honesty, there can't be all that many. The suit, yes, but the matching car, not so certain. What did his buffoon look like?"

"His what?"

"His buffoon, his hojo, his main man?"

"Oh, a big fellow built like a gorilla, about six foot ten or so, I would say, with a great flattened nose and horn-rimmed ears."

"What kind of ears?"

"You know, they stuck out on his head like some species of hard-plated lizards we have on New Burnt Norton. I'm not sure what they are called in English but they are plated with—"

"Yeah, yeah. Well there's nothing we can do about it now. Where are you staying?"

"The Holiday Inn, near the Coliseum."

"Well I'll take you over there now, after I lock up. I gotta drive in that direction anyway—I'm staying at my sister's and I borrowed her car."

In front of my hotel I clasped his hand firmly. "Good-bye, illustrious Joey," I said. For I knew now how temporary and even abrupt these relationships were in the modern world, and wished to make sure we parted strongly.

"Hey, listen," Joey said, "you in town for long? Why don't you stop by tomorrow night, if you're not doing anything? I'll close up early, and we can go out." He looked down at his steering wheel. "I just got divorced, ya know, and I'm kind of lonesome."

"But my friend!" I said. "That would be very fine indeed. I would be delighted to accept your invitation. And this would be a wonderful opportunity for you to get to know my fiancée, Maria Fishburn, who I will readily bring along."

On these terms we separated for the present.

I sat in my hotel room for some time unable to fall asleep. From where I sat on the bed I could see out the window of the hotel and down the street, where a man wheeled an enormous television set in a shopping cart.

Though I had not wished to tell Joey, my head hurt worse than ever. It throbbed as if something living inside it were trying to get out. At last I got up to inspect a painting of a ship at sea during a storm on one of the walls. It was fastened to the wall too tightly, however, for me to remove and put into the suitcase Air New Burnt Norton had given me as a promotional gimmick or gift. Not that I wanted the painting, exactly, but it would have been easy for me to sell it to some unsuspecting native back on New Burnt Norton as a work of art made by a real American.

Yet how could I ever go back to New Burnt Norton and all those trees? It was like a white light had been flashed in front of my eyes, blinding me permanently to anything else I might ever see again. I didn't know how I would be able to live without the excitement and energy of the city.

The television set made a continual buzzing noise. I wasn't certain if it were possible to shut if off, and so, to its constant burr, I lay until it began to be light.

In the morning I dragged myself down to the All-American Coffee Shop and ate several bird's eggs, French toast, bacon, juice, Rice Krispies, and coffee. The bill came to twenty-three dollars.

14

Always before, for the past several years at least, there had been with me the feeling on New Burnt Norton: What am I doing here? I do not belong; I was not meant to be a savage in the wilderness chopping constant trees for firewood. Yet there was now with me the feeling that I had never been meant to get away. My marriages, my pigs, my fungus jungle life were embedded in me too deeply. It ran through me like a streak of white fat in my center. There was no getting around it; there was no way I would ever learn to be civilized *enough*. My animal self was too raw and hot to tame.

After breakfast it occurred to me I might call Maria, who would no doubt rush immediately to my side to soothe and ingratiate as my wives would have done back home. Now, in my condition it required no small manipulation of the telephone; for this instrument in my stupor I found difficult to surmise. It required much determination on my part to figure out which number was associated with which little hole. And once I began to spin the section containing the holes, they were no longer associated with the correct number. But finally I managed to dial forth.

"Darling," the sleepy voice of Maria said, "it's you. I was still asleep, and having the nicest dream about you. Did you remember you're supposed to go to the museum today for the press conference?"

"Oh, yes," I said. "And also, I have an important invitation to bring you. For last night, I became friendly with a most prestigious man, the famous Joe. No doubt you have heard of him."

"No, darling, I haven't," Maria said.

"Joe, of Joe's Pizza, would like to take us out for the evening. I accepted for us both." For I was very proud that I had made a friend, and also that I had a place to take Maria, in order to repay her for the cocktail party event.

"I just can't, Mgungu," Maria said. "But you go. That will be nice for you. Now remember, I'm thinking of you, and I'll talk to you very soon." Thereupon she put down the phone.

Though I had a map to find my way to the museum, I found myself listlessly walking across town in the wrong direction. I thought wistfully of Maria, whom I had scarcely seen, and wondered if she might not be a vision or sprite or demon, the sort of ghost often seen lurking about the outskirts of my village. Yet never before had one been able to lure me away. The pavement burned my feet like a collar and leash on my neck, and the eyes of the passersby smiled grimly, more real than those of any of my ancient ancestors supposedly up there haunting the jungle.

Finally, without half paying attention, I stopped at a delicatessen near, according to my map, the Diamond District, though the streets were mere cement. For several minutes I stood outside, unable to form a decision as to whether I was hungry or not. Yet I was savage: therefore I must eat to survive.

So I went in and gazed: at the gefilte fish swimming in placental jelly, the papery pink slabs of corned beef rippling in fat, the pickled herring embedded with soft, rubbery stingers floating in a pool of cream. On top of the counter were several curled Danish lying wrapped in plastic. Faced with so much choice, my appetite left me and I went and sat at one of the little tables to decide what to eat.

Still, I knew whatever I chose I would be sure to want something different after I had tasted it. Something sweet? A piece of pineapple cheese cake? Or a knish or a Chinese egg roll. Which? Which? Each food called out to me alone.

Now, I had been having problems with my cigarette habit. This smoking had become a religious-type ritual to me and in fact I had done it from a very early age. And to smoke was very necessary with me. There was more to me than just a muscular man, but also a cloud of smoke. Where there was this cloud of smoke there had to be a human being. But in the mountains, to make my cigarettes I added ginger leaves to my rolled-up leaves of tobacco; my wives cultivated this tobacco and the ginger in the gardens and they, too, all smoked, as did even the littlest of my children. Thus we knew that we were not just prisoners of the mountain and the government but a force to be reckoned with. The smoke rose from the mouth of each of us like a gullet of steam.

The ginger leaf gave the cigarette a coolish, sweet taste I had been unable to replicate since leaving. And I longed for this taste deeply. What was I to do? I had a little pouch of tobacco, and also some rolling paper, but of the ginger leaf I had not. Yet in the window of this deli was a plant, the leaves of which were scrawny and sparse but did not entirely disresemble those of the ginger plant. So I got up and stripped the leaves from the vegetation, and then I returned to my place, where I began to manufacture a cigarette with the only type of cigarette rolling paper I had, which made long tenuous cigarettes. But everywhere there seemed to be some kind of a ban on smoking. Great signs adorned every wall, proclaiming NO SMOKING, and whenever there were more than one or two people in the room I was forced to put out my cigarette.

This was due, I thought, to the great American fear of death and disease, two items that were common enough, as I may have mentioned, in New Burnt Norton. But I was not prepared for my cigarettes being so violently grabbed from me and stepped on. I debated further in the delicatessen as I carefully rolled up a cigarette and inserted the plant leaves and some sweet spice from my little pouch. Should I get a roast beef sandwich? Might that not be too much to eat, so shortly after breakfast? Or something simpler: tuna on a roll and a side order of Jell-O with fruit cocktail? Maybe even something whipped up in the blender, like a strawberry-banana milkshake!

Everyone eating in the delicatessen was the sort of person I envied for the easy way they seemed to have accepted their lives. One old dad had on bright green trousers, hands trembling with the palsy as he lifted his spoon to his mouth. A spindly woman wore a plastic reptile coat that drooped open as if she were shedding. Two young women with matching stunted noses pecked away at equal dishes of gravel. As I smoked, around me they all began to look up and sniff, saying, "What's burning? Something's on fire." Which as it happened was not due to the hatred of smoking but something else, which was that the smell of the fresh leaves and the tobacco was abnormal.

A plump baby butterfly of a woman rolled out from behind the deli counter, a big bow of a mouth drawn on her lips with some fuchsia-colored unguent, and waddled up to me. "I'm sorry, that's not allowed in here," she said in a voice heavily painted in some accent. I looked at her in surprise. I could clearly see a man across the room smoking a cigarette. I could not understand why I was the one being picked on. She did not seem like the type of woman who would be upset by the white tusk I had shoved through my nose earlier that day. It hardly seemed fair. "But—" I said.

"Put it out or you'll have to leave. Don't make me call the cops. Don't give me any trouble, please. I got enough trouble."

"Well, all right, but—" The cigarette was forcibly removed from my fingers and snuffed out into an ashtray. Then she unrolled it and began picking at the tobacco, lifting it between her fingers to sniff.

"Hashish, isn't it? I may seem to you to be an old woman, but I know a thing or two. Tch, tch. What people won't try and get away with. But I'm not so dumb, am I? Am I?" Then, examining me more closely, she said, "Where you from, anyway?"

"New Burnt Norton."

"Aha, I thought you were familiar. You're the cannibal! I read a little about you coming to the International Dance Festival in the paper. Tch, tch. I, too, am a stranger in this country and have been for many years. Just a minute please, don't go away." She called into the back room. "Hey Mikey, get out here, will you? We got a cannibal out here, can you believe it?" In the room the heads of the eaters swiveled like turkeys. From the back emerged a huge turbanned gentleman with a long swaggering mustache curling down around both sides of his face and beard. He wiped his hands on a blood-speckled cloth he carefully hung up on a hook.

The fat woman sighed and seated herself at my table. "It's my breath. I'm very short of it," she said. "Hey, Mikey, guess who this is? He's the cannibal we read about in the paper."

Mikey looked me over placidly and began to run a side of meat through the electric slicer.

"My dear man, I feel for you very much," she said. Her eyes, quite whitish, were either rheumy with disease or emotion. "I know what it is like to be in this city and alone with strange customs. I don't intend any offense when I tell you that you must not smoke hashish in a public place in this country, whatever you are allowed to do when you are at home. In any case, a young man like you should not need to smoke that stuff, which is very bad for your health. And believe me, I have seen what it can do, although to you I may just seem like an old lady." She turned to Mikey, who now appeared to be grinding knives. "These young people think they have invented everything and don't realize the world has been around a good deal longer than their lifetime."

"Lady, I'm in my fifties, more or less," I could not resist saying.

"So, you're in your fifties! And has that kept you out of trouble? No, there's no telling anybody anything. Who wants to listen. Now I will bring you a sandwich and then we will talk. What do they call you?

"Mgungu."

"Mgungu! I couldn't possibly call you that. I will call you Perry, after an old friend of mine, an admirer from the North.

And me, you will call me Sophie, although I might have made you call me Mrs. Tuckermann, since I am the owner of the delicatessen, or even Mama Tuckermann, since that is the name of the delicatessen. But I am not asking you to call me by any of those names except Sophie."

Still I would have liked to have had a cigarette and sat tapping my foot impatiently and wondering whether or not something would happen to me if I were late for the photo session and the important press conference afterward. For although it is true I do not have much of a sense of time, as is true of many native peoples without wristwatches, I have more than enough sense of worry to make up for its absence.

Mrs. Tuckermann reappeared at the side of my table holding a large sandwich on a paper plate. She had taken off her white, grease-spotted apron and now visible was her dress of beautiful purple-and-white chiffon with a jabot of shreds of cloth at the neck. On her feet were tiny pointed black boots buttoning up the sides, and at the instep near her toes were huge bulges which signified the presence of corns. A thick pair of spectacles adorned the end of her nose and on one corner of the lenses were a pair of initials "N.N." in fancy curling letters of gold.

"Your initials—" I said.

"They were out of S and T when I got the glasses," she said, sitting again heavily. Her looping fleshy arms flattened against the tablecloth; with one hand she took my shoulder briefly and the force of her clutching was much greater than I had expected. "My daughter's idea," she said. "Who needs new glasses? I got nothing I want to see." She pushed the sandwich in front of me and for herself sipped from a paper cup filled with iced tea and cubes of lemon.

The sandwich was piled high with various types of sliced bread in light beige, dark brown, and marbelized colors. Some of the slices of bread had little seeds stuck into them. Many pieces were quite soggy and dripping from the salads that had been glued between the slices, puddles of cole slaw and layers of damp potato salad with hard lumps in it.

In between the salads and the breads were slices of turkey and greenish spiced salami. I tried to pick up the sandwich and nodded my thanks to Sophie Tuckermann. Her butterfly-bow mouth bobbled with interest as she waited for me to take the first bite, but most of the inside of the sandwich slipped and fell out in a heap onto the paper plate on top of the pimpled pickle.

"So, what do you think? Ever eaten delicatessen before? You're not going to find a better deli sandwich in this city, let me tell you. That's a secret. Mikey may be a foreigner, but nobody makes a better delicatessen sandwich than him. All kosher meats." A thick string of gristle lodged itself between my teeth and I attempted to pull it free surreptitiously with my little finger. Out of nervous habit whenever I talked to strangers my forehead perspired, and briefly I wiped it off with a paper napkin. "I know just how you feel," my new friend said. "I'm practically indestructible, although I fall apart constantly. You think it's easy, running a place like this? You try it. Standing behind that counter all day. There's always some maniac coming in and trying to rob the place or smoke a hashish cigarette. It's no bowl of Jell-O, believe me. Eat your sandwich—it didn't cost you anything. So, where are you from, anyway? New Guinea? Is that what they said? I guess you don't have too easy a life either. So tell me, what I'd really like to know is, what kind of self-defense you got there anyway? What do you use?"

"Well, we used to use stone axes, bludgeon each other to death, that sort of thing. Also we had arrows, barbed arrows that once they went in you couldn't pull them out. But none of that's allowed anymore; the government came in and ended war twenty years ago."

Sophie looked disappointed. "Yeah? So what do you use now, for hunting, I mean. You got guns? Or still arrows?"

"To be perfectly honest with you, there isn't too much animal life on New Burnt Norton anymore. I don't do too much hunting."

"Yeah? Well, how do you stay in such good shape? The

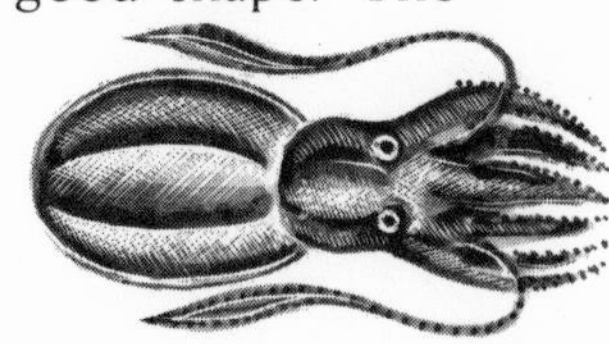

caveman diet I read about? You eat too many of those sandwiches, a person your height will have to go on a diet. Diet, diet, that's all anyone is talking about anymore. My daughter says I should go on one; my doctor tells me I'm going to have to lose some weight; how am I supposed to lose any when I work around the food all day? I hardly eat a thing, a piece of cucumber once in a while, a nibble here and a nibble there, I should starve myself and I still wouldn't be a raving beauty. I've been through too much, Perry, to suffer for my sins anymore. Things I couldn't even begin to tell you about. And you have, too, I suppose, I can see from your eyes. Who hasn't though, except for most of the population who aren't even human beings, forgive me."

"I don't know, actually. I don't do too much physical activity, I think, what you were asking me about before. Mostly my wives and children do the work. I have a hammock."

The sandwich was now flattened by the force of its own juice. It lay in a dead lump on the plate. Sophie looked at it with interest. "You like karate?" she said.

"I really don't know."

"In a city like this you got to know how to defend yourself. Mikey here is very good at it. His hands are registered with the police. Somebody like that around, I feel safe. One night he was coming out of his karate class and he was walking down a dark street. I told him, Mikey, find a class you can take that's in a safer area, but he doesn't listen to me. He still makes his wife wear saris. Suddenly he was being followed; someone came up behind him and stuck a gun in his ribs. Mikey was being mugged. So he turned around and cracked him in the face, kapow, one two! He heard a snap; he had broken the man's nose. The man left him alone after that. Am I right, Mikey?" Mikey did not turn around from his sawing. "He doesn't talk much. Now, for you, it's a different story. You're from a tribe. Many years ago everybody here used to live in tribes. Even if you were not such a hot person personally, you knew your tribe was the greatest. The burden was not on the individual. But here, we got one individual pitted against the next. Each person has got to struggle to survive on his own. Everyone competes, competes, competes all the time. There's a delicatessen up the street; there's a delicatessen down the street; I have to figure out how I'm going to stay in business without going broke. Am I right?"

"I guess so."

"Now, let me ask you something, a personal question. You don't have to answer if you don't want to, although I think you can be honest with me: What kind of family relationships could you possibly have, being a savage? Let me ask you that."

So I found myself telling her about Maria Fishburn: how she had lured me away, for I was a sucker when it came to the hope of intellectual communication, and had been starved for it back on my island home. "I cannot figure her out. What did she want to go and ask me to marry her for? This is a most strange thing, for her nature is no longer a seductive one. Surely a motivation is lacking. She has all the money necessary for independence —also the looks, the brains, the youth. Not that I myself am without attribute, but I am a man fifty-five years old, savage and hardly literate, barely speak English, three wives already I don't know what to do with . . ."

"So she wants to have children, maybe," Sophie said. "A virile man is a hard thing to find in the modern twentieth century."

"I'm not a good father, I can assure you of that," I said. "Why, one time I . . . never mind."

"A troubled girl," Sophie said.

"Yes, but what is making her so unhappy? Life is short and should be lived plainly, yet for her I believe she has the sense that unless excitement happens she is not alive at all."

"This is the way it is," Sophie said, and one of her stubby hands reached forward to clutch my sandwich. "Everybody has to have something, even if it is only raising pigs and wives and being a native dancer in a dance festival, or being an investment banker, or a train conductor. But from what you tell me, this person has nothing. Well, sadly, in this day, this is true of nearly everyone I meet, for each of them is unfulfilled and feels he or she has nothing, only a TV set and a very little desire—to purchase things in a shopping mall. For me, it doesn't matter, most days I'm glad just to be alive, but this is due to past circumstances in my life which taught me severe lessons."

I stood and said I must depart, that I would be late for the photo session and press conference. But I felt the better for speaking out to a grumpy and maternal being.

Sophie took a bite of my crushed sandwich. "Here I have the meats of the world," she said, "and around me the people are not people in themselves but only in what they are brainwashed into believing. But this is what I want to tell you. I have this feeling about you, a real strong feeling, and that is something I don't get often anymore. The feeling is this: I think everything will all work out for you as it is meant to. Even if you don't want it as it is. So you got nothing to worry about, take my word for it."

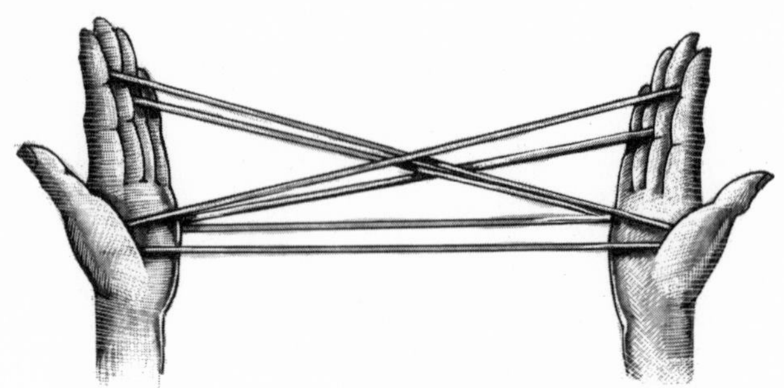

15

In one sense this man Parker Junius reminded me of some sort of sea creature that had crawled onto land and now was disguised as a human kind. When I arrived at the museum I had once more the opportunity to observe this genius of a man. For behind his thick glasses, the lenses like two truncated telescope lenses, were his eyes, nearly without whites and with a kind of liquid moisture to them that could only come from a cetaceous creature used to living under water. His skin was a kind of mottled paper, with blotches here and there, the texture of which was very fine and nearly translucent, with the interesting veins and waterways beating beneath.

And then, as I have mentioned, the two doggish eyebrows, thick and enforested, meeting together in the center of the nose, with the whiskery guard hairs protruding some distance above the matted hair and extending below the edge of his glasses where they were thereby magnified as were his eyes. And the giddy white hair that also sprang out of his head, tufted above each ear. He may very well have at one time been a sort of octopus, with that freckled face, tender eating only when beaten with a mallet or meat hammer.

Inside the place where the press conference was to be held, a room known as the Auditorium, conditions were very good, with the walls being made of an icelike steel, and the room being very spacious, although the floor, of wood, was covered with chairs, hundreds of chairs covered in red fabric and sadly cemented to the floor, so that a great deal of space was occupied.

On a raised platform a young, bearded man with a belly,

who was as it turned out not affiliated with any magazine or newspaper but was the museum photographer accustomed to primitive people and places, was busy setting up all kinds of lights and lampposts, some of which were switched on so that the room felt baked in a porcine brilliance as the light bounced off the walls.

Truly I wanted to make a good impression. For despite the fact that it was Maria's family who (in honor of the deceased Oscar Fishburn) had been the main financial support of the Museum of Primitive Cultures, she, Maria, had not been able to simply tell Parker Junius that I was coming to the dance festival (which, it now appeared, she had known about as far back as her first visit to my village on New Burnt Norton) but had to get Parker to personally invite me, which took some pleading on her part. In the end he agreed to do so, in a very dry and academic manner, sending a formal telegram to my hotel in Jaranekta.

I should have understood that a man of his stature knew which tribes had dancing, and which did not. But being naïve and full of life, I thought a great trick had been pulled over on the American peoples, that they had invited me, a man who had no dancing, to a dance festival at a museum.

"Mgungu," Parker Junius called from the stage, "come over here. This is Arthur Gornell, the photographer." The man appeared to be sweating profusely; he approached me at an oblique angle and nervously shook my outstretched hand in a nearly twitching frenzy.

"What's the matter, Arthur Gornell?" I said politely, for I was not used to such spasms, and he appeared to be trying to crawl around behind me, or at least stay to one side.

"He's a little nervous this afternoon," Parker drawled in his wealthy voice. "We've been photographing the various natives entered in the dance festival over the past few days, and he's had some rather unfortunate experiences. It brought back, I'm afraid, terrible memories for him of an expedition up the Amazon some years back." Arthur flashed a ghastly smile at me, revealing a yellow and jagged set of carved teeth, while one hand flew to his little belly.

"Come with me upstairs," Parker Junius said. "It's going to take him a while to get these lights rearranged." And he took me in an elevator to the top floor of the building. Here—as he explained, one of his conditions of accepting the prominent position of running a museum more complex than a giant corporation—he had a group of young boys locked up. They were hard at work constructing what he was currently interested in. For this man Parker was considered in his own right to be a very good artist.

In this large room, lit by skylights, the troupe of boys were standing around a statue, nearly ten feet tall, of a huge, spindly, nude woman and surrounded by scaffolding. "We're having trouble getting her to stand up," one of the boys called over to us. This statue, at present of plaster of Paris, was going to be bronzed when complete, and she was very spindly and tenuous, as if Parker Junius's idea of women was that they should be draw out of webs or made from thread. He earned a tremendous amount of money from making and marketing this type of statue, and would earn even more from the movie he planned to create next: It was to be a horror film about a computer that talked with the dead, due to a microchip designed by a scientist to receive brain waves from beyond the grave. He had plans eventually to go to Hollywood. Thus in a sense he should never have been as shocked by me as he claimed he was. And yet I think now that perhaps he believed in keeping his art separate from his life. He was considered nearly as good an artist as he was businessman and museum curator.

But in person he did seem ineffectual, that much must be said for him. His hand went out to one of the boys who was about to topple from the scaffolding and hardly appeared of any assistance whatsoever, clinging like the most tentacled fingers of an octopus to the boy's back. I, too, strove to help, and saw Parker's eyes unblinking behind his glasses, in much the same way that an octopus will, when caught, study the man who has caught it with a cold and calculated interest. I understood then he was indeed powerful and important.

After this we went back downstairs, where I was positioned on the stage under the lights. Soon, in the heat, I began to perspire, with green trickling rapidly down my arms, but as I was not wearing any shirt, per request of Parker Junius, I simply held my arms down at my sides. He stood nearby. Though he was in the heat from the lights he was not affected, and simply basked like a shark under water in the sun, and with his damp hand wriggling on my arm, he adjusted my position so Arthur could snap the shot.

"This is just a photo session for the museum, Mgungu," Parker Junius said. "Don't be nervous. The newspapers and magazine reporters will be coming in a little while. By the way, I wanted to tell you that you've been chosen—"

Here he paused, while a black youth, presumably eight feet tall, with red hennaed hair, who carried a basketball and was dressed in a smear of varicolored paints, in colors such as yellow and red, came out from behind a screen. He had apparently been dressing, and now wore a pair of dungarees and basketball sneakers, while thrown over the screen was a complex costume made of matted fibers like a hula dress, with an elaborate headpiece made of rotten fruits, such as persimmons and grapefruits, and sharpened spoons and forks that pointed in every direction. The giant grunted and scowled at the photographer, who noticeably quavered.

"Thank you very much, MiCarwo," Parker Junius said to the apparition, who bounced his basketball violently against the floor. "MiCarwo is a Watusi who is also participating in the dance festival. I am sure you will be seeing more of him. Perhaps you have already met. He, too, is staying at the Holiday Inn. MiCarwo, this is Mgungu, from the island of New Burnt Norton."

MiCarwo shrugged and began scratching at his flaky war paint, which powdered onto the floor in little clumps.

"MiCarwo saw a film last night," Parker Junius said. "It was about street gangs in New York City, and it made him very angry. You don't know any street gangs for MiCarwo to join, do you, Arthur?"

"No," Arthur whispered and hid behind his camera, which he began to adjust.

"That will be all for this afternoon, MiCarwo. Now, remember, you are going to be dancing in Central Park tomorrow afternoon for the documentary crew. Are you going to remember that?" MiCarwo glared at the floor. "Are you going to be able to find your way back to the hotel now, MiCarwo?" Parker Junius spoke clearly and distinctly, as if talking to a duck. His tone of voice sounded very familiar, but then I remembered that he spoke to everyone that way, or at least had spoken to me that way at the cocktail party. MiCarwo did not respond. He couldn't have been much more than eighteen or nineteen years old, and was very high and proud in his spirit.

"Okay, okay, I'll call a cab," Parker Junius said, and Arthur Gornell scurried over to the telephone. He was that glad to see MiCarwo go. "MiCarwo says he's angry that he has to walk everywhere. He says at home they all drive dune buggies and that he will go home now unless he is allowed to take a cab on a full-time basis. To be perfectly honest with you, Mgungu, I don't know why I bother. I'm completely exhausted at this point. I specifically asked that they send over a Watusi who spoke English, and MiCarwo spoke it perfectly well for the first few days he was over here, but after he got mugged on the subway something happened to him and he couldn't speak a word. All he wants to do is join a street gang and play basketball for the New York Knicks. He keeps asking me to take him to some stores where he can buy brassieres for his girlfriends back home. All these visitors with their requests for brassieres! Is there some kind of Third World shortage? I don't have time.

"I wish you would take him up, Mgungu. Maybe if you devoted some energy to him he would straighten out. As far as dancing goes, he can do it, but he's very self-conscious about it, although only ten years ago we were making the most wonderful films about the dancing of the young Watusi boys. He says people are laughing at him, though. This whole festival is turning out to be a disaster. The Polynesian girls' troupe has done nothing but pick up men since they got over here. Half the time I can't even get hold of them in the hotel. During the day they're too tired to dance since they've been out at discotheques at night. The Whirling Dervishes have refused to come out of their room for three days unless I send up a goat for them to sacrifice. Where am I supposed to get a goat? The hotel doesn't even allow any animals in it. I have three assistants supposedly helping me on this project and where are they? Off trying to round up the dancers to steer them from one event to the next, and the festival starts quite soon."

The Watusi had by now left the studio, scrabbling fiercely with the lock on the door, which the photographer finally undid for him, hesitantly approaching his side. I could hear the basketball bouncing down the stairs.

"Anyway, Mgungu, I have some good news for you. I didn't want to say while MiCarwo was in the room—he understands English intermittently, and he would only sulk. I've decided to use you for our feature-face about the dance festival. These people coming in a few moments are going to test you for the cover shot of *Time* magazine. I think you have one of the most interesting faces of any of the dancers in the festival—you are the oldest participant, and you speak the most fluent English. And you are the only cannibal. Just don't let on that you don't know how to dance."

"But," I said, "how did you know?"

"Oh, come on," Parker Junius said. "Mgungu." He spoke my name in a very sarcastic tone of voice, like I had made it up or something, and his wet and fishy hand clasped my arm. "I am the curator of an anthropological art museum. I do have a faint inkling, just an idea that is, of which tribes 'boogie' and which don't, heh-heh, speaking metaphorically, that is." And his watery eyes winked at me. "That will just be our little secret, won't it? And before the dance festival starts I'll show you how to do the fox trot—nobody will recognize where that comes from, if you just do it as I show you."

The photographer busied himself with his camera, swinging his little belly out of the way. "Between you and me and Arthur, all right, Mgungu?" Parker Junius said. "And Maria Fishburn." And I understood that to mean that I had been invited to the festival because of her and not because of who I was, and I cringed. "Now, I'm going to ask you to put on this little loincloth, all right, Mgungu?" Parker Junius said. "I think that will just make matters a little easier, since it is a civilized part of the world you are currently visiting. I think people will just be too curious to know what's under that yellow penis gourd you've got on, and I don't think that's the kind of publicity we want to get." From his leather bag he removed a tiny piece of wrinkled silk cloth of a blighted pink color and laced through at one end with a little piece of string. "Oh, darn," Parker Junius said. "Look, it's all wrinkled. I don't know how that could have happened."

He walked over to the other side of the room, where an ironing board was set up, and an iron. "I'm glad you put this out, Arthur, that was a good idea. A lot of the costumes have needed ironing, haven't they? Well, a lot of them have been in storage for a long time." He plugged in the iron. "Mgungu, I'm going to have to make some phone calls. You know how to iron, don't you?"

I nodded. "Oh, certainly, sir. Mr. Parker Junius." For I continued to be ashamed and embarrassed that he knew I was in fact no dancer but had been invited to this country to satisfy a woman's desire. And he even showed me, briefly, how to run the iron along the piece of silk.

"Well, excuse me," he said. "I'll be back in just a minute, and then I'd like to have Arthur do the shots of you we'll be using in the museum catalogue and maybe we'll have a chance to talk about what you should say to the reporters." He picked up the telephone and retired with it to a mirrored room that contained a bathtub and a toilet. I resolved to use this toilet when he was through on the telephone, for I loved whenever possible to try a toilet out. It was an object to which, after years of only the portable chemical johnnies, and before that only a hole in the ground, I could never grow tired. Each time I sat on one of these objects I had pleasure.

I picked up the iron, which was hardly warmed up at all, and began to run it along the little piece of dull pink fabric I had been told to wear. And to my horror, a large portion of cloth melted, poof, like that, under the weight of the iron. A little black smoke curled upward and I was very upset. "Oh, my goodness," I said, "I don't believe that I have been so terrible."

"What's the matter?" the photographer Arthur said softly, approaching the ironing board.

"I have just melted this loincloth and Parker Junius will be very angry. What a fool I am, oh."

Arthur held up the loincloth and there was a large hole that extended through it on both sides. At that moment, despite his timidity, the fact did strike me that Arthur was a very nice fellow and quite human. "Sheesh," he said. "Nice going. Where did you say you were from?"

"New Burnt Norton."

"And it's going to be too late to get anything else. What are you from, a low I.Q. tribe or something? They say Pygmies aren't too bright."

"I'm not a Pygmy, my dear friend."

"Yeah, sure. Just a cannibal." Of course I knew his words were jovial and jesting. "Well," he said, "I don't know what we're going to use, but we can't shoot you with what you've got on. The board of directors hates nudity, unless it's a couple of tribal tits." For, as I perhaps have mentioned, I was wearing a penis gourd, and had pulled a pair of trousers on over me just for the walk to the delicatessen and the photo session, which I did agree looked very strange and even obscene by American standards, though American standards had proved themselves thus far to be most peculiar indeed. Parker Junius continued to remain on the phone in the toilet, and Arthur said he did not know what to do. "Wait a minute," he said, "what about my bandanna?" From his pocket he removed a large red bandanna, which he said was from the island of Woolworth, and tied it around my waist, making the knot in the back and allowing the larger part to hang down in front. "Just don't turn around," he said. "Believe me, they want to see a native, but some of these female reporters will rape you if they see what you've got." As I say, a friendly fellow.

When Parker Junius emerged from the telephone, he saw what I had on and he said, "Where's the loincloth?"

"It didn't fit," Arthur said.

"What are you talking about?" Parker Junius said. "A loincloth, I'm sure, is one size fits all."

"I melted it," I said.

"You what?"

"My anxiety at using the iron caused it simply to melt."

And he examined the mottled pink loincloth and saw that it was mostly indeed melted. Only a smear on the ironing board remained to show what had once been the majority of the object. "But that was a valuable antique from the museum collection!" he said in disbelief. "Do you have any kind of idea how the objects are kept in the museum warehouse? That loincloth has for twenty years been in a room kept year round at a controlled temperature. No daylight is allowed to touch the objects and all air that enters the storage area is triple ventilated. And it was collected with great difficulty twenty years ago by the great collector Minton Heathcliffe on the last expedition he made! For twenty years nothing has come along to harm it. Why, that large spot on the back of it was actually tested and shown to be Minton's own blood! His heirs will kill me! Oh, this is terrible."

"Sorry, Mr. Parker Junius," I said, and even then more tears were coming into my eyes, and I wanted to burn myself or damage myself in some way with the same iron, now very hot, that I had damaged this article of clothing with.

"It was only out of the goodness of my heart that I was going to let you wear this loincloth! I wanted you to look nice for the photo session! Well, I don't think you should get this marvelous chance, which most people, myself included, would give their eyeteeth for, to appear on the cover of *Time* magazine. No, I don't think you should be allowed to at all. After all, there are plenty of other people I can ask."

I was despairing, and longed for the soothing presence of Maria, or at least for some Joy Paul Guilford to alleviate. I jittered and rummaged my body, wondering if I should attempt to leave in chagrin. But it was too late for such thoughts. The reporters and photographers had knocked on the door, and Arthur was meekly letting them in.

16

The reporters entered the room, and Parker Junius stopped snarling at me and stared with silent anger and disgust. "Come in, come in," he said to the crew, of whom there were at least ten or a dozen.

They stood around scuffling their feet and looking at me, as if I was not what they had hoped for at all. They were like an unusual pack of mixed primates—the lady chimpanzee with her long upper lip and hairy face, wiry and frail, clutching a little chittering pad in her paw; a big red gibbon from the *New York Post* with long arms nearly to the ground, chewing a wad of gum; and various other lesser monkeys, the Spider monk, the mandrill, the night lemur from *Vanity Fair,* all fumbling about in various ways.

"Hello, everyone," Parker Junius said. "I guess I've met most of you before. I'm Parker Junius, creator and curator of the Museum of Primitive Cultures. In a short time, as I presume you know, the museum is holding its first International Dance Festival. This is a joyous celebration of dance from around the world, and I am proud to be able to say that almost every country asked to participate in the festival was able to send their greatest dancers to take part. We have representatives from Turkey, from eleven African nations, from Polynesia—the list goes on and on. The festival will commence over the weekend, when the Museum of Primitive Cultures, in conjunction with WGBH and Lincoln Center, will host a series of dance and cross-cultural events throughout the city, beginning at the U.N. Plaza and ending three weeks later in the fountain at Lincoln Center. The schedules are contained inside the press packets; I hope you'll all be able to attend at least some of the events. But the reason I have called this press conference this afternoon is to introduce you to a special member of our international dance competition, a person whom we have come to consider the quintessential emblem of this festival and the feeling of international peace represented throughout the competition. I would like to introduce to you now, Mr. Mgungu Yabba Mgungu . . ."

I noticed that the reporter from *Time* magazine was not taking notes, but had merely switched on a tiny tape recorder and was now scratching absently at his fleas. This, too, came as a surprise to me, but then I thought: yes, why shouldn't civilized people have fleas! Who was I to assume that civilization meant an end to parasites! Parker Junius, as he was introducing me, gave me a fearful scowl as if reminding me to straighten up, and his red lips pursed in disgust, exactly like a little mouth.

". . . from the island of New Burnt Norton. He belongs to a tribe that is very nearly extinct, a tribe with unique skin pigmentation, of a wonderful and distinctive eggplant hue. Mr. Mgungu is a reformed cannibal." This did give some attention from the crowd, and they looked at me as if half hoping for a little action. "I say 'reformed' in the sense that some twenty-odd years ago cannibalism was outlawed on the island of New Burnt Norton, and Mr. Mgungu naturally at that point stopped. But once a taste for human flesh is acquired it is never lost, as I'm sure many of you can attest to." Here the audience chuckled, and I realized that what I was bearing witness to was that thing known as innuendo. "Am I correct in describing your background, Mgungu?" Parker Junius said.

I hesitated a little. My very arms and legs had grown quite numb when I realized who Parker Junius was talking about, that I was the one being referred to. How was I to be expected to speak to people I wasn't on friendly speaking terms with? I could not bend even the slightest joint in any of my body, and even there was a skunky smell to me, impenetrable, that I could not dispose of, the smell of fear. I was a gentleman with stage fright.

"Mr. Mgungu?"

"To be perfectly honest with you, and I hope this is the correct time to say this, I was never much of a cannibal in the first place, and vastly preferred to slaughter a baby pig. I am a pig raiser and have a substantial herd—" I would have gone on, but Mr. Parker Junius was staring at me ferociously with a look that would have dignified the most noble and Rousseau-type of savage. But luckily, for Parker Junius I mean, not one of them was listening to my answer and the questions next came so thick and fast it did not matter that there was not time for me to respond in between one of them.

"Mr. Mgungu, where is New Burnt Norton?" "Dr. Mugnu, how is it that you happen to speak English?" "Magnungu, when was the last time you ate human flesh—seriously now?" "Mugnu, what does human flesh taste like? Is it true that once tasted the taste for it never leaves you?" "Your skin—is it really purple, or is that some kind of stain?"

And they asked me other various personal questions about myself, and I told them about Yerba, Oola, and Nitsa. "And who does the work around the house? Or houses? You or them?"

"Oh, the wives, purely. It is for me to decide which pigs to breed and to rest myself in a hammock. For having three wives is a tiring thing for a man."

The lady simian scowled and wrote furiously. "Do you all live together?"

"No, we each have our own home."

"So, do you take turns living with each wife?"

"Oh, no, to be sure. It is not correct for the men to live with the women. The men, they have their own house. Should a woman enter it, over five years of age, it would be contaminated. For women carry with them a certain substance, which I guess in English you would call anti-*moodla*. That is to say, something that counteracts the effects of *moodla*."

"And what is *moodla*, exactly?"

"This thing called *moodla* is a very spiritual thing and hard to come by. What it is, is dangerous and powerful. Beyond this I cannot explain, aside to say that I myself am not gifted with much of it and it is in effect my *moodla* for which I at present search."

But mostly this gang was not listening, or so I felt, though they were a very selective group. I let them try some of my special blend of tobacco, which they were pleased to do, and I was able to relax and enjoy this friendly bunch. I relaxed so much, in fact, that I did not see Parker Junius shaking his head in the background and trying to usher the team out.

"What do I think of America?" I said. "Mostly, it reminds me of the old days back on New Burnt Norton, before the government came in and killed off most of the Greater Pimbas and ninety-nine percent of the Lesser Pimbas. Those were the days all right, oh boy. As you say in this country, I remember those were the days when a man could do as he pleased. Yerba's father irritated me highly, and so one day when the old man came to pay a visit on his daughter and son-in-law, I ate him. And, heh-heh," for here I was laughing and temporarily could not speak, "my grandfather used to say he had eaten better men than some of those sitting on the dummy Legislative Council they set up to trick the natives into believing they had any power in the government. Heh-heh." I expected the audience to laugh, but there was only a brief silence, so maybe I was not speaking so good. "Now, if you are finished," I said, "I have a few questions about this country I would like to ask you." And frantically Arthur began taking photographs of me and standing directly in front of me, so I had a hard time addressing my audience. This was a tactic on the part of Parker Junius, I later learned, to divert them from myself, who constantly blubbered like a fool and put his foot in it.

From my pants' pocket I removed a piece of paper I had clipped. "I would like very much," I said, "if you would explain this important question, asked of a very wise man or guru, which I have not been able to understand, as it is no doubt an American problem."

So aloud I read:

> *Dear Dr. Fox, We have a small, mixed-breed two-year-old dog. Ever since he was five months old, he has permitted other male dogs to mount him as though he were a female. This is quite an embarrassment to my wife and myself. He's not exclusively homosexual, since he does not mount other males, and he does become quite excited when he discovers a female in heat. Other dogs initiate the mounting after they have been around him a short while. He is a friendly little fellow, a good companion, and a good watchdog. He has been examined by our vet and has no serious health problems. Can you explain this sexual deviancy?*

My audience appeared, I thought, quite interested. "What does this mean?" I said. "What is it that this personage is truly asking?"

The lady reporter looked as if she had smelled something bad and I heard her mumble, "This guy is obviously a fake." The photographers looked at each other and did not respond. The youthful initiate with the hairy arms finally shrugged and shook his head.

"The questioner speaks falsely?" I said. Yet no one responded. "This is not something you can explain? Ah, well, it is the same with many of my customs, too."

"What does Dr. Fox answer?" from the back someone did call.

"Oh, he says there is no such thing as deviation, to allow the dog to do as it likes. This issue genuinely concerns people?" I did honestly want to know, yet still they shuffled their feet and looked away. "Also, I don't understand American sense of humor at all," I said. "I have some more questions I am going to ask you, but first, a recipe I would like to impart."

If this seems like a rapid switch from stage fright, believe me I had now relaxed and was a real ham. They did love it, or so I thought, and lapped it up, and I was sorry I had not decided earlier to go on the stage. "I have read your *Cosmopolitan* magazine on the airplane, and I have read your *New York Times*, and I know you to be a people interested in food. This is a recipe, a very old recipe, been handed down in my family, the Lesser Pimbas, for years." The lady reporter looked highly interested and exchanged pads, as if she were going to take personal notes on this subject. "Okay," I said. "Recipe time. Take the root of a certain wild plant—it has yellow leaves, it is called in other languages *aboodahbee*; the parings of the claw of the giant cassowary; the bony snout of a garfish—this is very difficult to come by, since my people live in the mountains and the trade routes to the water are circuitous and long—and wrap this in squares of a banana leaf." And I paused, finished.

But the audience waited expectantly. "And what do you have when you are done?" a reporter asked. He had stopped scribbling.

"Just that," I said. "Now, perhaps you could explain these jokes to me? For as I have mentioned, I understand not at all this American sense of fun." From my same pocket I removed a stack of cartoons I had cut out from *The New Yorker* and began to read them out loud. "Here is one. A man and a woman are sitting on a bench. The woman is saying, 'Pardon me, sir. You are being beeped.' What is meant by 'being beeped'?"

But there was no reply, although one man did say, "Well, you see, it's like this. Being beeped is when—" Unfortunately he was hushed up by the members of the press, as if there was some secret by being a native I could not be allowed to know, and I suspected this was the case. Tribal secrets, etcetera, there are even in my own group, a tribe I have mentioned singularly lacking in superstitions and customs.

And there were various others that I tried to read, but with little reluctance the group of them, who had seated themselves after some time on the floor, stood up and were being shown the door by Parker Junius. But the last person to leave did cry out to me, "Oh, one last question before I go, sir. What would you most like to be able to take with you when you leave the United States?"

"Ah," I said, "this is a thing I have thought some time about. And I have decided: a pinball machine and a dishwasher I have seen in a Sears catalogue. This dishwasher has a front made of glass and it is possible to watch the dishes being cleaned."

"Thank you." And he did depart.

But as I said, they had seemed like a friendly and likable bunch, and I would have called them sincere, whatever that means. So imagine my shock when the different headlines appeared on Friday, saying things like HE'LL EAT MANHATTAN and TALL TALES FROM PRIMITIVE MAN. And here I thought I had made things so perfectly simple to them!

And the articles said how I did not know how to iron, and how I was afraid to use the subway or change a lightbulb, and how this was due to my own inability to adjust and be flexible. I was portrayed as a stupid and unliberated man, mostly whining about how horrible it was to be fifty-five years old and how I was considering divorce from my three wives and marriage to a twenty-five-year-old American, something I did not remember saying.

In fact, when had I said anything at all of a controversial nature, and why was I made out to be such a namby-pamby? Plus, three-fourths of the facts were wrong, and even the nicest of them had some little jeering remark to make about me (though I was wrong to take it to be about me personally, since I knew they were referring to primitives as a whole): "An obsession with homosexuality"; "Not really so very savage—the life has all but dwindled from the wild, and those savages left are obsessed with material possessions, pinball machines and dishwashing liquid"; "Mgungu has enrolled his wives in his own personal cargo cult, trying to turn yams into gold, while his children operate swindles so he can make it rich and go to Argentina." And so on and so forth. It was vicious stuff, and when I saw it, I resolved to quit the festival, which was due shortly to start.

Had it not been for my head, smaller than life on the front page of the *Time* magazine, I definitely would have done so. As it turned out, I got caught up in other events during the festival anyway. But for now, Parker Junius had made sure I did not have any work to do, which was generous of him to a fault, considering that they had paid for me to fly over and were paying my hotel bill simply to have my face there at the festival. And I was indeed a face, and many people recognized me and asked for my autograph and ran with curious looks if I made a fierce face, fearful, no doubt, of the cannibal. Which pleased me a great deal.

But this was not yet due to happen for another few days, and then under totally other circumstances.

At present, after the photographers had left, Parker Junius simply scowled at me and said, "Well, Mgungu, I do hope you're happy. You have certainly made a fool of yourself without any help from anyone else. I begged you to shut up, I really did. And what the results will be I cannot say. It is my belief that your attempt to bait them will lead only to laughter on their parts once they quit this place. But apparently you know about these things better than I do."

"No, no, not at all," I said.

"Please, take that silly pen out of your nose. I thought someone was going to tell you about that days ago," Parker Junius said. "Listen to me. If you are going to dress like a savage, then I suggest you do it like an uncivilized one, and wear a boar's tusk or something a bit more natural than a Mark Cross ball-point pen. I'll see if I can find a carved tusk for you at the museum if you don't have one of your own."

"I am indeed sorry," I said.

"Mgungu, I'm older than you, but only slightly. Still, I would like to tell you something. Maria is a lovely girl, but she tires of her obsessions quickly. Be grateful to her; don't resent her. After all, it's only because of your association with her that I was able to invite you to be in the festival."

"I should have taken those Arthur Murray lessons."

"Well, well," Parker Junius said, "I can see that you're a man in search of something. But as for what you are looking for, I really don't know. It may be your *moodla*; but I can tell you from the start that no one in this godforsaken country will be able to help you there. They are all too busy looking for their own. I would suggest you see a psychic to find out what is going to become of you. Here's the address." He scribbled something down on a piece of paper. "Across from Macy's. Ask for Brian. Don't bother seeing anyone else if he's not there."

"Oh, but, sir," I said, "why are you being so kind to me after what I have done? There is no need, and I am as your slave."

"Why am I being so kind to you? After the disgrace your interviews will probably bring upon my museum? The only thing I can tell you is because, as Flaubert said, *'Madame Bovary, c'est moi.'* Do you know what that means?"

"I guess. Madame Bovary, she is me," I translated.

"No, no, don't thank me. You may be a fool, Mgungu, and a fifty-five-year-old fool at that, but we are still friends under the skin or in the blood, however you want to call the shots. I have understanding for you, Mgungu, and maybe even a little *moodla*, and that is more than anyone else in this country will find for you, I can guarantee that. Now I want you very much to come in one day during the week and have breakfast with me—we have much to discuss. I dine each morning here at the museum. Until then, just try to keep your nose clean, all right?"

"Of course, of course," I said. "I look forward so to our intellectual conversation. Might I add, I feel deeply terrible about burning that lovely loincloth. Usually, you know, I am a pretty good ironer. Maybe there is something wrong with your iron?"

And though he did not respond I smiled at him and wended to the door. Arthur helped me with the locks, saying nervously, "Well, I'll be seeing you. I'll see you very soon. Yes, good-bye. See you shortly." Meanwhile shaking his hand into mine as though a magic spider was being transferred from one palm to another, as is the custom.

"See you shorty"? I thought when I was again outside. See you shorty. What did that mean? Was I to take it as an insult? How strange everyone was, and yet, how infinitely good to me and how charming. That was the word for it—infinitely charming!

In my silly way I believed then that we would all be friends for a long, long time.

17

Look, you do want to go out tonight, don't you? How tired are you, anyway?" Joey said when I came into the pizza parlor.

"So-so," I said. I was filled with sorrow for myself, but did not wish to reveal this. "I had expected my fiancée, Maria, to join us, but as usual she has some sort of business meeting. Probably I am an embarrassment to her, being a primitive type of guy, and this is why she continues to make up excuses. Okay, so I have problems. Who doesn't? Maybe I am immature for my age, but I am also extremely short, which more than compensates."

"Yeah? You're not too tired though, are you? Let me ask you something—how much of this city have you gotten to see anyway, since you've been here?" Joey said. "Not much, I bet. What'd they do, take you around to a couple of museums and stuff? Maybe the Statue of Liberty, the World Trade Center?"

"Something like that. Oh, I was extremely happy in the jungle with my wives and the mosquitoes until she arrived and moved in to the Methodist mission below, thinking of rescuing me and taking me to civilization, a greater prize than her cousin Oscar Fishburn had ever thought of, and also a way to get even with her family."

"Let me tell you," Joey said, "I know all about it. My wife, before we split up, was from Minneapolis, and all the time her relatives would come and stay with us. Didn't cost them a thing. Free place to stay, free pizza—my wife knew it got on my nerves, and she encouraged it."

I had hoped we would indulge in a pizza before commencing, but Joey said, "Come on, we better get going. I've got a place I'd love to show you. If you're not too tired, that is. My cousin runs it. He'll show us a good time. You're a friend of mine, and any friend of mine is a friend of my cousin Guich. At least, this is generally the case."

Joey's car, an ancient Rambler, was halfway up onto the sidewalk in front of the restaurant. The door on the passenger side was tied shut with a piece of rope. "You may have to get in on my side," he said. "There's no point in keeping a decent machine in this city, that's for sure." The car started with a dull groan and a chuffing and would not move until he had given the accelerator a ferocious kick. Joey's driving took us erratically weaving through taxicabs down Seventh Avenue. Dangling from the rearview mirror was an assortment of toys, or perhaps they were something from the Catholic religion, which I understood to be composed of a great many items. There was a collection of stuffed dice, and shapeless faces made of green goo, and a black licorice-type substance. Bobbing on the dashboard itself was a felt or velveteen dog of fierce proportion, and in its mouth was a small human hand made of plastic.

"Yeah, I see you looking at that dog. Guess that's something you can identify with, huh, Mgungu? Oh, look, I didn't insult you or anything, did I? Christ, look, I didn't mean anything by it. I guess I was just thinking where I read in the paper you were a cannibal or something. I haven't got any objection, let me tell you. My cousin will get a kick out of that, I guess."

"No, no, I beg you," I said. "Please do not reveal this truth about me. But allow me to go out for once as an independent being."

"Well, okay," Joey said. "Sure." He stopped speaking in order to execute a turn of the automobile, which did not downshift regularly. Parked in the intersection was a vehicle stripped of its wheels, and peering into it as we pulled up alongside, I could see it was missing most of the interior. There was no way to get around it. "Son-of-a-bitch," Joey said, unrolling his window and spitting out it. "Just left there in the middle of the intersection. This is just the way it is, Mgungu. This city sucks. I mean it." To back up would have meant pulling into the intersection and already there were several cars behind us honking for us to move. "Can't you see there's a fucking car dumped here, you stupid bastard?" Joey screamed out the window at the car behind us. "What the fuck is wrong with you, do you mind my asking!"

I could not help but exclaim that his temper surprised me, but to this Joey explained his behavior was normal and American, and not to vocalize in this instance would have been wrong.

As it turned out, cousin Guich owned not a skin joint on 42nd Street, as I had imagined, but a very fashionable nightclub or discotheque, I guess it was called, in an old customs warehouse over on the west side by the Hudson, where at one time the great ocean liners of the world used to dock and even the freight ships, and where they still did, only now there were fewer of them.

The building was on the far side of a ruined district called the West Side Highway, partially on land, and partially on an enormous rotting pier that extended far out into the river. "My cousin cleaned it up somewhat," Joey explained. "Like, he got all those windows on this one side repaired, although he wasn't going to at first. The thing is, ya see, he wanted to keep the original nature of the place intact."

Joey pulled the car into the parking lot in front of the building, cursing the expense of the place, for it was going to cost him ten dollars to leave the car there for the evening, although he explained to the lady parking-lot attendant he was cousins with Guich who owned the place. The lady, dressed in a leather costume with spiked protrusions, was not impressed.

The building was of brick and extended for what must have been half a mile along the waterfront. It was true that the windows in the front were all neatly there, three stories of them, made of black glass. Above the second floor and below the third a huge sign said in peeling print, UNITED STATES CUSTOMS WAREHOUSE NO. 29. "That's where he got the name from," Joey said. "Warehouse 29. Get it?"

I nodded. Here and there in the darkness I could see with my acute eyes, a large rat or two, scuttling about their business. From the interior of the building emerged a muffled noise, and louder than that was the dull rapping of the Hudson water against the pier, swish swash, like a slap in the face. The smell of fish water was very loud here, and a smell of decay.

Before we went in, Joey suggested we walk along the water for a few blocks. Only a short ways away was another warehouse or shipping building, and in this one the windows were cracked like shrunken eyes and it was very dark. Farther down along the West Side Highway there was in fact actually docked a huge mother ship. "Probably the QE2," Joey said, with the lights strung along it twinkling like a dim party from the past.

Leaning over the iron railing that was strung along the edge of the road, I could see strange things float by in the water, lard mattresses and plastic bags filled with air and objects, even human bodies or curled and wrinkled fetuses, though this was my judgment based merely on what I had read in the papers.

Across the other side of the river was New Jersey, stupid and listless. "You should have seen this area before my cousin moved in and took over," Joey said. "This place was a disaster area. I wouldn't have been too happy about walking around here at night, let me tell you. It was a stroke of genius, doing what he did. I'm surprised you haven't heard of it, Mgungu. Everyone has. It's the most difficult place, at this time, to get into. And I mean in the world, it's the most difficult place to get into."

Who would want to? I thought, and above me, in the rusted rafters of a building, the pigeons crapped and cooed. "And besides that, the property value of the entire neighborhood has gone up, since Warehouse 29 opened," Joey said, "and is experiencing urban renewal." Whatever that was. "Come on, I'll take you inside. I want you to see it. You're going to love it—yes, there's nowhere else like it."

It was true that as we approached the building, this time from the downtown side, walking back up to it, it did appear, as I pointed out, "The roof is falling in at one end in a minor sort of way."

"Of course," Joey said contemptuously. "My cousin put an incredible amount of money into this place. It was falling apart when he got it—leased from the city for a dollar a year—and so far I think he's put fifteen or twenty million into it, but he didn't want to change it too much. Part of its charm is the original seediness. Yes, my cousin Guich is a genius and an artist." He glanced over at me to see if I was taking all this in. "Lately he's been written up all over the place—*Interview*, *People*—and he's thinking of forming a record label."

"Where would he glue it?" I said.

"What?" Joey said.

"The record label—where would he glue the label?"

"Heh-heh," Joey said. I decided not to pursue the question. We went past the klieg lights and the repaired windows—though I noticed that on the back side of the building, the side where the roof was falling in, that only the windows on the first floor had been repaired, and the ones on top were smashed completely—and around to the other side, where part way down the dock an enormous crowd had collected in front of a dimly lit door.

"What's that?" I said.

"I told you," Joey said. "Warehouse 29 is the most difficult place to get into in the country—"

"But why?" I could not stop myself from saying it, and Joey gave me a look of disgust, as if to say, I can't believe anyone could be so stupid.

"—and all these people are trying to get in. But it's doubtful on any one given evening, that Guich will let them in. As I have said, he's very selective."

When we got up to the door I saw that the crowd was indeed large and may have contained some five hundred people. The costumes were a sight to behold. As we got closer the colors became more distinctive, and the various types of fur, feathers, and precious metals used in the costumes became apparent. A man in a sleek seal tuxedo, standing some distance away on the dock, said to us as we passed, "Help me, please. A rotten board gave out under my foot as I was walking toward the door, and my foot got caught in it and I can't get out. Help me, please."

So I grabbed hold of him and pulled him out. "Oh, thank you," he said and ran to the edge of the pier where he took out from inside his coat a little package that he threw over the edge. "Would you believe it," he called to me, "all of these people are so desperate to get in over there, not one of them could bother to come over and help me out of my hole?" I said that I found this hard to believe, and was about to ask this friendly if strange gentleman his name, but he disappeared into the crowd.

"Come on, come on," Joey said, tugging at my arm, for now he was caught up in the fierce beat of the crowd, and the people who stood bored as birds at the edge and waited with an air of false nonchalance for those that they were with to make the door magically open so they could be dragged in.

Then a face separated itself out of the crowd, a greasy-head with large fish-blue eyes and a flaring nose that pressed itself right up into my face. Its hair was all chopped into little bits, black makeup around its eyes, and when I took a step back in startlement I noticed it had on a leather jacket covered with primitive etchings and wore blue patent-leather boots. "You!" I said. "It's you—my old friend and companion! What are you doing here?" For the face and body belonged to that of Kent Gable, familiar to me since my airplane trip, yet a personage whom I had lost any hope of seeing. "My friend!" I said, with gladness and surprise.

"Is that really you, Mgungu?" Kent said. "Crikey, I never thought I'd see you again. How come you never called? I was certain that by now the fate I was warning you about would have befallen you. Bloody 'ell, am I glad to see you!"

"But you will join us now, will you not?" I said, for Joey was already thrusting his way through the crowd.

Joey turned around to wave me forward. "Oh, Christ," he said, looking at Kent. "I can't believe you know one of *those*."

But I assured him he was mistaken. "Believe me, Joey, when I say that if you can be friends with a cannibal, you can most certainly be friends with a rock-and-roll star who has been taken away more than once by alien beings from a UFO."

At this Joey conceded that possibly he had made a mistake, and there were introductions all round.

"But tell me, Kent," I said, "how did it go for you on the show of today?"

"The 'Today' show?" Kent said. "Not so good. Unfortunately, the interviewer started to question me, in a very patronizing way, and I couldn't help myself, I became enraged and physically attacked him. Put him in hospital, I did. I'm very ashamed. They've invited me back to apologize." He looked most mournful.

"But, my friend," I said, "what a piece of luck, bumping into you like this."

With that Kent agreed, and as we crept slowly through the crowd, I told him everything that had happened to me since last we parted, and together we reminisced about what good times we had once had.

At last we reached the front of the crowd. The door was tiny and made of gold and the crowd heaved and pressed itself against it. "I can't see," I said. "What are they doing?" I backed up and climbed on top of the iron railing that surrounded the door entrance, not that I trusted it, for it wiggled and seemed likely to collapse, but I was eager to see what was transpiring. What was happening was this: a person would knock on the door of gold, and at the top of this gold door, about two-thirds of the way up, a tiny window would open, two sides that folded inward, also made of gold. And a face would be at this window and the face would say, "What is the password?" and whoever was closest to the door, or the person who had knocked at this door (for sometimes someone would knock and by the time the door had opened the person had been carried off in the pushing throng and crowd), the one closest to the door would say a magic word.

Sometimes this person would lean forward and whisper it, and sometimes the word would be shouted, and the words were of every kind imaginable, such as "Venezuela!" "Cocorico!" "Conquistadores!" "The Amazon!" and "To see what he could see!"

Sometimes the little face on the side of the tiny door would say, "That's right," and the gold door would open a crack and a strong hand would reach out and grab whoever had said the magic word and that person would grab hold of whoever he had come with and they would be dragged in.

The crowd sighed and moved back and forth restlessly. If the

word was whispered and the person was let in, a great shout would go up—"What was the word? What did he say?" If the word was spoken out loud, a sound of impatience would rise up from the people, for once the word was spoken out loud and heard by many it could no longer be used. At least, this is what Joey explained to me, and he also said, "You see, every night is a theme night. My cousin picks the theme, and there are only a certain number of words, prechosen, of course, that can be used as the password. And also it is based on whether or not he likes the way you look—that, too, is a part of it, and either he or his assistant must decide that when they open the little door to hear the password."

As we were talking, Kent listening to us but not speaking, only smiling in a happy way, a long, low-slung car with its belly nuzzled to the ground like a cat pulled up to the building. And it was a red car, and it drove straight into the middle of the crowd, and the crowd stepped back some distance. Some of them were even shoved into the iron railing, and had I not gotten down from it quickly I might have been forced or tossed into the water by the sheer force of the mass of men.

The car stopped and from this car two people got out, a man dressed in red with a pair of dark glasses on, and a woman who kept her head ducked under her arm as if she were some kind of water bird. The man, too, was like a bird, a kind of peacock. And the crowd made little cackling noises; the very air around this couple was electric and a trifle *moodla*. The man walked strongly through the crowd, which had backed off, and he knocked on the gold door. The little face popped out, and the man did not say a word before the door swung open, this time all the way, and the man and woman walked in.

The crowd surged forward as if hoping to catch a last glimpse of this couple and the world inside the warehouse. The red car started the engine and pulled forward again, driving to the end of the dock, where the chauffeur turned it around and drove back through the crowd. And the crowd was silent for some thirty seconds and in awe.

"Did you see that?" Joey said.

"Yes," I said, and even I was impressed. "Who were they?"

"I don't know," Joey said. "I don't really keep up on these things. Probably some count and countess. Or it may have been Mick Jagger, a well-known star, and his newest lady friend, a Japanese bassoonist. Guich will tell us. He knows everything and knows who everybody is."

Gradually one or two people did manage to guess the correct password and were let in. How empty it must be in there, I thought. There could not possibly be as many people inside as there were outside. Meanwhile the crowd grew and grew and the low tugboats passed in the night, honking and groaning on the Hudson. "Well, what do you say?" Joey said. "Are you ready to go in?"

"What have we been waiting for?" Kent said. "I thought it was just that you couldn't get in."

I nodded agreement. "Are you kidding?" Joey said. I could see he was collecting his breath. "I'll hang on to your arm then," he said, ignoring Kent. "So we don't get separated." We plunged into the crowd, Joey mumbling excuses and dragging me along behind him, while I held on to Kent's arm. The faces painted blue and purple in the crowd looked at us angrily as we tried to get through them, and some of them dug me in the ribs with their elbows or gave me a sharp punch across the upper arm. But I could not back up, for Joey was holding on to my arm too severely and dragging me through the mob with great strength.

At last it was our turn at the golden door. Joey began to punch on this door, as did several others—only they were knocking politely. He banged and banged, and I began to think the evening was over and the place was closed for the night, though judging from the waiting crowd this could not be the case.

Finally the little shuttered window opened and a small white face looked out. "What do you want?" the face said blankly.

"Let me in, you old son-of-a-bitch!" Joey said joyfully, and the face swolled briefly and the door opened and we were pulled in. Due to the extreme brightness of the waterfront lights that had shone in front, my eyes took some time to adjust and at first all I could see was the little puppet, surrounded by some bodyguards or assistants. "Joey, why do you do things like that?" the little puppet man whined. "How do you think it makes me look? I told you before, if you want to come by, call me during the afternoon, and I'll tell you one of the passwords for the evening. Or if you can't get hold of me first, just make something up, and I'll let you in."

"Sure thing," Joey said, slapping his frail cousin around and planting a big kiss on the face of him. "Hey listen, I got a couple friends with me tonight I want to introduce. Just so you don't think you're the only one around with famous friends. This is—" And then he remembered what I had made him promise earlier, that he would not reveal my identity to anyone because it embarrassed me. "—This is my friend Kent Gable, a well-known rock-and-roll star."

Joey's cousin Guich looked at Kent and then stared at me for a long time. "Who's this?" he said.

I kicked Joey between the shins. "This is my friend . . . Cotton Mather," Joey said. "He works as . . . a janitor, a janitor in the building where my pizza parlor is. By the way, Guich, the business is doing real well. Not that I'm in the same league as you are, but . . ."

His cousin continued to look at me attentively, as if he had seen me someplace before, but luckily he did not look impressed. "A rock-and-roll star," he said at last. "Well, stick around with me for a little while. I have some people I want you to meet."

Kent gave the two of us a demure smile, missing but a few teeth, and a nearly naked Oriental girl, naked, that is, except for a long pair of gloves that went up to her arms and covered her entire body, came over to us and asked if she could show Joey and me through the door. "Well, farewell then, Kent," I said, for Joey's cousin was leading him astray.

"Hey, Mgungu," Kent said, "let's meet up tomorrow, shall we? I want to do a bit of shopping, and we could have tea."

I said this would be most fine, for then we could speak in person, and also I might purchase some presents for my wives, and I waved him off. Then I began to look around. Where we were standing appeared to be an old elevator shaft and it went up miles in the darkness. The room was filled with a heavy dense and perfumed smoke that had already begun to have an insinuating effect on me, for it must have been some kind of opiated smoke. How odd that the elevator shaft appeared to go for hundreds of feet above me, and I imagined then that the elevator was beginning to descend, and might perhaps crush us all; therefore I knew that I was not myself, but hallucinating. And the girl said to us, "Come on, we better go into the other room before the elevator comes down, for I am a little frightened when this happens."

We went into the other room, which appeared acres long and was filled with rubble and piles of garbage and satin pink upholstery, as well as many stuffed buffaloes, wallabies, and a huge skeleton of a dinosaur. There were various people lying on these sofas and doing things off in the corner. There were little cars—Dodg'em carts from an amusement park—and there were various people driving around in these. "Can I take your coats?" the girl said, and I noticed we were divided from the rest of the room by a counter where another girl was taking money. But Joey's cousin, trying to escape the descending elevator, I imagine, came running in from the other room, a white-faced doll, and told this girl that we were his guests, we didn't have to pay. Joey looked relieved, because, as he whispered to me, "Who feels like paying thirty-five bucks apiece just to enjoy ourselves?"

We got into these Dodg'em carts and drove to the other end of the room. It was that far away, with Joey steering around the garbage and the decay and the sleeping people. We were nearly hit once, however, by a drunken driver weaving in and out of the potted palms.

At the far end where we were driving to was a dance floor, somewhat elevated and revolving, with the most peculiar lights, different sorts of neon and laser beams and music that was loud and rhythmic.

Joey and I wandered around past the dance floor, and I could not help but study closely and observe these persons tossing and throbbing and lounging on chairs, each in the throes of personal experience. He led me up a flight of stairs; it was impossible to see, but everywhere were various pairs of eyes, glowing redly in the dark.

We emerged on the second floor, a real disaster, with great pools of rancid water that looked to me to be, with all the electrical equipment around, a strong hazard. But as I have said, I know little about these things. On the second floor, which was only one part of the building, for some of it had been ripped away to create a higher ceiling for the first floor, there was a gigantic castle that Joey said his cousin had obtained through a contact on Disney's World and had not decided what to do with. There were piles and racks of theater clothing, for use of the guests, and there were mannequins so real-looking they actually spoke, and I did not know they were not real until I bumped into one and excused myself.

Inside this castle were all kinds of rooms, containing banquets made of plastic grapefruits, and hamburgers, and waffles, and I had to be prevented by Joey from sitting down to dine. One room held thousands of Ping-Pong balls, another giant stalks of gold wheat fifteen feet tall. Another room Joey refused to enter, saying it contained many bats and a foul smell. "I don't know if you noticed," Joey said, "my cousin is not really a well guy. He has problems and is, I would say, somewhat neurotic. Anyway, this is the way it is, and I guess who doesn't have problems today? So the guy has not gone out in daylight for fifteen years. He's rich enough: he can hire other people to do it for him. Are you hungry? They got real food downstairs."

So we returned to the dance floor to get some drinks and some food, for here was a region selling various sorts of seafood out of barrels that they would cook for you right then and there—you could choose your own lobster, and each lobster had a little nameplate round its neck with its name, such as "Fred" and "Mary" and "Lewis"—I suppose in order that the purchaser might feel on friendly terms with the food. There were blue-green crabs and flopping fish and oysters sitting merrily on beds of ice. The whole scene was quite gay and made my head throb as if it had no need for the rest of my body.

At last I excused myself, for I spotted a room marked MEN, and in here there were people of every nationality and sex gathered. Sitting on a pink satin chair was a handsome fellow wearing red cowboy boots that came up to his thighs; he held a tiny platter on which was placed a white substance which he was in the processs either of inhaling or sticking into his ears, I could not determine which. Now in my village the insertion of a substance into the ears would have been a more shameful thing than the act of masturbating in public. Yet I sensed this man's pride in his boots, and I thought I would be friendly; therefore I approached him and said, "I must tell you, you have made me very happy, for when I saw you I thought; Now what more could I possibly want to see for the rest of my life? For here I am in a place where a man may freely wear thigh-high cowboy boots and stick things in his ears, without shame. And I wonder what could possibly happen to me next, for at this minute I am ready to go home and retire."

The man stood up as if to respond, but at that moment I saw in the mirror behind his head the man in a luminous green suit; he was talking to Maria Fishburn, who was wearing a shimmering seaweed-green gown of a netlike filigree and beneath it she had on nothing, but the nipples of her breasts were painted blue.

My heart nearly stopped. I thought, Well, I have made a mistake, imagining it to be her in the swish of the crazy men's-room light; obviously it is not her, but possibly the resemblance is due to the fact that this person is another member of the Fishburn family tribe.

Yet when she paused briefly in front of the mirror to remove her contact lens and replace it, I knew it was her. "Hurry up," the man in the lime green suit called, and she turned and followed him. The two of them went into one of the little toilet booths. I did not know what to do, so I stood in front of the door, hurt and surprised, waiting for Maria to emerge. She had told me earlier that she was too fatigued to join me this evening, that her plans were otherwise. Yet here she was!

My honor was threatened and truly I was angry; yet also deeply injured. Were we not engaged? She had said herself we were to be man and wife; our phone conversations were long and loving. Yet for me a telephone relationship was not enough.

Though I waited and waited, neither she nor the man in the lime green suit emerged. At last I burst down the door, thinking to obtain explanation.

But all that was behind the door was another door, which I opened to find myself directly on the dance floor. A man grabbed my arm and pulled me, and I was caught up in the dancing. Not knowing any of the steps I could do nothing but stand still. The crowd hummed and throbbed to the music, thousands of bodies, except for mine, moving as one. The dance floor turned, the music was exceedingly loud, but though I looked with piercing gaze, of Maria Fishburn I saw no sight.

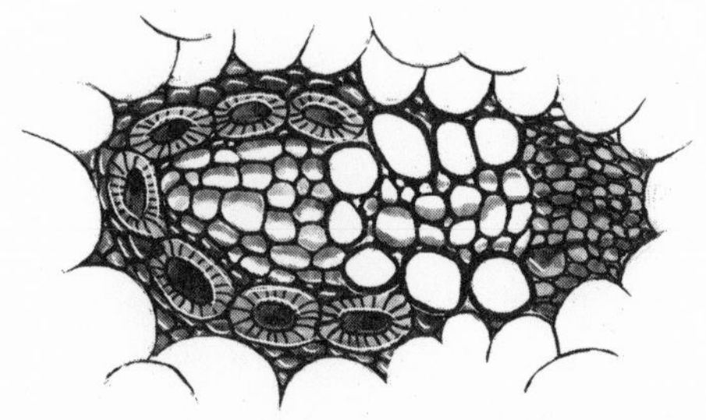

18

nd I had an alien feeling. The only time this feeling did not swirl in the thick air around my forehead, air rich and dense with thoughts however dumb, was in the morning. I loved breakfast, and there was nothing now I had to look forward to more than my breakfast at the museum with Parker Junius, who had invited me to partake.

I rose very early, at perhaps six o'clock, for I could not sleep, and went out onto the empty streets that reminded me, at that time of day, of morning in the mountains of New Burnt Norton.

In my house in New Burnt Norton—I thought with homesickness—the fire on the floor would be out by sunrise, which meant the shrill whine of the mosquitoes, driven away at night by the smoke, had started up again. Outside the door to the men's house, the steam would not yet have burned off and hung nearly on top of the vegetation, the mountaintop still lost in a milk-white nothingness. This is how a day begins: firstly the children wake up the women, who open the pigsty and let the pigs out. Some of them go to the door of the house to grunt at me, and it is possible to feel them shifting their bulk as they rub backs and sides against the scratchy straw of the walls, nearly pushing the house down in their lust to stop their itches. Other pigs are in the courtyard, rooting and churning the dirt with their pink rubber noses, wrinkled like an elephant's trunk and tough as a cactus. And the smoke was clearing, or the steam, and the red ginger flowers like hot open mouths fluttered as did the brilliant orange marigolds. Yerba each morning went across the yard to the stone fireplace to roast sweet potatoes for my breakfast. The little children walked about shaking with the cold and wiping their dripping noses; they rubbed their hands together to keep their fingers warm, and they hugged themselves and jumped up and down while waiting for the yams to get done to eat. My sons woke up hacking and spitting and coughing as they stirred about in a feeble attempt to awaken. Then I threatened to beat one unless he would stoke the fire. And it would still be dark inside the hut so the red tips from the cigarettes glowed as we waited for breakfast. And in the sun outside the door the copper wings of a black hornet glimmered.

Invariably hungry I stopped on the way to the museum at an Orange Julius, where I got myself a chili hotdog and also a large glass of drink made partially from fruit and partially from chemicals with lumps of gelatine floating in it. And then I proceeded.

The light on the street, at this hour, was excellent. There was a flatness about it and yet a lucidness to it as if everything had been bathed in gray and liquid Lucite. The buildings had a soft edge to them; they were in colors of old-rose brick and dull green mildew, as well as a smooth chalky color. As I have said, I am a man for whom many things are too strong—this time of the morning was one of them, and my over-observance of this caused everything to be very alive and wavering. My skin was sensitive and probably needed to be oiled; but I felt it was this way due to the intense light of day where only previously it had been dark. Meanwhile the taxis were honking and the air was cool and still nearly sweet and I was alone in my dark sunglasses. Around my neck I had a label bearing the legend *Guaranteed For a Year* that I had found only recently in the hotel lobby and that I could not resist stringing on a string around my neck, and insisting to myself that I wear it.

Upon reaching the museum I observed how its imposing face was set like a large tooth on a block of similar structures, only with large garage and glass doors instead of normal small ones. The museum was still closed for visitors; it was too early in the day. But the doorman knew me and let me in with a key on a large metal hoop looped to his belt. There were also offices upstairs for the museum administration. It was not purely a museum. There was a cafeteria where museum patrons could go, but my being admitted this early in the day was something special. The doorman let me in and I can assure you this was unlike the majority of people in the city of Manhattan. Why, out of sixteen million, only a very few, possibly ten or fifteen, were able to enter the museum at that time of day.

Inside, the fluorescent lights were not yet turned on. In the dark, the totem poles, some of which were forty feet high, had snarling faces and hooked noses, very poignant. I came upon a room with various types of Inca gold and jewelry. I stopped here in the dark and peered in the glass cabinets filled with glittering trinkets. Though I could see these things but dimly, there was a primitive and rich feel to these objects, and the squat, flat faces of the modern-day Peruvian Indians, whose photographs lined the wall, enormous photographs perhaps some seven feet across, seemed resigned and stolid, as if a great deal of life had been drained off them since the Spanish conquests. There were rooms filled with Maori masks, whiskery and ridiculous, and old stone and bone faces. Of course there was nothing made by the Lesser Pimbas; as I have said we had no art or voodoo kits. But I tell you, the junk in that place, though filled with feeling, was not very good, if I may be so bold as to say so. It was uncivilized and brutal stuff, and it was a sorry sight to see how low man could sink before moving up.

In the back of the museum was a little garden, roofed over, that was not part of the museum, though it was filled with certain primitive objects, Mayan stone carved blocks, Egyptian wahoos, a head from Easter Island, and also a tremendous sack-like nude called Henry Moore, or so a sign said. There were various ivies that covered the brick wall at the back and sprang rampantly from assorted pots. Also there were peppery geraniums like screaming-meemies in red and pink colors, and there were several small tables made from latticed metal, with chairs to match and strawberry-colored umbrellas that said CINZANO. As I stood looking out I was approached by a big lady in a white coat and a little cap. "I am Serafina," she said. "You are the cannibal? Go and sit in the garden. I will bring you breakfast. I am staff cook. Parker Junius, he is coming. You like cereal? I bring." As she went by I could not help myself and pinched her loudly on her broad bottom, so reminiscent of Yerba's huge tush and filling me with longing, which did not go over well with her. She scowled but returned a few moments later, bringing me coffee and Wheat Chex.

I liked them best soggy, and indeed I had to wait until the milk had thoroughly disapproved and soaked in, meanwhile sipping the black coffee. Sitting there this was my favorite time of day, alone in the garden with the little singing flowers and the ominous statues glowering at me in the honking air, for it was chilly. I could not help but think of Maria and the night before. Could she possibly have seen me and fled? Yet how loving she was on the phone. I wanted only to be closer to her. If she was to be my wife, at least I'd like her to be in the same apartment. But perhaps, being no doubt young, and pure, also virginal, she was merely having nervous jitters.

While preoccupied thus, Parker Junius came in, abrupt and in a hurry. "Where's Maria?" he said.

"I—" I said.

"She couldn't make it? That's too bad, because I had some things I wanted to talk to her about. She mentioned to me you plan to marry. As her guardian, there are financial consequences to discuss." He took off his glasses and wiped them voraciously. Then he picked up the little bell and began jangling it, making a gleeful sight in the peaceful garden as he waved the little bell with his giddy tufted hair framing his face.

With the tinkling sound of the bell the cook Serafina came running, for she loved him and approved him as gratifying to his position and also because he was not a bottom-pinching cannibal. For him she rapidly wheeled a little tea cart and carried his coffee in a pot.

This cart was filled with glorious filled and stuffed cakes. There were blueberry and cranberry crumb cakes, simply loaded with crumbs, and there were strawberry tartlets not commonly known for breakfast and heaped with rustic strawberries shimmering with glaze, and there were prune-whip stars, and hummocks of cheesecake, and gooey Danish from which protruded raisins and nuts and pineapple mush-up. For this was the interesting thing about Parker Junius: He ate nothing but dessert. Nothing but dessert had parted his lips for nearly two years, since his heart attack.

"This heart attack," he told me in between bites of a sleek chocolate cake, black as a seal and densely fudgy, the name of which was blackout cake, and it was three layers thick, "arrived two years ago, and since then my appetite has not been the same. Over one summer vacation I planned to go to Greece, but on the Fourth of July weekend I suffered a heart attack while walking from the store back to my apartment building. I was on my way back from grocery shopping, carrying two large bags, and a waterfall of air—you know what a waterfall is, don't you, Mgungu?"

"Why, yes," I said.

"Of course," he said, "What am I saying, you're from New Burnt Norton. For a minute I thought you were one of the ones from the Kalahari Desert—anyway, this waterfall of air gushed into my throat at the same time a giant hand seemed to swoop down from out of nowhere and squeeze my ribs. In front of me each molecule of oxygen hung heavy and swollen, shimmering in the heat. I remember everything seemed tremendously enlarged; you can have no idea of what this experience was like. My doorman carried me inside. The shock of the air conditioning after the heat was as if two scabs had been ripped from the place my eyes once were. Since then, I've only felt like eating dessert." And he helped himself, after scraping the last of the blackout cake from the plate, to a slice of pie stuffed with pecans. I could not help but be fascinated by him, with his curious sprockets of hair and a perpetually surprised look on his face. "You know, Mgungu," he said, "now that you are getting married to Maria, I wonder if you have any idea of what you are getting yourself into."

"Oh sure," I said. "Plenty." Though in fact we looked at each other dubiously.

"I wish you would think twice about the whole business," he said. "She is a mysterious young lady, and very dissatisfied with herself. I am far too busy with the museum and with my boys and artwork to have much time to devote to her. Of course, it's her family's money that supports the museum, and I've known her since she was a tiny infant. But she's a grown woman now, and I can't keep an eye on her day and night." He looked at me meaningfully. "You know she was institutionalized some years back. I don't know what she's up to these days, but from what reaches my ears—which is very little—she may be involved with things she shouldn't be."

"Such as?" I said.

"I really can't go into it," he said. "However, I do know that Maria has this idea that she is invincible, which is not true. She's a strange girl. She's always associated with the wrong type, an act of rebellion possibly for being born rich. Why, even as far back as Vassar she had a boyfriend who claimed to be an art dealer, but who in fact—"

I felt obligated to interrupt any possible slander against her. "She is a very pure girl, spiritually and intellectually speaking, though perhaps a little mixed up in the head," I said.

"You don't know the world around you, Mgungu," Parker Junius said, "and perhaps you don't know how to distinguish between the subjective and objective aspects of your life."

"That is the effect of the Joy Paul Guilford over a period of years on my brain, possibly," I said.

"No, no, no," Parker Junius said, "By what I said I mean this: you see the world around you as a scene painted for scene painting's sake, when in fact it is not only highly representative but also symbolic. And these symbols you are not interpreting, but simply letting pass you by. Oh, this may sound surprising, coming from me, but in fact it is what I have come to believe. You have character, yes, although it is not a character I would wholeheartedly approve. But a person like Maria Fishburn doesn't have any character except for the role she tries out. Now, how do you think you fit into her picture?"

"I guess I'm not sure."

"Aha! You see? Well, it's like this—she has constructed a Platonic ideal in her mind of you, and once you fail her in this role—for she imagines you in a part as well as herself, though her part is a leading role—I'm afraid there will be grave consequences. As for the danger she is possibly currently in, why, she has no idea that it is not a part she is merely playing for excitement—but it is real life. I believe you are aware of what is real life and what is not, aren't you, Mgungu? I guess, which is why, although to be honest, I disapprove of her marriage to you—and by the way, you are going to divorce your other three wives, aren't you?—you may perhaps be able to help her out. I told her parents if anything ever happened to them I would try and look out for her, but the girl is as stubborn as an oyster."

"What kind of common criminal is Reynard Lopato?" I asked suddenly.

"What? How do you know about Reynard Lopato?" he said, and a strange and fearful look came onto his face, like a marmoset with two sprouts of lard-white fur above each ear.

"I don't," I said, "But I've heard mention of him."

"Oh," he said, with what I believed to be relief, and out of nervousness tipped some coffee onto his lap. "He's just common."

"I see," I said.

He pushed his platter away and sipped the last of his coffee before standing up. "Well, I must be off," he said. "It was pleasant speaking with you. So glad you could come." He tried to smooth down his free-sprouting hair, which rapidly hopped up again. His eyes had glazed like those of a fresh-killed animal, indicating to me he had much to think about and a great deal on his mind, while his gold glasses reminded me of the Methodist missionary, my former teacher, the crisp teacher, whom my father had killed after a minor altercation.

What had happened was this—he had come down to the school, my father, to bring me and my sisters back up to the village to help with the digging of a new garden. The missionary was new to the area, and as it turned out he had very fatty limbs. He was replacing an old missionary who had retired and gone back to Brighton, England. He was not a person who was aware of the correct way to behave, and he had white, white skin that rapidly turned pink and burst open in blisters, although this was when roasted and not when still alive.

In any case, he refused to allow my sisters and myself to leave the school, and at that moment my father decided to take the missionary's gramophone, which included a set of Hawaiian ukulele marching music as well as the Django Reinhardt records and a few scratched hymns. Naturally the missionary refused to give up his possessions, there was a brief tussle, and the teacher was laid out in the missionary position for roasting. My mother and stepmothers came down. It was a time for celebration. I got to keep the teacher's glasses, which I wore for several days until I got a headache and my eyes started to hurt.

The glasses may still be up in the rafters of my house someplace, for all I know. As I say, he had not been a pleasant missionary, forcing us to sing foul songs, etc. When once I asked him how his wristwatch worked, he said I would know when I got older, a sorry answer if I ever have heard one. It was from him that I developed my suspicion of people and my certain brutal cynicism usually lacking in most primitive people. The death of the missionary proved to be the death of my father, for some time later he was finally tracked down by the New Burnt Norton version of Canadian Mounties or Texas Rangers and was brought to prison, where he was tortured to death. Though I am sure simply because he wore similar glasses did not mean Parker Junius was the same as the missionary at all. I was not one to jump to conclusions.

"Well, I must push off," Parker Junius said, standing and putting down his coffee cup from which he sipped the last drop. "By the way, my secretary is typing up a list of the various times and places you'll be dancing. Pick it up any time you feel like stopping by."

"But wait—!" I said, for surely Parker Junius must have understood I could not participate absolutely. But it was too late, for he had already pushed off.

After he left I, too, started about my daily rounds, though I could not depart without carrying with me several large pieces of cake from the tea tray and additionally both cups and saucers. For although Maria Fishburn was giving me twenty-five dollars a week spending money, a generous sum, and a Kool Kash Kard as well (though no instructions on how to use it), I was not able to break myself of my need to acquire man-made possessions and any kind of freebie.

Then I went off to visit Kent Gable, and also to simply observe the great jaw of the city, for this was how, since becoming an American of leisure, I spent my days.

Only now, due to Parker Junius's mention, I was very worried, wondering what I could do, if anything, about Maria Fishburn, who was indeed a very strange girl and incomprehensible, I saw now, from the very day I had met her. And what she was involved in, and what I could do about it, I did not know. How was I to explain to Parker Junius that I had never even been in her apartment and that there was nothing in common between us? And yet I was fond of the girl, as much as I was able, though perhaps for the wrong reason, which was that I was in love with her. And I determined to rescue her, if only from herself. This seemed to me that I had found a task in life, and something worthy of a cause.

19

Do you mind if we stop in here for a minute?" I said to Kent as we passed a store that sold women's stockings and underwear. It was a tiny shop set far back from the street-front and I wouldn't have noticed it had it not been for all the plastic nude and nippleless torsos dressed up in satin garter belts and crotchless underpanties striped purple and green. "I want to buy some brassieres for the wives. It shouldn't take very long."

"Yeah, sure, why not?" But he looked slightly impatient and glanced at his watch once or twice as we went into the shop.

There were two men and a lady crowded behind a tiny glass counter. One of the men had a pointed pink head, hairless and shaped like an arrow, the other wore a hatchet mustache of grayish color. The woman, mean and slim, was garbed, I suspected, beneath her shapeless spotted dress, in the most exotic underwear the shop had to offer. I did not doubt for a minute what went on among the three of them when there were no customers in the shop. Behind the men were box after box containing the articles of clothing and stockings, and under the glass were rows of socks and underpants, laid out neatly as fishes. Against the far wall, leaving barely any space between the counter and the rest of the room, was a long rack of negligees, flittering gently in the gust of wind our arrival had let into the shop.

"I'd like to buy some brassieres," I said.

"What size?" the man with the chopper mustache said. He came out from behind the counter to look at me more closely.

"What you got stuck in your nose?" he said. "What's that, some kind of a fountain pen?"

"Ballpoint."

He shook his head. The other man blew his nose loudly into a handkerchief and went over to the woman, muttering to her about something while the two of them straightened boxes of stockings. "All right, all right, so you got a pen stuck in your nose. What size bras do you want?"

"I'm not sure, really," I said. I looked at Kent, who was gazing at himself in an absentminded way in the mirror at one end of the room. He bent over to brush at some mud stuck to his patent-leather cowboy boots. "I guess I want some very large ones. And some medium-sized ones."

"Very large? That's some help. What do you mean, very large? Is that a size? You talking about a thirty-eight C? A forty D? How am I supposed to know? What do you want me to do, mind read?"

"Maybe if I could just see some of what you have—"

"What should I do, open every box in the house? Give me a rough idea, an estimate even, maybe I can help you."

"Okay. Well, one of them is about this big, I would guess—" I held up my two hands cupped several feet in front of my chest.

"*Gott in Himmel,* I don't know. Let me see what I can do. Who knows what I got when you hold up your hands like that. Maxi, bring me the box of things on the top at your end there. It's way on the top. I don't know what it says, you know which one I'm talking about." The woman got up on a small stepladder and took down a box covered with dust, from close to the ceiling.

The hatchet mustache opened the box in front of me with soft hands and gently removed a layer of tissue. Inside, the white garments were made of some kind of very tough and thick elastic. The brassiere part was built into a kind of boned corset that when I held it up to myself came to well below my waist and ended in dangling metal clips to hold up stockings.

1. Facsimile of a drawing of New Burnt Norton, from an English volume on islands of the South Pacific, 1859.

2. Oscar Fishburn, Maria's cousin, shortly before his disappearance from New Burnt Norton, where he had gone in search of the rare death's-head butterfly. No traces of his body were ever found, except for his gold Rolex wristwatch and a native wearing a T-shirt that said "Save Water, Shower with a Friend."

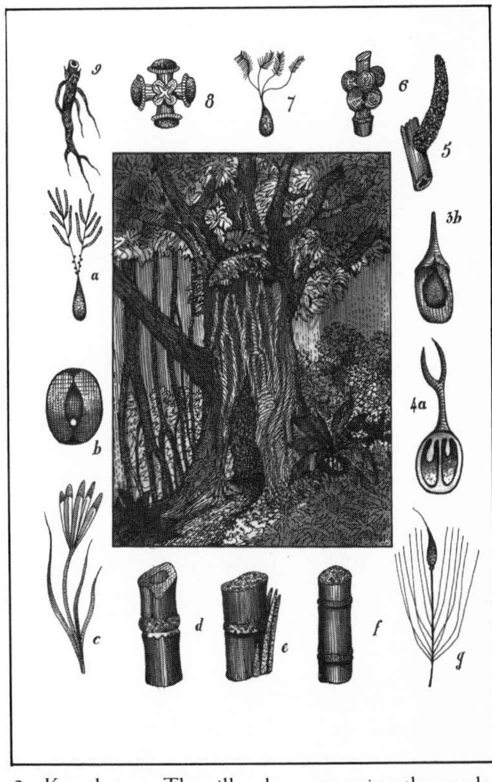

3. Kapok tree. The silky down covering the seeds of this tropical tree is often used for stuffing pillows.

4. Maria Fishburn and her mother, Eloise Fishburn, shortly before the plane crash in which both of Maria's parents were killed.

5. The Fishburn family home. (*DC/Small World Photos*)

6. A caboose, invented by Albany Phillip Fishburn I, on which the Fishburn fortune was founded.

7. The first meeting of Maria and Mgungu Yabba Mgungu, taken with a self-timing camera.

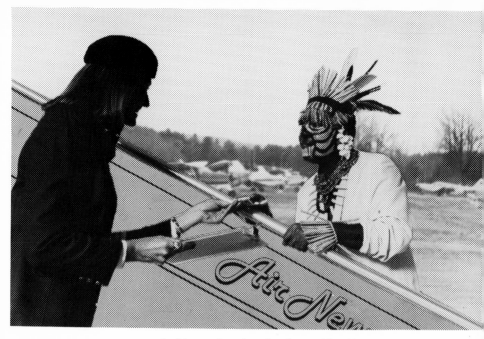

8. Mgungu boarding the plane to New York.

9. A "Welcome" fruit basket similar to the one sent to Mgungu.

KENT GABLE

10. The record album cover of Kent Gable, who befriended Mgungu on the plane trip.

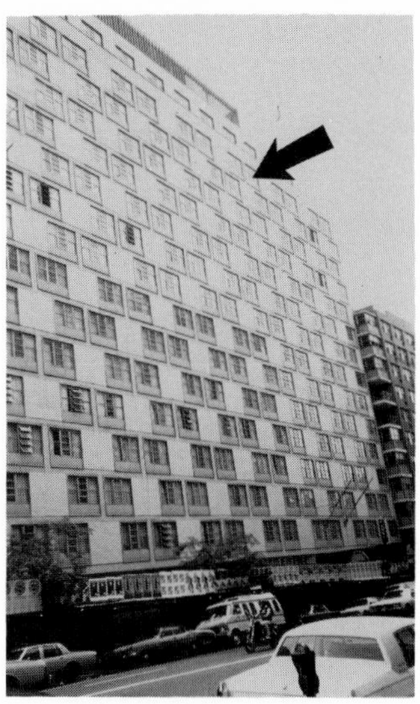

11. The site of the Holiday Inn. Arrow indicates fifteenth floor.

12. An impromptu performance by Kent in the Greek-American House of Belly Dancing. "The music was like a pig being killed and seemed to shred the very fiber of the air." (*Courtesy Alexander Takodopoulis*)

13. Sophie Tuckermann, owner of Mama Tuckermann's. She was later to found the "Free Mgungu" society.

14. The table altar found in Mgungu's Holiday Inn hotel room.

15. Parker Junius, curator of the Museum of Primitive Cultures.

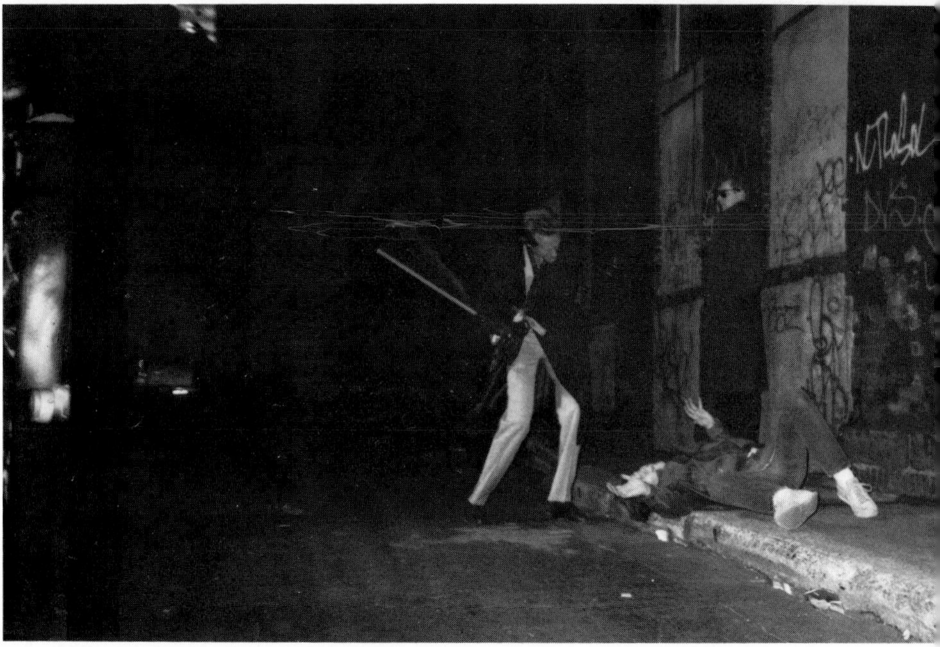

16. Photograph taken behind Joe's Pizza by Mgungu of Reynard Lopato, common criminal and art dealer.

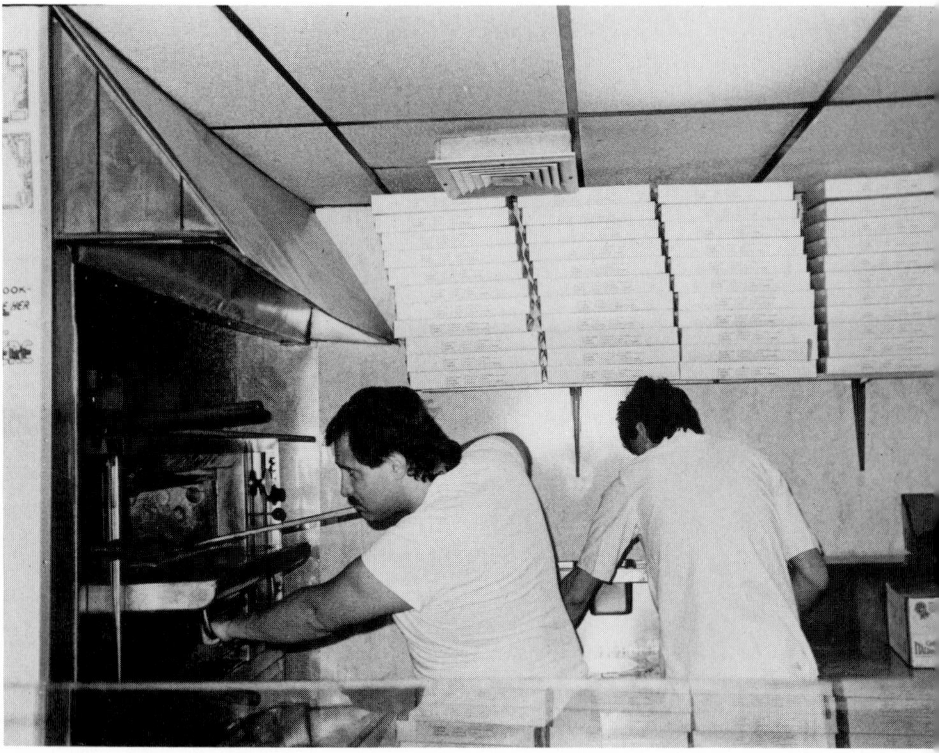

17. Joey Tarrantino in his pizza parlor.

NTERNATIONAL DANCE
FESTIVAL

Museum of Primitive Cultures. MPC

18. Poster from the first annual International Dance Festival, now a collector's item.

19. The wedding of Maria and Mgungu at Tavern on the Green.

20. Warehouse 29, located in an abandoned warehouse on a pier on the Hudson River, before its destruction in one of Manhattan's most infamous nightclub disasters.

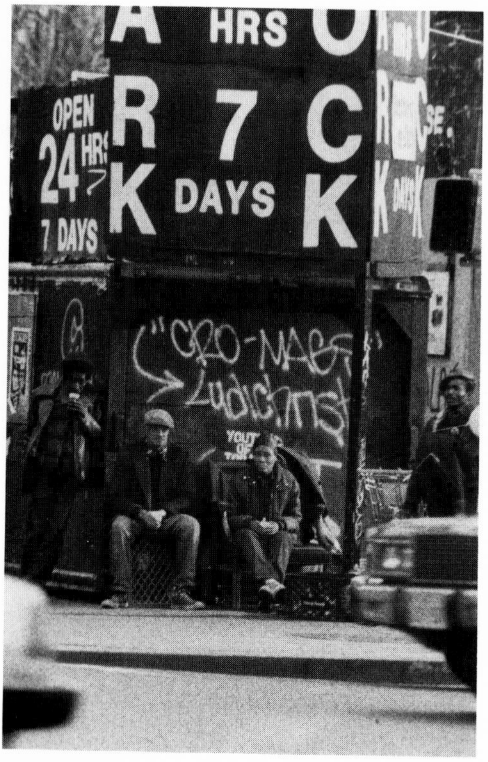

21. A number of street-people who associated with Mgungu following his eviction from the Holiday Inn.

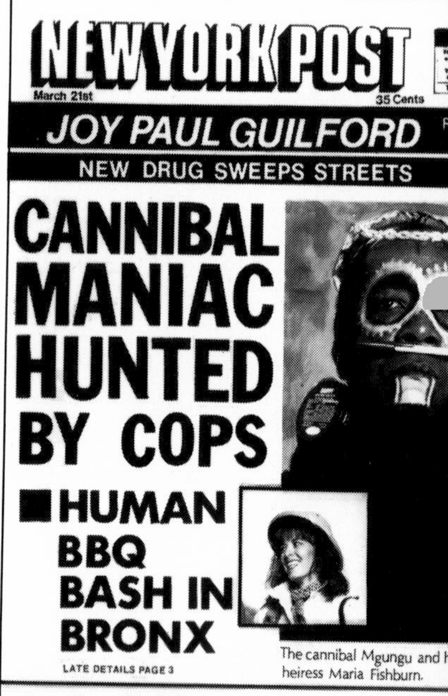

NEW YORK POST

March 21st — 35 Cents

JOY PAUL GUILFORD

NEW DRUG SWEEPS STREETS

CANNIBAL MANIAC HUNTED BY COPS

■ HUMAN BBQ BASH IN BRONX

LATE DETAILS PAGE 3

The cannibal Mgungu and h[illegible] heiress Maria Fishburn.

U.S. REPORTER SEIZ

We've created a monste

22. *New York Post* front page.

23. *Time* magazine cover.

24. Co-op City, the Bronx, where Mgungu was taken by Reynard Lopato and Mikhail for "an American picnic in the country."

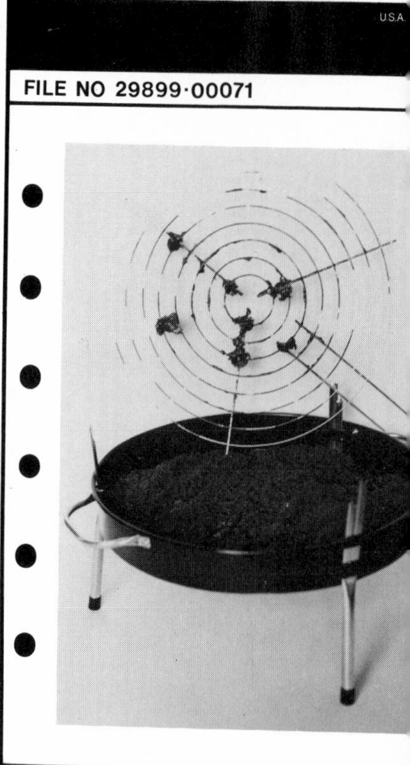

25. Police file photo of the abandoned barbecue grill at the site of the picnic. Other evidence included a portion of a femur carried off by a stray dog.

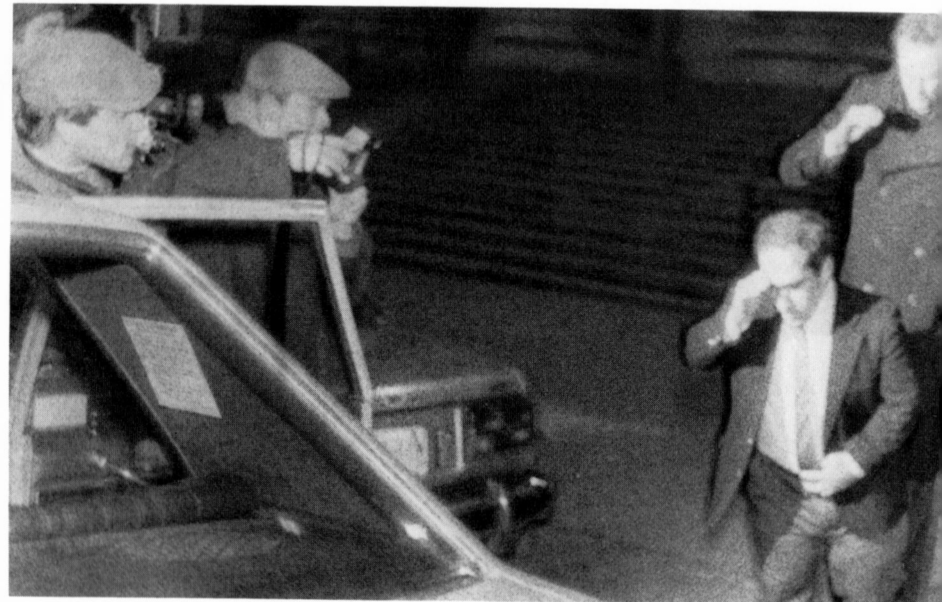

26. Reynard Lopato and Mikhail dodging photographers.

27. Courtroom sketch. On the left is Mgungu's attorney, Mr. Kirk.

the advice of his attorney, Mgungu wore
l" clothing for his arraignment in court, but
nged in the bathroom.

29. The victim.

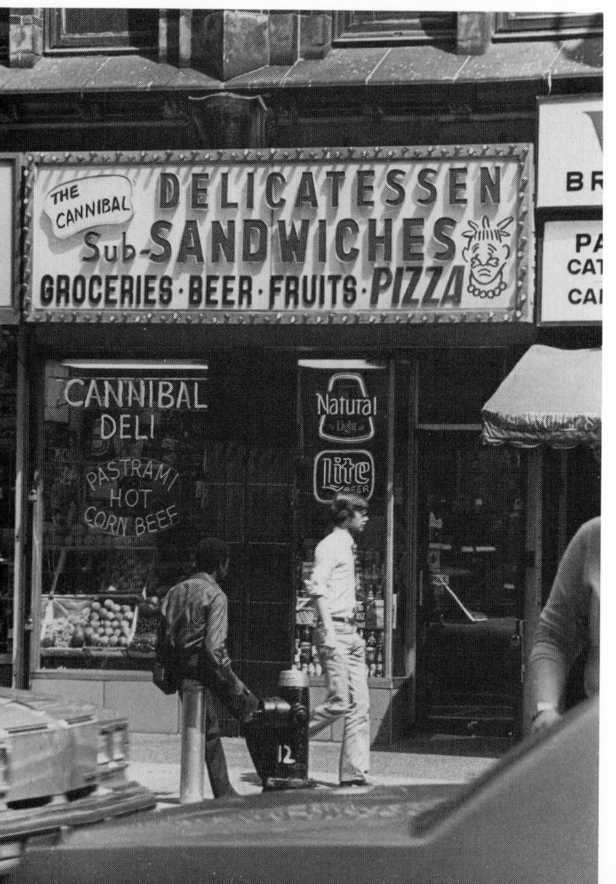

30. (*above*) Photo from a *New York Times* article about a man allegedly raised among the Lesser Pimbas.

31. (*left*) The Cannibal Deli, formerly Mama Tuckermann's.

And the cups of the brassiere were made of concentric circles of fabric terminating in two points like stingers.

"Hey, this stuff isn't new, is it?" said Kent, coming in to look at the box of things with some interest.

"No, no, I'll let you have it for half price. They don't even make this material anymore; it's a little yellowed now. You won't find it anyplace else."

"When is it from?"

"Nineteen forty-seven. Look, it was eight dollars then, I'll let you have it for half of that, four bucks, tax included."

"I don't really think it's what I'm looking for."

"You don't know what you're looking for, do you? You don't tell me, how am I supposed to guess? I'm not a mind reader."

I tried to smile. "Yes, you're right."

"You tell me you need something that big, you're going to want something with some kind of support in it too, unless it's not for a woman you're talking about." And he looked at Kent and me suspiciously. "We get all kinds in here. You'd be surprised."

"Maybe she's not that big."

"I didn't think so," he said sternly. "You should find out the size first, always."

"Could I see something with colors?"

"Well, I'll see what I've got, I don't know." He pulled out a box of varicolored brassieres in silky fabrics, some with underwires and some without, and some with little removable rubber pads and other devices. For Yerba I took some with big splotched spotted dots of purple and red and green, for Oola I chose some smaller-sized ones in a shell-colored pink, and for Nitsa I got some cheerful red ones with circles like eyes cut out for the nipples. Then also I took some stockings with seams up the back and for Oola a pair of high-heeled slippers with pink fur or fluff stuck on.

Then, laden with these packages and Kent's violin case, we went out into the street, past the bald pink-headed man who had ignored me in the shop and who was now sitting in the store window removing the panties from the nude ladies and was putting on them instead new brassieres and pinning little signs to parts of the body with price tags.

The wind was howling very fierce and the slush in the great droopy trails dripped around our feet. We passed a restaurant sleazy from the outside in appearance, with a cardboard harem dancer in the window revolving endlessly, by means of electricity. Her stomach kept constantly twisting and churning. Kent said, "This looks a bit like home. Let's go in for a coffee. I could use a cigarette."

And on entering he removed his large velvet hat, which I may have neglected to mention he wore, a hat that matched in color directly his scabrous shirt, and with the removal of this snow-encrusted hat his ears plunged out directly from his head, as if before they had been pinned closely down, and they glowed redly from the cold. Under his hat his hair was stumpy and troubled, and his appearance was frightening, except that the look in his eye was glazed and vegetarian, for he did not have the eyes of a meat eater. Also his physique was not so good but was filled with flab. "I don't need muscles to play the violin," he said to me, judging what I was thinking I guess from my scrutiny of him. He looked at me. "I'm dying for a cuppa, but I can't stand the way they make it in this country. It's never strong enough." When the waiter approached he said, "I'd like a cup of tea with two bags, please."

The waiter was delighted to serve, as we were the only ones in the place, and this waiter had a mop of greasy hair that dangled in front of his forehead and a shiny black-and-white plastic pin that said ALEXANDER. Nearly immediately he winked at me. And though all I ordered was a cup of coffee, shortly this waiter returned with a cup of coffee and a coiled roll with a lump of something red and gooey in the center. "For you, something special," he said to me. "Thank you; you're welcome."

The walls of this place were decorated with photographs of belly dancers, and it was called the Greek-American House of

Belly Dancing. I guess it was a night-time place. As I said, it was empty now. "Thank you; you're welcome," I said, thinking this might be a Greek-American way of speaking. Also I began to unwrap my package of brassieres, for I could not bear to leave anything in a state of purity but always had to examine each purchase and remove any pins, labels, or plastic covering, simply for the thrill of touching something new and uncontaminated. Then I stopped myself short. "Oh, my dear friend," I said to Kent, "please excuse my rudeness. For here we are, having our hot drinks over a table, and of course I should be having a conversation."

Then I paused and began, for I knew this was what civilized people did, and I was pleased. "So it is," I said. "A life in the United States. How was I to know what people said or did is not the same at all as what they mean? As in my own country, some customs are startlingly different, and cannot be guessed at. For instance, let us say a nice fat bunch of yams are being passed out by the wives. Do not smile. The more scowling that is done, the more yams you will be handed. Why is this? Because nobody has to give you anything to please you when you are already pleased. When you want something, you frown and look away. Then you are always given a lot, so you won't be angry."

"I see," said Kent.

"However, in this country, from what I have learned, the reverse is not the case, but is based on a monetary system. Though luckily for me, I was able rapidly to adjust to this custom, since I am able to view money only as green pieces of colored paper, and hand it away easily. And what is valuable to me is not to everyone else. The effluvia of society—empty beer cans, a string of moldy chilies, a sprung umbrella—by accident I paid good money for these, not knowing what they were. Yet still I value this junk highly. That is why, Kent, so often since arriving I have ended up as a remnant of a prehistoric race, watching with dull and uncomprehending eyes the busy and inexplicable activities of this civilization."

"Pass the sugar, please," Kent said, "and I'll have a bit of that sticky bun, if you're not going to eat it, mate."

"And I must say," I went on, pleased with the direction our discussion had taken, "that often the city does appear to me cruel and unyielding, the shapes grotesque and unnatural, more oddly juxtaposed than any of the strangest formations on New Burnt Norton; the twisted and red mountains, the vegetation humid and suffocating, are far more normal than this."

"Oh, yeah," Kent said, his mouth full of bun.

"Therefore, due to these physical differences in environment, customs must naturally vary from one place to the next," I concluded. "And if not brought up with the jargon, a person would not know what it was all about. But forgive me, my friend. My time is up. You must speak now. For we are having a *conversation*."

To my surprise, Kent seemed to know the custom of which I spoke, for he took a deep breath and began to talk rapidly. "How did I decide to become a rock-and-roll star?" Kent said. "It's like this: I was very good in school, I was a maths major. However, I thought—I don't want to be an accountant for the rest of my life—that was what I was going to be, you see—and so I went down to a vocational guidance center—it cost me seventy quid, and I had to fill out thousands of questionnaires. And when I was done they said, 'Oh, you should be a famous rock-and-roll star.' Well, that sounded okay, so I approached the record companies, each one, but none of them were interested in me. I played the guitar, you see, and I played the violin, and I played rather well. But, I thought, Well, this is what I was meant to be, and for so many quid I wasn't going to give up easily. A few weeks later there was a record convention in a big fancy hotel. And so I went to it and chained myself and my amplifier to a car engine (I'm not saying this was an original idea, mind you) and plugged it into the battery of the car. Well, it knocked me right out. Electrocuted me, it did. And when the guy came back to his car—he was president of a large company, I had made sure of that—he was so upset to find me half dead and chained to his car, he signed me up and put together Kent Gable and the Experience. And then we had a hit single in England, so I'm well on my way, you see. The only problem is, at this point, everybody I meet is either nobody, and therefore beneath me, or somebody, and therefore too far above me to associate with me."

"Oh, yes," I said, "and what is vocational guidance?"

"Oh, there's no point in going into that. You'd never understand. Though maybe you should go for it, if you remain undecided."

"Undecided?" I said.

"As to what you are or what you are going to do."

I was very surprised that he was aware of this aspect of me.

"Well, look," he said, "don't look at me that way. I'm going to talk about this just to give you some idea. What is my philosophy? It's like this—for you, things are simple. Many years ago during the days when people were simpler, we used to live in the trees. Through my music I'm trying to recapture some of that feeling, that emotion. For you, however, you are nearer to the trees than the rest of us. When you accept that, you will be fine. If not, however, you maybe should see a vocational guidance counselor."

"Yes, but what is this thing called vocational guidance?"

"I'm going downstairs for just a minute. Will you come with me?" he said, not answering my question.

"Okay, certainly, my friend, but why?"

"I have something I want to show you."

I followed him downstairs. These stairs plunged steeply, and below was a narrow greasy hall with a lightbulb hanging barely from the ceiling. We passed several grimy storage rooms laden with boxes. He pushed open the door marked MEN and said, "Come on in."

"But is there room for more than one?" I said.

And he said, "Oh, sure."

When we were therein he turned on the light, exposing a little rust-stained sink and a toilet around which was a little dripping puddle on the floor and continually flushing. So he jiggled the handle to prevent it from further flushing. And I approached it as if to urinate, thinking, perhaps, he was afraid to enter the basement alone, seeing how New York is a dangerous place, and thus asked me to come with him.

And he unzipped his fly, revealing a partially erect and fairly small penis, which he displayed to me.

"Uh-huh," I said, "very nice, Kent." For as you can see I did not know what this was all about but assumed it to be some English or European custom, or even something American I had not yet been exposed to.

However I did grasp what it was he was getting at when he asked me to take this object into my mouth, and without derision I said, "I am not able to."

"What's wrong, then?"

"I am a man fifty-five years old," I said, "and while in my past I might have been interested—I don't know—at this point I'm not even sure how much interest I feel in women anymore." Which was a lie; I was interested in women, or at least in my wives, who did know how to turn me on, as they say; however, I believed this the best thing to mention, as I did not want to lose his friendship. For I did really admire him, with his white calcified skin of a chalklike texture, and his shrubbery for hair and nail pins through his cheek.

I had always wanted to know exactly what a rock star was, or was like.

I pissed, and when I turned around his strange hands were washing themselves in the sink bowl. "So tell me," I said, "what is the pleasure in something like this for the other guy? Is there anything in it for him?"

"Oh, sure," he said. "You should try it, then you'd see."

But still I deigned, and we returned upstairs, and when the employees saw his violin in its case resting under the table they asked him to play. For they recognized him; they had seen his face on the cover of his records and also knew he was playing in the city. "But I have no amplifier," he said, and they showed him where the belly-dancing band daily stored their equipment, on a little platform or stage. So he plugged it in and began to saw away; the music was like a pig being killed and seemed to shred at the very fiber of the air.

I didn't see how he could not be aware of what he was doing: I put my hands over my ears, for it seemed to me that soon a visible hole would be torn in the molecules of oxygen, due to his playing. Oh, it was simply terrible, yet meanwhile the employees, and our waiter Alexander, stood around clapping their hands.

And finally a recognizable tune began to emerge: it was "Sweet Georgia Brown" he was playing. Things began to stir in my bowel. I could feel things moving around down there, over which I had no control. This was simply due to the electric frequencies emerging. For I had never actually heard rock music in person, and I supposed this was the point of it, to get the *moodla* stirring around down there inside one.

I nearly let out an involuntary curdle. It was all I could do to keep the groaning and the noise within my throat. Combined with the feedback noises that emerged from the amplifier, and the way he sawed away at the popular air, his chin wibbling over the edge of his violin, it was certainly something. Though they asked him to continue, he shortly stopped. "It sounds terrible," he said. "I need to go and collect the proper parts. I lost all my equipment," he explained to them, "and now I need to refurbish this instrument." They applauded politely and said the coffee and tea were on the house, in addition to the little cake Alexander the waiter had given me because he had taken a liking to me.

I told them I would most definitely come back for a meal, or at least stop in to say hello, but that first I had to go downstairs again to use the facilities, for the instrumentation had stirred me up inside and it was necessary for me to relieve my bowels. And so I went back into the dingy basement; no sooner had I seated myself on the nice smooth toilet than there was a banging on the door. "Who's there?" I said.

"It's me," a voice said. "Please let me in."

Yet the voice did not sound quite familiar enough. "Who is it?" I said. "I cannot let you in. Go away please. Without meaning to hurt your feelings, I lack sexual interest at this moment."

"Very good," the voice said. "Thank you; you're welcome." And the footsteps went away.

Kent and I went back out onto the street, and Kent assured me that despite what had happened before we would still be friends; that in fact we might even meet again soon, for I invited him to my wedding.

So we shook hands; his were very strange, though in what respect I cannot say. And I wandered off alone, thinking to myself, I should have gotten from him some advice about Maria Fishburn, for he seems to know a great deal and is a young and modern fellow; perhaps he could have told me what to do about Maria Fishburn. I thought and thought, until my feet were soaked. And everything seemed most strange to me, yet about this strangeness there was nothing, I believed, that I could do.

20

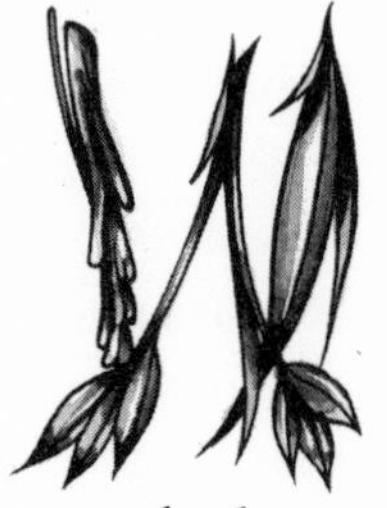

ell, so it must be remembered that all this time Maria was preparing for this wedding of ours. In many ways I felt this to be a mistake, for perhaps I sensed in my heart that she was not ready for conjugal bliss; yet this wedding was something she claimed to want desperately, and would speak about with me on the phone frequently, and the preparations were to be elaborate and also extravagant. When I tried to make her understand, late at night, that I felt some hesitation, she grew very angry and would hear nothing of it.

"I want this to be a real Marin-county-type wedding," was what she said. "Out behind the Tavern on the Green, because I know how claustrophobic you get when you're trapped indoors. And we'll have a judge to marry us instead of a clergyman. Because I want this to be a reconfirmation of an already working relationship, not something we need to do to formulate one."

"Yeah, of course," I said, not understanding in the least.

"What were your other three weddings like?" she said. She claimed to be able to talk better to me when she didn't have to look at me, and I was fond of her warm, breathy voice emerging from the little telephone device so late at night, and was better able to appreciate her than when I had to see her in a nightclub from afar, which made me nervous.

"What were my other three weddings like?" I said. "Well, I tell you. They were not like the one we are to have, my dear. For one thing, I am sure that—being experienced as I am—I know now how to make it a happy thing for us both." I had become quite debonair in my Americanization, and knew slightly better what to say to a girl.

Then I heard her gentle and strange weeping on the other end of the phone. Tears were peculiar to me, being foreign to the nature of New Burnt Norton women. "What is the matter, dear heart?"

"Oh, I don't know, Mgungu," she said. "I should be happy, but I'm not. I feel all mixed up. If only I had been born on New Burnt Norton and was one of your wives, belonging to a tribe. Yes, that's it. I wish I belonged to a tribe. I want to take the place of a tribe for you, Mgungu, if I can. I'll be your complete tribe. You're not legally married to your other wives, are you?"

Then she asked me if I minded getting divorced, since I was doing it for her, and she didn't care if I did it after we got married. "Sure," I said, in a nervous state. "No problem." I didn't want to tell her that there was no such thing as divorce among the Lesser Pimbas, that once two people decided to be married that was it, even though there was no ceremony.

"Oh, Mgungu," she said. "I guess I'm sorry to be making you marry me, when you were better off up in the mountains of New Burnt Norton." This was the first time she had, I felt, spoken so openly with me.

"But I don't think so," I said, deeply touched. "I'm very glad and happy to be marrying you. This is the life I have always longed for, I think. I was not meant to be an uncivilized man, but rather have always thought of myself as one being accustomed to and needing products, as well as being a child of technology. And if what is bothering you is the fact that you feel bad at taking me away from my other wives, let us send them some gifts, divorce gifts so to speak, maybe a set of walkie-talkies or a CD player, or perhaps several sets of falsies, something to cheer them up, heh-heh."

But Maria did not respond. She had such a sophisticated sense of humor that the only things she found funny were the ones she thought up herself.

Now, my visa was due to expire in only a few weeks hence, and I did go to see if I could get it renewed, in order that I might be able to stay in the country on my own merits, without necessarily having to become a bride. I went to the New Burnt Norton embassy, which was hardly an embassy at all but an office on the third floor of a building in the east 40s. It was empty except for a petite secretary eating a box of Chicken Dixie Drumstick crackers. She did not offer one to me. "I am here to apply for an extension of my visa, lady," I said. "In order that I do not have to go through with this marriage to an American girl whom I dearly love yet I feel may be a mistake."

"I advise you, sugar," the receptionist said, "to come back in a few hours." She crunched down firmly on another cracker and looked dreamily down at her desk.

"I'll wait," I said, and sat down in the waiting room. No one

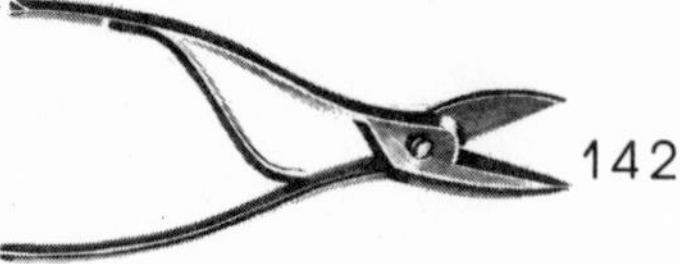

else was there, and though there were a few magazines lying around the room, these were primarily from 1967.

After several hours the secretary spoke again. "I advise you to come back tomorrow, sugar," she said. "I don't think he's coming in today."

So I sat and thought: I was still jittery of the idea of marriage; no doubt three times had been enough, for a person such as myself. Yet I had to ask—did I love Maria? And the answer came back to me that I did.

So at the appointed time I began to walk from my hotel over to where the wedding was to take place: outside behind that chapel known as Tavern on the Green.

No one had told me there were to be white Rolls-Royces to take each of us from our respective homes to the garden in back of the restaurant. Therefore when I emerged from the lobby onto the street I ignored the large car parked there, thinking, Oh, it is only another movie star staying at the hotel and waiting to be driven everywhere. I walked straight by it and shivered in a blustery fashion, trying to hold my head up, for the weather was not yet springlike. In fact I still wore my fur coat, and as usual, to please Maria, beneath it had on practically nothing.

Now on my feet instead of my former stinking sneakers I had on a pair of little nasty boots Maria had found for me as a prewedding present and arranged to have delivered to my door. And these little boots had shark's teeth painted in the front, and from the sides, shark's fins stuck out. These boots did please me very much, and in watching them I kept my head down in order to witness my feet swim along the pavement. How was I supposed to know everyone was frantically looking for me, trying to place me inside the white Rolls-Royce? Finally, I understand, it left for the wedding, empty except for my friend Joey, who had been sent to the hotel to look for me. I did not mean to make trouble, and gladly I would have ridden in it had I known, which is how I happened to arrive late to my own wedding and thoroughly damp in the feet.

As I trudged up Eighth Avenue toward the park, I did feel pretty good about the way things were between Maria and myself right now. Even though I had never been inside Maria's apartment, and even though there had never been anything physical between us, we seemed to be well suited for each other. "When we are married," she said, "we'll get a big apartment, and I'll get you any credit cards you want. Oh, Mgungu, if only you knew how you make me feel! So innocent! So primitive! I would hate for you ever to have to hear the lurid details of my past, when with you I am so youthful and naïve. I want to be a babe in your arms! Which is your favorite?"

"What?"

"Your favorite credit card, stupid: MasterCard? Visa? Diners' Club?"

"I don't know," I said.

"What do you mean, you don't know?" she said, "*Schvartze.*"

Which was her way of letting me know I had made a faux pas. But I was accustomed to behavior of this sort and appreciated the hint. And she told me I should invite my friends to the wedding; I invited a few friends, the people I had met in my travails that I was so dearly fond of, and so on this cold afternoon, when the weather should have been warmer, but had mysteriously dropped to some thirty-five degrees in temperature, a lush slush hailing from the sky, I went to the Tavern on the Green to be wed.

Across the courtyard I could see Maria in her wedding gown made of silver parachute material, fluttering and whipping in the wind, and surrounded by an entourage of Parker Junius and a group of what may have been her relatives, as well as the judge who was to marry us.

Then rushing up to me, bleating and running up against the heels of each other, came the herd of reporters and photographers I had just met days before at Parker Junius's studio. I smiled at them, seeing as they were familiar and friendly, ill prepared for their raucous outbursts. "And now, give us a smile please!" said one. "No, not a smile—look savage!" "Hey, big boy! This way!" This last speaking was the man I had met from the *Post,* red and shivering in the cold, his fingers fumbling with the shutter of his camera. "Over here, Mgungu!" This was spoken by still another. How was I to know this was to be such a production? To me, after all, getting married should not have been any big deal. I was no spring chicken, I will admit that, and I had just casually walked over to the restaurant from the Holiday Inn, never expecting a major celebration. "Look as though you are about to carry out a head-hunting raid; that's it, you've got it! Now hold it, hold it! That's fine, just like that!"

And so I grimaced and twisted my face for the benefit of the wedding photographers and for the news media. I tried to please, really I did.

On one side of the courtyard was a huge orange tent, nearly as big as a circus tent, and the sides of it flapped and snapped in the rough winds. The whole thing seemed nearly likely to fall over, but I did not dream it had anything to do with the wedding. "What's that for?" I said to my friend the lady gymnast reporter. Quickly she noted this down in her notebook. "That's for your wedding," I was told. "Didn't you know?" And they looked at me as if it was readily apparent.

Now Maria came up to me, approached by her flanking warriors. "Darling," she said, stooping to give me a peck on the cheek. Her dress, I now saw more clearly, was slit nearly down to her navel or upper thighs and was highly revealing. Whether or not this was due to the ill effects of the wind I did not know, but the photographers posed the two of us together and then appeared to be thrusting their cameras up her dress. Well, this may perhaps have been an American obsession; it did seem to be harmless.

It was a real hurly-burly, my wedding. Parker Junius was wearing a tuxedo and smoking a cigarette with a bored appearance on his face, although how he could not have been freezing I don't know. I think he would have liked to say something to me—some words of wisdom, perhaps—but never having been married himself he didn't know how. Also there were various relatives of Maria's, and these were mostly a group of dowagers in venerable fur coats, nearly bald in patches . . . and there was the man in the green luminous suit, ominous, scowling angrily, with a narrow fox head, and I ducked my face in order to prevent recognition. I hoped he would not identify me with the scene that had taken place in the alleyway behind the pizza parlor.

Also there were many interesting faces left over from the cocktail party I had attended, and these included the black-haired lady who had tried to seduce me, and the young Argentinian playwright that the party had been held in honor of, with his white white hair all covered up by a large beret, and other people such as Maria's veterinarian, and her old nanny from childhood, and two young ladies named Nicole and Edit. And also there were friends of mine: Kent Gable, the rock-and-roll star, obviously very stoned and weaving back and forth until he flopped onto the ground (he was quickly taken up by the black-haired lady, I am pleased to relate) and there was Joey, reeking of garlic and pizza, elegant in a white suit, who whispered to me, "Where were you? I hadda go over to the hotel to look for you! You were supposed to be riding in the limo, ya dodo."

"Please, everyone," Maria said, "let's go inside the tent." Nearby a large tent had been set up; as the guests trooped inside, she approached and spat, catlike, into my ear, "This is all for you, darling. Do you like it?"

Around the sides of the tent various passersby, strangers to both Maria and myself, I later learned, had gathered, and these now followed us inside, everyone assuming they were friends of the opposite person, who had invited them to the wedding. For the most part these strangers were base in nature, shabby and covered in the accumulation of much dirt. The smell of these folks created quite a competition with the smell of the gardenias, white and wilting in the cold, inside the tent. One man carried a bag of empty beer cans, while a crazed youth held a Doberman pinscher on a chain. Out of one corner of my eye I saw him painting the tent walls with a can of spray paint.

There were perhaps some ten or fifteen of these gate crashers altogether, each more fearful in appearance than the next: some even dressed in slinky outfits Maria said were made of the loathe polyester. Had the guards checking the invitation list been at the door as they were supposed to, these people would have never been admitted, but as it was the guards had been sent out to look for me and had not yet returned.

"Darling Mgungu, what does this remind you of?" Maria said to me, now bending to speak again into my ear, which caused her silverine dress to flop lower than ever on her chest, setting off another rush of photographic clicks. I only hoped the dress would not droop low enough to reveal her little clove-colored nipples; such a personal note would have been, I felt, rather embarrassing to her at some later date, as this was not how women displayed themselves in civilization. "What does all this remind you of?" Maria said again.

"I don't know," I said.

"You don't know?" she said bitterly, and the guests, huddled in the cold inside the tent, turned to stare. "You don't know?"

"Sorry, dear."

"But this was to have been a surprise especially for you! Doesn't this remind you of the tent we slept in on the way down from Mt. Bawwaar-Yaas?" It was true the light inside the tent was orange, due to the orange walls of the tent, and several electric heaters set up at the side of the tent were now turned on, and surprisingly rapidly the air became warmer than the air outside and quite steamy. There were two long tables set up in the tent, covered with plates and white cloths, and at one end a band stood waiting, a group of men with steel drums. "Well, come on!" Maria said. "What are we waiting for?" With that remark another frenzy of camera clicking took place, and the group of us moved down en masse toward one end of the tent.

Here the judge stood before us and began to speak. "Just a minute," Maria said, interrupting. "I just want to make sure of something before you begin. Are you any religion in particular?

I know I asked you this before, but I just want to make sure while there are witnesses around."

"No," the judge said. He was a quite frail fellow draped in overly heavy robes, though I'm certain he was the warmest of any of us, save perhaps the old ladies in their bald furs. He looked startled. "No, I am interdenominational."

"Are you sure?"

"Why, yes," he said.

"You have no particular religion you practice, no certain beliefs? Because the reason I am asking you this is that my fiancé is a savage, a very pure one, and I wouldn't want him to have to go through any kind of ceremony with modern mumbo-jumbo."

"I am quite sure," the judge said in an annoyed voice.

"Good," she said. "Of course, I knew before I hired you anyway."

With that, the wedding commenced, a queer ritual indeed. After some incantations on the part of the judge, it was apparent that we were married. On that note the steel band started up, everyone applauded, Maria pulled me toward her to kiss her, although my kiss did not land anywhere except on her cheek. I felt my heart was breaking like a rare china plate.

"Oh, darling," she said, "let's try and be happy, even just for a short time. Guess what? I searched and searched, and I found a band that played music from New Guinea." And she pointed over to the band of steel-drum players. "It wasn't easy, believe me. That's the same as what they play on New Burnt Norton, isn't it? I mean, music from New Guinea is very similar to music from New Burnt Norton?"

"Oh, yes," I said, seeing her eager face look into mine. I did not have the *moodla* to tell her that the only sound that would have been music to me at that moment would have been the squealing of my pigs and the squabbling of my wives—my other wives, I mean.

But, apart from this tiny moment, all in all it was a delightful wedding. Everyone was most congratulatory, though I grew nervous when the man in the luminous green suit approached. I was fearful, for I thought he would be angry, remembering how I had badly beaten him in the alleyway behind Joe's Pizza some time ago; and I did not want to have to bruise him again, here in public. But he introduced himself, the famous Reynard Lopato, and said that although he did indeed remember me from the alleyway, all was forgiven and he hoped we could be friends.

"Very good, then!" I said, slapping him loudly on the back. He returned the affection, for he kept one thin hand on my shoulders and remained quite close to me, even going so far as to insist on sitting next to me at the meal. And the wedding food consisted of: a piece of chicken per person, some creamed peas, some mashed potatoes, and a spear of broccoli. It was a sit-down meal, too.

Now during the meal I commented to Reynard that he had a very unusual body odor or after-shave, which I had previously smelled only infrequently during my life, and that was during the preparation of Joy Paul Guilford. But before this remark could develop into a narrative, an unfortunate incident occurred: Someone shouted out that the tent was on fire. Everyone jumped up; small flames were leaping up. It appeared that one of the electric heaters being used to warm the tent had been placed too close to the tent wall and had begun by first melting that section of the wall, which in the heat caught fire.

By this point the flames were quite large, and Joey and myself jumped up and doused this wall of flame with champagne. However, my foot touched the heater, which was not turned off, and at the same time my feet were very wet from the slush on the ground. A terrible jolt went through me; it was said that I was very nearly electrocuted. And it might, in the long run, have proved to be the best thing if I had actually been killed. It did cause the old dowagers to scream and cackle though, boy, I tell you.

However, it was too late, and the rest of the meal had to be finished with one wall gone and that side open completely to the bitter wind, and also to the public, who clustered and stared near the perimeter. The napkins and food blew about a great deal, and I had to reestablish myself in my fur coat, which I had taken off for the occasion.

At last there was the wedding cake, huge white and dry slabs of it. A great deal of fun, Maria and I carving, with a little interracial candy couple, white and purple, made of spun sugar, perched at the top. I did not know these were meant to be saved as a pentimento of the occasion and gaily popped them into my mouth, demolishing them in one melting crunch, to Maria's perturbance. But it was my first American wedding, that must be remembered, so some mistakes were granted. And Maria smiled joyfully, whenever her picture was snapped, which was nearly continuously.

The steel band unfortunately knew only one song—Maria had found them playing in front of a theater and had hired them without troubling to listen to them very long. They played over and over again, inviting the customers to get up and dance to "Yellow Bird." But as we were all quite cold, Maria got up and gave a little speech, which went something like: "This is simply an affirmation of an already working relationship. Although Mgungu and I come from cultures extremely different, this is proof positive that love overcomes these differences and transcends race, creed, and color—"and everyone went home, carrying with them hunks of the large cake.

Maria got into the white Rolls-Royce and despite the fact that for some reason the guests were throwing things at her, I followed and got into the car, expecting to go with her.

But at her block she breathed sweetly in my ear and said, "Why don't we wait until we take our honeymoon, Mgungu? I'm planning something for us right now, and I want it to be really special. Until then, why don't you just stay at the Holiday Inn, since all your things are there?"

Being a malleable fellow, I presumed this was the general custom in the United States, or at least in Manhattan.

21

So we shook hands, me grasping hers gingerly, for she had a firm grip, like a sticky baby taking hold. And I watched her get out of the car in her silver coat, which she handed to me. "Do you mind taking this to the cleaner's later?" she said. "For some of the silver has gotten a little tarnished from where the champagne got spilled on me." I said I didn't mind, and she kissed me wearily and sweetly on the cheek.

Standing in front of her building were two men, rather burly, in steel-gray suits and attractive black hats. "Why, hello there, Maria," one said. "We've been waiting for you."

"Say, Maria," the other one said, "we didn't expect you to have company." And he put his hand over her shoulder. She was looking down at the ground; her head raised up on her spindly neck when he spoke, and I noticed how very brown she had become, due to many hours partaken under a sun lamp. The man called to me, "We'll see you later on; we just have to talk to Maria here."

"Ah, yes," I said. "The press conference is something I know all about."

"Well, Maria," he said, "what do you say?"

"I'll just go and tell Mgungu good-bye," she said, and broke away from the man's grasp to come to the car window. "Mgungu," she said in a low voice, "I just want to tell you: I may not see you for a while. I don't want you to worry. I've done something silly—but I'll get it straightened out—I just have to talk to these guys. Just tell me—do you forgive me?"

"Forgive you?" I said. "For what? I can assure you, your behavior is merely that of a typical female, scattery and full of excess emotion." She did look tired; I saw there were large white circles under each eye and I wanted to say: "Get some rest. Let me come in with you and I'll vacuum the floors and clean the ashtrays." But I knew this was not the appropriate thing to say with the reporters standing by on our wedding evening.

"Just say it," she said.

"Of course," I said. "I do forgive. If you forgive me." She leaned in the window and kissed me again.

"Maria—?" the man said. "We won't keep you long." And strangely he bent to pick up some of the granular bits of rice or crystal that had been flung at us by the guests and had now fallen out of Maria's clothes onto the sidewalk. And these bits of hail he threw once more at me in the car. Then Maria went into the building followed by the newspaper reporters.

My car waited; I did not tell the driver where to go. Meanwhile I went through the pockets of her jacket, cleaning them out before taking it to the cleaners. I saw she had the habit of tracing my name over and over on scraps of papers and then crossing it out in several vicious swipes, the lifetime habit of a twelve-year-old; along with these were bits of paper with half-finished notes of instruction for the preparation of Joy Paul Guilford, for she had often tried to get me to explain this to her, to no avail. These particles of paper now fell to the floor of the auto in a confetti cloud as I rummaged my own pocket for a light, for I had been given a wedding cigar I was anxious to smoke. I bent over to gather these items up. I did not want to throw the papers away—I knew what kind of voodoo even the most unconscious person could inadvertently work.

When I sat up I asked the driver to pull away for a few blocks, and gazing back I saw the lights to her apartment go on and I knew she was now inside. And I wondered what it was like up there in her vast apartment, for I knew it had to be vast, her being very rich, although I had never seen it, and no food in the refrigerator except for a wrinkled lemon and a bottle of Evian, for this much she had told me.

Also she had decided to convert one room of her apartment into a studio, where a teacher came in once a week to teach her to make jewelry. She was going to have an aim in life, she had realized some time before, and was going to be a famous jewelry designer. So she was learning to make extraordinary flowers out of glass and the shells of eggs, flowers that were so close to flowers in nature the difference was nearly impossible to tell except for one thing: the glass flowers always broke after they were worn for a short while.

At last I told the driver to take me home, home being still the Holiday Inn. But once there I changed my mind and directed him to a bar I had seen a few blocks downtown. This club was seedy, and there were big sticky splotches on the table, but I was not particular and went in anyway.

I had several drinks—a Piña Colada, a strawberry Daiquiri, a Pink Squirrel, and a variety of others. Soon I was depressed and my head hurt.

At another table a tremendously substantial man rooted through a bowl of French fries. I watched him for a while; he had a fascinating air and perhaps was a person of importance, though why I believed this I couldn't say.

Shortly thereafter he asked if he could join me. "Certainly," I said, and was even glad for the company, not being able to refuse. There was a floor show; on the stage a woman was dancing naked or nearly naked, except for a couple of breasts, removing various parts of a cowboy costume. Her breasts were monumental and seemed to belong to a person other than herself. They hardly bounced at all, and stuck straight out. "That there's a man," my friend kept saying excitedly. "He had an operation ten years ago and kept getting silicone shots into him to give him tits. Her measurements are forty-two, twenty-four, thirty-five. Incredible, isn't it?"

Also I remember he kept asking me how much I thought he

earned. "Seriously, you're not from this country. What do you think a guy like me makes?"

"I have no idea."

"No, really, take a guess."

"I don't know what the salaries are like in this country."

"Well, just give a guess, make it wild, I don't care."

"Thirty thousand dollars."

"Thirty thou, huh? Not bad, not bad, considering that you really are a primitive kind of guy from a place where I understand they don't pay you in money but in stone axes or something, from what I've read. No, I make closer to ninety."

"Thousand?"

"Yup. Ninety thousand buckeroos." I didn't know whether to believe him. Meanwhile while he talked I kept thinking: Am I a mensch or a mouse? Wait a minute, Mgungu! Is this any way for a person to be behaving? And I thought, Enough of this garbage, I am going to visit Maria now, and though not to screw her or rape her or anything certainly, we are married and I will make her some chicken noodle soup and maybe life will start to be different.

For it was my lawful duty as an American husband to try and act like one. I even smiled to myself, thinking, I will go over there right now and the look on her face will be surprised, but she will understand and let me in and I will lead an American life.

I will have a "relationship."

I was like a dragonfly in the morning; dew clung to me in excitement, I fluttered my arms like wings, I was ready to begin. "Excuse me, kind sir," I said to my powerful friend, built like a meat cleaver or a herd of buffalo, "I wish you all the best of success in any future endeavor."

And I blew a kiss to the man or woman who had had artificial breasts attached, and she stopped her act to wave back at me with a look in her eye that said: hither and yon. This I took to be a lucky sign.

So I was right with the world, temporarily, and felt very strong, as if my *moodla* was between my two hands and I could mold it and direct it to take me anywhere. And I grabbed a cab; decisive action is always good for the soul.

I got off at her apartment after tipping the driver; I still had problems with giving tips and always in a cab spent the entire trip worrying about how much the tip was going to amount to. But I managed, and I walked inside, snapping my neck at the doorman to indicate to him: Don't give me any grief, for I am very strong inside myself right now, despite the excellent security precautions of this building. I went straight up without further commitment, trembling now a trifle in my knees, always one of my weakest joints.

I knocked on the door of the apartment.

Nobody was home, and this was obviously not the case. I rang the bell and rang it, and finally was answered. The man who answered the door—one of the two reporters who had met Maria when she stepped out of her great white wedding Rolls-Royce—looked at me, and his eyes were like two squinting glittering green stones, maybe emeralds, Maria's favorite rock.

This guy looked at me, but did not speak. Then finally I said, "May I come in?" But my voice, due to nerves, did not speak in English but in Lesser Pimbanese, the first time this had happened to me. And I thought: I am the victim of some kind of hoax, though what this hoax might be I could not say.

Another minute passed.

Then came to the door the man Reynard I had met that afternoon at the wedding. He wore still his luminous green suit filled with sprinkles and sparkles. He said, "Why hello there, Mgungu. I'm very glad to see you. These men are from a magazine, conducting an interview with Maria this evening. It may be better if you go away and come back tomorrow." He lowered his voice. "It's an important interview. It may help her, you know, to sell her jewelry, which she very much wants to do.

You understand." He made it apparent that to enter would have been in bad form and impolite, also he and the other man stood there so I could not go in.

As I did not want to incur her wrath I went away, though not before Reynard had invited me to go on a little excursion with him and a friend the following day, which he thought of right at that minute. "A wonderful idea!" he said. "And it will be good if we can get to know each other and become friends! Also the weather is due to warm up! I understand, man, that it is going to become hot! So, I tell you what: I'll pick you up at your hotel in the morning. And as for Maria,"—and he lowered his voice again,—"don't worry about her. You know how she is, I guess. She wants me to tell you that she may be going away for a little while. But she's going to call you, probably."

Here I hesitated, wondering if I should demand to be let in, but not being familiar with American protocol, and also slightly drunk, I went back downstairs and resigned myself to my room alone in the Holiday Inn.

Though I did think: What was Reynard doing there in her apartment?

But I had neglected to ask; and as it was now very late I did not want to call and disturb.

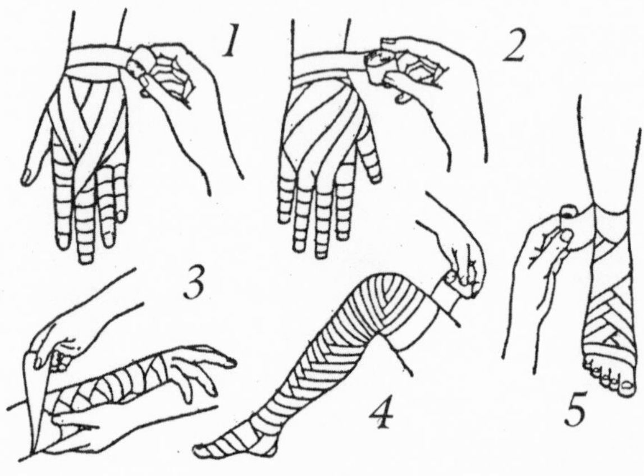

22

In the morning Reynard met me in the lobby and led me out to the car, a lengthy limousine. It was a hot day, unnaturally.

There was a small dwarf on the back seat who kept jumping up and down and finally climbed over my lap. He wore white buckskin ankle boots and with one hand groomed his slender muskrat mustache. When he peered into my face I noticed there were flecks of dandruff in his eyebrows. "I want to sit next to the window," he said. "I hope you don't mind. But I often get violently ill when I'm forced to sit in the middle. I have a tendency toward carsickness, and I'm afraid to say that when I get carsick I generally throw up, usually on the person who happens to be sitting next to me. And as I've just eaten a rather large meal—" He made a gesture with his hand, and I slid over into the center, next to Reynard, as the dwarf scrambled over me. When he got next to the window he began to play with the electric buttons, making the window go first down and then up, pressing another button that automatically slid open a little table laden with shimmering decanters in pink, blue, and clear glass.

"You're letting all the air out," Reynard said. This caused the dwarf to open and shut the window several more times in rapid succession, looking over at Reynard as he did so, his small, deeply set eyes shining with pleasure. Then he began to bounce up and down on the seat again, half standing in order to look out the window. When we stopped at a light he began to shriek at a man walking a Great Dane, "You have no right keeping such a large dog in the city! I hope when your dog shits you break your back carrying the crap around in a little bag!" He shook his fist vehemently at the man, who looked up in an uninterested way at the little dwarf bounding up and down on the seat of the lime green Cadillac. "Asshole!" His voice was nearly as loud as a bullhorn or one of those small shriek alarms I had sometimes heard ladies set off in the city to frighten away suspected muggers or indeed just any person who happened to be walking too close to them. On the other hand, perhaps it was my appearance rather than my distance that set these alarms off so frequently.

"I can't stand dogs," he explained to me with an angelic smile. "They give me a lot of trouble, you can imagine." Then he bellowed out the window at a woman wheeling a shopping cart and a giant schnauzer. "You should be put to sleep!"

"Sit down, Mikhail," Reynard said, reaching across me and roughly pulling the dwarf down on the seat. With this the dwarf gave me a sharp kick in the thigh and, with his little muscular legs (I later learned he was a bodybuilder and had even won the Mr. Miniature America contest several years running before becoming ill), this was not pleasant treatment.

"I don't want you to touch me, Reynard!" the dwarf shouted. "I've had it with your bullying. What do you have to be so macho for all the time? You could have accomplished the same thing by simply asking me to sit down." He scowled at Reynard and stepped onto the floor and walked over to the table, where he poured himself a shot of amber liquor into a stubby shot glass.

"Oh, for Christ's sake, I'm sorry," Reynard said. "I swear, I'm sorry, just forget about it, all right? Look, you don't want a drink now, do you, Mikhail? Honestly, why don't you just wait a while until we get there—what do you want to start drinking so early in the day for? You know how you get when you drink, Mikhail—why don't you just put it down for now?"

The driver had slid open the glass window that separated the front of the limousine from the back in order to be able to listen. "Shut that window!" Reynard said. "Shut that window! I told you, Mr. Jack, that when you drive this car you are to behave like a driver, and, unless I tell you, that window is to remain shut!" The dwarf laughed gaily, a deep chuckling laugh, and then as he rubbed his small stomach he swallowed his drink. "Aw, for Christ's sakes, I asked you—" Reynard said. He leaned forward to take the glass from the dwarf but the dwarf held on to it firmly and walked to the window and pushed the open button. He leaned his head out, resting his chin against the base of the open window like a dog, head into the wind, his small hands clutching the side of the wall. We drove across town, and near the Museum of Primitive Cultures I saw my mentor, Parker Junius, crossing the street with an air both dazed and stupefied. "Hey!" I said, "There's my—" But before I could finish the dwarf let out a low, dull moan that stretched from one side of the car to the other.

"What is it?" Reynard said, crushing out his cigarette and sliding down the seat over to where the dwarf had slumped against the door. "What's the matter, honey?"

The dwarf weakly pushed him away. "He's out there, Reynard. I just saw him. Back up. You've got to back up. I just saw him at the corner of Fifty-third. Go back I tell you! Back up!"

"Now, now, Mikhail, honey, you probably just thought you saw him—"

"No I didn't, I tell you, he was walking his damn dog, that goddamn Rottweiler watchdog. I'd recognize that pink, naked behind anywhere and that ugly dripping jaw. Now, you swore to me, Reynard, you'd get him when I found him, and I found him!" The dwarf's fists were punching out at Reynard but Reynard made no move to fend them off, only reached out to try and soothe the dwarf.

"I know I said I would, honey, but this just isn't the right time or place. I can't just stop the car in broad daylight and get out to grab this guy."

"Why not, you took *him* with us, didn't you?" the dwarf said, pointing at me.

"That's different; he's coming with us of his own free will. I promise you, when the right opportunity comes along—"

"Oh, for Christ's sake, let me out here," the dwarf said, attempting to swing the door open as the car stopped at the lights.

"No!" Reynard said, and grabbed the dwarf around the waist. "Keep the doors locked, Jack!" The dwarf began to struggle and landed stinging kicks to my shins.

With many million people in Manhattan I had put myself in a car with this couple. How alone I felt and like a leaf trembling on a bald tree. I reached over and poured myself a drink and lit a cigarette. Half smiling, the two of them stopped their battling and examined me with a curious insectlike look. "Is something wrong?" the dwarf said with a quick lick of his lips.

And I sat staring at the two of them, the large-headed dwarf and Reynard the art dealer, with his skin like ambergris in his neon-green suit. And they sat looking at me, until finally an amused look came over my face and I determined to try and enjoy myself, for here I was after all in the United States of America, where everyone was supposed to know how to have a good time. I did not perhaps yet know what constituted a good time, but I could not believe that these two would endure anything for very long that was not a good time, with the wonderful interior of the Cadillac glowing and silky in its green and the little pull-down curtains over the windows made of dark and luminous velvet that swayed and wrestled with the rocking of the car. For the dwarf had now pulled these curtains across, and with a small cooing sound he leaned over into the lap of Reynard and said sweetly, in a small Shirley Temple voice, "Reynard, let's stop uptown first."

"I don't want to stop uptown. I'm in a hurry, Mikhail. You'll be sick. I don't want that. That stuff always makes you sick. Now, we're going to have a barbecue this afternoon. I told you already. You're going to like that. We're going right now out to the country for this picnic. What you want to waste time stopping uptown for."

The dwarf's face turned sullen. "Fuck you, Reynard. I want to stop uptown. What harm can it do you, fifteen minutes is all, I promise you. What's a picnic to me anyway without stopping uptown first?"

He reached forward to pour himself another drink but stopped and tossed his silvery hair back when Reynard said, "All right, all right. Just don't have anything else to drink, you have to promise me, and we'll go uptown first. I can't stand it when you drink—you can't hold your liquor at all." He leaned forward and spoke into the intercom to the driver. "Okay, Spareribs. Let's go uptown first. Mikhail wants to stop off at Mrs. Irian's."

"Spareribs!" The dwarf thought this was uproariously funny. "Spareribs! I like it!" He lit himself a cigarette with a lighter made of a large block of steely blue metal. The cigarette he took out of a case made of alligator. It was a pink cigarette with a gold tip. The other cigarettes in the box were various pastel colors. His nails were carefully lacquered and buffed, and each was perfectly round like the interior of some shell. And he held the cigarette with great dignity and perfection, but his hands, quite short and stubby, were like the ridiculous hands of some overweight child. "What do you do?" I asked him.

The dwarf looked at me quite coldly. "What do I do? What is it that I do? Why don't you tell him, Reynard?" He carefully rolled the ash of his cigarette in a circle in the brass ashtray attached to the arm of the seat.

"Mikhail is a writer," Reynard said. "He has a piece in this week's *New York* magazine."

The dwarf examined me once again, this time more fondly. "I may seem a ludicrous figure to you," he said, and held out the alligator case of cigarettes to me, putting it back in his breast pocket after I shook my head. "But inside this body there resides a mind. And, I have come to discover, after nearly a lifetime of learning and despair, that there is little connection between the body and that blob of substance floating up there on the top of it. A frail spine perhaps." He tossed his hair back. "When are we going to get there?" he said irritably, and with a thin pink handkerchief he drew from his lapel he wiped his head, on which had appeared white beads of perspiration. The car, stuck in a morass of traffic, coughed in the heat. The fumes of the exhaust rose up even through the cool, air-conditioned air.

"We could take the West Side Highway," I suggested, in a sense proud of my knowledge of Manhattan.

"The West Side Highway," the dwarf scoffed. "My god, the thing is shut down and what's still open is a disaster area. How would you like to be up there when the whole place collapses?" He barked doggishly and drew in on his cigarette. Reynard looked at him with strong affection.

And the car crawled uptown, dodging pedestrians who flung themselves in front of the wheels, to the disgust of the dwarf who insisted on shouting to the driver through the intercom that the next time one of the jaywalkers did that they were to be run over; and up Broadway on streets frowsy with rubble and detritus, old newspapers blowing in the gristy wind of late spring, past the Chinese-Mexican and the Italian-Indian restaurants until finally the dwarf, impatient now and nervous with excitement or his one drink, told the driver to pull over and double park.

Then to my surprise he snatched up my hand by the wrist and pulled me along with him out of the car and we trotted or raced between the bodies of the students, for we were near a college university campus, and into a tiny and dark shop set between a bar and a liquor store and loaded with queer things in the windows. There were huge rabbits and wobbling bears, but I did not have a chance to look further, for the dwarf, bursting through the door, pulled me in beside him.

My eyes were unused to the dark after the light of the street and briefly I could not see the interior of the shop. "My dear Mrs. Irian," the dwarf said, "here is someone I have brought to see you. This gentleman has arrived all the way from New Burnt Norton for a dance festival in this city and I felt it important for me to bring this savage by to see you during his short stay in this country."

I was laden suddenly by the smell of chocolate. The store, dark and musty, was heavily fruited with this chocolate scent and the walls covered with trays and racks of varieties of chocolate. There was no one that the dwarf could possibly have been speaking to. A drop of water from the air conditioner outside had fallen on my head and now dribbled down to the end of my nose. "Well, what do you think?" the dwarf said proudly, tugging at my arm. "Mrs. Irian is one of the last of her kind. No one in the city make chocolates like these anymore. She keeps her daughter back there." He pointed through a beaded curtain. "Working, working. The poor girl is kept dipping chocolates for ten hours a day. They have to hire a doorman to keep the place from being mobbed at Christmas. They ship anywhere in the world, you know."

Each tray of candy was labeled and marked with the contents and there was not one inch of free space in the shop; it was like the interior of some swell children's book, maybe *Poor Little Rich Girl*. "Let me tell you what I want," the dwarf said, seemingly into empty air, and then I saw that behind the counter was a tall, immensely thin woman. She had crooked hands and a delicate scent I could smell even through the heavy odor of chocolate. Her eyes, rheumed and white, did not comprehend the dwarf before her. "What do you want, I haven't got all day," she said dully. The dwarf smiled gleefully. "Pure strawberry syrup," the dwarf said. "One bottle. *Madre mía*." He tried to go around behind the counter but the woman stopped him. "No," she said, putting out her arm. "No come back here. Not for customers." The dwarf bowed slightly and, sighing, returned around to the correct side. "A can of coconut snow," he went on, "a quarter pound drained orange peel, a half pound rum-raisin fudge, a package of crystallized kumquats."

Mrs. Irian could only fill his orders in a rather crabbed way, so slowly as to be less than methodical but nearly sluggish. Yet the dwarf was almost dancing in the aisle and rushed around behind the counter, this time managing to jump up and give Mrs. Irian a hug and peck on the cheek before she could make him leave. "Ah, *madre mia*," he said. "Glaće clementines—give me eight, no, ten of them! Half-pound dried candy carrots and half of honey papaya! A pound of strawberry cordials, a quarter-pound of ivory and bittersweet breakup! A pound of mixed marshmallows: mint, maple, coconut, and chocolate! Two pounds of cashew clusters, pecan delight, chocolate pretzels. Bittermints and buttermints—a box of each. A quarter-pound mint lentils and a half-pound chocolate coffee beans. Almond roca—that's for Reynard, I don't like it myself—and a half-pound box of Italian nougat, although my dentist says it's ruining my bridge. Give me one pound hand-dipped chocolates filled with creams, jellies, fruits, and nuts—those twenty-dollar-a-pound ones against the wall if you don't mind, Mrs. Irian. Some Gianduitto and some Perugina. Some peanut-butter nonpareils—just make a bagful of them, I don't care what they weigh—and some heavenly hash. And for Jacko in the front let me have a box of chocolate cherries."

The old lady behind the counter puttered slowly, filling his order by dishing out one piece of candy at a time into a weighing tray. Then finally, for me, the dwarf chose a chocolate Easter bunny, a rabbit three feet tall and decorated with bloodshot and bloodthirsty eyes of marbleized marzipan. It was on sale for half price. Thrusting this rabbit and the bags of candies into my arms, the dwarf danced out into the hot street, nearly slamming the door in my face behind him.

The lady behind the counter had not uttered another word except to mutter slowly and complain under her breath. And yet she looked at the dwarf with delight and affection. After he had scampered out into the street she said to me as I tried to swing the door open by pushing my naked back up into it, "Ah, that Mr. Mikhail, he a crazy one. He's a writer, you don't know that? And someday we'll all be in his book. He's a crazy one, that Mr. Mikhail."

Well, at least he was shorter than me.

Jack the driver started the car again and Mikhail scattered the bags of chocolates along the facing seat in the back. The car left Manhattan and shortly passed a cemetery. At this the dwarf, who had been slumped slightly on the seat gorging on his bags of candy, perked up and leaned his large head out the window once more. The stem of his neck, so delicate, held up his face like the reed of some too-thin flower, and it was easy to understand why Reynard seemed so fond of him. "The cemetery!" he said with pleasure, looking at me. "The cemetery, where all of us most someday go. Unless, that is . . ." and he did not continue.

"Unless what?" I said.

"Unless you choose cremation, or burial at sea." The cemetery stretched for nearly miles or at least acres, like thousands of skyscrapers in miniature, mimicking the skyline behind us. "Why, there's hardly room for a body to be stuck under one of those little stones," the dwarf said. "They must be buried in those graves several layers deep, don't you think, Reynard? Tenement dwelling, huh?"

Reynard laughed uproariously, like a giggling fox, as if that was the funniest thing he had ever heard, and he slapped me on the back. "Tenement dwelling!" he repeated. "Tenement dwelling!" He continued to laugh.

Behind us the outline of the city was grim and jagged, a metallic vision. The glittering windows of the buildings shone like speckled flecks of mica. Then appeared through the green windows of the car the monotonous towers of some tall buildings, grisly and cold bones. "Co-op City," Reynard said in a dull voice. "Pull off over here, Jack. This is it."

"We're here then," I said. "Very good. I am pleased, for never have I been on this American thing, a picnic."

"That's right," Reynard said, and with this he took his knife and began to clean his fingernails. And the dwarf trembled and wriggled with pleasure in his seat. It was then I began to remember clearly, of that night some nights ago, in the back alleyway behind Joe's Pizza, for the Reynard I was with now seemed at once to resemble the man I had seen then.

23

n truth I was afraid. The small eyes of the dwarf gleamed with a cool luster, and his parrot tongue darted out to smooth his lips at the same time two of his fingers reached up to flatten his muskrat mustache. He was laughable and yet not a person to be laughed at, I felt.

Across the road was a chain and the car stopped short in front of it. Passing cars buzzed like angry tropical bees as they went by. Some of the green limousine jutted out into the slow lane of traffic and this was causing problems. "Get out," Reynard said to me, as if I was no more than a slave, and at that moment this was all I could believe myself to be.

He tossed a set of keys after me and pointed to the chain that stretched across the road. At one end of it a huge padlock linked the chain to a post. The key did not fit into the padlock and I had to jostle with it until it unclicked. The nose of the car edged closer to me and then when I had unlocked the chain the car pulled across and over onto the other side of the road. "Lock it up now," Reynard said. The car continued to pull down the dirt road and I stood looking after it, certain it was going to go on without me, but Reynard unrolled the window and with a sugary smile said, "Is something wrong, Mgungu?" So I went and climbed in.

The car was on a winding gravel road in the middle of a bleak stretch of field-surrounded acres distant by a cyclone fence. The dwarf sprayed some after-shave on himself from a bottle in a little mahogany cupboard beneath the seat. A thin fragrance filled the car, the mist of a greenhouse or a grove of orange trees, cutting through the powdery cigarette smoke.

"Like it, Reynard?" the dwarf said sarcastically.

"Very nice."

"Yes? You like it? You like?" The dwarf for some reason sounded very angry and with a small leap to where Reynard was sitting he tried to spray Reynard's wrist with some of the tropical fragrance.

"Cut it out!" Reynard said, but the dwarf continued to shoot at Reynard until the whole car was reeking with the overpowering smell, like some kind of fruit gone bad in the heat.

"Who does this belong to, Reynard?" the dwarf said angrily. "Which of your ladyfriends left this here in the car? This is no after-shave, Reynard. Just tell me, where did you get it?"

"I don't know, Mikhail," Reynard said wearily. "Just put it down; I don't know where it came from. Maybe Tony left it here."

"It would be far better for all concerned if you would tell me right now where it came from," the dwarf said. "I want to know, Reynard, and I will know. Otherwise I would like to get out right now and I will walk back."

"Oh, come on, Mikhail, you can't walk back. Now cut it out —we came out here for a barbecue; you know I don't use this car all the time. Maybe Tony left it here, maybe Eva. How am I supposed to know? Jack, who was in here who would have left this perfume crap?" The driver did not hear through the glass. "Open up that glass, Jack! Do you hear me?" Reynard said. Finally he turned the intercom on and brittlely snapped at the driver to slide open the glass between the front and the back.

"You asked me not to."

"Well, now I'm asking you to. Who left this perfume?" he said, holding it up.

"I think it belongs to that fashion editor for the magazine who was in here the other day, boss," the driver said. When he said "boss" he slurred the word like a knife across a tomato. The dwarf slumped back down in the seat and Reynard looked relieved.

"There, you see? Now what are you being such an idiot for,

Mikhail, man?" Reynard said. As we drove bumpily down the road, the piles of garbage rising high on either side of the car, stacks and mounds of old tires, cinder bricks, empty cans, and bottles half plowed under a sea of powdery red sand, a sea gull preening itself on top of a small mountain of dirt, Mikhail began to speak.

As it turned out, the dwarf was not a novelist, though he had written a book years before at age twenty-two, but now wrote a monthly column for *Interview* magazine, a newspaper, in which he basically repeated, word for word, any interesting conversation he might have had over the month before. He was most fond of death-row killers or movie stars who had undergone sex-change operations. A lot of the time he spent in Florida or Switzerland with his doctor, discussing and testing various sheep-embryo injections as a means of rejuvenation, and though Mikhail denied it, Reynard insisted that the dwarf participated in these experiments in the hopes that he would grow in stature. It was true he did have a marvelous head of shimmering silver hair.

The dwarf opened the door, sniffed the air, and then shut it again. "This is your idea of a place to have a picnic?" he said to Reynard. "I love it!"

"I thought you would," Reynard said with some pleasure, and tried to help the dwarf out of the car.

"I can't step outside just yet, however. I'm afraid the odor has made me quite weak. Anyway, as I was saying," the dwarf addressed me once more, "this sixty-year-old woman I knew down in Florida was receiving the monkey-gland treatment. She had the body of a thirty-year-old when the treatments were complete. Yes, the body of a wonderful thirty-year-old, and not an ounce of unnecessary fat on her. But her mind had disintegrated completely. She had not a brain left in her head, nary a whit. I'm afraid to say, when the treatments were complete, she had the mind of a monkey." He looked at me expectantly.

Constantly I was receiving facts such as these. Yes, these

facts seemed to be a necessary part of life here. And yet I could not add them up together so that they supplied me with any useful information.

As if reading my mind, the dwarf asked me, "When were you born?"

"I'm not sure, actually. It may have been some fifty-five years previously." Which was going to bring me close to sixty, soon, I realized, and though I may have already had the mind of a monkey I was far from the body of a thirty-year-old. Still it had never occurred to me that youth was a particular asset. It seemed to me that, at least on New Burnt Norton, the older one got the more one was entitled to.

"No, what I meant was, what month of the year?"

"I don't know. In the Lesser Pimbas this is not important. Most of the children die before too long anyway, and we have not the astrological signs in any case."

"What do they die of? Disease?"

"No, competition. The older children take the food of the younger ones when they are no longer nursing. This is part of the survival of the fittest, you understand?"

The dwarf blinked his eyes. "This is interesting. Reynard, turn the tape recorder on. I may decide to use this for next month's issue." Reynard nearly purred with excitement, for I supposed he was glad to be taking part in something actually to appear in *Interview* magazine, and his catty eyes stretched wider, nearly reaching over to each side of his head. "But, you're actually fifty-five years old? I can't believe that, really! You certainly don't look it. My goodness, your skin is practically smooth as milk! And purple as they come, aren't you? What is the diet like over in New Burnt Norton? I'm sure Dr. O. would be interested in hearing about that."

"Oh, mostly sweet potatoes, cooked several ways. Broiled sweet potatoes, boiled sweet potatoes, sometimes a sweet-potatoes pie. I have three wives. Each cooks in a different way. Curried sweet potatoes, for example."

With this the two of them looked at me with what appeared

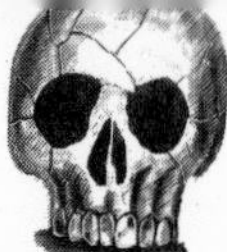

to be disapproval, though for what reason I could not say. I examined the recent wristwatch I had been newly given by Maria. Finally the dwarf tapped on the glass of the front of the car.

"Jack, would you set up the things for the picnic?" he said.

"Is it that I mentioned I am not monogamous?" I said, "or may it be that you did not know I had other wives besides Maria Fishburn?"

Reynard and the dwarf did not say anything but looked out the window as the driver, nearly as tall as the dwarf and myself put together, and wearing a short-sleeved Harvard sweatshirt, unloaded from the trunk a small hibachi and a bag of charcoal. Then he took out a Styrofoam cooler and several beach chairs. These he arranged on the inner side of a heap of old bottles and bedsprings, letting the old tires, garbage, and cardboard cartons serve as a sort of windbreak. Here on this flat stretch of sand the wind was indeed fierce. The smell of smoke was arid and acrid, and the smoke from the hibachi was turned to blow in the opposite direction from where the three of us arranged ourselves on the beach chairs around the blanket. But there was still no way of escaping the stench of rotting garbage and incineration.

In the distance the bony towers of the Co-op City jutted up severe and stark. There were no trees, though far away near the cyclone fence a bald trunk grew up and some children played baseball on a dirt-crusted diamond. The dwarf asked me to stand up, and he rearranged the chairs so that we faced the skyline of Manhattan. He placed each chair deliberately and firmly as if he were moving a couch to a new position in the living room. I noted a large and friendly-looking rat, so fat as to be nearly obese, rustling around among the rubble. Its two yellowed teeth gave it a smiling appearance. "A picnic!" the dwarf hummed with delight, spreading out on the blanket before us some grapes, large linen napkins he weighed down with a bone-handled knife, shiny paper plates decorated with a picture of a lobster wearing a bib, a large white and frosted cake topped with tiny slivers of mandarin orange, some pieces of fried chicken and some slabs of green honeydew melon he unwrapped from the plastic wrapping that then quickly became covered with particles of cocoa-colored soot. "Balducci's" he said to me. "They always do a nice spread. Are you familiar with them?"

Jack the driver skulked ominously. "I started the fire, you know," he said. "It should be ready in a few minutes." He wandered off, kicking at used tires and empty beer cans. In a minute, however, he returned, saying, "Look at this, Reynard! Heh-heh, what do you think of this?" He had picked up a box full of Baby Ruth bars, uneaten and completely wrapped, though rather wet.

"Put that down," Reynard said, knocking the box out of his hand. He thrust into Jack's hand some slabs of meat wrapped up in white greased paper that the driver began to unwrap. "Cook this," he said. "How do you like your steak cooked?" he said to me. "Well-done, medium, or rare?" The driver began to pile the steaks all together in a heap. They were pink and quite bloody against the white page.

"I'm no chef," Jack said sullenly.

"It doesn't matter to me," I said. "How does everyone else like it done?"

"Oh, no, this isn't for us," Reynard said. "This is just for you—the rest of us are going to eat this chicken here. This is just a special treat for you, our foreign guest. And a friend of our dear friend, Maria Fishburn."

"Well, but how very nice," I said. "But I please hope you will also have some of the meat meant for me. It appears to be a great quantity you have purchased, and though a savage I have at this point a fairly small stomach. In any case, I guess I prefer it medium to well-done. Not too red, but rather delicately charred on the outside. How nice a barbecue will be, reminding me of the way we cook at home, though generally there the meat is roasted on leaves underground over some hot rocks."

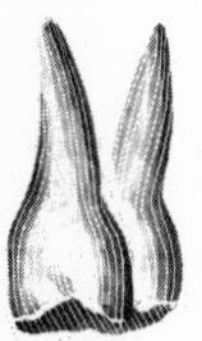

The dwarf had picked up a large thigh of the fowl and was

eating it with one side of his mouth. "My teeth are bothering me again, Reynard," he said. "I don't want to think I'm going to have to see the dentist. Though actually I don't mind the dentist I have now. A nice fellow. He gives me laughing gas. Giggle, giggle, then I'm out like a lightbulb until he gives me the oxy. And the most wonderful hallucinations! I don't suppose you've ever taken drugs, Mgungu, have you?"

"Well, I—" I started to say.

"Of course you have, what am I saying?" the dwarf said. "It's thanks to you and your drugs that we're here on this fabulous *picnic!* And it's thanks to you that no doubt I'll shortly be fabulously *wealthy!*" And he clasped his little hands over his mouth. "Oh, hush my mouth," he said.

"What, my friend?" I said. "For I do not comprehend."

Now it may be predicted that I should have listened to the dwarf's words more closely, but it must be remembered that the dwarf was an erratic personage and had behaved irrationally and unpredictably in his words and actions to me before. So when he began to sing a little tune and continually wiped his forehead with his pink handkerchief, his muskrat mustache drooping at the corners, I merely assumed he had lost his marbles. I myself felt irritable. Constantly the wind blew up in our faces, covering all with a fine garbagy grit that seemed nearly edible.

In the distance the children playing baseball seemed not so much to be playing but rather beating one another with sticks, though in the haze it was not possible to see clearly. The driver skulked impatiently, turning the pieces of meat over on the fire with a pointed stick. "This charcoal won't stay lit," he said. "I'm going to put some pieces of wood on the fire and then it'll cook faster. Got any marshmallows, Mikhail, for afterward?"

"We'll see, Jack," the dwarf said.

"You know, I'm not even that hungry," I said. "I hope you're not going to all this trouble just for my sake."

"No, not at all," Reynard said politely, lighting himself a slender cigar. He had stepped behind the car for a few minutes, possibly to relieve himself, and now he had tremendous difficulty with the cigarette lighter, which shot out a flame nearly a foot and a half long, visible even from my position.

"Did it hurt when you got your nose pierced?" the dwarf said.

"You know, I don't even remember," I said. "Who remembers these things? Sure it hurt, I guess. It wasn't done under any laughing gas, I'll tell you that. Chop chop, they've put a hole through your nose. What hurts is afterward. I tell you, it's worse if you're a woman. Every time somebody dies a few of them have to get a finger cut off out of sympathy. Anyway, my nose. It's done about age nine or ten with a group of tribal boys all the same age. Only in my case, there were no other boys my age. No, I was the last Lesser Pimba of my generation. But, since then I've managed, with careful management, to propagate the tribe some. Oh, sure, we're still an endangered species, entitled to special benefits. You asked me before what we eat over in N.B.N. Sweet potatoes, yes, I may have mentioned. Also a lot of cereal, especially a baby cereal vitamin enriched and fortified and complete with dried powdered milk. This is sent up by the government for the children, but it is necessary, too, for the adults to eat. Also we have the Kellogg's Coco-Krispies. Anyway, I was thinking,"—for now with the smell of roasting meat so close and sweet to my nose I felt like talking extremely—"you may perhaps like to someday pay my tribe a visit. Well, you are welcome. We would love to have you there. I know my wives would enjoy to meet you. We don't get to have many visitors. And as for keeping young, well, I tell you it is the boredom of the environs that keeps one forever young, this at least is my conclusion so far, though these days the jet planes do pass awfully close overhead on Mt. Bawwaar-Yaas. Why, only a short while ago a lady was remarking on the muscular shape of my ass. I think this is something you may like to see, with your concern and interest in the human body. For I understand it is unlike the rear end of Americans."

As if from nowhere a hungry wolfish dog appeared at the edge of the smoky fire. It was spindle-ribbed and with a bony and meat-eating appearance to its eyes, although it slunk fearfully on the opposite side of the fire. "Scat," the dwarf said, "scat." And he feebly tried to throw a stick at it. "Where is Reynard? Jack, get rid of this monstrous hound!"

Reynard had disappeared off on the other side of a small mountain of garbage, and the car driver grinned dopily at the frantic dwarf. "The food is done," Jack said. He wiped his hands over the front of his shirt and then ran them back through his hair. The dwarf was now jumping up and down and trying to scramble up a high system of broken pipes, though the dog was displaying no interest in him.

"Scram," I said to the dog, but the dog merely slunk off a little distance farther. It was a combination Doberman pinscher, from what I could distinguish. Jack put the meat in a pile on the plate and tossed what looked like a T-bone to the dog. At this moment Reynard returned from urination behind the far side of the limousine and saw the dog grab the bone in its mouth and race off with it toward the garbage heap.

"Hey, what the fuck are you doing," he said furiously. "Jesus! Who gave the fucking bone to the dog?" Jack hung his head. "My god, you are retarded, you big moron! What a jerk!" He shook Jack by the shoulders and cuffed him in the head. "What were you thinking of? That dog isn't going to carry that bone around forever. Sooner or later he's going to get tired of carrying it, he's going to leave it someplace, someone is going to find it, and then we're all going to be in trouble. You just eat this meat," he said, thrusting the plate of meat at me. "And you come with me, Jack, and help me get the bone back. You stupid bastard."

"I'm sorry, Reynard," Jack said. "I just wanted to feed the dog." The two of them set off in a churning motion through the sand after the dog. I helped myself to a large steak, picking it up between my fingers. "Plenty of meat," I said.

"Reynard is very worried about animals," the dwarf said. "Sometimes a dog might get a bone stuck in his throat and choke to death. He would hate to be responsible for that. How's the meat."

"Oh," I said, swallowing. "I'm so sorry. It's just that sometimes I forget my manners. Won't you have some?"

"No!" the dwarf said.

"Are you quite sure?" I said. "It's really very good."

"No, no, no!" he said vehemently.

"You see," I said, between mouthfuls, "On New Burnt Norton the men eat first, sometimes tossing a few scraps to any of the women or children standing around. And the chief men eat first of all. At least, that was the way it was during my father's time. Say, what kind of meat is this? It's very good. Not steak, certainly, however."

The dwarf shrugged. "I don't know," he said. "I'm a vegetarian, though I do eat seafood and sometimes a bit of poultry. Reynard said that was steak he had bought for you, so I guess it is. Maybe it's beefalo."

"Beefalo? Well, you don't say. There is a taste to it both familiar and yet very distant, a taste I don't remember and yet one which I feel I know quite distinctly," I said.

The dwarf hesitated and put down his chicken. Then he went to the car and opened the door briefly, returning a minute later with his cigarettes.

"I really don't know," he said.

"Well, perhaps it's veal," I said. "Maybe a veal chop, though these aren't exactly chops and really I have never tasted such juicy veal. Do you know what kind of marinade he's used? It must be the eating outdoors that makes everything taste so delicious. It really is good, although you know, I usually feel apprehensive about veal, knowing how they milk-force those calves."

The dwarf agreed and lit up a blue pastel cigarette. "Eat up, eat up," he said. "who knows when Reynard and Jack will be back from rescuing the dog. I hope it's all right." I was surprised at his change in attitude, and yet, there was something so sincere about the little dwarf worrying about a dog choking to death on a splintery bone, that, though not a young dwarf, he appeared at that moment very lovable.

"What a kindly soul you are!" I said. He modestly examined his clear white fingernails.

Then, through the dirt, attracted by the smell of roasting flesh, came the baseball-playing children who stood in a circle around us looking wary and greedy. "Well, there certainly does seem to be a lot of meat here," I said. "Are you sure you won't have any of it?"

"No, no, it's just for you," Mikhail said. "I can assure you, you were meant to have it all."

"Well, then perhaps I can just give some of it to these kids here. They do look hungry and even ominous for sure," I said, as they swung their baseball bats backward and front, reminding me in a sense of my own children now up in the mountains of New Burnt Norton, eating their cold cereal to which they need only have added water to produce a complete vitamin-fortified meal.

"No!" said the dwarf shrilly. "Oh, Christ, I wish Reynard was back. This whole thing has been a mistake. Look, the stuff is for you. Finish it please, and I will tell you the subject matter of my latest piece. Exclusive. Come to think of it, Reynard will probably have some of the meat when he gets back after all, and I know he will be angry if you give it away as it was very expensive. We'll take it home with us if you're not hungry. Oh, what a life." He moaned slightly.

"Okay, okay," I said. "I'll drop the subject." He was certainly an adorable dwarf, and yet I myself felt that the dwarf's behavior was highly erratic—first angry at the dog, then worried over its well-being; at first to appear so generous and gift-giving and then yet to be so stingy over a few pieces of meat. "So what is the exclusive story you were about to relate?'

"Something I clipped out of the newspaper," the dwarf said. And from a slender sharkskin billfold in his inner pocket he removed a piece of paper and from it read, " 'At about six twenty-eight this morning a man unstrapped his artificial leg, carefully placed it on a Manhattan subway platform, and plunged to his death in front of an IRT train. Police identified the man as Irving Bass, and said he was about fifty. They said they were able to identify him because his name was taped to the artificial leg on the platform at the 34th Street station.' I'll be meeting soon with a lot of people who knew Irving Bass, and some who didn't. I'm anxious to learn what happened to the wooden leg. I think it'll make a great piece." As the dwarf spoke one of the children darted in like a nasty fish and snatched a hunk of meat from the plate before me. I made no move to stop him but looked at the view of the skyline, rather, and the dwarf, furious, jumped up and down shrieking, "Stop him, stop him!" until he was quite red in the face and then he sat down heavily on the chair. The child in any case had dropped the meat into the dirt, fascinated by the dwarf's presentation. At this the children, with mocking grins on their battered and chip-toothed faces, moved in closer, hooting at the dwarf and desirous of getting nearer the meat, as children are in my own land. "Did that child take any of the meat?" the dwarf said in an exhausted voice. "Did it have any bones in it?" His face was damp and spongy and his hand tugged rapidly at his nervous little mustache.

"Hey, din't I see you on TV?" one of the boys said to me. His nose moved in toward the dwarf like a rat and his companions also nudged in closer, causing the dwarf to stand up on his chair.

"How did I ever get into this one?" he said. "The life of crime and barbecue picnics is not for me, I realize now." Then he bellowed, "Reynard!"

"Please," he said to me pleadingly, "just get me into the car, all right? I think I've seen this film one too many times before, and I know what happens next."

So I stepped over to help the little man off the chair and

move him into the car, for for all his earlier energy he did appear very delicate now of constitution indeed, but he snapped out angrily, "Whatever you do, just hang on to the meat!"

Meanwhile the children, not even proper children but really very overgrown and with yellow broken tusks of teeth and cornrowed hair or weaselly whiskers and beards on their faces, had pushed up closer to the dwarf and seemed likely to make off with him as if they had found some foreign and tropical bird in their midst and were now eager to pluck him. But holding the platter of meat I pushed and shoved them away, which they allowed me to do out of fascination. And then with the dwarf under my other arm I half-carried him to the car and put him inside. The dwarf out of the way, the children turned their attention to the picnic buffet spread out over the ground, and, seating themselves on the chairs and the blanket, they devoured the crisp blue and green grapes and, pouring the chilled wine into the silver plastic cups we had brought with us, they toasted the open air and the Co-op City. Each had snatched up a chicken bone or breast and, waving it freely, they plunged into the food.

Reynard came back, followed by Jack, who carried the wolfish starving dog, now lying limp over his outstretched arms, and when he saw the boys at the barbecue he trotted over to them with snarled lip and, speaking what must have been a few choice words I could not overhear, he managed to drive them off quite quickly. They slunk back into the rubble, even looking fearfully behind them from time to time, and tossed the chicken bones down as if no longer with any appetite for life.

The dwarf popped out of the car and stepped up to Jack to examine the dog. "What happened?" the dwarf said.

"Ah, we couldn't get it in time. The dog dropped the bone, we couldn't find where it left it, Jack threw a rock at it, which killed it, and when we got up to it was when we saw it didn't have the bone anymore and the dog was dead. We're just going to have to forget about it."

"Forget about it!" the dwarf trilled. "You fool! At least if you had left the dog alive it would have led you back to the femur or T-bone, whatever it was it dropped. How can we forget about it? Someone's sure to come across it, now or later!"

"Ah, who's going to know. Some kid? Anyway, where you going to find it out in this mess? Don't worry about it," Reynard said. "He doesn't like to litter," he said to me. Jack put the dog down on the ground. With a sleek movement the dwarf stepped up to it and began to stroke the limp side of the dog, smoothing its black-and-tawn-colored fur back into place. His small hands flicked back and forth over its side. "Those kids get any of the barbecue?" Reynard said.

"No, no, I don't think so," the dwarf said, "thanks to Mgungu here. But they did grab the rest of the meal, and I would have liked some more chicken, I think. Is there anything left to drink?" But they had taken with them not only the wine but the entire Thermos full of lemonade.

"Have some of the steak," I said, for I was still holding the platter, but the dwarf looked quite disgusted.

"What, is that all you've eaten of it?" Reynard said. "Come on, eat up." And with a fork he picked up off the ground and wiped clean on his knee he attempted to feed me some particles of the meat.

"I'll have some," Jack said, using the bottom of his sweatshirt to wipe his neck and head. Though I held it out to him, Reynard shook his head in vehement disgust, and the driver did not touch it but rather looked ashamed. "Sorry," he said. "I changed my mind. I'm not very hungry." And though the dwarf was very sick from the chocolates, and Jack started the car to put the air conditioning on, no one was in a hurry to go but insisted on waiting until I was finished with my meal. But the quantity of meat was so vast I was soon stuffed.

"Come on, eat some more," Reynard said, and they all watched me eagerly.

"No, really, I can't," I said, wiping my chin free of grease. "I'm stuffed." The meat, though delicious, sweet and fatty, was, I found shortly, really quite sickening.

So Reynard took me out for a walk to give me a fresh appetite, and pointed out to me the tower of Co-op City where the Son of Sam killer had lived, and the tower where a rapist of young girls lived quite happily to this day. And he instructed me in the various outlines of the Manhattan skyline, and to which each building was attributed.

Then we returned to the car for more food.

And I ate and ate, my stomach swelling and growing bloated, and the dwarf dozed on the back seat in the lime cool. And the sun was going down and the lights flickering on in Manhattan and the sun illuminating all in an elastic gold-and-pink light.

Finally I was done and had consumed the entire platter of meat alone, groaning in pain. A real New Burnt Norton feast, as I told them, as in New Burnt Norton one gorged when there was food and starved when there was not. Jack and the dwarf went out to bury the bones left over, for, as they pointed out, there was no point in adding more garbage to the garbage simply because there was already garbage out there.

"After all," the dwarf said, "if people hadn't brought garbage here to begin with, there wouldn't be any garbage now, and this might have been a very nice place."

In the darkening light the jackal faces of the juvenile delinquents appeared again around the car and they began to throw little moist objects, which hit the windows with a slap. These tiny gabs appeared to be bits of fatty particles of meat, prechewed, although it may have actually been mucous or small balls of wet napkins they were flinging. "Fuck," said Reynard, "let's get out of here." And Jack started up the car. Feeling quite ill, I stretched out across the floor, resting my head against the seat behind me, and in the growing gloom we drove back to the city, the velvet curtains swaying in the dusk.

24

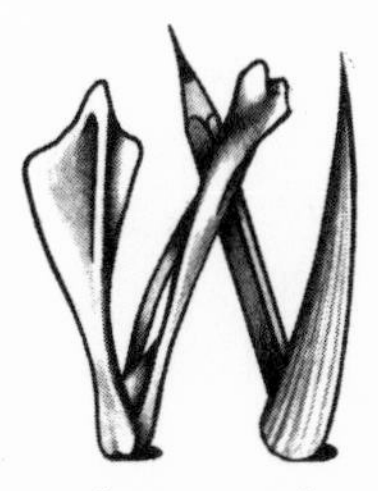

hen I opened my eyes the dwarf, like a nervous snail, was curled up in front of a small table that had miraculously unfolded from the ceiling, shuffling a deck of cards he laid out before him in a cross-shaped pattern. "Don't you want me to do you, Reynard?" he said. He looked at me and noticed my eyes had now opened. "I want to read Reynard's cards for him, but he doesn't want to hear his fortune."

"I have to go, Mikhail," Reynard said. "Maybe later on."

"He's very nervous about hearing his future," the dwarf said. "And no wonder. I wouldn't want to hear what was going to happen to me if I were Reynard either. Come to think of it, I'm not sure I want to find out what's going to happen to me." We were back in Manhattan, and the limo dropped Reynard off at the Four Seasons, a large restaurant by appearance. Before he got out, however, Reynard said a strange thing: "Take care of yourself, Mgungu. It's been real." And though I waited to hear the rest of the sentence—It's been real what? real nice? real interesting? a real good time?—who knew what he was going to say, the end of the sentence was not forthcoming, and as for taking care of myself, I hardly saw what that had to do with anything. The dwarf, clamping a green cigarette between his rubbery lips, asked me where I wanted to go.

"Back to the Holiday Inn, I guess, if that's all right with you," I said. Yet after these words were uttered, my food must have reached its digestive peak, for I felt abruptly forceful, and my thoughts and heart were full of energy. "I know what," I said. "I'll go back to my hotel and check out. Then I'll move into Maria's place. This nonsense of living apart must come to an end. For we can reside in the same apartment, at least." After I said this, it was a good thing, and I felt much better for having done so. And it was the first time I had felt such control in a long time.

"No, wait," the dwarf said suddenly, although the car was not moving. He twitched slightly and knocked the deck of cards to the green rug on the floor. Then he threw himself on the floor and began to try and pick them up. He was not a well dwarf, I decided. "Don't you want to go out to dinner or something first?" he said.

"Dinner?" I said. "I don't think I'll eat again as long as I live. Come with me over to the hotel first, though, and I'll have a coffee or a drink if you want while you eat."

But now the dwarf looked unhappier than ever. "Yes, I'll come with you," he said. We left Jack waiting outside the hotel with the car while we went upstairs. In the lobby I told the hotel clerk at the front desk that I was planning to check out and that he should send the bill to the Museum of Primitive Cultures, which was planning to take care of it as previously mentioned. The dwarf clutched at my arm anxiously and kept trying to steer me over to the bar, a hole off one side of the lobby decorated like a Swahili village complete with hair-covered bongo drums nearly four feet tall.

But I said I just wanted to go upstairs first and despite his apparent protestations we took the elevator to my disastrous room, which the maids had not touched since my arrival, due to certain reasons I will explain later.

In the room the dwarf did not look well and said, "I can't bear the stink of air freshener. It reminds me exactly of a happy day in the pine forest, if you know what I mean. I'm just going to open the window." For the hotel, though air conditioned and on the eighth floor, did have several windows that actually opened and closed, which, as I had come to learn, was highly unusual. But a patch of bird smear had never been cleaned off the largest window in the entire time I had been there, and I wondered now if I would miss it, having come to learn the outline of it so intimately, the blashy blob on the top of the glass trickling into teary lines near the bottom.

The dwarf pulled over a chair and stood on it to swing open the window, but to his shock and mine the entire window came off in his hands, leaving a screenless and gaping hole on the eighth floor out into the world. He sat down on the ground and, snickering nervously, leaned the window up against the radiator-coolant system and walked to the other side of the room.

At that point another strange thing happened—a large, greasy pigeon, which had been perched on the window ledge as if waiting for something, chose to fly flappingly into the room through the hole. It was an unusual bird, brown and white as opposed to the usual gray specimen, and around its neck was a prismatic ring of color formed most queerly, I believed, from various oily substances on the bird's feathers. And with its intelligent eye it saw the table and landed upon it, then twisted its thin neck and began to flap its way about the room as if hoping now to get out, as if it must have made some sort of mistake in coming in, which it had. But it could not find the window again, and I determined that the bird was in some way damaged or even mentally defective.

An abrupt knock came to the door and then it was flung open. Apparently the visitors had their own key, and in fact it was the hotel clerk I had just spoken with downstairs and the manager, with a dry fringe of friable hair that came down over his aviator goggles. The hotel clerk was tattooed with pimples. "Mr. Mugnu?" the hotel manager said.

"Mgungu," I said. "Mgungu Yabba Mgungu."

The manager gazed at the flapping flight of the fowl and at the dwarf, who had gotten himself into the bed with the knocking on the door. For what reason I couldn't say. I imagined he was not feeling too well, for he pulled the covers up way over his head, and lay on what must have been his side, curled fetally as if trying to disappear. Although he gradually pushed the covers down beneath his chin to throw a word or two into the conversation that ensued.

"I understand you're planning to check out tonight."

"That is correct," I said. "I've just gotten married and I'm moving into my wife's apartment. I would have moved out last night, but I couldn't find her, strangely enough, and I understand she may have gone away for the weekend. A busy lady, that woman, and constantly forced to look after and maintain her body. But not only her body, her many business affairs, one of the difficulties, I understand, of owning money. One must be constantly managing it."

However, no one appeared to be listening to me.

The hotel clerk had picked up the smashed skull that stood before my framed picture of Jackie Kennedy Onassis. The skull had belonged to some member of the Greater Pimbas; I mean, it had once been a member of some living enemy, known to us as the Greater Pimbas, being greater not in intelligence but in stature and numbers, and it had a large hole in the thinnest forepart of the temple. This was where the brains had been spooned out after the head had been roasted and the skin peeled.

Well. Why I had it was I needed some object to remind me of home, and this skull, taken by my grandfather in some minor ambush, had always been the one he was most proud of. I'm not sure exactly why; it may have been an ambush they had given to commemorate a certain occasion—the discovery, for example, by the tribesmen of the "jet plane," an event I had always heard recalled with much laughter and ridicule as well as pleasure. The idea of human beings flying around in something so small always cracked them up.

Though the hotel clerk and the manager were briefly intrigued with the silver-framed portrait of Jackie O., I was surprised at the length of time they examined the skull and the shortness of time with which they examined the portrait of the beautiful and well-known goddess. Well, it was becoming easy, as I may have mentioned, for me to be tolerant of other religions, particularly since my own was not a very religious tribe except where it came to the Jacqueline Kennedy Onassis portrait. Now the hotel clerk held up this skull, an object polished smooth and yellowed, for my grandfather had used it as a pillow for many years before getting one of Dacron polyester fiberfill through an old Sears, Roebuck catalogue.

Meanwhile the manager had of his own accord begun to go through my things, looking quite white and shocked, which explained why he did not ask my permission to do so. It was difficult in any case for him to sift his way through my belongings, which had been flung to every portion of the room. With my weekly $25 wealth I had simply bought new articles of clothing instead of taking the old things to the laundry, and thus there were hundreds of filthy socks and Jockey shorts participating in giving my room the illusion of a home.

"My gosh," he said, holding up one slice of bread after the next (for a while I had felt the need to buy packages of Wonder Bread, which I would then squish and save temporarily) and flinging them back down. "My gosh, what has been going on here?"

"You can't do that," the dwarf said, getting out from under the blankets. "This man has just married Maria Fishburn and now owns nearly fifty million dollars. Or at least one and a half. He is here because of a dance festival held by the Museum of Primitive Cultures, and Parker Junius has promised to take care of the bill including any additional phone calls. It is illegal for you to touch his things. You cannot search an American citizen's belongings without a search warrant."

The manager stopped briefly and held up a number of the brassieres I had been collecting for my wives. From underneath it he pulled a plastic bag full of my special tobacco mixed with leaves and began to sniff it. "I just spoke with them over at the museum," he said. "Someone was working there late, or there would have been no one there at all, so you were lucky. They have no such record of a Mr. Mgungu participating in the festival. Parker Junius is in the hospital, having just suffered a heart attack, and cannot be disturbed."

"Oh, no!" I said, deeply struck. I began to head for the door. "I must visit immediately."

"No visitors. No calls. I already checked," the manager said.

I was like a man stricken and beside himself and did not know what to do. This terrible thing was beyond comprehension. The pigeon still flapping mercilessly around the room came to roost near the manager as if hoping for a handout of grain or bread crumbs. I held up a slice of Wonder Bread. "Here birda birda," I said.

The manager irritably pushed the bird off the back of the chair. The bird let out a squawk and, rising slowly and with several false starts, flapped over to the lamp, where it sat miserably on top. "What is in this bag, sirrah?" the manager said. "I would like to know what has been going on here."

The hotel clerk was now opening my drawers and finding empty can after empty can. There were cans of peas, okra, and mixed vegetables as well as Libby's sliced peaches in light syrup, bags of every shape and size, and tins that once contained Danish butter cookies. There were also old egg cartons, yogurt containers, and little paper bags from McDonald's, and bits of cellophane and Saran wrap. What is my explanation for this? It is like this—how could I bring myself to throw any of these things out when I knew how handy they would have come in over on Mt. Bawwaar-Yaas? We could have used the empty tin cans to keep grubs in, those little greasy bags from McDonald's could have been put to use as stationery, not to mention those empty firm yogurt containers that only smelled slightly, although I had washed them out several times. Yes, I was in fact like Heidi, *Heidi* being one of the books I had in my library up there—by now the rats or pigs had probably eaten it, and my eyes prickled thinking of that poor Heidi devoured by rats; anyway, I was in fact like Heidi, who when she was down in Hamburg saved all the white rolls for her grandmother up in the Alps, since the poor old lady had no teeth and couldn't eat the tough black peasant rolls. Well maybe it was in fact a peasanty or peasantish thing to do, saving all those empty cans and bottles for my wives to keep their gewgaws and pawpaws in, but really wasn't it also a matter of sound ecology?

Here I had been keeping all that stuff carefully and now it was being swept away into the garbage by the manager in one blow. How many times at first had the maids come in and cleaned my collection away, forcing me to start all over again, before I put permanently the DO NOT DISTURB sign on my door. It was not an easy life I was leading, and now the manager spoke again like a screaming mouse, "Get rid of that bird! You're going to have to leave. These birds bring with them germs, salmonella and schistosomiasis. I don't know how you ever brought it in here—there are no pets allowed in this hotel." The hotel clerk pointed out that the window was broken and reached up to rub his pimples. "All of your belongings and your passport will have to be left here until you can pay," the manager said. "I don't know if you realize what kind of trouble you are in."

"He can't leave his passport!" the dwarf burst out.

"Why not?" I said. "It's a very simple matter—I'll leave my stuff here, go and scout up Maria. However long it takes, I can surely track her down with my jungle nose—and I'll get her to pay up the bill. Then the museum will pay her back."

"You can't do that!" the dwarf said. "You're leaving the country! Tomorrow! You need your passport."

"No, I'm not," I said with surprise.

"The bill comes to four thousand dollars and seventy-nine cents," the manager said disapprovingly.

"How could that be?" Mikhail said. "He hasn't been here that long!"

"What's your involvement with all this?" the manager said, giving him a look.

"None!" Mikhail said. "None at all! Anyway," he said frantically, "Mgungu's a rich man. You have a joint checking account, don't you—since Maria's disappeared you don't need to find her, you can pay on your own."

"Unfortunately we have not cleared a joint checking account with the bank," I said. "She did give me a Kool Kash Kard but that is only good for hundred-dollar withdrawals maximum. And I don't know how to use it. But what are you so worried for? No wonder you are fearful of aging. I'm not worried."

"I'm not worried either!" Mikhail said. "It's just that you shouldn't have to go through this nonsense—you're a rich man now and a foreigner to our country. You should be treated with respect or there will be serious repercussions." He looked at the manager severely. "This man is going to be on the cover of *Time* magazine. I'd take care of the bill for you, Mgungu, but unfortunately I just paid my alimony and I'm a little skint at the moment." The dwarf was anxiously pacing back and forth and finally, snatching up the pigeon, he threw it out the window. It appeared to struggle violently against gravity for a minute to fly back inside or at least land on the window ledge once more, but was picked up by a gust of wind. How it had ever gotten up so high in the first place was a mystery, and then I wondered if perhaps the dwarf had not in fact done something to the bird, because it could not get its wings to working again. Though it flapped it seemed to be falling down to Eighth Avenue below. It simply could not get itself to stay up in the air and at last fell like a plummeting bullet. "You can't do this!" the dwarf said hysterically. "Where will this man go?" But the manager escorted the two of us to the door, making sure we were not carrying anything with us.

"I'm not going to call the police in," the manager said.

"No, not the police," the dwarf said.

"Although you have a skull here and a bag of what is quite obviously drugs," the manager continued. "If you promise me you will have the money first thing in the morning. I'm afraid I won't, in this instance, be able to accept a check unless it's certified by the bank. Don't you have any credit cards?" And he looked at me hopefully for the last time.

"I'm sorry, not yet," I said. "I've only just married into money recently. Yesterday in fact." And I half expected a congratulations, which seemed to me would have been in order, but the manager merely shook his head once more and said, "My gosh, I never expected this job would be like this," while the small dwarf grabbed at the manager's sleeve again and again, which I did not think was much good for diplomatic matters.

Out on the street the dwarf seemed literally to be on the edge of collapse. "You better take it easy," I said. "Maybe you should go home. Reynard was right, alcohol doesn't agree with you."

"I can't let you out of my sight," he said. "Where are you going to go now?"

"Over to Maria's," I said. "I have the key. Maybe she'll be there, or maybe she's left a note I simply didn't see before."

"No, no, no," the dwarf said.

"What's your problem?" I said. "I'm not so savage as I may seem. You can tell me. Is there some reason I can't go over there? A surprise party, maybe, similar to the ones I've read about so often? I've never had a surprise party before."

"No, no, no," the dwarf said. "*Au contraire.* I didn't mean a thing by it, only I'm so upset your passport being taken away and all. Of course you can go to Maria's apartment—it's your home now."

"Why, I'm an American citizen now, aren't I," I said.

"Yes, but you still need your passport," he said, "if you ever want to leave this country and go back to New Burnt Norton and your three wives where you were probably much happier leading a cannibal existence. Do you have the keys to Maria's apartment?"

"Oh, sure," I said.

"Can I see?" he said.

"Okay." I shrugged and held them out in my hand. With that

the dwarf took them up and I swear either deliberately or because he was the clumsiest dwarf on record dropped them straight into the grating over which we were standing. "Nice going, Mikhail," I said. Still I was fond of the little demented soul.

"Look, you can stay with me tonight," he said brightly. "I should have suggested that earlier."

"No, look," I said, "I'll get them out, no trouble." I bought some chewing gum at a nearby kiosk, and, chewing up a morass of it, I attached it to the end of my girdle of dogs' teeth I took from around my waist, and made uncircular, so it was now like a weighted string with a great wad of wet gum. And astonishingly I managed to recover the keys.

"Still, why don't you stay at my house," the dwarf said desperately. "I'm lonesome, and I can't bear to be alone."

"Okay," I said, sympathetically. "I will—but I want to just go over to the apartment first and leave a message for her and just see if perhaps she is there."

"You can't do that," the dwarf said, but I still had not gotten the point, and, the dwarf trailing alongside and followed by Jack in the green limousine whom both of us had forgotten, we went over to Maria's.

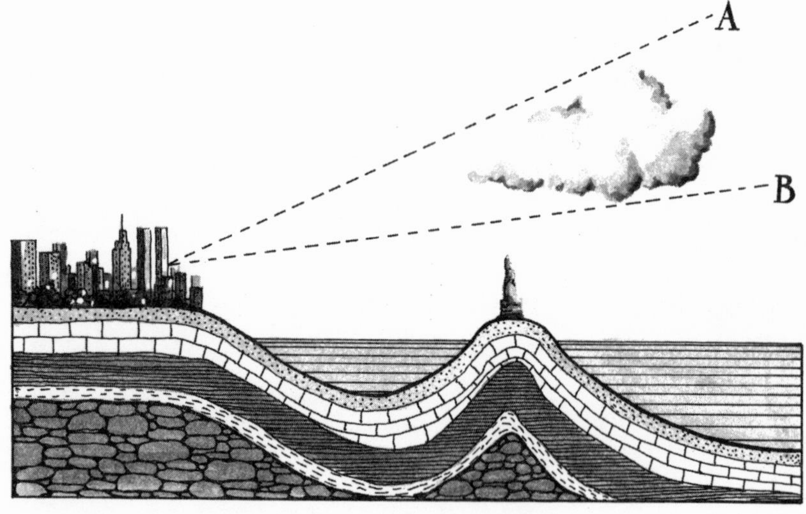

25

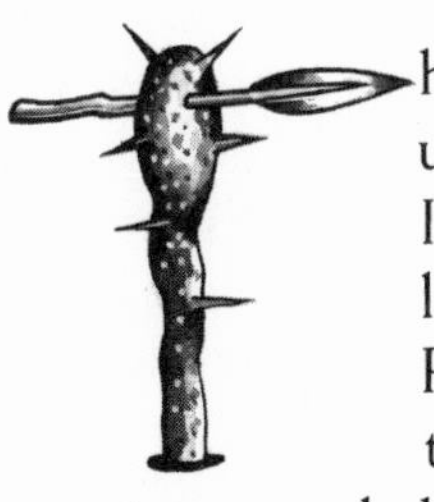

The doorman did not recognize me, giving me an unfamiliar stare and approaching me near where I stood next to the elevator. In the center of the lobby, a small fountain, made of bayonets of Plexiglas that pointed up from a low murky trough of water, jutted out into the room. The water, recycled through its various portions, made the bubbling sound of a toilet being flushed, and tiny colored lights blinked on and off. Momentarily I considered taking a refreshing dip.

"Can I help you?" the doorman said.

"I live here now," I said.

But the doorman gave me a suspicious glare. "I.D., please," he said.

"I don't have one yet," I said. "I'm Mr. Fishburn now."

The dwarf, running his short and pinkish hands through his silver hair, whimpered at my side and said, "I feel hungry. Maybe we could just stop at the coffee shop on the corner for something to eat, since you're obviously not going to be allowed to go in."

"No, that's all right," the doorman said, relaxing perceptibly. "I recognize you now. You're the cannibal, huh?"

"That's right," I said, and to the dwarf, "there's probably plenty of food upstairs. I'll get you a bite to eat up there."

"So, you married Ms. Fishburn, huh?" the doorman said. "Well, that should change things for her somewhat, I guess, huh?"

"Oh, I don't just want to rush indoors and eat," the dwarf said.

"I guess so," I said to the doorman and was about to turn and follow the dwarf out, but when the elevator opened I changed my mind and got in. The dwarf turned around and joined me; Jack the driver followed on our heels. The doorman waved good-bye and the three of us stepped into the elevator along with a woman bearing faint resemblance to a very rich and bejeweled chicken who had seen better days. She must have been out walking her dog, a sleek and bald-bodied type of chihuahua or Mexican naked dog, totally furless except for a long ridge of fur that grew along its spine. This dog wore a jaunty pink hat, the same type of hat such as children wear at birthday parties, only knitted out of pink wool. The dwarf, in a paroxysm of anger at the sight of the dog (although he might actually have been full of fear), stood behind me in the elevator during our upward descent, glowering at the dog, who drunkenly tossed his head from side to side, trying to shake off the little hat. Jack the driver was unnoticing of the hound and would have stepped on it as we were leaving the elevator, had I not clutched his arm and with all my strength pulled to swerve him to one side and away from the dog.

"Watch yourself," I said to Jack, as despite my efforts he seemed determined to unconsciously injure or maim this dog on the way out. The chicken lady was riding up to the twenty-fourth floor, while we were getting out on the twenty-second—but Jack did not understand my friendly attempt to maneuver him out of the way and, knocking me against the elevator wall like a lion shaking off a fly, said, "Huh?"

I banged into the lady, though luckily not crushing the miniature hound, and said, "Excuse me, so sorry," as I tried to step out of the elevator, the door of which Jack was now blocking as if waiting for an explanation of why I had told him to "watch himself." For some reason it was only now the tiny dog caught sight of the dwarf and fell in love with him—why this should be I don't know, except that the dwarf was by far nearest the dog's height—and the dwarf continued to back up, although he was already as nearly in the far corner as he could get. "Shoo!" he kept telling the dog. "Go home, sir! Bad boy." The feathered creature did nothing to call off her dog but watched as it jumped up against the nervous dwarf's legs.

"Why did you tell me to watch myself," Jack said dangerously at the door, holding the doors of the elevator open again as they automatically tried to shut on him.

"You were going to step on the dog," I said, nursing my sore arm from where I had been slapped against the wall. I took the dwarf's hand and tried to pull him out around the dog, but the animal's pink leash was in the way blocking us, and the woman, with the blank expression of some avian flightless creature on her face, could apparently make no move to help any of us but stood looking. Finally I moved the dwarf around the far side of the dancing dog wriggling its tail at the dwarf's proximity. As we managed to get out at last, the jeweled and spectacled fowl took notice of us for the first time and then as the doors to the elevators closed I heard her saying to the dog, "Sit down, my darling Betsy."

The dwarf, removed from his phobia or angst, managed to calm down at once. But at the door to the apartment he earnestly held on to my arm when I tried to fit the key in the lock, and he began frantically ringing the doorbell, over and over again, as if chiming some kind of Oriental gong. "What are you doing that for?" I said.

"Well," the dwarf said, "just in case she came home unexpectedly. It would be awful to walk in on her unannounced on what is your honeymoon. Suppose she was waiting to surprise you, naked perhaps and in the living room, and the three of us walked in? How embarrassing and even cruel." And he rang the doorbell two or three more times in succession.

But the door unlocked and we moved into the hall, all done in creamy pink and puce art deco, two large satin-covered chairs in the shape of oyster shells, which I remembered from Maria's description, that Paloma Picasso had thrown out in a fit of pique and Maria had shipped from Paris, while above our heads a chandelier made of shimmering coral-colored beads trembled like an old lady's necklace. I took the boys' coats and hung them up in the closet, not noticing as I should have that the hall light was already on, but saying instead, "What's that funny smell?" For it was as if I were back in the faintly steaming jungle of New Burnt Norton with the smell of growth and vegetation around me.

And on one end of the little front room or lobby the staircase curled upward to the upstairs. To the side the hall went off to the various rooms and on the other side, which is where I went now, into the dining room and the kitchen. "Come on, you guys," I said, "let's look at what is in the refrigerator to eat, seeing as you're so hungry."

And despite their feeble protestations we passed through the dining room, with its long table of carved precious woods, with a terrace on one side through the French doors and the collection of Orrefors crystal lining the glass cabinets along one wall and then into the kitchen, all High Technology and Cuisine Minceur, though what those things were I had only heard in passing speech and they had not yet become real to me.

In the refrigerator I found nothing but a carton of spoiled milk, some lank and limp celery stalks, and a small jar of caviar, which to me was only fish eggs. This I offered to Mikhail and Jack, though the jar was so tiny I could hardly see how it would do them any good and a price tag on top said $108.59. Putting the jar on a plate with some old egg matzohs I found in a box in the cupboard, I showed it to them, but at this both of them shook their heads.

I opened the freezer, where aside from a carton of Häagen-Dazs ice cream in a chocolate flavor there was nothing but a tremendous pile of wrapped and stacked meats, frozen.

"Ice cream, anyone?" I said, but they both shook their heads, looking glum, though Jack was meanwhile pacing back and forth like an animal grown too big for its cage. "Well then, why don't we move into the living room, where I believe we will be more comfortable," I said.

"No," the dwarf said, "I'm perfectly fine here." For with great difficulty he had lifted himself up onto one of the tall bar-type stools that served as the seats for the kitchen-counter breakfast table.

But I had learned to pay no attention to what the dwarf said and went into the living room, followed grimly by the two of them, and turned the light on, and there crouched behind the sofa in the middle of the room, holding a huge carving knife and with a slightly puzzled expression on his face, was Reynard.

And before him stretched out on a plastic tarpaulin was a white body, human and missing various limbs such as the head and both arms. There was a great deal of blood surrounding the body and even spattered out onto the white rug, and Reynard stood there holding the knife and the dwarf stood trembling over to one side, while Jack, who had removed some sort of knife from his own pocket, now placed the tip of it in the small of my back.

26

It was quite obviously a female body. This was noticeable by many of its attributes which I am unfortunately here too delicate to mention.

"Maybe you'd better sit down," Reynard said, and Jack's knife, like some delicate bird's beak, perhaps a sort of woodpecker, pressed rather deeply into one of the lumps of my spine, directing me over to the red sofa, where I proceeded to sit.

"Oh, Jack, put the knife away," Reynard said, "you big baboon with a tendency to be overdramatic." His own knife was a very large, stainless-steel blade, an expensive chef's knife made in France I believe, the name of which escapes me now, and was covered in a rather gory assortment of blood. Also on the ground was a large pair of shears and a neatly laid-out assortment of butcher's cleavers and meat-tenderizing hammers, all arranged on another of those thick plastic tarpaulins of the same sort as the body was lying on. "I'm sorry you had to come in upon this misunderstanding," Reynard said. "For it is a misunderstanding, though whether or not you want to believe that is up to you. As you may know, I am a good friend of your former wife's. After going out to dinner I stopped over here to leave her a message or perhaps to see if she had gotten back yet and I found this body and this assortment. She was apparently involved in some kind of criminal activity and fled the scene when it was too late." He pointed to the collection of equipment on the ground and looked aghast at the knife in his hand. "I had the keys to let myself in. You can imagine my surprise. This is horrible, although a very neat job. I can imagine full well, man, how you must be in a state of shock." Here the dwarf let out a tiny whimper of the sort of which he was so adept.

"But this is no time to panic. This is New York City. This sort of thing happens all the time. The thing to do now is to find out what has happened to your wife and how you can help her. I suspect you will be blamed for this. How are we to prove you did not do it? Indeed, for all I know you may have done it. I think the best thing to do will be to get you out of the country and meanwhile I will consult my lawyer."

The décor of the living room was in red and white, which struck me at that moment as eminently suitable. A door to one side led out to the terrace, the same terrace that also extended from the dining room. I was narrowly in a state of shock, as Reynard had foretold, though my behavior may in fact on recounting appear to be callous. Still there was little I could do, momentarily. "Whose body do you suspect that of being?" I said.

"There is little way of telling as the head appears to be missing," Reynard said. "You will leave the country as soon as possible." And he looked at me fiercely with his red-rimmed eyes.

"They kept his passport at the hotel" the dwarf said.

"Then we must get it back," Reynard said, "to help our friend. Are you hungry?" I shook my head. "Maybe in a little while then," he said. "We are going to have to think of something to do with you. Do you have any money?" I shook my head again. "But you can write a check."

"No," the dwarf said, "he doesn't have a joint checking account."

"Son-of-a-bitch," Reynard said.

"Only a Kool Kash Kard," I said.

"How much money can you withdraw?" Reynard said.

"Up to one hundred dollars."

"But if you go to different machines you can draw one hundred dollars at each."

"I don't know how these things work," I said. "Whatever you say, though."

"Where do you have your account?" Reynard said.

"Rational Bank of Manhattan."

"Then you and Mikhail will go out and Jack and I will try and clean up here. I'll think of what to do, believe me. I won't leave you in the lurch, I'm not that kind of person. Mikhail can vouch for that, can't you, Mikhail? Mikhail is a very well known writer, I don't know if you've been aware of that. But generally, well-known people would not get themselves into any dangerous kind of scrape, nor would they leave someone in the lurch."

I nodded. Reynard's green suit flickered eerily in the reddish living-room light.

The dwarf led me docilely outside and down in the elevator. What I thought was, this could not possibly be happening to me. I had to get away. My life a violent mess seemed to be too much of a joke to be true. And now with a new wife who appeared to be a killer of some kind. If possible I would have taken a vacation from myself.

"This is New York," the dwarf kept saying. "Things like this happen all the time. It's not your fault. You just have to accept these things for the way they are and try and cut your losses while you can."

I felt extremely resentful of Maria Fishburn for putting this over me. Yet I could not believe she would have duped me. How much deader a white person looked than someone purple! And the blood so much bloodier against a white rug. She had never liked me very much in any case, I now realized, and this would be just the sort of stunt she would pull, marrying a poor dumb savage only to lay a murder rap on him. At first what her purpose had been in marrying me was quite unfathomable. Yet now it did begin to make sense.

"How do you feel?" the dwarf said.

How did I feel? I felt like a nervous idiot. Just walking around, the two of us were, trying to get to the Rational Bank of Manhattan, although why I could no longer remember. An insect flew into my eye and I rubbed at it frantically. It was a painful and trying moment. Oh, Jackie Kennedy Onassis, I prayed, suddenly turning to religion in a time of need, and thinking of the small snapshot of her I kept in a little voodoo or fetish bag around my neck, please allow me to wake up and find this is not happening to me. "This cannot be happening to me," I said.

"But it is," the dwarf said helpfully. "I tried to stop you, you know."

"I know," I said. "Just let me wake up in my hammock on the side of Mt. Bawwaar-Yaas, just let me wake up as president-elect of the Lesser Pimbas in my New Burnt Norton home, and I promise you I will keep my mouth shut and not whine for a life greater than myself again."

"Mmm," the dwarf said thoughtfully, lighting a yellow cigarette.

Then a curious thing happened. I saw an object and, stooping over, picked it up. It appeared to me, and the dwarf agreed, that I had found an Indian arrowhead, completely intact. Where had it come from? It was quite obviously a sign of some kind, although the dwarf insisted it had probably been dropped by some Indian-arrowhead collector. "However," I said, "wasn't this island once owned by American Indians?" The dwarf reluctantly confirmed this.

Briefly I felt slightly better. Then my worrisome thoughts appeared again. How do you manage to survive, Parker Junius, I addressed him in my head, thinking how his gill-less floundering and pompous inadequacy had taken him to the position of curator of the Museum of Primitive Cultures. Then I remembered he was now in the hospital, having suffered a heart attack. But I did not believe he could have ever felt the way I was feeling at this monent. How nice it must be not to have this burden on oneself, this desperate crawling and scrabbling on the inside of something trying to get out.

My life was ruined. I might not have been happy before, but I was not unhappy, and content as a dog. Next to me the dwarf walked frantically, a frittering, spineless creature of whom I could not help but be fond, trying to steer me to the Kool Kash machine at the Rational Bank.

The first machine we came to, some seven blocks beneath Maria's apartment address, was out of order. It was bent and demolished, a big gaping hole where one was meant to deposit the card, as if someone in a frantic rush had tried to pull all the money out of it, and the front of it was smeared with excrement or old pizza. "Where is there another machine?" the dwarf said.

"Across town," I said, "some five or eight blocks, I believe." And I was very impatient with my own desperate thoughts quivering in my head and longed, as they had suggested, to get my Kool Kash and my passport back and flee the country and have done with the mess once and for all. Yes, that is what I would do, I would use the Kool Kash Kard four hundred and fifty times, until I had collected enough hundred-dollar bills to pay off my hotel bill, collect my passport, and buy an airline ticket to take me back to N.B.N. So we proceeded to the next bank location, readily accessible, and I said my thought out loud. "Animals don't have to worry about a thing."

"That's true," the dwarf said. "They aren't aware of death."

"What about the elephant graveyard?" I said.

"Well, that's instinctive," the dwarf said.

"People, however," I said, "they worry about death."

"Well, that's modernism for you," the dwarf said. "Me, I'm all for the Epicurean life. Don't worry about it so much. We'll get you out of this. Trust me."

What a fantastic smell there was on the air, a hot night of young spring onions. Was I in love with Maria Fishburn? Was this part of the issue? Love was not an emotion we had over there in the primitive island. Love is something extraneous and for those highly civilized. We had mostly in the Lesser Pimbas the emotions of food, hunger, clothing, and sometimes hysterical weeping for five or ten minutes at the death of a friend or beloved child. Still, I thought of her hair like hard glass that broke off to the touch and her silky eyes like the eyes of a seal behind her comical prescription glasses. For she had never really grown accustomed to contact lenses, even with the new ultra-thin so popular on the market after our return from New Burnt Norton. And now there was a feeling of time running out, of something slippery and necessary oozing between my fingers, now that it was to be my last few hours in the United States. And on a breeze came the scent of some cheap perfume, on top of that of the spring onions. I heard water trickling somewhere underground, and above that, the dull rush of the subway. The trees with speckled fingers waved tentatively, uncertain as to their stature here in the city. I did not want to lose this, did not want to lose any of this and return to my fungus jungle life.

The next machine we came to appeared to be in order and the dwarf showed me how to insert my card and punch in the various numbers and the password, which Maria had once whispered to me, SWORDFISH. But the machine, blinking and relentless, took my card and would not return it. The dwarf was nearly in tears and hammered and banged on the machine, but the machine did not smile and my card was gone from sight. I suggested I return with the dwarf to his house and possibly get some sleep. I felt very tired. My adolescence was perhaps, at age fifty-five, over at last.

27

I felt a tightening stricture cross the top of my head as we approached the dwarf's place of residence, and this pressure became a louder and harder thrumming or sobbing, as if the being inside me was trying to escape and would now use any means of force to do so. And in the dim night we walked uptown, the dwarf earnestly depressed at my side, very sincere over the fact that I had lost my only means of support, the Kool Kash Kard, and struggling to keep up with me as I now struggled to get away from myself. How was I to know, innocent and stupid as I was, that his spontaneous moments were calculated long in advance? "Hey," Mikhail said breathlessly, "wait up."

And I halted abruptly and said, "Oh, I am very sorry, my friend, forgive me for I am not myself. Here I am fifty-five years old and in such a mess. This is not an American thing to be and I presume that I am still at this point an American citizen. I cannot help but think, Who did that body belong to? and where is my wife? What terrible thing could she have been involved in to have such a demolished and depraved object lying around her pad? She must have been in some very serious trouble indeed, to commit such a crime or allow such a crime to be committed on her premises. For tribal warfare, if not allowed in New Burnt Norton, can certainly not be allowed here, no?"

And the dwarf shrugged his weary shoulders and stroked his mole-fur mustache. "The way I see it, Mgungu Yabba Mgungu," he said, "everything about you is struggling to get out. You didn't realize that if you couldn't find what you were looking for in your own backyard, you had never really lost it in the first place." And he pulled the alligator cigarette case from his pocket.

At this a soft sound of ripping rope escaped from my throat and I nearly fell to my knees. "But!" I said, and clutched the dwarf by both shoulders, turning him to face me, "but exactly! And how did you know, even?" The dwarf had nothing to say but a wise smile. "Here!" I said. "I want you to have this!" From my neck I removed the necklace made of a human jawbone and tried to hang it around his neck. But the dwarf shuddered and wriggled out of it before I had properly strung it. It hung down nearly to his waist, his height being so much shorter than my own, and I made as if to shorten the string, but he said, "Yuck. I'm afraid I find it rather disgusting. Please, you keep it. I have enough nightmares of my own."

"But," I said, surprised, "you don't find this here jawbone attractive?" And I held the V of bone up into his face. "Look how smooth, how polished and like yellow silk, stained and pitted slightly here and there with red ocher, due to some chemical interference, possibly pollution. And how delicate and how perfect. Here at each end I have bored a hole through after much laborious labor using primitive tools—believe me, I did not even have a little hand drill readily purchasable in a hardware store but had to use the ancient awl of my grandfather, so broke was I on New Burnt Norton." Then I took out my Indian arrowhead. "See the resemblance between the one and the other!" I said. "This, too, was carved by hand or using I would imagine a piece of flint and has remained here untouched for a considerable length of time. What was it doing here? How could it lie here undisturbed for so long? And yet the passage of time has poured right over it and left it untouched. Why, perhaps it may have slipped right in out of another time, dropped through a hole which is sometimes torn in the spiderweb of the air."

"This may in fact be possible," the dwarf said, "possible." But he looked dubious. "My doctor now is working on a medication to regenerate pubic hair. People feel older, my doctor tells me, when they lose their pubic hair. In fact this makes them feel older than when they actually lose the hair on their heads. People need a nice strong crop of pubic hair. Still, as I have said, my doctor is working on a means to regenerate not only the pubic hair but also the head and facial hair. With time and effort, he says, the human body can live to be well over two hundred years old—it is simply degeneration that causes us to die, and this is easily correctable."

"Just think of the additional mistakes to be made in that length of time," I sighed.

"Oh, knock it off," the dwarf said. "That is the wrong attitude. You're going to have to start fighting this terrible attitude of yours, Mgungu. This is New York City. These things happen. I don't understand how you, a cannibal and lacking in the basic emotions, can be so shaken over a thing like this. Let me tell you, this is new for me, too. Yes, I have interviewed pregnant lady stabbers and in fact I have had sex with a man shortly to be electrocuted for killing with malice and then watched only minutes, all right it was more in fact like several hours, later, as he spasmed to death on the electric chair and though I could not smell it I knew what the air must be like inside that room. And I have seen what the dead leave over; I have seen that room behind the electric chair where the possessions of the murdered—for they are murdered, Mgungu, we killed them, you and I—lie uncollected, their *Encyclopædia Britannicas* and baby pictures, the condoms they will never use and the newspaper articles they have so carefully saved, yes those are usually their favorite possessions—you would not believe how carefully they collect every article pertaining to their crimes and how neatly these articles are clipped out and pressed into a scrapbook, as if it is only through these articles that they can prove to themselves they were ever alive. And their report cards from elementary school and old yellowed letters, the detritus of a criminal lifetime, although it is not as much as would be expected. And old undershirts that no one ever comes to collect. This is a special room they have got there, Mgungu, a special room right behind that electric-chair room, and that is the only reason it is for. A sort of museum warehouse of the dead. Why, I bet they could even charge and make money—there are more people than you would believe who would get a kick out of looking at that junk. And then at least the average taxpayer would not have to pay so much money just to get one of these criminals knocked over. Because it costs at least fifteen hundred dollars to electrocute someone, and even then they are rendered useless because electrocution damages the organs so they can't be transplanted."

"What does this have to do with me, however, and my predicament? I thought you were going to offer me some advice," I said stupidly.

"Now, yes, if I had the money I would go now to the hotel and get you out of the country, for I know how you must be suffering. And I am not the sort of person to hoard money. If I have the money I will give it to my friends, I will just give that money away. But anyway, I would prefer not to discuss this, but rather I think we should talk about you. But you must promise now to tell me the truth."

"Yes, certainly." I said. "But what about? And why?"

"It may come in handy in the future. I want you to consider me your closest friend."

"Of course!" I said, and I was very much flattered. I admired the dwarf's large and oversize head and his petite feet. For truth to tell I had not a very best friend during my male adult years, and hardly had a friend during my childhood years since there were few people on New Burnt Norton with whom I was compatible. And I was not used, therefore, to the companionship of others. For it was impossible to be friends with my wives, who were too dissimilar from myself.

But when I agreed to be the dwarf's closest friend I should have remembered my friends Joey and Kent Gable and indeed many others I had met during my trip, even Maria Fishburn. So here I had made a betrayal without thinking and simply out of flattery and it was right for this I be punished. I should have by this age learned something, whether it was about loyalty or integrity or something like that. Joey had never mentioned that we were friends or not, but I should have remembered him and turned to him, who would no doubt have rescued me. And instead I had forgotten about him completely. Even still I could have turned to Parker Junius, though he was in the hospital, or at least could have sent the old fool a get-well card, though I suppose I held him in some resentment since he had not taken care of the bill at the Holiday Inn. And yet all these people had dropped out of my head in my fascination with these new and strange creatures, the famous dwarf and Reynard, who, despite his foxy grin, was very dangerous.

"Now, don't take this the wrong way," the dwarf said, "although you are welcome to if you want. But I find you very attractive, as a person, and yes, as a man."

"You do?" I said. This came to me as a shock and almost a blow to the system, that anyone could find me attractive. What a strange life! And everything took on a significance not its own, in my crazed state. My life, which had previously kicked forward drop by drop, with each minute as clear and real and boring as the next, suddenly zoomed about. Which direction was up and which then was down? For the city buildings loomed broken on all sides and the sidewalk might as well have been the sky. Like a hideous garbled joke I did not understand, we passed on the street a gigantic pile of meat, uncooked and pale pink. Why, there were pounds of it, streaked with fat and stacked or thrown up next to a series of garbage cans awaiting collection. It must have been an entire side of beef or who knew what, a whole huge mountain of meat, and on top of it was a vast quantity of raw frozen peas, dull green and dented and puckered, the way frozen peas often are. They had not yet even thawed. "Do you see that?" I said. "What the hell is all that meat doing here?" For it was most peculiar and even stranger, I warranted, than my finding the Indian arrowhead, which was quite obviously an easily interpreted symbol.

And with this the dwarf's mouth wrinkled up, a little crumpled plum, and he began to weep. "I think you should go away," he said.

"What?" I said.

"Please, just leave," the dwarf said. "Oh, I just feel so guilty. You must try and escape, while you can."

"What do you mean by this?" I said.

"Nothing," Mikhail said. "I don't mean a thing. Pay me no mind. Well, I'll see you around. Here we are at my apartment, though it is not my own but only a temporary sublet until I can afford to move back into my co-op, which is larger even than Maria's and which I've rented out for the time being. I'm sorry. I really can't ask you up. It's just I can't bear it anymore."

"But why?"

"There are some people I simply can't stand being with. Don't take it personally, but I am an emotional and sensitive person. I only hope you will grow to understand me and even admire me more and more as time goes by." Then as we passed a tree in front of his building he stopped to give it a saddened and heavy kick with his little miniature boots like a child's. And I realized that with all this activity the night had passed and it was now dawn and the sun was coming up.

"Well, okay," I said, for the dwarf's behavior I did find very puzzling. And to think of the way he was kicking that harmless and defenseless old tree! My heart went out to it. "If you really can't stand me, I must surely leave."

28

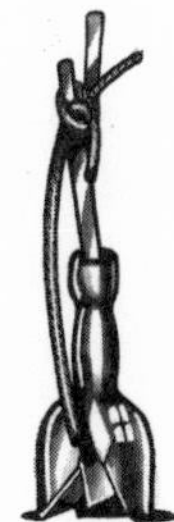
was at a terrible loss and did not know what to do with myself. I was penniless and the excitement and troubles had rendered me quite famished. During the early part of the day I wandered through Central Park, near the zoo and the merry-go-round, picking up peanuts and old pieces of Cracker Jacks from the ground.

Many people thought I was a clown or roustabout and it was true with my naked and bald chest painted in rings and the rhinoceros beetles stuck onto my nose, and the gay curling feather thrust through my kinked hairdo I did resemble the white-faced mime or the fire-eater or the group of medieval singers in their decorative and pointed hats, each of whom gave me a nod as if acknowledging me as one of themselves. "Look at the clown, Anita!" I heard the blond taloned mother of one child say, and I plaintively stretched out my hands toward the infant, who, chuckling with laughter, thrust her box of Junior Mints out at me as if to pour one into my hands and then did not know whether or not to continue laughing when I took the box, poured all the candy down my throat, and returned it to her.

Yet the nervous rattling in my stomach did not cease. I found half an uneaten banana, dank and overripe, and then I saw a child in a blue dress, temporarily abandoned by its parents, holding a hotdog plastered with mustard and candy-spittle. The child gazed at me for a moment with a look astonished and fascinated as I bent down as if to pat the tyke on the head and then snatched the gnawed dog, devouring it in two hungry gulps. As if I had unleashed a stopper the child burst into angry tears. For a moment I was half tempted to take the red balloon the child was holding as well, but as I saw two figures like charging water buffalo approaching the calf, I turned and fled in a hurry.

After that I devoted time to trying to catch the slow and sluggish pigeons who waddled sedately near the benches and between the legs of the strollers. Each time I got close enough to one to nearly grab it, it would take off in a frantic squawk and a flap of wings with a speed that was surprising. "What is that man doing?" said a woman spindly as a pencil, who strolled with a speckled gentleman. "Leonard? Just look at him, will you?" she said, as I tried to creep up behind individual pigeons each in turn.

Finally I worked out a method of fixing up a loop on a piece of string I took from my net bag, and, placing it on the ground near where a group of elderly ladies and feeble men were feeding the pigeons dried crumbs, I waited for one to step into the loop so I could then pull it tight.

The pigeons strutted closer and closer to my string as the crumbs were scattered in every direction and at last a particularly plump brown-and-white bird with two blue-encrusted eyes came nearer and nearer and finally one clawed foot just touched the inside of my loop of string. "Yaha!" I said in delight and pulled the loop of string shut, catching the pigeon by its foot. It let out a bird yell and tipped over onto one side, screeching frantically, but this alone was enough to cause the old ladies to step up in a fright and one of the braver and more bold fluttered over to me angrily, saying, "Sir, leave that bird alone! Leave go that bird at once or I shall call the policeman over here!"

The other ladies circled angrily and fiercely as if desirous to peck me to death, saying such things as, "For shame! A grown man like you and a poor defenseless pigeon!" and, "That man is sick! Oh, how terrible a world this is! He should be locked up!" until I was forced to release the pigeon and ambled off as if such a thing had never occurred, saying only once or twice aloud, "The bird had something wrong with it. I was only trying to catch it to help repair it." And I stopped on the pathway to retrieve a crust of chewy rye bread, hardly stale at all, that had been thrown for the pigeons and sparrows, while the ladies went, "Tch, tch tch. Can you believe it," and shook their heads.

As I passed a gnarled and badly carved up tree with a sign on it that said SILVER MAPLE TREE, a voice from beneath it said, "You're giving us a bad name." It came from a lone guitarist, who was kneeling in a pile of dust beneath the tree trunk, a velvet cloth spread before him covered with coins and bills. "Why don't you get your act together instead of bugging the birds? I've been watching you," he continued. "You're new here and so I'll clue you in. Don't bother the birds or the people, friend. All of us here work together, and if you give us a bad name we're all in trouble. So we'll throw you out of the park before we let that happen. Why don't you just cool it before something like that has to happen?" And with this friendly message he picked up his guitar and, strumming a tuneless chord, sang, "Bangladesh, Bangladesh, I've never seen such a mess, all those people dying." Nearly immediately a delicate man passing by threw a fifty-cent piece onto the cloth and the guitarist gave him a nod and went on with his tune.

But what kind of act could I have put on? Then I saw a bunch of squirrels nibbling nervously next to a field of baseball players and my stomach groaned in anticipation. I joined a group of boys engaged in throwing rocks at the animals, but I am afraid due to my years of rest and recovery and the fact that hunting was illegal on New Burnt Norton, besides the fact that all the native animals were extinct there, I was not the hunter I once was, and all of the squirrels were too fast for me. And the boys soon lost interest in their project of molestation.

I wandered until I came upon an aged squirrel, struggling with little clutching legs to clamber up the side of a tree called RED OAK TREE and pulling itself up little by little.

It was a poor specimen of a squirrel with hoary white fur grizzled and nearly frosted on its body and a glazed eye that glared at me suspiciously as it humped along. "Toukey, toukey," I said, "come over here, my pet." And as it reached a branch and paused to cleanse its whiskers I gave out a chortling yell and smashed at it with a stick.

The squirrel, with a surprised and bitter look, fell from its branch, arms waving frantically, and plunged to the ground, where I rushed up to it and beat it severely with a stick until its small body lay bruised and trembling on the muddy spring ground. The tail flopped back and forth miserably. I had killed a meal, and with eagerness bent forward to pick it up. But I had unfortunately not damaged the squirrel as much as I had thought, for when I picked it up a breath of life came back into it and it bit me viciously on the hand, sinking its two buck-toothed fangs into the fleshy place between finger and thumb.

"Yaaugh!" I said and, shaking the squirrel loose, threw it back to the ground, where it began to chitter ferociously and charged around the tree trunk in a deranged and rabid circle. I began to follow it, trying to block and feint its mad and unsteady path, kneeling and wheeling in the darkening afternoon as I tried to stop it.

Thus, unnoticed to myself and the rodent a policeman approached, swaggering a stick and sprouting a nearly greenish mustache. "What's the matter here?" he said ominously, and I looked up at him from where I knelt on my knees. "What are you, bothering this animal? Some kind of a squirrel pervert?"

"Officer," I said, "there's something wrong with this squirrel—I don't know if it's sick or what. I was walking along and I saw some kids who may have been throwing rocks at it or something. I think it may have been hit."

The officer looked sympathetic and jumped sharply to one side as the squirrel took a swerve for his feet. "Yeah," he said, "you may be right. Jeez, these kids. Look, I don't know, I could call the ASPCA or something but they probably won't even bother to show up. It's just a squirrel. I don't know what they could do for it anyway."

"Poor little thing," I said.

"Yeah," the policeman said, "it's a crime. You're in this city for a while, you become immune to anything. You don't get many people who would even bother stopping for a squirrel like this. What are you, from out of town or something? That looks like some kind of native costume you've got on."

"Yeah, I'm from a place near New Guinea."

"Oh, yeah? I got a cousin stationed over there. Guy named Mitch Sawyer—maybe you know him. Well, look, I don't know what I can do for this animal. Maybe the best thing is to put it out of its misery."

"Oh, I suppose so. Though I don't think that will be easy to do, catching it, I mean."

"Nah, nah, that's okay, that's what we're trained for. I'll just give it a knock in the head." And the next time it passed, shrilling and chirping bitterly, the policeman gave it a knock alongside its head with his baton and it fell dead at his feet. He picked at it gingerly with one of his feet, and before he could stop me I had swung it up by the tail eagerly. "Better not touch it, could get fleas or bubonic plague or something," he said. "Who knows what these rats get into? Though I guess a squirrel isn't the same thing as a rat, is it? It's a rat with a tail? Anyway, give it to me, I'll take it and throw it away so nobody can get at it."

"Oh, look, that's all right," I said. "As long as I've already touched it there's no point in your getting contaminated, too. I'll just find something to wrap it in and throw it where no one can get to it."

"Well, okay." The officer shrugged as he ambled off. "Look, I'm sure you've been told this a thousand times since you've been here, but you really shouldn't be in the park at night. It's getting late. Why don't you go home, buddy?"

At this remark I nearly broke into tears, being volatile in my hunger, and also realizing I had no home and no place to go. "Good-bye," I called, "and thank you." And I looked after him gratefully as I began to pluck some of the fur off the limp body of the squirrel and gutted its tiny interior with my arrowhead. I managed to get two nice little bite-sized fillets off the tree-climber, and then, scooping some dirt on the intestines and remains with the blade of my knife, I crawled off the pathway to a small cave I found between a grouping of boulders. Here I collected some sticks and twigs and arranged them into a heap, and lighting this campfire I now spitted the squirrel meat and held it and turned it over the flames until it was nicely charred. It made a pleasant toothsome and I began to wish I had managed to catch several, or even a dozen more. My stomach groaning and churning in hunger, I doused the fire with my foot until it was nothing but a bed of warm embers, and, creeping close to it, tried to drift off to sleep.

29

hen I awoke I began without reason to walk downtown. By now it was somewhat past six in the morning—judging from the position of the sun it might have been nine or even twelve. How tedious a thing it was, I thought, to be without greenbacks in the civilized world. I might even at that moment have turned to knavery, had not I seen, on the corner near Columbus Circle, a man waving a ten-dollar bill in the air and shouting, "Commies! Fucking Commies!"

I approached his side. "Sir, might you not share that money with me?" I said. "For $10 is enough to share, and we are all Americans and friends here."

The man looked at me wildly; I wondered perhaps if he suffered from rabies or Tay-Sachs disease. "Are you a Communist or a Capitalist?" he said, holding out the bill in his fingers.

I thought about this for a time. "Where I come from, it may

be said that in a sense it is a Commune," I said. "For we all work as one for the good of the whole." The man snatched the bill away. "But on the other hand, as I am the President and Chief-elect, everyone is actually working for me." At this the man pressed the bill into my hand.

"Take the money!" he said. "Kill the Commies!"

I must have been growing wiser in my civilized ways, for without questioning his deed I took the money and walked on.

The pavement was strangely tarry and hot with the globs of chewing gum round grinning faces on the ground. And the smell of excrement rose up from the traces of feces that remained on the curb and sidewalk after people had wiped up after their dogs, a curious practice. Now before me the trees with their scrawny branches seemed hardly vegetation but thin men growing out of the ground, and the faces of the women on their way to work were not fresh but already puttified with smears of makeup running from beneath their eyes. I had a feeling that something was terribly wrong.

Still I ambled down the avenue in a downtownwardly direction, with the hinking and plinking of taxis in my ears and a state of misery in my body, but at least some money now with which to buy myself the time of day. On the side street I saw a Hickory House Coffee Shop and I went in, pushing the heavy, sticky glass doors open into the cool interior and the plastic leather seats. Before I could ease myself into one of them and get a cup of coffee the chef or cook, in a narrow white hat like an unrisen pie, snapped, "I'm sorry, you can't come in here."

"What?" I said. I looked at him, certain he could not be talking to me, but was probably addressing some old sorrowful bum behind me who so frequently in Manhattan wandered into the wrong place. In fact I did look around behind me, and then to the side, but though the restaurant was quite crowded with people, there was no one else he was talking to except me. "What?" I said again. "I didn't hear you, I think."

"Look, I don't want to cause a scene, but I'll call the cops unless you just leave quietly. Come back at ten tonight, that's

when we throw out the food. Now come on, I'll help you up," for his words had caused me to slump into a vacant seat. He even had a kindly look on his face and his meaty hands were smeared with breakfast butter.

"Help me up!" I repeated, hardly able to believe what I had heard. "Help me up! No thank you, indeed." And stunned and bewildered I walked back out onto the street. I could not even take a step or two before I was forced to stop and rest myself, leaning my head against the cool glass window of the Hickory House Coffee Shop. I pressed my face against the silky chilled surface. The goldfish customers looked at me from the other side of the fishtank. Their mouths were open and I wondered how it was they didn't just swallow so much food and drown. My head was aching and I was quite naturally swaying with exhaustion—so strangely was I weak and fatigued—but I managed to unplaster myself from the glass and continue on my unknown path.

Before me now was a huge McDonald's, all gold-yellow and three stories high, tucked in among the other shops. At least here was a place I would be welcome! Inside I waited on line to purchase a large object like shimmering baked tripe, called the Egg McMuffin. This I covered in ketchup, though the girl was reluctant to give me as much as I would have liked. In addition I received a large black coffee and a thick, pale fruit drink, made, I was told by the man behind me on line, from a mixture of pulverized wood pulp and the skins of banana blended and combined with artificial purple flavor.

With these trophies on a tray I found a seat, a tiny plastic seat cemented firmly to the ground in front of an even tinier table made of false wood or *wood of the gods,* as I had heard this style of Formica referred to. I gazed around me, sniffing the cool air rich with old hamburger juice and fried tallow and intestines, and though normally I would have found these odors delightful, I now felt queasy; the sides of the room started to grow dim and then dimmer and then moved in quite quickly and close to me, while the roaring in my head grew louder and more loud. Now everything was perfectly black and my head felt as if it had been made on Jupiter, so thick and globular it seemed at this time.

It may very well have become enlarged in size; in any event my head collapsed over to one side and the rest of me followed. Maybe I was overcome with an American ague; maybe it was a recurrence of my old brain injury received at Joey's; maybe it was squirrel-poisoning, or the consequences of my emotional trauma; but all I can say for certain at this time is that everything grew very black and then I rested.

When I awoke I was on the ground, with a group of egg-eating breakfast customers looking down at me with disinterested interest. "My food!" I said, springing up and glancing around on the table. "Who has taken my Egg McMuffin?" But alas, everything I had purchased was gone.

However, a man in a bowler hat with a nice tan, carrying a cane, was kind enough to buy me a coffee himself and bring it to me, insisting I sit again in a chair. In an accent like Kent Gable's he said, "There, there, my good man, you must take it easy for a while. When was the last time you've had anything to eat? Can't you get yourself into one of those programs to dry out?"

"What?" I said, furious now with myself and those around me. "Is that what you think? That I'm a drunk?" And I half-tried to bare my teeth, in the old spirit, but all that came out was a sorry moan.

"Now, now, it's really quite all right, you know," the gentleman said, "didn't mean anything by it." And he scurried off, leaving me all alone.

After some time I did feel resuscitated and stood up, determined to find out what had happened to my Egg McMuffin and coffee and fruit drink. At each table where people were eating those same foods or something similar I stopped to glare and ask them where they had gotten the items. Then I soon saw that this would not work and that perhaps it had even been a busboy who had thrown my food away. I then waited until various customers had left and sat down to finish up what they had not eaten.

Various chunks and crusts of Eggs McMuffin lay dying at the bottom of the little boxes, and on some plates were pancakes, very succulent and rubbery. So I filled myself, though I was beginning to learn the effect of myself on these people when not in the company of a museum representative or Maria Fishburn. My hair now was quite matted and wrinkled, filled still with wilted feathers, and my bare chest had lost its oiled hue.

When I had eaten my fill I slowly pushed through the revolving doors, waiting until someone else stepped in to push them around for me, for I was by now as weak and unsteady on my feet as the dwarf or any other New York bum.

As if drawn by an invisible string I continued to make my way downtown. For some reason—here another small blank spot remains—I found myself on a bus headed toward what would be the south of the island. I seated myself in one of the seats marked FOR THE ELDERLY OR HANDICAPPED. Across from me sat a lady with a hat decorated with small plumed feathers and a series of tremendous moles creeping across her face like mice. Also there was a woman wearing a leopard-skin print raincoat, and a man with great sheets of dandruff decorating his blue shoulders. The faces shook back and forth on their stems at the sight of me, a garden of disapproving flowers. I was understanding that perhaps I was not in such good shape today, though what might have happened to me I still could not fathom.

Even the bus driver looked horrified, and soon I had cleared a round space of seats beside me that stretched some distance down the bus. When I realized what I was doing to those around me I stumbled up and asked to be let off.

Behind me the door swung shut with a pneumatic sigh. In any case, I now, away from the crowds, felt myself to be perfectly at ease. The coffee had taken some effect, and it was a lovely day. Down here there seemed to be a nice breeze coming in off the East River, or perhaps even from the bottom of the island, a nice reeky fish smell that reminded me of a hot day down in Jaranekta. Where I was, when I got to the corner, was on the Bowery and East Houston.

The shaking feverish chills of strange American origin came over me again and I sat down on a stoop to rest. I was wrong to feel the coffee and egg had created an improvement; consumed with an endless trembling and thoroughly weak once more I put my head down on the pigeon-encrusted step. The tinny sunlight felt shattering to my eyes and I tried to keep them shut, wishing above anything that I had kept a shirt with me from my suitcase in the hotel instead of insisting on prancing about in all my native nudity. And though I was not disturbing a soul but rather merely resting before standing up again, trying to revive my strength, wouldn't you know it but a policeman appeared on the scene and, prodding me with a delicate toe encased in a heavy black shoe, he asked me to move along.

"Now, I don't want to have to disturb you on a nice day like this. Sleep it off, go ahead. Just do it someplace else where I'm not around, okay, buddy?" he said, and he looked at me with a squint that suggested I had better do what he said.

Nearly weeping with fear and fatigue I got unsteadily to my feet and surely would have been led off to the station or the hospital when at my side a strangely dressed man nearly half-bent over, took my elbow and with a ferocious stink of fish and urine about him said in a slurred, demented voice, "This is my pal. What for are you bothering him? Leave him alone, you hear me?"

"Sure, sure," the policeman said, listless and indifferent.

"A Vietnam vet'rin," the bum said to me. "Yes, indeed."

"You are?" I said.

"Me?" the companion said. "Heh-heh! That's a laugh! You and me were friends over there, don't you remember? Man, you farther gone than I am!"

"Sorry," I said, "I think you've made a mistake," and expected he would then release me, but instead he clutched me more firmly and I tried to concentrate on keeping up with his athletic erratic path. Finally he led me into a small rubbish-strewn park and there pushed room for us on a green park bench filled with other similar kinds on this hot day. Through my bleary eyes I was able at last to examine his most unusual outfit: placed around his waist he wore the empty frame of a television set missing the glass, though with the vertical, brightness, and contrast buttons still attached. Also there was a small hole marked COLOR CORRECT-O-VISION, so I understood it must when working have been a color television set. Several miles of string, rope, and baling wire were wrapped around him, holding on not only the television set around his waist but various pieces of colored plastic and garbage bags. These presented a gay spectacle and in fact I had to admire him both to myself and out loud. Over some portion of his anatomy or television set he had draped a faded blue greatcoat, now buttonless and stained and pitted with the remains of a thousand nightmares.

"Yeah?" he said. "You like it? You like? Oh, brother, I thought you would. I've been waiting just to show it to you, I'm quite the dude in it, aren't I?" And he tilted his head back to howl with laughter, revealing long spinelike teeth, yellow and nearly gone.

From this great overcoat he delved deep inside and removed a half-empty bottle of one Thunderbird wine and, gazing at it somberly and lovingly, he unscrewed the cap, wiped off the top of the bottle, and presented it to me. "You first," he said. "In honor of my finding once again my brother who I had believed to be gone from the face of this earth forever."

I felt quite hesitant, depriving this man of what might very well have been his only source of support. And yet when pressed—"Here, come on, purpleman, it'll make you feel better,"—I could not rightly refuse. As I say, I had had this craving since rising, for something, who knew what, and I had not received such a generous and open offer since leaving New Burnt Norton. Here was something given eagerly and willingly, with a desire honest and undeniable. Who was I to rise above such an occasion and ruin this man's belief that he had found his brother? So I gave him a small salute and took a pull on the stuff, which had a cauterizing effect on the lungs going down and nearly did bring back pure and certain memories of the pomade or pombo Yerba used to cook up back on the mountainside of Bawwaar-Yaas.

"Ahh," I said, and wiped off my mouth, "you were right indeed."

"So," the friendly television-set man said, "you see? Just listen to Daddy-o."

"Ah," I said, and took another pull before returning the bottle. "Is that your name then?"

"Is what my name?"

"Daddy-o, my friend. Is that your name?"

This caused my friend to break down with laughter and he chortled until his most awkward television set shook up and down and he nearly fell off the bench with pleasure, causing several other old bums sitting alongside him to try and place stupefied kicks at him and ask him to fuck off. Finally, gasping, he drank slowly and cleanly from the bottle and placed it down at his side, holding on to it carefully with one hand all the while. "Daddy-o," he said. "Oh, I know you know. You my long lost son, that half-Vietnamese kid I got that whore from Hanoi knocked up with. Tha's right. My boy." And he looked at me fondly. "Yeah, why don't you just call me Daddy-o." There was even a tear perhaps in his pus-filled eye.

"Well, okay," I said. "I think the alcohol is doing me some good. What do you say we go over to the nearest liquor store and I'll buy us another bottle. Maybe I can knock this bug out of my system before it takes over completely."

Daddy-o's eyes, though quite yellow and irritated looking, even pus-filled as I have said, beneath his crazy hat of twine and Baggies, lit up at this and he gave me a slap on the knee. "Heh-heh," he said. "Well, all right! I knew you was a son of mine from the moment I met you!" And he drained the remains of his bottle and placed it under the bench, where it was snatched up by an old slug of a man who attempted a small battle over it with another to make sure there was nothing left in it at all. Carefully clutching my arm to make sure that I would not escape, he led me to a liquor store, tiny and on a corner and lined with shelf after shelf of metallic bottles of alcohol in indiscriminate shades and colorations. Daddy-o pointed out the shelves he subscribed to, those filled with bottles of Ripple and Thunderbird, prechilled in their own personal icebox. "The greatest thing since sliced bread," he said, I think, for he spoke his words in small clusters, dividing them into short ostensible groups of two and three and rendering those words on either side of them nearly incomprehensible. There was certainly not a full sentence that he had spoken so far, although in my blurred condition it made little difference to me.

"Look, I don't want that stuff," I said. "I just want something to warm me up," as the chills were now upon me and I wished something to burn through me as in a winter toddy. "What about some bourbon?" And with this Daddy-o let out another peak of screaming laughter such as I was already growing used to and nearly knocked some baskets of dollar bargain wine over onto the floor in his hysteria.

"You got any money," the manager or salesclerk of the store said, approaching us with a scrofulous look, as if accustomed to such antics and such clientele.

"Yes, I do," I said disdainfully, "and I would like a bottle of bourbon, please. A pint of Jack Daniel's."

The salesclerk, wrapping it up, asked for four dollars and thirty-five cents. Knowing how little this left me over with, I nearly asked him to put it back, but then, seeing the joyous face of my new friend, I said, "Ah, what the hell. You only live once, right?"

"For sure," Daddy-o said. "And quite frankly, I don't like the taste of other bourbons very much, although if presented with another brand I would drink it. But in your present condition, I don't want you to get sicker. Rather, you are merely looking to straighten yourself out."

Bewildered at this sudden outburst of logic from my friend, all I could say was, "Right," and I tried to help him negotiate the door once again with his massive television set. Then we returned to the park, where I cracked open the bottle and we rested out in the sun.

30

Perhaps my spirit was now broken, for I no longer cared about my past life and in fact began halfway to enjoy the new. To be perfectly honest with you, I made no attempt to find out what had happened to Maria Fishburn or anybody else for that matter, though sometimes I thought of Parker Junius in the hospital and wondered how he was doing.

It was booze booze booze all day long down in the bottle-and-slag heaps and I did love to drink. I was not bad at learning the ropes, believe me either, and many people half my age would not have made so quick an adjustment.

Oh very early each day would come the spitting and coughing and hawking and the urination against the wall, which was sometimes in Daddy-o's case filled with blood and agony, for he was not a well man and depended on me as much as I did on him. Then the examination of the various bottles lying around: was there anything left to drink in any of them. Each in turn was held up to the light for examination and shaken. There were others sleeping outdoors at this time of year—the place we generally chose to sleep was a kind of hole near the underside of a bridge and it was a good place for sleeping, cool on a hot night.

Then rising I gathered up the few belongings we had and attempted to straighten out Daddy-o, slapping him on the face one or two times to get a little life back into him. He didn't look good in the mornings. Without his TV he seemed naked, though he wore many rags; his eyes were yellower than ever and a lot of snot hung down from his nose, his fingers would be reaching up around inside of his mouth—he was always afraid he was losing the last of his teeth, which he was—and then with his cracked hands, split and fissured like the red powdery top of Mt. Bawwaar-Yaas, he rolled up a cigarette from a tin of old cigarette butts he kept next to his chest. That is, if there were any butts in it. But generally there managed to be enough for one smoke, which we would step out into the sun and share and look into the river, gagging and phlegmy as we spit back the night we had just passed.

And the sweet reek of old urine and perspiration in the morning, yes I did love those ancient smells and the inhalation of cheap tobacco as I assisted Daddy-o into his TV set and myself dressed to represent god knows what, in my small fur piece made of rat fur or marmot invested with fleas that Daddy-o had found in a rubbish heap and I wore even in the strongest heat, and still with my dogs' teeth and jawbone and naked chest and also carrying a large-sized lady's umbrella.

This I have to tell you was companionship, and the next thing was blinking in the light to stagger across town, neither of us saying anything, only trying to breathe and with bitter expressions on our faces and contempt.

Our territory extended up one side of East Houston from Broadway to the Bowery and beyond, though sometimes on a hot afternoon we moved over to the park or down by the side of the river. Directly across from the Bowery was a partially demolished building surrounded by a fence, and it was here we used to take a nap in the afternoon on the bed of bricks, or throw drunken stones at the wall on which was painted, now that I think of it—though it is blurred thinking I am thinking, for there is not much that was not blurred during those blurry, alcohol days—the outlines of two men, silhouettes, I guess you would call them. Sometimes one or another of us in a rage would fling bottles of stones at these figures, drunkenly flailing and swearing in despair and weeping tears of drunkenness. And whoever had worked themselves into the rage would generally end it by trying to throw himself under the wheels of the passing automobiles. But one or the other always stopped whoever was doing this. Daddy-o was very protective of me and vice versa.

Very soon I had come to look like him. On certain days, if we had a buck or two we hadn't spent on booze, which was rare, we would go over to the Volunteers of America store, where rack after rack was laden with stained and crumpled suits; bathrobes of silk paisley; smoking jackets; old Qiana shirts printed with penguins; Bermuda shorts and Lurex ties; dresses in lavender or yellow with pink spots and suit coats in size forty XX; green shimmering tuxedos with roaches breeding in the lapel pockets; platform-soled shoes with the platforms nearly six inches thick; the remnants of an entire civilization, in other words.

"You see," Daddy-o said, "it's very important that a man such as yourself dresses for his station in life. Now me, I got a look. But you, you we got to *cultivate*."

He swore up and down at the little old Spanish lady who ran the place, sitting behind her counter piled full of little religious altars and magical beads and pictures of Roberto Redford. She was very fond of me, though Daddy-o tried to introduce us time and time again. "You know Roberto Redford?" she said to me each time we went into the place. "His legs, they are too short for his body. This is a terrible thing, no? Here is a man, fully grown, and his legs are only one half the size they should be. His waist and his torso, they go down nearly to his knees."

"You stinking harlot." This is how Daddy-o spoke to her, although it was not personal, but how he spoke to any passing woman. "I know all about you and Roberto Redford. Whore! What have you got in this dump for my friend today. This man

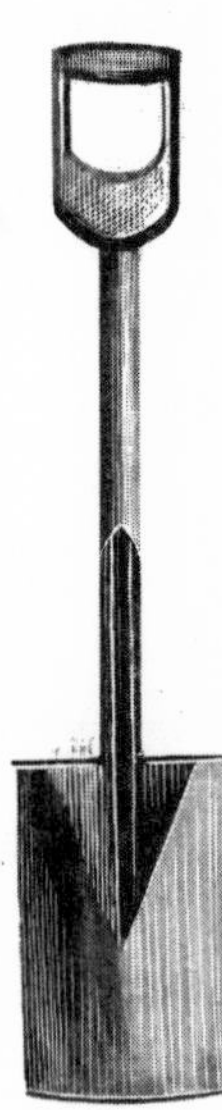

is a cannibal, didn't you know?" And he made a devouring motion with his mouth. "And he needs suitable clothes befitting his position."

"No, I din't know your friend he's a cannibal," the Spanish lady said, rearranging her rows of old dolls dressed up as Madonna, and turning her little candles. She grinned and gave me a wink. "What's this handsome cannibal doing in the company of an old bum like you?"

"This cannibal man, he's my son," Daddy-o said. "That's why he's in my company, slut face. Now shut your trap and show us the goods." Meanwhile while he spoke he had found a pink plastic raincoat and was examining it in the light of the air.

"Watch yourself and your language," the Spanish lady said. Her eyes and mouth rimmed with makeup caused her to resemble an old flamingo that had seen better days. "I'm not going to let you in here no more, if you talk like that, Daddy-o." To me she handed a pair of sunglasses, presumably not new in style, pointed up at the sides and made of red, plaid plastic any one of my sons or even my wives would have given some eyeteeth for.

"Put them on," Daddy-o suggested, and then stood back to stare at me. "Perfect fit. How much?"

"For you, twenty-five cents. For your friend, a dime."

"Okay," he said. "Throw in the raincoat and we'll take them."

And soon with these items I was dressed to kill; apparently it was necessary for me to dress like this, at least in Daddy-o's mind, and I did not mind complying, never having led this life before or having a mentor in it.

There was a group of us, as I may have mentioned; Harry, Kusa, Kato, Willadad, Daddy-o, Mel, and myself, and these other fellows—though they themselves apart from Daddy-o all dressed in vomit-colored bums' coats—appreciated and approved of my outfits, calling me "the soul brother from Africa" and certainly making me feel wanted.

Now even after all this it was still only early morning and the liquor stores not yet open, but we took our free cups of coffee from the Spanish lady and went to where there were a bunch of TV sets always turned on in the window of a shop on Broadway, and the two of us stood in front of it to watch the "Today" show. Though Daddy-o's feet were plunked into boat-sized shoes he could not stand still for long, for his legs had no ankles or calfs because something strange had happened to him over there in Vietnam and his legs were straight up and down, the legs of a two-legged buffalo, and me like a filthy punk rock-and-roll star, with my harlequin sunglasses I kept on to keep my eyes out of the light, for how they ached, my eyes, and stung like two bumblebees sitting right in my head.

We were both in a sorry state caused by this alcoholic condition, so after a time we did sit ourselves down on the pavement to watch the televisions. Now at first there was a beautiful model aged twenty-two years old—"Mm, mmm," Daddy-o said, and some dribble came off of his lip although he could not see and was practically blind as a bat due to some accident or other in which he had lost his glasses. "What a treat, hmm, my son?"

Now this young girl was explaining how she had managed to collect one million dollars which she had presented to the next guest on the show—he would be there following the commercial—in order that he might contact the aliens who had befriended him and whom he missed greatly. And using the money he had found them, and they were going to let him join them that very night.

"Now that certainly is something to do, isn't it?" Daddy-o said.

"What do you mean?" I said.

"I mean, that is really something, isn't it? Isn't it?"

"I guess."

"What do you mean, you guess? That really is something, isn't it? That girl collecting all that money to give to some guy to get ahold of the aliens? Huh? Isn't that something?" And he tried with his damaged legs to plant a kick on me.

"Yes, that's something. Now shut up, you're making me miss

the show, and I can't hardly hear it anyway, through the window of the store."

"I tell you," Daddy-o said, "If I had a million dollars I wouldn't be giving the money away like that. Would you? Huh?"

"No, I guess not."

"You guess not? Boy, you a fool if I ever saw one, who don't even know his own mind."

But I paid Daddy-o no attention, for there on the screen, to my wonderment, was Kent Gable, obtaining the interview. "But I know him!" I said. "He's a friend of mine!"

Now Kent explained that thanks to the girl he had found the aliens and that he would be joining them that night at 12:00 A.M. Eastern Standard Time; and he made his apologies and bid the people on the planet good-bye. "I can't tell you all how happy I am at last," he said.

"What is it like to be happy?" the interviewer said.

This cracked up Daddy-o. "Woowooo!" he howled and rolled over on the sidewalk. "Woowooo! Oh, I don't believe it! What is it like to be happy! You tell them, Mgungu! You tell them what it's like!"

By now I was used to his crazed laughter, and in fact I too had become prone to strange and sonorous cackling of my own that I would release unheeding of any humor in the surrounding conversation or air. But his was simply deranged, while mine was laughter given as I remembered involuntarily embarrassing moments from my past.

Now Daddy-o's laughter started me off too, as it made me remember when Kent Gable had escorted me into the bathroom in the Greek-American House of Belly Dancing, and pretty soon I was lying on the ground laughing also. And in a minute the rush hour pedestrians had started walking down to Wall Street and were jostling and hopping trying to get around the two of us rolling on the sidewalk in front of the television store in the morning sun. At this my sunglasses fell off my nose and cracked apart when somebody stepped on them. Daddy-o would have gotten up and started to demand money from the woman who had broken them, but his television set frame hindered him from sitting up and down too quickly, and by the time he got to his feet she was gone, and the owner of the store stepped out and asked us to move on.

And this brought me back down to earth, for I was terribly sad thinking of Kent's departure, and that we had not really had a proper good-bye.

Next we went over to a liquor store and looked in the window, gazing at the rows of bottles dreamily, which meant it was time to see what we would do for some cash.

We stood in the middle of the street, on the meridian that runs down East Houston. Daddy-o started swinging his TV from side to side and shifting from one foot to the next. "I got the blues," he sang. "I got the blues. Wa-wa-wa-wa. I got the blues."

"That's fine," I said. Daddy-o danced as the cars went by; therefore I took out my harmonica, an imaginary harmonica I removed from my pocket of the same kind I used to play up in my hammock on New Burnt Norton before my middle boy named Radiocity stole it and ran off in the woods to join the Greater Pimbas, who lived mostly now in a housing development.

I was playing the harmonica so Daddy-o might dance. And I, too, was a-dancing and he was a-dancing and the cars passed by. Then Willadad Brother showed up with Harry, and they were carrying buckets of soapy water and a little ammonia sprayer, mostly empty, that they had found, and a bunch of grease-covered rags. "All right!" Daddy-o said. "All right! Make ourself a little money, all right!" And I was puzzled, not being familiar at that time with what we were going to do.

"We are washing ourselves some windows, soul-brother," Harry said, and he took a swill of a pint of Old Grand-dad from the bottle in his pocket that was nearly empty, and the rest of us scowled at him. "You go find us a couple boxes to sit on,

Daddy-o," he said, and Daddy-o stepped as usual straight off into the traffic and walked between the cars as if they were not even there.

"He is going to get himself killed," said Willadad Brother, and we watched Daddy-o as he walked nearly directly into the side of a fast-moving car.

"That boy is crazy and nearly blind too," said Harry. He stepped up to a car as the lights turned red and went to work washing the window of that particular car. "No," the man said, unrolling the window. "No, thank you." But Harry kept on smearing the car window with grease and then dabbed a bit of ammonia on the window until the man was forced to hand him some change as the lights turned to green. Yes, I thought, I did like my new friends and found them most spontaneous, Harry strutting back to the meridian—for such a small thing truly did him good—and the group of us standing around shaking ourselves, because all of us at that moment would have liked something to drink. You would have to say that there was a certain tribal togetherness and a great amount of spirits. And that was what I loved and had missed and supplied me with much *moodla*. For while I loved Maria and Parker Junius and my uptown friends, I realized I had never known such spirituality with them, and this was where I belonged.

So I was happy and at ease.

Then the lights changed color again, and before the cars had stopped moving Daddy-o was out there holding up his greasy sponge and pointing to the windows and the drivers were shaking their heads no, no, no, no, go away. So he went over to a silver-colored Mercedes and, tapping on the side window, put in his hand for a donation. And yes, he was handed money. He came back over to where we were standing, strutting like a bull rooster with his wires and antennas and garbage bags trembling and shaking and he said, "Look at this. This man just gave me money *not* to wash his window."

"Let me see," I said, and pointed to his closed hand, but he would not show me how much he had made and carefully buried the coins inside some of the secret pockets he had inside the television set.

This was how the morning passed and even a little while into the afternoon when Harry collected enough from us for a couple of bottles, and because this was a group of friends he was trusted with the money and came back with two large bottles of the vino that we passed around.

A huge diesel truck pulled up and stopped when the lights changed to red and started honking. "What he want?" Willadad Brother said. I wet the rag and started to walk over to the truck, and the driver, a big fat fellow, handed out the window two bottles of red wine with some French name on it that reminded me of the days when I was on the cocktail-party circuit, a longer time ago it seemed than I was able to remember. And these bottles I brought over to the other men.

We stood around discussing and studying the labels and thinking of where we were going to get a corkscrew. "Thank you, brother!" I said to the truck driver when the lights changed. "I thank you sincerely, and bless you for your *moodla!*" And I turned and called to Daddy-o, "My friend, do come here and bless this good fellow!" Daddy-o stepped out into the street, where a fast-moving car in the fast lane clipped him on the side and knocked him down with a shattering sound.

"What are we going to do?" Willadad Brother said, and the car coming up behind Daddy-o's body slowed down and tried to stop but could not before it hit him again.

I ran to his body and placed myself over it, indecipherable with grief, but the men came and lifted me away and said it was necessary to put Daddy-o in the ambulance. As they lifted him up and took him away, I remembered the two of us, Daddy-o and me, riding the subway trying to collect some money by panhandling, Daddy-o in his television set doing a soft-shoe shuffle back and forth and the garlicky urine reek of the two of us as I played my mock harmonica, "Wa-wa-wa," and Daddy-o shuffled back and forth collecting money so the two of us could share in a bottle of booze.

And I remembered that cold-hearted blur that comes over you when you drink so much the entire world becomes invisible. And Daddy-o and me getting into a battle over some nonsense, but both of us too drunk to do serious damage to each other and falling down in a slag heap, not waking up until hours later in search of some more booze. I remembered all this and more. And I saw how this kind of life had aged me rapidly, though if I had not had Daddy-o there to teach me the ins and outs of survival I probably would have grown older much quicker.

I thought to myself, Well, maybe it is time you got out of this one, Mgungu. And I looked at the other men and realized for the first time how very much younger they were than myself, and that while I would miss their company more than I wanted to believe possible, I could little afford to lead such a life for much longer.

So I drank a conciliatory bottle that Willadad handed me, as he said sadly, "Here, Mgungu. Maybe this will be of some consolation to you." And I tried to make plans for how I was to get out of Manhattan, and yes, even the United States of America, without any cash and even without a passport.

And whether or not Daddy-o was dead or was going to die I didn't know but I did not feel that I was exactly carrying good luck around with me. My hand went straight to my neck; it seemed as if it had been sent directly to the jugular by a force not my own. And missing thereupon were my decorations. My GUARANTEED FOR A YEAR label and my jawbone necklace; both had gone. I piled through the contents of my fetish bag. Though this may seem to have been an inappropriate time to do so, these devices were important to me, and though unbelieving I believed it necessary for these objects to adorn me, thus offering my friends some protection from my ill *moodla*.

But there was nothing left in my fetish bag. All that was there was my picture of Jackie O., which I had managed to slip out of the hotel, now bent and cracked from being without a frame. And my friends the bums clustered around to gaze at her radiant visage; they were very much in awe, and the photograph was greatly manhandled from one person to the next.

And who knows what I would have done after the ambulance took Daddy-o's body away had I not gone back to washing windows and found myself scrubbing or rather dirtying the window of a long, large, green limousine, pale green and luminous and with much flashy and trashy equipment on it. And from the window a thin hand was beckoning, beckoning to me.

31

took a few steps back in surprise, bumping into the car stopped at the lights in the next aisle. The back window of the limousine unrolled the rest of the way automatically with a soft, rich hiss, and the face of Reynard stuck out shrill and foxy and his green suit did not appear to be looking so clean but was a little worn around the collar.

"Hello, Reynard," I said.

"Get in the car," Reynard said.

So I opened the door. What else could I do? There was nothing much left to move me one way or the other. And I waved to my young bum friends, Harry and Willadad and Mel, who stood drinking from their bottles of wine, and my heart felt engorged in my chest like a pig's bladder.

It might have been a drunken dream they were staring at, me in my pink raincoat and seedy, stinking clothes climbing into the elegant leopard of a car. "See you guys," I said, and the lights changed and the car pulled off and in the rearview mirror

I saw them standing behind and jumping up and down and hooting like monkeys.

Well. That was one period in my life, I thought. "Christ, you stink," Reynard said, and himself was swilling from a bottle of bourbon. A little bulldog of a man sat next to him, dressed in a suit with ponderous paunch.

"Let me have some of that," I said, and tried to take the botttle from Reynard.

"None for you, my man, you are staying off the stuff. What a stinking mess you are. Take a look at yourself. How old are you? Sixty? And you look every day of it. Where did I go wrong taking you under my wing the way I did and letting you in on things you had no right in knowing? Disappearing like that! Do you know, you missed the whole goddamn dance festival! I've been worried sick. Why didn't you come to me when you needed help?"

"I . . ." I said. "I didn't know where you lived."

"Well, it's lucky I found you when I did. Mgungu, I'd like you to meet Mr. Kirk over here. He's going to be your lawyer."

"Lawyer? I don't need a lawyer."

"Now, I want you to listen to him very closely, as he has worked out a little plan for how to get ahold of your money."

"Have you seen my wife?" I said.

"Well, that is bad news and that will come in time. But now, listen to this gentleman."

I had to listen to Mr. Kirk, a man of beet-red proportions and with a scar over one eye, handsome and fortyish, yet handsome in a very pockmarked and sinister way, as if a bulldog had a bad case of acne. He was very friendly and said in Brooklynese, a local jargon or one of the American dialects, "I'm real pleased to meet you, Mr. Mgungu. I saw your picture on the cover of *Time* magazine. It'll be an honor to tell my wife I met a real cannibal. I guess there aren't too many like you. Isn't that right." I nodded and pleaded silently with Reynard to give me a drink. "Now we're going to take you over right now to dry out, Mr. Mgungu, and when you come out we're going to set

you up very nicely and your financial situation will be a thing of the past. Whether or not we can get you out of the country is another story completely, but I'm working on that. All you have to do is sign these papers here and we'll be able to open up your checking account immediately and this will give us some control of Maria Fishburn's trust fund as well. Believe me, this was not an easy thing to do and you'll thank me for it later when you're feeling better. But for now it is safe to say that you won't be seeing Maria Fishburn again, and since you are her husband this is the way she would have wanted it."

"What do you mean, I won't be seeing Maria Fishburn again?" And the two men looked at each other.

"Maria—was involved in some kind of trouble," Reynard said.

"Your wife—has fled the country," Mr. Kirk said at the same time.

Finally Reynard said, "Well. I'll have to be honest with you, Mgungu. I guess you'll find out sooner or later. Your wife has committed suicide. Earlier today her body was dredged. Of course you realize what this means."

"What?"

"You are a rich man. But there is some terrible news I have to tell you."

"What is it?" and this I said in a suspicious tone, allowing nothing to be pulled over on me.

"That picnic . . . remember it?"

"Yeah?"

And Reynard looked at Mr. Kirk. "Mgungu, Maria was involved in certain criminal activities—that steak you ate—"

"What about it? I remember. It was good."

"It was human flesh, not steak."

"Oh, no! So we're all cannibals!" And I was more shocked than you would have believed possible, though that this should startle me to such a degree it is easy to doubt, considering how earlier I had capitalized on this asset. And yet it did. A sense of horror came to me.

"No, Mgungu. None of us was hungry. You were the only one who ate the meat. I'm afraid you're in a lot of trouble."

"But we're here to help you now," Mr. Kirk said. "The court will recognize you as a primitive and uncivilized person and will give you a reduced sentence. And when you come out you will have all that money."

"Court?" I said, and my voice rose an octave. "What court?"

"Mr. Kirk is a great lawyer," said Reynard. "What are you getting so upset for? Calm down." At that moment an insect flew in the window and landed on my hand. "Look at that," Reynard said, "somebody's visiting." It was a red bug, speckled, a black head. However, it sunk its little teeth into the back of my hand, biting me quite severely, and I shook it off, gritting my lips.

"I know little about the American legal situation," I said, "and I am no financier." This had been apparent to me from the days of the unsuccessful Feed the Infants swindle back on New Burnt Norton. But Mr. Kirk said not to worry, and Reynard poured us all drinks to toast to me, and drunkenly I made my mark on the various pages, signing *Mgungu Yabba Mgungu*.

Among the papers were my passport and my marriage certificate as well as my visa and smallpox vaccine papers, and my telegram inviting me to the International Dance Festival. It never occurred to me to ask where these things had all come from. "You'll be rich beyond your wildest dreams, Mgungu," they told me. "You can buy whatever you want."

But I was sullen and scowled out the window.

"If I get to the right people with the right amount of cash, you'll never have to see the inside of a court at all," Mr. Kirk boasted. And for my own good they said they were taking me to an alcohol rehabilitation center to dry me out, in case it was necessary for me to appear in front of a judge when the executors got through appointing Maria's estate. But here I was very firm, putting my foot down and insisting they let me out.

"I won't go to the dry-out center," I said, and I was filled with an unghastly desire. I would have jumped out at the stoplight if necessary, for I felt very oppressed and needed time to brood. And though usually I am not a very firm man they saw how strenuous I was and that I would have busted loose a window at that point.

So they agreed to let me leave; but only if I would meet them later that day at an appointed time at an uptown museum, a convenient locale, and then I would go with them to be rehabilitated. And believe me when I say that although they looked sinister I trusted them absolutely. Who else did I have to trust, if not them, but myself? And the way I was feeling about myself at that minute was none too good. Here I was trying to be civilized and all I had done so far in my time in the United States was to slip further into decomposition.

I think they were surprised they were letting me go so soon after finding me; but they had no intention of letting me disappear for good.

32

Boneless with grief, I saw then that I could never again be near people as long as I lived, and that in fact if there was a place in the world more isolated than New Burnt Norton it would be best for me to remove myself to it as soon as possible.

The car stopped at the lights. "Let me out here, please," I said. "I'm going to be sick."

"Okay, okay," Reynard said. "Where are you going?"

"I need to walk," I said. "I want to be alone." In my haste I would have strangled him to be free.

"Mgungu, I only came to help," Reynard said. "You don't want my help, fine."

Then I was stricken with guilt, and said indeed I appreciated all he had done for me.

"Well, all right then," Reynard said. "You go and be alone. It's all been a shock for you, I can see that. We'll pick you up, around four this afternoon, up in front of the Whitney museum. You know where that is?"

"Yes," I said.

"Got any money?"

"No."

"Well, I'll bring you some later on. I'll look after you from here on."

So I left them and began to walk. I walked endless blocks, the wind, though hot, chilling my inner ear, a metallic voice screaming and irritating the lining of my brain until it swelled and reddened . . . and this grinding of bones! This grating of gears! The shatter of lightbulbs on an empty floor! Would it never stop! I may have been suffering from the d. t.'s; I was as sensitive as a raw tooth exposed to the wind, the weight of the very air on my back pressed on me remorselessly. The bitter beams of light, the chiming of tin cans—I was sorry now to have let myself be so chiseled and peeled by the world, a receptacle, no, a receiver for the slightest current of words, as if my skin had been scraped like a slice of burnt toast.

And the two brittle lungs, gray and thinly etched and veined, opened and closed like a fish mouth. Each breath, so painful to me, had even become painful to the eyes of others, I could see as they passed around me leaving a wide berth. Why, I was no better than a common criminal! My entire body was covered in thick beads of oily sweat and in my throat something humid and rich had sprung to life like an egg.

But my god, how grotesque! This could not be me, a human being, stalking endlessly his reflection in the glass, but was instead some hideous animal, dank and sweaty with gray matted fur. My yellow teeth loomed long and the whites of my eyes were no longer clean and silky but discolored and speckled with blood like an ominous portent of the future, a return to animal life. And the hyena laughter and chuckles followed me down every street in the hot sunlight filled with ashes and soot.

However, in New York nothing remains the same for very long, and after all, had the dwarf not once told me himself that the emotions of the savage are short-lived?

And, quickly and callously, I hardened myself toward myself and the crime I had committed. Soon there was a solid grin pasted on my mouth as I walked along thinking of unknown colors and talking out loud to myself, saying over and over, "I have one and a half million dollars. I have one and a half billion dollars." What was I going to do with all that money?

Well, there were many things I had in mind. A sports car I had seen advertised in a magazine, for example, modeled on an antique car of the past with leather seats as soft as a bed of worms, costing nearly sixty thousand dollars and with long rolling fenders. A red mink coat was something else I had always wanted, and a television set the size of a movie screen. I decided I would outgrow my fear of machines, although for the car I would hire a chauffeur rather than drive.

As I walked I could see the green limousine on the street, following me patiently like a guard dog. "Go away!" I waved at them. "Leave me alone!" But the car did not move, and when I walked over to see what it was that they wanted from me the car leapt forward and pulled away, leaving me standing at the corner. I wondered if this was part of the protection plan they had told me about. But all I could do was shrug, glad they were gone. Glad they were gone? I will say this was highly unusual for me, for I was never glad to see anyone go but instead generally did anything to cling to people at the last second of departure.

I tried to put them out of my mind. I went into Bonwit Teller's to decide what presents to buy for my wives now that I was to be rich. In front of the store there was a sort of metallic statue or sculpture of chrome—a mockery, in a way, to me, for it was as if it was saying: "Look, Mgungu! Chrome out here on the sidewalk! While you are still in the stone age we have here a big slab of perfectly made chrome we call art!" But then, on the other hand, wasn't all New York saying this to me? Wasn't the whole world laughing, really, at my being such a primitive dull-witted guy?

I determined more than ever, since I was rich without being dependent on anyone else, to turn myself into a civilized man. I gave a kick at the big metal sculpture. Before I could go into the store, though, I passed through the dangerous-looking doors made of glass that whipped around and around without surcease. It took me a very long time before I could work up my courage to step in through them, though at last I plunged and went forth. And then, once inside, although mentally I had adjusted to the fact that I was now a bachelor millionaire of sorts, I realized I was still wearing the same old bum's clothing.

Oh, what luxury and cool banks of cosmetics. How sterile everything appeared, so clean and untouched by human hands. There were glassed banks and counters of little tubes of makeup, varying colors, troughs of lipstick in mauves and greens and blues, and jars of expensive slops and soaps in heavy glass boxes. And there were various brands: makeup for Oriental women and makeup for pale-haired women, and for women without any hair at all. And tweezers, pluckers, mincers, and teasers of every sort. There were places where a woman could sit down and have toiletries applied to her face by others! How my wives would have loved it, in particular my wife number four. And at the thought of Maria, sorry sparkles came into my eyes, for I remembered then that as she was not here I could not share it with her.

I ambled in and around this wonderful funhouse. When I stopped it was only to put on some blue shadow over my eyes, to remind myself of the sea on New Burnt Norton, which on a clear day was visible from the hemp-and-wood lookout tower my grandfather had built.

At each counter there were darling little free samples I saw many women helping to themselves, and of these I tasted many.

And I put on a yam-colored sticky stuff on my cheeks in two round splotches just as I had seen some women do to themselves. And now I was really enjoying myself, and I pretended briefly to be sweet, lost Maria Fishburn, who constantly wiped onto her face lipstick. I found a purple Christian Dior lipstick that seemed to be the same color that she would have worn and I put this on. And I looked at myself in the mirror and it was indeed the same color she would have worn, and briefly again I felt very sad.

Then I thought—forgetting I had no money—well, perhaps I should buy some of these little gooey sticky tubes for my wives and wait until I get the Bank Americard, the MasterCard, the Visa, and Diner's Club Card that had been promised me by Reynard and get them brassieres and other clothing then. I stopped in front of a gaudy-looking black metal counter where the makeup, meant for going out at night, was filled with glittery and shimmering gilt bits. "You can put it in your hair or your eyes," a woman dressed like Dracula was saying to a group of twelve-year-olds. And she flicked some coppery-gold powder into the air, where it caught a drift of air-conditioned wind and spinkled electrically.

"Oh, wow," the twelve-year-olds said.

And I determined this is what I would buy for the gals back home and I would get it back to them no matter what else happened.

I had to test it, though, and first I dipped my fingers into the little pots of stuff and began to put it on my hair, when I saw, only for a second, the hand of the lady Dracula behind the counter wave. And the next thing I knew a hand had clamped itself on my shoulder and I tried to shake it off, so engrossed was I in what I was currently doing. For these tubes of paint had a lot of magic power in them, or *moodla*. And I, too, longed to resemble the most ideal of birds after my drab days as a bum clad in a pink raincoat and a pair of broken sunglasses. For how important I believed it was for a person to be decorative, I have already described elsewhere in the text.

But the irritating hand remained still on my shoulder, and when I looked up, it was a guard.

"You're going to have to leave," he said.

I was escorted to the door, the man saying the whole way how guilty he felt. "For you and me are the real brothers, brother," he said. "Don't get me wrong. I don't approve of any of this shit. The rich get richer and the poor get poorer, and that's the truth."

"I am rich now," I could not help but say. "I'll buy you anything you want." For I had taken rather a liking to this man after overcoming my initial shock, and it was good to have a friend.

"Yeah, sure," and he smiled. "But seriously, I do hate to have to ask you to leave, and I hope there is no offense taken. Why shouldn't you be allowed to come in here when there are all these rich women with nothing to do all day but buy makeup? But for the prices they are paying they feel they are entitled to shop with members of their price range only. Shit, if I could afford to I would quit this job and get me a ranch out in the Panhandle. Hey, are you all right?" For suddenly I felt quite faint and weak and nearly disintegrated beneath my knees.

"Yes," I said, "not to worry. I'll be back when I get my credit cards."

"Yeah, sure," the guard said, helping me through the revolving doors. "Take care. Crazy old Pygmy," he said as he went back into the air-conditioned cool, meaning not for me to hear that, I am sure.

And as it was nearly time for me to meet Reynard and Mr. Kirk, I began to walk uptown to the museum, walking rather slowly to conserve my strength, and my new eye makeup glittering and flashing in the heat, as if my eye was winking individually at each person who passed by.

I wished I had taken them up on their advice and had gone back to Reynard's co-op to take a shower and get some new clothes, but the shock had been a great one, believe me, for a few minutes at least, and I had needed to be alone.

When I arrived at the museum I had additional time before they were due to arrive and so I decided to take a look around. Here I was more bewildered than I had been in the department store. For I had not previously the time nor inclination to see modern art. And while the objects in the Museum of Primitive Cultures—dried skulls and religious totems and carved canoes—were familiar to me in a certain standard way, resembling things I had seen in the *National Geographic,* this stuff here at the Whitney did not look like art at all. I was not sure if it was a joke, or perhaps if some kind of mistake had been made and I had come to the wrong place altogether.

To a large wooden crane, plastered with tar and feathers, was attached a kind of slanted ramp, and on the ramp lay a large cloth object spattered with black and resembling a dead or dying chicken.

On a wall was a canvas, entirely white, to which the artist had neglected, apparently, to fix the paint.

There were some broken clay pots and underneath them a ticking alarm clock.

There was a painting of a comic-book page; there was a painting of a soup can; there was a painting of a man so perfectly real that every pore and pimple was sadly visible; and there was a sculpture made apparently from crushed car parts.

And none of it was very well constructed, so that I felt I might have been more talented myself. But perhaps this was the point after all.

In this fashion the afternoon passed. Now, even an animal needs some privacy, and though I did not understand why, since Reynard and the lawyer had been so kind to me, and had not shown any disgust with my behavior, I could not contemplate seeing them in a few minutes and in my sorry state I could not bear to face them. So I went to clean myself in the bathroom, a room behind a door marked with a kind of square scowling shape I took to indicate MEN. It was empty, until I noticed a sign over the toilet that said: "LADIES, PLEASE FLUSH THE TOILET AND DON'T WET THE SEAT." And I wondered, were bathrooms here coeducational, as was the case at the nightclub Warehouse 29. But I was mistaken, for a young female entered, saw me, and, emitting a scream, struck me on the arm.

I did try to escape surreptitiously and continued my walk around the museum, but the female pointed me out to the guard, and I was asked to leave the museum due to my embarrassment and depravity. I had had no desire to lurk in the ladies' room, I can assure you, and it had been a pure mistake.

I was now very tired and rested outside behind a cement wall, thinking I would surely see Reynard and Mr. Kirk as they drove by. I watched a lot of different people enter that museum, and it was a sight to behold. I was sincerely sorry that the trip might come to them as a disappointment. It occurred to me I might warn the individuals as to the terrible condition inside the museum, but I did not feel myself fit to be in the company of other human beings.

I contemplated buying a bottle, or acquiring a deserted island off the coast of Maine and founding a possible utopia where I would live alone, unable to damage others. I was as emotional now as an adolescent with too many hormones, and suffering, too, perhaps from the tragic accident of Daddy-o, as well as from alcohol-withdrawal. I believe I would have abandoned civilization at that moment, taken my fifty million bucks and gone home, had I not at that minute seen a squad car pull up and rush with pointed guns into the museum.

A thought came: they were looking for me.

With that, another two squad cars pulled up, and also the green limousine of Reynard. And he, and the dwarf Mikhail, and Mr. Kirk stepped out of that limousine and took the additional cops into the building, as if they were going to point me out. At this I thought, Oh, Mgungu, you are a befuddled old native and paranoid. But something, perhaps an instinct, would not let me go back into the museum or near the car. So I turned and scuttled across the street in an uptown direction, keeping my head down low.

33

Now I was footloose and believed myself to be a common criminal. I might have thought I had made a terrible mistake, and that Reynard and the dwarf were seen with the police for reasons other than to set me up; but on passing a newsstand I saw the headlines, thick and black, trumpeting on the front page of the *New York Post, CANNIBAL MANIAC HUNTED BY COPS,* and I knew I had not made a feeble mistake.

"I have no money," I said to the newsagent.

"So?"

"So, I think you are going to allow me to have one of those newspapers, at the risk of your own termination," I said and bared my teeth, while allowing the rims of my eyes to flush suddenly red.

"What?" the newsagent said, not understanding. "Maybe I don't understand your accent."

"I said, lemme have a paper or you're going to get it right in the keester."

"Hey, what are you talking about, buddy?" the agent said. "I can't do that."

"See that headline?"

"Yeah."

"Well, that's about me. I want this paper, or you're going to be victim number two." Sadly I was forced to do this in order to receive these needed goods, otherwise most certainly this never would have occurred.

"Yeah, sure," he said. His eyes began to bulge and it was a sight to behold. "Have a paper. Take two. Take a *New York Times,* too," he said, scrabbling with the papers before him. "You want a *Interview? Vanity Fair? Spin? The New Yorker?* You need an extra copy to send home? Here, here."

"No, no thanks. The *Post* will be fine. Thank you very much, sir. I will long remember your generosity."

"You're not planning to come back here, are you?"

"No, I don't believe so.

"Can I have your autograph?"

"But I am delighted," I said, and signed my mark, Mgungu Yubba Mgungu, before bidding him good-bye. Then I absconded with my paper to a bench placed in the middle of Park Avenue and proceeded to read the various articles about the cannibal.

How terrible it was to see myself projected in such a light!

Basically, these articles stated that I had arrived in this country for a dance festival given by the Museum of Primitive Cultures, and had met and married the heiress Maria Fishburn with the prime motive of killing and eating her, in particular with the hopes of grasping her fortune. Remains of a still-unidentified body were discovered in her apartment by her friends, Reynard Lopato, described as a well-to-do art collector and dealer, and Mikhail Van Hoosen, the well-known author and journalist. They had come into the apartment and found me broiling a steak, and when questioned I gleefully showed them a number of other steaks in the deep freeze and also other parts of the body. The Museum of Primitive Cultures was currently having its financial affairs investigated by the state for evidence of their involvement in the case, as it was understood that the Fishburn family, and in particular Maria Fishburn, had long been supporters and patrons of the museum. There was a possibility of fraud in connection with the cannibal native of New Burnt Norton and the museum. Parker Junius, museum curator, had suffered a heart attack some time back and was currently installed at Mt. Sinai Hospital. Meanwhile, a ten-thousand-dollar reward had been put up by the family of Maria Fishburn for information leading to her disappearance, and another ten thousand had been added to this anonymously for information leading to my arrest.

Then there was a brief biography about me, stating how I was a primitive savage and immoral, spoke no English, was sixty-five years old, had three wives, and was unChristian. It was believed that if hungry or trapped I would repeat my actions, and that cannibals were known to have a particular fancy for young and fleshy girls. In fact women in the Manhattan area were advised to stay out of the parks and off the streets late at night.

Next there was an article about the history of cannibalism, and descriptions of Australian aborigines cooking white men at the turn of the century, and about how Captain Cook met his demise. There were some old-fashioned engravings of these cannibals in the act, reproduced in the paper; also there was an item on Page Six with a photograph of me, taken at the wedding. In it I was grinning foolishly, my decorative paint on my face lopsided and clownish.

And there was a brief interview with one Officer Marc Goldblatt, of the Ninth Precinct, who claimed to have found a man, several weeks earlier, in the park, who he believed to be the cannibal in question. "He was doing strange things with a squirrel," Officer Goldblatt said. "At the time, I believed him to be just another nut case. But there was something about the guy that made me think twice. I went back to look for him later but he was gone. I never seen anybody act that way with a squirrel before. You get them from time to time, though, at least I've heard about them. Squirrel freaks."

I kept leafing through the paper; just then a man sat down next to me with a portable transistor radio, through which a man's crackling voice announced, "1010 WINS. 24 Hour News. Coming up on the hour: the story of a man crushed by his own television set costume. Hit by a car, pieces of the set pierced him like shrapnel."

"Where's the goddamn ball game," the man said, twisting the dial.

"Wait!" I said. "I want to hear that."

Then the man looked at me as if he had not noticed me before. "Hey, aren't you the cannibal maniac?" he said and scurried off quickly into traffic.

For a few minutes, before I could begin to think about what

to do with my own fate, I mourned deeply. What stories that man could tell! Once, on seeing a man taking a hair out of his food, Daddy-o declaimed on the danger of swallowing this, relating how his friend Bronx Bronco—who had been drunk for three years straight without a sober day to break up the monotony—had swallowed a single hair which, taking root in his stomach, had grown to such a length that it had killed him before an operation could be performed.

I wept briefly, one tear droopy wet and hot from my pinkish eye. I sighed, honked my nose onto my sleeve—believe me, there were times when it was not enjoyable to have a deviated septum with articles sticking through it—and determined now to be master of my own life and to take hold of my own future. But what to do?

I could not begin to imagine how these awful rumors had been spread about me. Cannibalism? For a moment it crossed my mind that Maria Fishburn was in fact dead, as suggested by the article in the paper, or that something terrible had happened to her, but . . . I knew these rich people. I no longer had faith in Reynard and did not believe his story that she had killed herself. Why, she had probably just taken off for the Bahamas for a few days, on her honeymoon, and would return at the beginning of next week. Reynard himself had previously suggested that Maria might be in some kind of trouble, that some underworld figures had used her apartment as a slaughterhouse for an ill-doer. Or, as the dwarf had mentioned, a breaking-and-entering incident might have led to the murder of one of Maria's houseguests. It had been Reynard's advice that I lay low while they sorted the matter out; which I had done, without their help, and would continue to do until some better explanation placed itself before me.

Actually I still could not believe the whole thing was not some kind of mistake. It had little to do with me.

It seemed the best thing for me to do would be to give myself a disguise. But what kind of a disguise could I purchase with no money? Well, I would have to think of that later. The first thing, I had to go and see Parker Junius in the hospital and perhaps get some of the facts as to what the true story was. He would know the truth at least. I sincerely doubted he would turn me in, being rich enough not to need the money. My dear friend, with a heart attack! I wondered, too, what had brought that one on, for he had assured me that since his last one he had kept himself in the fittest of health. I had a strong longing to see the old fellow, and I beset myself in an uptownward direction, maintaining close to the walls, until I arrived at Mt. Sinai.

Then from the beginning, I entered.

I debated on bullying people in the lobby into lending me various parts to my disguise. From a man sitting in the corner, I might request a hat; from an Oriental lady I might beg a little pair of gilded earrings, and so on. But secondarily I decided this might not be wise. So instead, at the main desk I asked the receptionist in what room Parker Junius was staying. "He's on the eighth floor," she said. "Room eight-o-nine. But I believe he's stated he doesn't want any visitors. You can check with the floor nurse, though. Or I can call up for you."

"That's all right, sugarheart." I said. See how easily I found it to talk to Americans now? And particularly women—I just stuck in that "sugarheart" as if I had been living in the United States my whole life.

And I went up in the elevator quaking, surrounded by doctors and visitors and stout little nurses, expecting each of them to give a scream and leap on me; but not one of them recognized me. It was too busy a place; they had other things on their minds besides worrying about a cannibal. Perhaps since I was described as being sixty-five years of age in the paper I was less recognizable, since obviously people were expecting an older man.

On the eighth floor the nurse was not at the nurses' station. She was probably using the facilities or watching television off somewhere, or else participating in group sex. So I went directly on down the hall and into Room 809. And there he was, the wise man Parker Junius, lying prone and prostate on the bed.

Well, he looked just terrible, I can assure you. Lard white, his tufts of hair had sunken weakly onto his flaps of skin that decorated his face. He did not have on his glasses; they sat dismembered at the little table on the side. And also his face was quite remorseful in expression; though this was I presumed because he had removed his false teeth, which I never knew he wore until then, and now they swam in a glass at the head of the bed. There was a sink set against the wall, and the window looked out over a scene of construction, where men with jack-hammers pounded away. It was very noisy, and to speak one had to yell.

"My friend," I said, shutting the door, "I didn't know you wore false teeth. I am torn with sadness." I noted that hanging up in the open closet were his clothes; a striped sweater, a pair of white shorts, and a white shirt, along with a pair of sneakers —a real athletic outfit. "My friend, how did you land yourself in this dump!" I shouted.

Sadly all Parker Junius could do was groan from his bed, and one eye on his white face fluttered open weakly.

"What?" I said. "So tell me, how are you feeling?" And I would have slapped him on the back in my joy to see him and still alive, had I not been so worried about the approach of the nurse and constantly glancing at the door. He groaned again. "What?" I said. It was most difficult for me to hear him over the sawing and drilling of the construction, but this is what he said, in part: "I haven't many convictions; but I have three or four that I hold strongly. One is that people on the whole had better not devour their family, or at least their wives. Another is, that people in an advanced stage of pulmonary weakness had better not receive any upsetting news at all, and if you have come here to torture me, I suggest you leave at once."

"Me? Torture you?" I was shocked and hurt, but then realized my poor friend was more deranged and ill than I had thought. "My dear friend, I fear you have been sorely misinformed," I said. "Someone has been spreading terrible rumors about me. How I wish I had gotten to you first to explain what has happened. If only things had been different since my arrival to this country!"

"Ah, things are always different from what they might be," Parker Junius said. "If you wait for them to change, you will never do anything."

"Yeah, sure," I said. "Now, tell me, what is it you have heard?"

As it turned out, he had been playing squash or racquetball (what the difference is between those two sports anyway, I have never been able to figure out and have always longed to know) at the New York Athletic Club, where he played nearly three times a week or when the opportunity presented itself. While playing, a friend of his shouted onto the court—and believe me, from what Parker Junius said, I was led to understand the New York Athletic Club was not a place where shouting, or New Burnt Norton natives, were allowed—"Hey, I hear Maria Fishburn has disappeared, and the museum is under federal investigation! Why, you old goat, Parker!" And this was the shock that kicked old Junius's ticker over, sending him to the hospital via ambulance, on that evening some weeks before, when I had returned to my hotel only to be thrown out.

I remembered what he had told me about his former heart attack, seeing the molecules enlarged, and also the feeling of scabs being torn from his two eyes, a curious-sounding sensation indeed, and I asked him now if it was the same. "The same, and yet different," he said weakly. "I don't hate you anymore, Mgungu. I have always been fond of you, you know."

"Don't worry about it."

It did not look as if he would die. He said he had been feeling better until I came along, but I assured him I could not stay long, which seemed to pick him up a little bit. I tried to tell him the whole news story had been a mistake, that Maria Fishburn was alive someplace and well, that in any case I had long since stopped being a cannibal and would never now devour human flesh unless inadvertently, but he refused to listen. And here I had been hoping to get some true confessions from him!

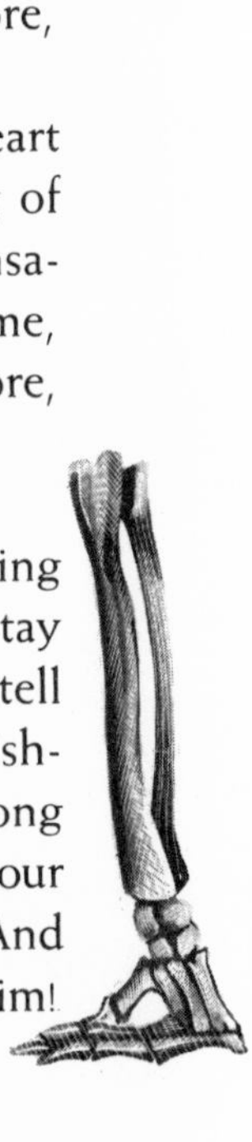

"Please bring me a glass of water," he said. Then, wetting his lips, he said, "You know, I've been rereading *The Portrait of a Lady*. Henry James. James is interested in civilization with a gloss, and he deals with characters who by their nature are sensitive to nuance and perceptions. What he is talking about is different ways of seeing. To start with, those differences are right on the surface: the look of things—statues, buildings, places."

"Yeah, sure," I said. Poor old fellow, his mind was wandering as usual. As he talked I was removing my soiled bum's garb and dressing myself in his lovely white athletic clothings. Oh, how pure they were, and smelling faintly of laundry bleach.

"Beyond that, he looks into relationships—relationships between the moral and the aesthetic. These things in some way are distinct. But before we get into that, let's look, Mgungu, in a more general way at what James is saying. There are a lot of statements in most books—particularly in *The Portrait of a Lady*—and it is always a temptation to stop and footnote these, don't you think?" And, rambling on, he made it aware that he was obviously quite far gone. I looked at his chart on the foot of the bed, and the vital signs were better than I would have expected. "What a different set of circumstances Isabel Archer had from those of Emma Bovary! And what does Isabel have in mind when she says she's worrying about her independence? If only Maria had worried about this just a trifle! And what does Isabel feel about sexual relationships—in the erotic overtones, the imagery carries a great deal of this. Is Isabel afraid of marriage? Yes. Does sex frighten her? I think so. Birds. We see a great many birds flying about."

"Do you want some more water?" I said. I held the glass up to his lips and he impatiently pushed it away.

"You might put it this way or you might not—what Isabel is looking for is someone who will measure up to a very high set of specifications. A new relationship is something she is always interested in, yet also something she tires of very quickly."

"Frankly," I said, "I really don't know what you're talking

about. I wish I did—but there it is—I'm not following a word of it. And for that I'm sorry."

"This whole business of acquisitiveness—getting rather than spending—is very important. Kant—the German eighteenth-century philosopher, you know—said, 'You should not regard people as merely a means but as ends unto themselves.' "

I couldn't believe he didn't think I knew who Kant was. The poor guy was pouring out his last thoughts as quickly as possible, one following the other with little train to his thought. Though, as I say, it was too noisy for me to hear everything, and due to his weakness Parker Junius spoke barely above a whisper. "*Ficelle*—do you know what that means, Mgungu?"

"No, I guess I don't, sir," I said. I took up his hand and held it tenderly between my own.

"*Ficelle*—a kind of thread or string—serves the same purpose, for Henry James and myself, as a confidant. You, Mgungu, have served as my *ficelle*, for this brief time."

"Sure."

Now the nurse came into the room and saw me there, holding his hand and dressed in white. "You aren't supposed to be in here," she said. "This man is very sick." And then her eyes flickered a little bit, and she stared at me hard and on purpose. It was very rude, especially for someone with as mean little eyes as the two she had plopped in her head. I don't usually take a dislike to people, but she was quite a little minx. "I know you!" she said with a squawk. "You're the cannibal maniac! What are you doing here! My god! What a vampire! This man isn't even dead and you hover like a buzzard! I read about you in the paper today!" And her face broke out in brilliant red blotches, fascinating to behold.

However. I put down Parker Junius's hand and I approached the nurse. "Are you planning to tell somebody about this?" I said sternly.

"Yes, of course," she said. "I'm going for help at once."

"Then I'm afraid I shall be forced to withhold you here against your will."

And I removed the top sheet from over Parker Junius, since there was nothing else in the room but my smelly clothes, and, holding on to the nurse's wrists with one hand—she was strong and did struggle, but I would not let go—I shredded the sheet into strips, using my other hand and my tough teeth.

Then I bound her to the bed, a great massive iron hospital bed, making sure she was tied so severely she could not escape. By now Parker Junius was tossing and turning in the bed, due I suppose to the narcotic drugs they had given him, if that was indeed the medication he had been given, and mumbling, "Oh, I'm so ashamed. How could this have happened?" This poor guy was quite delirious and did not know what he was saying, nor did he have any idea any longer of what was happening around him.

I gagged the nurse, and then I snuck out down the corridor and left the hospital, muttering under my breath and praying no one else would identify me on the way.

34

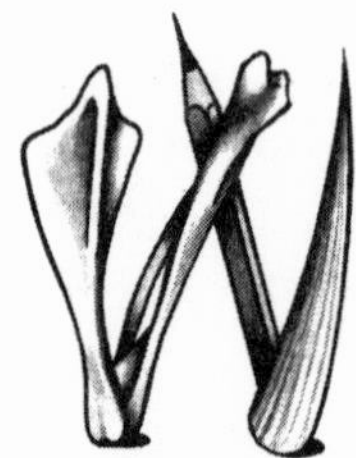

hen I sat perched in my kapok tree on New Burnt Norton, weeping over the death of my little piggy, I never expected that only a few years later I would be dressed in tennis shorts and wandering around an all-night grocery store, evading the police and knowing not what to do.

How little time it took for me to make a mess!

There is a certain fruit, inedible, that the children use to play games with in the village; it is the color and shape of an orange, with smooth, lightly pocked skin. Inside this fruit is an object warped and convoluted as the human brain, a strange deformation. Who knows what the point of such a fruit is, or even at any given time what may be found inside it?

At least, these were the thoughts that ran through my head, and I thought: I must now take my life into my own hands. I must begin to live. For up to this time I had been a victim of circumstance, allowing myself, though not without desire, to be whipped here and there, hither and yon, from cocktail party to press conference and picnic. What a drag. And my thoughts continued: I really should now attempt a firm action, thus revealing my true *moodla*—but what to do, what to do? And a bitter smile crossed my lips, for this was ironic.

After leaving the hospital I trudged about for some hours, finally dozing off on a park bench, after covering myself with some newspapers to remain hidden. These I found, when I awoke, had left the lovely starched and white clothing of Parker Junius slightly blackened and even a few words of the newsprint had worn off on various places; viz: on my chest was written the word *CAN* and also *DEVOURS*. I would have to have these articles cleaned before returning them, no doubt about it. And with my two forefingers I wiped two circles around my eyes, and rubbed my forehead, for I was more than a little weary.

Now the city looked an ugly place to me, with the buildings leering and toothful on the street, becoming everywhere a set of jaws. Even the darkened windows of the buildings were eyes, and there were few cars and trucks on the avenues and even fewer passersby. The gritty pavement was tiring to my feet, and the sky not dark enough for night-time but a snarling pin. I longed for the cool, mushy ground of New Burnt Norton and the sky like a helmet, perfectly round, with its heavy white clouds and stars of twirling, probing needles, calm and sharp.

I walked over to the Hudson, past the Broadway bums, no longer a friendly crowd dozing dead in the doorways but relics of my distant past. How I wished Daddy-o were with me, and I debated going to rouse my pal Joey, pizzamaker deluxe, only he lived somewhere in Brooklyn, I believed, and I did not know how to make my way to this country.

The city was looking quite hateful, and the cars like powerful tigers seemed likely to run me over.

Also everywhere I saw the police, or imagined I did, and saw my own head placed on a platter with an apple in its mouth and the words "Ten Thousand Dollars" written before it. And the sight of blood, which usually did not bother me, continually came back at me: the dried and crispy blood on the white plastic tarpaulin at Maria's apartment, and the swollen head of the dwarf with his little bloody or chocolate-smeared hands.

And as I walked along the riverside I came to Warehouse 29, the fashionable disco.

Even at this hour, which was really not so terribly late, they were lined up in front of the place, wearing their mysterious costumes and resembling Americans such as Dionysus, Darryl Strawberry, Batman and Robin as well as King Kong and other heros. And I determined to go inside, without receiving any aid.

Yet I was nervous, and considered the shame and humiliation of not being admitted, but I thrust my way through the crowd in a fierce fashion. And the crowd parted, with different persons snarling, "Watch it!" and "Well, really, tootsie, if you need to get in *that* much!" and other bitternesses. When I arrived at the door I stopped, and could not remember what to do; but to my surprise the little window swung open and the moist white face of Joey's cousin appeared like a frightened lemur and I was admitted without further adieu.

Inside everything was quite different and not at all as it had been. Now, instead of rubble and detritus piled everywhere, the ground was of a highly polished metal and covered with an oil slick. There was no longer an elevator shaft, but instead near the entrance was a large swimming pool, blue and reeking of chlorine with colored lights flickering under the surface. Various people were swimming in it, in time to the music, and one man appeared to be drowning. I was shown into a room with tiny wobbly tables by a girl with a red mouth the size of a saucer and the color of gobs of raw meat. On the walls were a lot of paintings; what these were of I could not determine. No liquor was served, but only various kinds of ice cream in various flavors, described as "blueberry cheesecake, pralines and cream, honey pot," etc.

The ice creams were brought to me, unbidden, and I wondered why I was being so strangely accepted here and had not been asked to pay any money at the gate, nor had I requested any of the ice creams. . . . But I ate them anyway. And these ice creams, of which many varieties were brought to me, one after the next, were molded into nude male and female torsos and were decorated with creams and condiments of different sorts. The ice creams were served by women and men naked from the belly up.

The women's breasts were assorted shapes and sizes with nipples colored from very red to a delicate pink to an orange brown. Some of them reminded me of Yerba's, very large and cup-shaped nipples set on the ends of pendulous breasts; others were younger and springier.

But sexually exciting I could not find them, and in fact I was rather revolted to observe them so close to my food, as if an unworthy fly had approached. The men also were covered in vituperative oil or sweat, and wore jogging shorts or jock straps. Joey's cousin appeared and came up to me, his beady eyes hidden behind dark glasses, and he was most deferential and unctuous and also familiar with me, shaking my hand several times between his moist and hot one. It was like shaking hands with a jellyfish, as if we were old friends, and I thought, Well, perhaps I will make a new friend tonight after all, and perhaps he will advise me.

He sat down, his bodyguards or stooges standing ready behind his chair, and he was served some dishes of ice creams. "Liquor license," Guich was explaining, between bites of a vanilla goo mixed with slabs of banana, a terrible thing I thought, to do to a banana. "Very difficult to get one—we had one here but it was revoked. So until I can get a new one the place is a 'juice bar.' What do you think?"

"Oh, sure," I said, and I wondered if he had not heard about the reward on my head and my alleged cannibal and animalism. And suddenly he shoved up under my nose a tube of something resembling a nasal decongestant at the same time pounding me on the back, so that I was forced to cough and inhale very deeply.

When I breathed in the room turned very cold and I felt extremely dizzy. In addition the room spun around me a brief time before it stopped, and the spoonful of ice creams I was holding landed on my cheek. "Amyl nitrate," he said.

"Oh, certainly," I said.

"Like it? Ever had it before?"

"Actually I have not." And I experienced a feeling of isolation, but it lasted only briefly and I was able to smile at my friend. "Come on," he said and led me out through the disco, and the crowds bowed and scraped before the two of us.

Through a special door he unlocked with a key, he led me into the basement filled with pipes and crackling electrical wires. The Hudson was very near us; the basement was underground on shore and the river ran rapidly to the right of our ears, hissing and gurgling in a torrential fashion. Although I may not be correctly interpreting what I saw, the room, which on the floor was dirt, appeared to be filled with gray powdery toads, difficult to avoid stepping on, though they did hop out of the way at our approach.

And he removed a quantity of white powder and showed me how to ingest it through the nostrils, difficult to do with a deviated septum in the way, I can assure you. I did not want to mention to him that there was something vulgar and even obscene about the two of us in the basement stuffing this cleanser powder up our noses—for it did taste like Ajax, a brand of bathroom cleanser—but that if this was to be his thing and he was now my friend, I would go along with it. It certainly did numb the head, this stuff, if that can be said to be entertainment.

Then we returned upstairs and I went to the dance floor and began to dance wildly, without remembering that this was something of which I had no idea of how to do. A waitress kept bringing me shots of bourbon, and these, too, I consumed. And snowflakes fell from the ceiling of the room, turning once they hit the floor into flakes of soap powder, so I constantly skidded on these and fell, hitting my head every which way and that. From time to time I let loose with a cannibal scream that went something like "Yaaaauuuuggggghhhh!" which seemed to be well appreciated by my companions.

Soon it seemed to me that we were all doing one great big tribal dance festival, and I nearly believed this was what Parker Junius had intended, and strangely I forgot that the dance festival was over and imagined it was taking place now, while different photographers flashed my picture and the other dancers kept a wide berth around me, though pointing at me and staring, due I suppose to the greatness and majesty with which I danced. "The president-elect of the Lesser Pimbas!" I shouted, "Owner of one hundred pigs and nearly four wives! Heir apparent to a million bucks! MasterCard, Visa, American Express!" I was carried away briefly.

At last I went over to one of the sofas to lie down, realizing I was perhaps not so young as I felt anymore, and then I passed out, dimly imagining before I did so that I could see Maria Fishburn swimming naked in the pool with Reynard, who wore his green suit. And I wondered how it was that his suit was not ruined in the water.

Thus I suppose, asleep on the couch, some time passed.

When I awoke I was choking heavily and the room was filled with a thick, black smoke. Also there was the smell of burning popcorn and my eyes and lungs were seared as if bathed in some kind of acidic bath. "Hey!" I said, and sat up, "something's burning!"

The dance floor was empty and there was no one in sight, though a record, badly warped and woozy, continued to play. "Someone's left a hamster in the rain," a man sang. Pushing through the smoke I saw great flames spouting at one far-off end of the room and could not see at all in any other direction so boiling and intense was the heat and the fog.

I ripped up a pillow from the couch and, placing it over my mouth and part of my face, I staggered from the room and tried to find the exit. Meanwhile I saw some men chopping a hole into the wall from the outside, and they were firemen, who, when they saw me, said, "Here, get this guy!" and then helped me out.

Luckily they were very busy and unrecognizing of me, and went back to their duty of chopping down the walls of the building. Outside a vast crowd had gathered, consisting of the people who had gotten into the discotheque and been evacuated, and those who had not gotten in, but who still appeared to want to. The police were now rounding up these people and backing them off the pier. Otherwise they might have returned like lemmings.

And the fire engines were spraying water from the hydrants, and I saw that the whole backside of the building was up in flames and that the pier appeared ready to collapse into the water. There were police everywhere. I thought it a good thing for me to get out of the area. Some firemen standing outside wanted to give me oxygen, and said I had better go to the hospital.

But I knew I must escape. I staggered back and tried to walk some ways out of sight. More and more police cars appeared, as did several new fire trucks, now numbering nearly a dozen in all. It was a huge fire. There were flames everywhere, the air was filled with dense black smoke, and everyone had to be cleared from the area. Even the police cars backed away.

Some boats arrived and sprayed water from the Hudson into the fire. But it was no use. The flames shot higher, the building burned, and at last the whole of Warehouse 29 and the pier collapsed into the river.

Gathering up my strength I moved on. Soon I began to trot a little; I wanted to get away as far as possible from the source of the police. And I was brutal in my exhaustion.

At last I saw a Spanish grocery store and it was filled with light. I thought, I am without money, therefore I will take what I need. There is certainly enough stuff for all, here in this country. What I take will not be missed. For my throat was most dry and parched, and I could have used something to eat, too. I did not stop to think that in my present condition I might cause some attention; I did not know that I was black with smoke and reeked of bourbon, also granules of soap were stuck to my skin. Thus my white athletic clothes were ripped and disheveled, and somewhere along the line somebody had tied a long purple scarf around my neck.

But without thinking, I went into the all-night bodega.

There was a burly man positioned in my path; he was buying a fifty-pound bag of dog food and a six-pack of beer. Had his dog suddenly grown hungry in the middle of the night? I could not imagine, but from his appearance, so much larger than mine, I hesitated to ask him. I no longer trusted strangers, nor felt myself friendly to them.

So I looked about. And into my pockets I loaded a small container of yogurt, also some various mini-snacks and quick-energy bars. Then I removed some hen's eggs from their boxes and thrust them up under my shirt, doing so very quickly, for I saw a person, standing by the freezer, who was taking from it every frozen fried-chicken TV dinner that there was and eying me suspiciously. I debated taking one of these myself, but realized I had no microwave.

I made as if to leave the store, but at this exact moment I caught sight of two policemen entering. And then, in an overhead curvature mirror I saw myself reflected, and I saw how blackened and grimy I was, and the deranged whites of my eyes. "That guy over there!" the man at the cash register shouted to the police, and pointed to me. "He's a shoplifter!"

I began to bolt for the door; one of the policemen sped after and grabbed me, crushing the eggs that lay beneath my shirt. "What the fuck!" the policeman said. "I think I just broke something." And some yellow yolk trickled out from beneath my clothes.

So, though I was caught and arrested for shoplifting, when they took my name at the precinct they soon realized who I was: they had caught the cannibal maniac and he was me.

35

Often here in my cell I receive the sound of a single saxophone. This music has been at times astonishingly loud. The *wah-wah-wah* throbs on the air like the cry of some giant bird, probably a cassowary. From another floor or cell block this mocking voice comes, falling upon my mental spirits like a parrot being strangulated. Never before have I realized how closely the sound of this instrument, the sax, sounds like the voice of a human being, and a human being, at that, brought to the lowest of the low, the place where sadness passes into a grisly despair. This sound echoes off the steel and cement walls, and with each note the *oo-oo-ooos* bounce around and turn into *wah-wah-wahs*, until it resembles a whole orchestra of hyenas, weeping and mocking itself and me.

A short time after my pretrial incarceration a number of publishing companies came sniffling around offering me great sums and quantities of money for the rights to my life story. And there was more promised if I could write it myself, which I was well able to do and with plenty of time on my hand.

Mr. Kirk had disappeared—but luckily after this I was able to get in touch with him, though not without some difficulty. He operated out of an office in Brooklyn answered not by himself or a secretary, but by a machine that did not return calls but left a brief space for the caller to leave a message. As I was allowed only one phone call a day it took me several weeks to reach him. It was not until the news about the money I received from Crown Publishers to write my memoirs hit the newsstand that I heard from him at all. So surprised was I when I did get to speak to him that I said, "Is this you or your machine?"

There was a pause as if Mr. Kirk was thinking and then he said, "This is me." He had been working on my case, he said, and was anxious to find out several things from me. "First of all, what did you do after you found out you had been given all that advance money? You didn't get it recently, of that I am aware, but must have had access to it for several weeks. I wish you had let me know."

"Well, I did try to get in touch with you, Mr. Kirk, but I am afraid to say that while I was waiting for you to return my calls I went very much berserk."

"In what respect?"

"I indulged myself in every whim. I found, I am ashamed to say this to you, Mr. Kirk, that I had a terrible desire to receive products through the mail. The very idea of getting a package or a letter began to obsess me. In one week alone I went through more than forty thousand dollars writing away for products, however unbelievable this may seem to you."

"Products? What sort of products?" Mr. Kirk coughed or barked irritably into the phone.

"Well—cheeses, for example. I joined the Cheese of the World Club. And rupture devices."

"I really don't understand what you're talking about, Mr.

Mgungu—forgive me if I sound obtuse. Forty thousand dollars?"

"It was the Florida Perma-Mobile that ran the cost up—but let me read you some of the ads for the things I sent away for —just a minute here." And from a greasy billfold and passport wallet I took out a stack of newspaper ads I had clipped from various newspapers. " *'LONGER NAILS EASY AS A-B-C—IN MINUTES! AMAZING! Like movie stars with amazing STA-LONG NAIL BUILDER.'* I bought three sets at seven dollars each. *'HAIR OFF FACE LIPS CHIN ARMS LEGS—Now Happy! I had ugly, superfluous hair, was unloved, discouraged. Tried many things, even razors.'* That didn't work, by the way, and I tried to return it; there was a money-back guarantee but I never got my money back—maybe you could look into that if you get a chance. *'Now! Let me show you how hand reflexology can bring you instant relief from pains all over the body. Cure specific ailments . . .' 'Find Buried Treasure, locates buried gold silver coins, old weapons. Works through earth, vegetation. Discriminating models available.'* I ended up purchasing the one at two hundred and thirty-nine bucks. *'Now! Get Four Real Old Buffalo Nickels Only One Dollar.'* And for four ninety-five plus postage and handling I received a book of astounding new psychic prophecies, including *'How the CURE FOR OLD AGE will be discovered when a new area in the brain is found with amazing health powers that could be the miracle key to faith healing—When a DICTATOR WILL SEIZE POWER in the U.S. and later become the FIRST EMPEROR OF THE MODERN WORLD. Learn the astounding signs that point to a person that is alive today! When a NEW WORLD PLAGUE will needlessly kill millions because they do not know about a simple precaution!'* Truly these are exciting times that are upon us."

"Christ! My god, man, forty thousand dollars! It's not human!" I heard Mr. Kirk take a long suck on his pipe.

"For seven dollars a carat I took on an amazing opportunity for collectors of authentic gemstones to purchase genuine emeralds, cut by hand, ready to set! In presentation pouch with certificate of authenticity, signed by a leading Fifth Avenue jeweler! How could I resist an opportunity such as that, Mr. Kirk?"

"How many carats did you buy?"

"Hundreds! Thousands! I don't know! . . . *'Away with those curlers! For twelve ninety-five at long last a permanent wave that lasts and lasts!'* Now I may put away once and for always my curling iron and curlers. All I need to do is comb my hair with the new *Ondulamatic comb.* Immediately, at just one stroke of the comb, my hair will become wavy and it will stay wavy. *'Apply it cold, without electricity! The secret of this sensational Permanent wave comb lies in its double set of teeth! . . .'* For nineteen thousand, nine hundred, and ninety-nine dollars I acquired a home in Florida *'NOW! While prices are still low!'* In order to *'ESCAPE FREEZING WEATHER AND SNOW'* I purchased a *'completely furnished two-bedroom Perma-Mobile home plus a sixty-by-ninety landscaped lot with car port, utility room, Florida room, patio, and sidewalk included!'* All by mail! . . .Ten bucks bought me *'the amazing diet secret of a desperate housewife'* . . . fifteen dollars and I had information telling me how to *'duplicate sounds that trigger automatically Astral Projection and Out-of-Body Experiences!'* . . . I got free information, too, Mr. Kirk, don't get me wrong, I wasn't out to spend money if something was available for free. I received information for psoriasis sufferers, stopping hiccups, brochures on how to get a university degree by mail and job opportunities in New Zealand."

"Well, how much of the money from your book advance is left, Mgungu?"

"None, I'm afraid."

"You know, Mgungu, retaining a lawyer is quite expensive."

"But what about my wife's money? For am I not a wealthy man?"

"Unfortunately, no. Remember those papers you signed, back in Reynard's car? There have been tremendous problems with the Fishburn estate, and—"

I could not believe what I was hearing. "But sir, did you not promise to help me? Am I to remain a prisoner here forever, then?"

"No, no, no," Mr. Kirk said. "Of course not. I understand you're a foreigner; you don't understand the American legal system. Of course I won't abandon you. My assistant and I will be working on your case; I just won't be able to devote the time to it that I would if I were on retainer, that's all."

"Mr. Kirk, you are a very good man, and I thank you after all," I said.

"If you think of something, or want to speak to me for any reason, don't hesitate to call. You have my number. If I'm not in, my machine will be. I'll be in touch." And with these words he hung up, leaving me alone in the smeary phone booth, with the guard on the other side knocking and tapping for me to come out and go back to my cell.

36

or a while a group of supporters marched almost daily in front of the prison, holding signs. These signs said various things such as RELEASE MGUNGU, SOLEDAD BROTHER #2, PROTEIN DEFICIENCY SHOULD NOT BE PUNISHED, and other phrases and sayings. Some of these people had marched from California, stopping in Washington, D.C., on the way, and others were young civil libertarians and civil-rights workers. There was a group of students from the Columbia School of Law; also there were several famous political activists in the group, and these included movie stars and American Indians of a tribe who claimed to have eaten human flesh in the not too distant past as part of a religious ritual that included peyote. These last demanded to be arrested too, if I were not released.

So I was quite well known, as I say, for a while, and while it lasted it was a lot of fun. At night these supporters would be pictured on the television news inside the jail, and some of them were trying to eat nothing but meat for my cause and had eaten meat and meat alone for twenty-two days.

Also my case was discussed on a half-hour special, with F. Lee Bailey interjecting, about "Mgungu, a cannibal from New Burnt Norton who inadvertently ate his American wife." The conclusion was that I would probably be pardoned by the governor in the near future. There was an interview with the activist movie star, who, since the end of the Vietnam War had found many things to complain about. I was the third cause he had taken up that year, the one before me being the San Andreas fault, whatever that was.

Meanwhile my new friends would sit around after the news each night arguing my case, for they had all studied law in great detail, hoping to be able to release themselves from jail. And I had plenty of friends in jail. There was Murdoch, who would later be given ten to twenty for buggery of thirteen-year-old girls, and there was Bad Omen, a suburban cat burglar who had attended the Rhode Island School of Design. He had even once had a one-man show at the Whitney, a sculpture made from piles of ladies' underwear he had stolen. And they were a bunch of great guys, I mean, really, although they were murderers and rapists and drug dealers and various other felons. But you know, once you got to know them they were really nice, and though it is true on frequent mornings some prisoner would wake up stabbed to death with a shiv or maybe raped or would have had some other injustice committed to his person, this was due purely to environmental stress and it was understandable that these were tough guys.

They were always nice to me, though, calling me their celebrity and the Man Maniac, which was apparently a term of endearment, and offering to get me any kind of intoxicant or drug I would want, or even various types of sex, despite the trouble this would have gotten the fellows into.

And even the room would sometimes go into a kind of hush when I came in to watch the news. They didn't get to see many cannibals, I guess. "You see," Murdoch said, "it's like this, Mgungu. You've committed a likable crime, and also you're a foreigner. If they could of caught Reynard and pinned something on him, then your story would have held up. They would have put the blame on Reynard Lopato and then it would have been okay to let you go. But as it stands, Reynard is nowhere to be found, they caught the dwarf, who of course denied everything, and what's your word against his? They had to blame somebody, and that guy's a famous writer and knows all the ins and outs—ever read his book *Dried Blood*? He obviously spent years studying that case and probably had the best lawyers in the country advising him on this number. If we could only get those kids who saw you that afternoon at Co-op City. Shit. Would you recognize them if you saw any of them?"

"I don't know," I said truthfully. "People in this country look pretty much alike to me, white or black."

"My sister, she lives in Co-op City," Dagmor spoke up, although the news was over and he was trying to concentrate on a Bugs Bunny cartoon. "She has a bunch of kids, five or six maybe, and I bet some of them are that age. How old you say those kids were?"

"Fifteen, sixteen," I said.

"You want me to ask her?" Dagmor said.

"You asshole," Bad Omen said. "Five thousand people live in Co-op City. What makes you think any of your sister's kids would be the ones Mgungu saw?"

"Don't call him an asshole, Bad Omen, you have a bigger one than anybody here," Murdoch said. "Let him ask. Maybe his sister's kids are the same ones. Knowing Dagmor, I wouldn't be surprised. What else does Mgungu have to go by? It's worth a chance, anyway."

As I have mentioned, they were a bunch of real friends. They loaned me their lawbooks and showed me how to study up, though it did not do me much good. I used to get a lot of mail, too, some of it forwarded to me from the Holiday Inn during that brief period when I had been a practicing millionaire and had gone berserk writing away for products. Lately I seemed to be receiving a spate of Frederick's of Hollywood clothing I must have ordered in a frenzy, for I had no memory of it—crotchless underwear, nippleless brassieres, spike-heeled shoes tufted with pink fur, that sort of thing.

And there were hate letters, and letters from men across the country, mostly from Texas, saying they had often felt like doing exactly as I had done and didn't blame me at all. And there were people writing for recipes, and there were letters from women enclosing nude photographs and offering to marry me when I got out, or even saying they would come and get married to me while I was still in jail.

It was most unusual, but meanwhile my case was being appealed by Mr. Kirk, or so he said. And the time, although passing, was seeming to take forever. The court processes were very slow, and for every one step forward my case took, Mr. Kirk said something had come along to put it back two. But each time there was a good reason that this happened.

And the prison board offered to let me go to school, inside the jail of course, and I began to take two courses, geology and weaving. I had thought of taking a course in writing poetry, but I didn't, and why this was, is not absolutely clear to me.

One day during the period when I still thought there was some hope of getting out, I was paged to come to the visiting room on the grounds that there was a visitor. It seemed I no longer knew anybody on the outside, a fact that did pain me. I did not know who could possibly be visiting me and I was highly surprised to find Sophie Tuckermann, delicatessen owner and philosopher, on the other side of the Plexiglas wall.

"You look terrible," was the first thing she said. "What's the matter with you, you might have aged a million years."

"Really?" I said. I was worried and put my hand up to my face, almost expecting to feel furrowed wrinkles on my sebaceous skin.

"*Ach du lieber,* my little *affenpinscher,*" she said. "This is terrible to see you."

"Well, you look just fine," I said. "I'm glad to see you, my friend."

But in truth she did not look great and also appeared to have aged, so I inferred she was projecting her own feelings onto me. She was hunched, her eyes drooped, the folds of skin on her forehead and at her jowls were baggier than ever. This was the aging process for you. "So," she said, "I grow younger while you get older. Am I right? Ha! That's the way of the world, isn't it, Pierre?"

"Perry," I said.

"What?"

"Perry, you used to call me Perry."

"So? Who asked you? I used to call you Perry, whatever—that sounds unlikely to me. I don't know any Perry. So now I'm calling you Pierre. It's not all right with you? You don't like it, I'll leave."

"No, no, it's all right," I said.

"So tough luck, I'll stay. What are you complaining about, then?"

"I'm not complaining."

"Ach, Pierre, I told you not to get involved with that girl, what was her name, Marie?"

"Maria Fishburn," I said.

"I told you, stay away from her, she's not good for you, she's got nothing in her brain but dollar bills. So. But did you listen? No, you, a foreigner, were smarter than an old lady who had lived in this country for thirty years. Did it get you anywhere, Mr. Smartness? Here, I brought you a sandwich." And from her bag she removed a sandwich on a water roll. It was wrapped in a few paper napkins, through which the juice had soaked mightily, like an old diaper. And she squeezed this sandwich under the space of the Plexiglas divider, flattening it further.

I looked surreptitiously at the guard.

"No, it's all right," she said. "I brought one for him also, so he told me it's all right to give this to you. It's good, isn't it?" she called over to the guard.

"Yeah, sure," he said. He was wolfing on the sandwich voraciously.

"Don't eat it so fast, mister, you'll get a bellyache," she said to him. To me she said, "So what are you waiting for? Eat, eat. Or as you say in your country, *mangia, mangia*." And she laughed. "Pretty good, huh? See? Even me, an old Jewish lady, can learn to speak a foreign language. How's my accent?"

"Good," I said. The sandwich, soggy straight through, was even more grisly than I remembered them having been in the past. It was some kind of meat with a lot of mustard, though what the meat could be I did not want to think about. It was white and sweet and had the texture of a sponge. Even briefly the thought crossed my mind that another terrible joke was being played on me.

"Turkey roll," she said. "It's good, huh? You don't get food like this here, I bet. What do they keep you on, mashed potatoes? Ha! I bet. You look like you could afford to lose some weight, what did I tell you. I think what they're feeding you here is making you paler in skin coloring, a kind of mauve."

This may in fact have been true. It was a known fact, at least it was a known fact that some of my father's relatives used to believe, that a man resembled whatever victims he ate. That was why they always tried to eat one of the Greater Pimbas, who in life had been very powerful. They would eat the brains and the palms of the hands first, in an attempt to transpose the victim's intelligence and strength to the diner. The rest of the body went to the women and kids. But my father and my grandfather, too, had agreed that this was a lot of guff and merely a primitive superstition. Also it was wasteful of a lot of fine meat.

Still, there may have been something to it, for I had been reading recently that there was a lot of truth in primitive folklore.

"Let me ask you a question," Sophie Tuckermann said. "You and me got a lot in common. We both been through wars of our own kind. You used to fight in wars, didn't you?"

"Yes," I said. "But it was a long time ago we used to have intertribal wars."

"Well, same here," she said. "Only maybe not so long ago, nor for you either. So here's the question: What happens when you got hit in those wars? You didn't have any doctors, did you? You're a primitive man—do you feel any pain?"

"Well," I said, "it's like this: when a man gets hit with an arrow in a war, he has to think fast. He has to get away as fast as he can; otherwise somebody's going to come up and finish him off with a stone ax. Then it's dinnertime, and you know what that means. Not that it makes any difference if you're dead—it's only if you're still partially alive that it's a sorry deal." I put down the terrible sandwich. It lay like a mountain before me on the table. "It's difficult to run," I said, "with an arrow sticking out of your body. It's pretty heavy jungle up there and a lot of brush to run through if you're trying to get away and there's a three-foot stick coming out of your ribs. So the best thing to do is to break off the arrow close to the wound."

"*Oy gevalt,*" Sophie Tuckermann said. "You Pimbas!" But she was obviously fascinated.

"More often than not, if the wound is only in the flesh, the arrowhead rots away in time. And although the wounded person might feel sick for a while, he usually wouldn't die. But if the arrow is wedged in a knee joint or under the jawbone, or in the spine, it's not very comfortable, and if he's left crippled, well, then a lot of times he's put out in the woods to die."

"Just like the Eskimos on the ice floes," Sophie Tuckermann said.

"What?"

"You know, the Eskimos. If you get too old they put you out on an ice floe for the polar bears."

"Oh, no," I said. "We revere our old people. It's just the sick ones we don't like. They interfere with the *moodla* of the village."

"*Moodla?* I don't think you've explained this to me."

"It's like this—once in a war far from the village I was hit in the buttocks with an arrow. I walked for three days to get back to the village, the arrowhead sticking in my derriere the whole time. Because I was young and my *moodla* in war then was very strong, I felt very little pain. And let's face it—pain is simply an inevitable part of human existence, isn't it?"

"I suppose so." She sighed and stood up to go.

"Hey, wait a minute," I said. "Where are you going? Don't go yet—visiting hours aren't over. I don't get many visitors."

"No," she said, "I gotta go. I got a meeting in a little while. Oh! I almost forgot the reason why I came here, what I came to tell you. Wait another minute before I tell you. Don't you want to know about Mikey? You don't even ask me about Mikey. Tch, tch. You must learn to cultivate an interest in others, Pierre, despite your own present situation. That is the gentlemanly thing to do."

"Okay, okay," I said. "You mean the big guy with the turban who worked behind the counter in the delicatessen?"

"That's who I mean. Well, some good news has happened to him. He's going to be on Johnny Carson, he's going to show how to make delicatessen sandwiches."

"Well, I declare," I said, having heard this expression on a television show the night before.

"Yes, you may well declare," she said. "And if you're not going to eat that sandwich I may as well take it back. Mikey is really going places, and you, Pierre, what is going to become of you?"

I had not expected such a caring outburst from a calm philosopher such as Sophie Tuckermann, and there really were tears in her white eyes.

"*Ach du Lieber,* Pierre, I worry about you when I am not with you, though you may not believe this. Your story and your problems are what keep me up at night. Well, now I really must be off. I have a meeting with the Free Mgungu Fan Club, of which I am chapter president."

"The Free Mgungu Fan Club?" I said. "I haven't heard anything about this. And chapter president?"

"Well, chapter president-elect. Already there are several divisions or branches, of which the New York chapter is the largest."

"But what is it for?" I said.

"What is it for? What do you think it's for, you great ape. Why, we have a collection of memorabilia associated with you and your New York escapades. Also we write letters to our congressmen asking for your release. After all, who in this country today is not a cannibal in some way or another, and why should you be locked up simply because you were more honest about your need for human flesh? That last is part of a speech I am presenting this afternoon." And with her bags she began walking to the door, under the wary eye of the guard. I was shocked to see she now used an aluminum walker to get around and could only move a few steps at a time, placing the walker a few feet in front of her and then slowly edging her way up to it while clumsily holding on. It was a tragic sight.

"But wait a minute," I said. "Don't you understand? I was duped! I had no idea I was committing cannibalism! I gave it up a long time ago and only rarely today even wonder how a lady with a particularly delicate-looking haunch would taste."

Sophie Tuckermann then turned before she walked out the door. "You can't fool me, Mgungu," she said. "For why do the fish stay together in a herd, all jammed up together like that, when there is plenty of free space around them? Because it is meant to be, that's all. Fish are not bright enough to see their way through to the world around them. Or maybe they are lonesome. Or it might be for protection. I don't know. A bigger fish comes along, grabs one of them; maybe each fish feels it is less likely he personally will be grabbed if there are ten thousand fish on either side of him."

That lady was a real philosopher. But what she was talking about I did not know.

"The club is knitting you a sweater with a saying on it," she said. "I'll bring it to you when it's finished."

"What does it say?" I said.

" 'YUM-YUM,' " she said.

And though I spluttered again that it had not been a voluntary or conscious action on my part she left, saying, "That is what happens to those who do not stay where they belong." But she was a firm advocate for my stand, and she appeared often on the news over the next few years, holding up the sweater they had knitted for me, and saying how honest actions should not be punished, and she also visited me frequently, each time bringing me sandwiches from her shop, now renamed the Cannibal Deli and doing a brisk trade.

As I mentioned earlier, I was at this time taking several courses, my favorite of which was geology. I found I loved to study the rocks, in particular the various formations and fomentations they took, and the names, such as oolitic limestone, Manhattan schist, iron pyrite, carborundum, beryl, topaz, quartz crystal, gypsum, and many others. Each rock to me in the classroom was like an edible material, and even sometimes I would surreptitiously touch these small sample stones, used for identification purposes, with my tongue.

I read about volcanoes and even created a small one out of chemicals in the classroom, though I was not able to duplicate completely the different substances that spewed forth from these conical hills, the molten lavas and tephra and magmas, all at an exceedingly hot degree. This was a great love I developed for rocks, and there was a certain inanimate relationship that developed between me and stone.

Soon I had read so vastly I knew more than the teacher, a red-headed girl from C.C.N.Y. who came once a week to volunteer her time to the prisoners and who taught the course in the hopes of finding a husband. I could tell you about any sort of geological formation you would want to know, and could even determine the dip and strike of a bed of rocks, quite an accomplishment for a man who had never before known very much about anything.

Of course, it is true there was not much use for these skills inside the prison, and even less outside, though during the recreation periods I used to go out in the yard and pick up pebbles, which were mostly the same various quartz and granite chips. But I was vastly satisfied and began to work toward my high-school equivalency test, in the thought that someday I could perhaps work as a great geologist and even discover some continent.

I admit I was sadly deluded at this particular time.

As far as weaving went, there, too, I proved quite adept, which helped me to overcome some of my insecurity, which, according to the prison psychologist, I had a great deal of. I learned how to set up little hand looms and the prison even had a larger loom to be operated with the feet. I felt that here was another valuable skill to be used when I got back to New Burnt Norton. I could show my wives how to operate one of these little six-strand hand looms, using local sticks and llama wool I would import from Peru. And we would not only be able to weave our own woolen clothing, but perhaps we could sell some of the work to the tourists at the city airport.

As I say, I was a little *meshuggeneh* at this time. It did not occur to me until later that it was too hot on New Burnt Norton to wear woolen clothing.

37

s for my poor friend Joey, with his burly jaw and slovenly appearance, what was to become of him? For he was genuinely fond of me, and as far as I was concerned he was what might be called a good buddy and a man after my own heart. I see him still, slobbering over his pizza pie, or deftly flipping dough in the air, white and powdery, with his short hands, reminding me for some reason of Dante the Italian, and also the word *chiaroscuro*, graceful as ladies' hands as they pinched and molded the dough.

Unfortunately he put the pizza parlor up as collateral while gambling on the horses and he lost everything. He went to work as a bodyguard for his cousin Guich. After Warehouse 29 burned down it turned out that the electrical wiring had been illegal in some respect and the insurance people would not pay. Over forty people were killed in the fire, and Guich was sued for fifty million dollars. Even though he claimed to be broke, Guich still allowed Joey to serve as his bodyguard while he opened a chain of steak restaurants out on Long Island, but soon the pressure drove Guich from the country. Luckily he had managed to invest some money previously in a Brazilian emerald mine set deep in the Amazon jungle, which produced a miraculous lode when the highway being cut through the jungle was complete. The mine provided jobs for nearly two thousand primitive Indians, who before the emerald mine offered them employment had had nothing to do but stand along the edge of the highway waiting for the cars to begin coming through.

But Joey was again without a job. He came to visit me shortly after this in jail, and he did not look at all well. One of his arms was in a sling and he was strapped with wrapping paper or some kind of cloth around his ribs.

"Yeah," he said to me. Though he spoke cheerfully he seemed reluctant to look at me. "I got in a little altercation with one of the clientele at Guich's Steak Barn out on the island. The guy claimed the meat was tough—he suggested it might not have been beef—he didn't like the chopped liver at the salad bar and said it wasn't kosher. He wanted his money back. So I asked him to leave. Next thing I know, the guy went berserk. Started throwing steak knives, cheesecake. I tried to get him to go outside; he took up a volume of the *Encyclopædia Britannica* he had on the seat next to him. I never knew what hit me."

"An encyclopedia?"

"That's what I said. I never even noticed it. This guy starts hitting me with it. *A* through *Aur*. A real thick volume. You know I never liked getting too involved."

"I know."

"It wasn't my scene anyway, you know?"

"Yeah." I was not really able to believe him and suspected his injuries might have been related to his gambling.

"So, how you doing, anyway?" he said. He looked around at the Plexiglas and chicken-wire wall that separated the prisoners from the visitors in the visiting room. The wall was smeared and badly scratched. It was even difficult to make out his face on the other side. "They treating you all right here? You getting any tougher? You always were too sensitive, you know. Took things too personal, like."

"I tell you," I said, "you really want to know what gets to me?"

"Sure," he said and appeared to inspect a scratch or a blemish on his forearm.

"This endless brushing of teeth! Day in, day out. I don't want to have to have root canal work done! For years as an uncivilized person I neglected to brush my teeth and never felt the slightest twinge of guilt. I'm sick, sick unto death, I tell you, of the endless bristles and tubes of Crest."

"Yeah, sure," Joey said. His hand went to rub his prickly blue chin, "Mind if I smoke?"

"No," I said. "Go right ahead. I'm actually thinking of quitting. For I'm civilized now, somewhat. Or I'm trying. Yes, dandruff shampoo! I can hardly stand it. The jock itch, the crotch rot, the toenail clippers, the diaper rash. It's one thing to have these things when you're a dull-eyed savage; it's to be expected even. But this is New York City."

"Diaper rash?" Joey said.

"Sophie Tuckermann was right," I said. "I am going to have to go on a diet pretty soon. Do I look like I've put on a lot of weight? Hmm?"

"No, no. You look fine."

"Are you sure? How can you tell with this scratched Plexiglas in front of me, anyway?"

"No, no. You're fine, don't worry about it. Just start lifting weights or something."

"Maybe. I was thinking of taking up racquetball. They have pretty decent courts here, you know. On New Burnt Norton the diet, monotonous it is true, always left me slim and without constipation. Of course, it is also true that many children were undernourished there and suffered from beriberi, but not me. A diet! I won't be able to stand it. I am not able to bear the pain of hunger with much grace, you know."

"I don't know, Mgungu," Joey said. "I don't know what to tell you. So tell me: how did you like New York? When you were out, I mean. I guess I took you to a few places that weren't in the guidebooks, didn't I, huh? You know, quite frankly, I wouldn't mind going off to N.B.N. myself. Of course, it might not be that interesting after a few years, but I think I'm getting tired of being interested. I could use a little boredom for the next twenty or thirty years. Listen, you say you got three wives there? And a little village up in the mountains? Jeez, I don't know, how would you feel if I just went there to sort of look after things until you get out of here? You know, my former wife, a social worker, recently got remarried to another social worker. You'd think that would be the last I'd hear from her, but no, she's still bugging me for alimony. I could really get into leaving the country. Sure, I want to help contribute to the support of the kid, but frankly, I'm not much of a father."

"You have children, Joey? I didn't know."

"Yeah, I got one, a girl. She can't stand me, says I've got hairy arms. I tell you, I didn't get along with one wife so good, but three, that's another story. I wonder if I could handle that. I mean, sure, I guess you probably would have to be a diplomat and even a good manager to get along with all three of them, but, I mean, what the hell, I've always been good at that—I've always considered myself the executive type and anything would be better than that one-on-one that constitutes a marriage in this country." And here he gave me a little wink and would have nudged me had not the Plexiglas wall been in the way.

"Oh, Joey," I said, "you woops are all alike."

And he chuckled a little and was able at last to look me in the eye. "The word is *wop*, Mgungu. You'll never learn, will you? You and me, boy, we was real friends for a while there though, wasn't we? I mean, it may not have seemed so at the time, but in retrospect, we really were close. I remember you used to come in the shop and we'd sit around eating pizza. I make pretty good pizza, huh? You used to say you'd never tasted anything like it. I guess they don't make pizza over on N.B.N. I lost the shop, you know, did I tell you?"

"Yeah," I said, "you mentioned on the phone."

"Yeah, it was due to a horse, Gotta Angle. A very pretty horse, one of the prettiest horses you'd care to see. I was a little in debt due to some purchases I rang up on a MasterCard, you know, and I felt like I was on a lucky streak, so I went to the track and got in over my head . . . I was thinking of buying a cake or something to bring you," he said suddenly, "but I didn't know what flavor you liked. I thought you might be allergic to chocolate or something. Pretty dumb I guess, I don't know why I thought you might be. My grandmother used to be allergic to chocolate. If she even got a taste of it her face would swell up like a ballon and she got hives, you know, big red welts, it was not a pretty sight, I can tell you, and she used to go to bed with a sick headache." He put his head down on the table and began to weep, and his blue-black hair, curly and stiff, shone up at me like a piece of graphite.

"I'm sorry about your grandmother," I said.

"Oh, Jesus, I'm sorry," he said. "It's just that it's so terrible, seeing you in here like this. You're such a good guy, Mgungu, I want you to know that. I bet you don't even feel short, do you?"

"Oh, is that what is wrong? No, don't worry about it."

"Christ, Mgungu, I'm such a mess. I'm forty-three years old, I got no family; owning a pizza parlor was as big-time as I'm ever going to get, and I couldn't even hold on to that. My whole life has been a waste."

"Don't say that," I said.

"You know, when I was eighteen, I used to just hang around, doing nothing. I got into trouble, just to provide myself with a little stimulation. But the way I looked at it, I had my whole life ahead of me. I never thought the whole business would go by so quickly, with nothing of dignity accomplished."

"But what is there to accomplish," I said, "other than human being-ness?"

"I wish to God now I had become a rock-and-roll star."

I was a little surprised. "I see," I said. And I thought of my friend Kent Gable, who was by now no doubt on the other planet, with his alien friends from the UFO.

"But the thing is, rock-and-roll stars keep late hours, and my eyes get tired if I wear my contacts for too long."

"Maria Fishburn used to have trouble with her contact lenses," I said.

"Anyway," Joey said, "you're the one who should be complaining. Some friend I am. I come here, you're in prison, and

I start crying. Sheesh." He signed mournfully, for my friend was indeed in a mournful mood.

"Look," I said suddenly. "Why don't you go to New Burnt Norton and live up in the village for a while? I mean it. I know by now my wives have probably picked up some dodo instead of me—you know how women are; if it's not one man another will do just the same—and the place is probably falling apart. I would really be grateful if you would go there and oust this guy and take over for me."

"Are you serious?" Joey said. "Nah, you really can't be serious."

"Sure I am," I said. "You're my friend. I would much rather have you screwing around with my wives and fixing the chemical latrines than some stranger. Of course, you would have to promise to leave if I ever get out of this place."

"Huh?" he said, "Oh, yeah, sure, sure. No, I was just thinking. Do you mean it? Because if you do . . . Maybe you're right. After all, somebody has to be out there in the wild . . . or else the whole world will be the same and civilized. Don't you think?"

"Yeah."

"I wouldn't even have to brush my teeth if it would make you feel good to think of somebody out there not flossing. I can't believe you're serious, though."

"Yeah, I told you, I mean it. What's to stop you?"

"Well, I might just take you up on that offer. I just might do that. I really might. Do you think I would make a good savage?" And he mashed his nose down with the end of his thumb and pretended to thrust a finger through it.

"Well, I don't know," I said. "Sure, why not? As good as I was, I guess. It's an acquired characteristic. I think."

"Why not?" he said thoughtfully. "After all, you were just as good a civilized person as I was. Neither of us seems to have made too much of a success out of it. But listen, there's something I've got to ask you, and I hope you won't take offense. Are you really a cannibal?"

"Put it this way," I said. "I'm not a vegetarian."

"Yeah," he said. "Well, I guess if you can get used to eating my pizza, I can get used to just about anything, too . . ."

And we sat for some minutes, silently looking at each other from opposite sides of the smeary Plexiglas with its netting of chicken wire sealed in between, until Joey began to clean his fingernails and the guard called, "Time, everybody. All visitors must leave the visiting room. Visiting hours are over. That's all folks! " And the white and black and Spanish ladies, weeping and shuffling their enormous handbags, left the room, dragging off the sleepy children.

"Look," he said quickly. "I'll be back before I go. I'll keep in touch, and I'll let you know how things are going."

But I did not hear from him for several years, and then only by accident. One day in my job as janitor for the prison (Mr. Kirk was still pleading my case, and I was on a work-study program the institution was offering at the time) I happened to be going through an old stack of *New York Times*es before throwing them out, and I saw an article about a man who had been "discovered" by a group of explorers on their way to the Mt. Bawwaar-Yaas pyramid. In the article it said that he spoke no English and it was believed that as a child he had been kidnapped by the Lesser Pimbas, now essentially an extinct group, from a Methodist Mission. He was completely uncivilized, the journalist said, and this was an excellent opportunity for sociologists to study the effects of environment versus heredity. There was even a photograph of him looking quite content in a hammock. It was, although blurred, most definitely Joey. In the background I could barely make out the figure of Nitsa, scowling and noticeably pregnant. So I guessed he was all right.

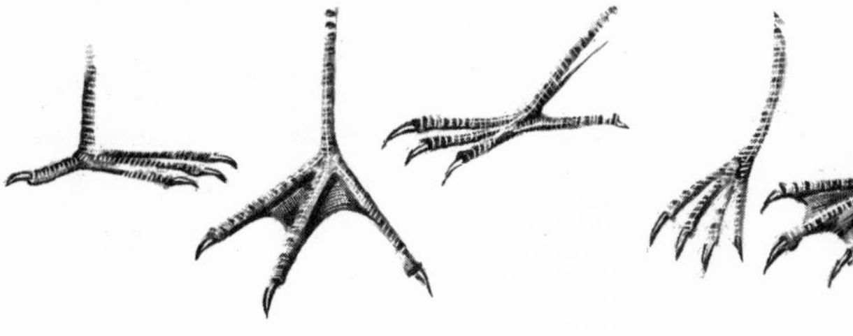

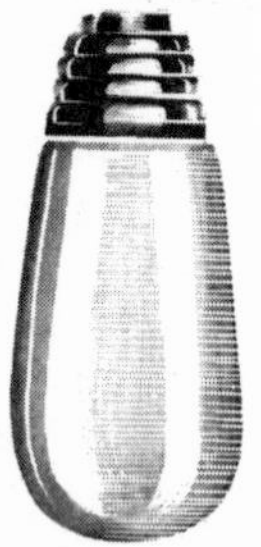

Like Grodzin's marble-cake theory, my life has proven hard to chew. I have not related everything that has happened to me since my arrival in the U.S.A.; a good deal of it, and probably the most important parts, I have left out.

But then, I'm savage, really, and not too literate and was never good at expressing myself. Still I have plenty of time on my hands that must be put to some kind of use. As I say, I'm interested in rocks of all kinds, though there are not too many of them here. But I have written to several sources asking that they be sent to me. Rocks seem essential; they are, after all, the true roots of what this planet, and therefore what we, are made of. And many rocks have with them a kind of inner peace and security hitherto unnoticed by me. I might even be tempted to say rocks contain a kind of *moodla;* primitive to be sure, and inert, but *moodla* nevertheless.

Someday soon Maria Fishburn will probably return. Then this whole mess will be dropped and I can get on with whatever it was I was doing before I ended up here. I used to raise pigs; that might be something for me to return to, perhaps on a farm. Specialized breeding is not so easy as it might seem. Nowadays it is done mostly scientifically, with special artificial-inseminating devices. Still I have always had an affinity for these animals—I could probably be put to some use.

Meanwhile if I could just get my hands on that little dwarf I would like to wring his neck, friendly as he has been to me in the past. Mr. Kirk promises he will try and get ahold of him. The way I feel about it, you see, is that there are two different types of people, not just primitive and civilized, but those who plod along right through what they want to do as if there were walls outlining their lives, and everything were serious and goal-oriented. These will use any opportunity to trample on those lesser than themselves. And then there are the other kind, constantly making mistakes; well, this is me.

There was a doctor here for a few weeks, conducting experiments on me. He was a psychiatrist named Dr. Turin and he had several interesting things to tell. The first was about the puffer fish. This is a fish that swells up to the touch, a defense mechanism when it is caught, to render it unswallowable to the predator. This fish bears with it a toxin most poisonous to man. I believe it is located behind the fish's ear. If this poison is eaten a man becomes paralyzed. His lungs are frozen and he is unable to breathe. However, the Japanese are a people fond of eating raw fish; and in Japan there are one or two gentlemen licensed to remove this puffer-fish gland to enable it edible. Why they must be licensed is this: if the blade nicks the gland, the toxin escapes imperceptibly into the fish and the dining customer dies. But the best chefs are able with their deft knives to remove all of this gland except for a tiny portion. And they are able to leave enough behind so that the person eating the fish experiences a tiny twinge of pleasure. The mouth and nose are numbed, and the eating experience is sensational.

"Very good," I said to Dr. Turin, "but why are you telling this to me?" He had me wired up to a sort of machine—part of it was a bio-feedback machine, and there were other attachments, some not so pleasant.

"You tell me, Mr. Mgungu," he said. "What do you make of that story?"

He was a cryptic man, but I was learning to respond.

As I say, I had been in therapy for some weeks, which according to my lawyer was supposed to do me a lot of good. The room was well lighted; also the chair I was attached to. At least this made a pleasant change from my cell, which I found far too small and hemming for a man used to mountainous vistas.

"You know, Dr. Turin," I said, "sometimes a person will get into my head, and there I'll be, stuck with that person walking around up there, uninvited. And that person will be talking and breathing as if it were not me, but three-dimensional. And it has been this way with many of the friends I have made here in the United States. They continue to walk around inside me though they are not here, as vivid and real, though I may have met them but once, or though no longer alive. But with you, it's a different story. How many times have I listened and listened to you, trying to make some sense out of what you are saying, but to no avail?"

"I don't know," he said. "This is something to think about."

And in my head I saw the lush palm trees and the hedged gardens with the pigs rooting about, and the thin and feathery acacias, and the cocoa trees lining the road in Jaranekta below, sprouting hard-cased, multicolored pods bright with violent mauves and yellow and red-orange. And I knew I had made a mistake.

Also I thought of Maria Fishburn, only twenty-two when I had first met her, and so pompous for one so young. "Does the punishment fit the crime, Dr. Turin?" I said. "Please answer me straight out for once."

But to this he had only a thin-lipped smile.

"All right, then, I have a story for you," I said. "If a wife needs to sew something on New Burnt Norton, you know we have not the needle and the thread. So she approaches me with a sharp stick, a stick she has specially sharpened herself until the nose of it is shrill and pointed and the branch itself stripped of bark. And she hands this stick to me; with it I make many jagged incisions along the calves of this wife, until the blood trickles down her legs, thick and dark. And meanwhile the wife has made a little cup or bowl out of a banana leaf, neatly folded, and she holds this bowl under the incisions to catch the blood. And when she has enough as she wants, she takes it and while it has not yet dried uses this blood to hold her seams together, or to fix whatever it is she is trying to mend. Blood makes a good glue, Dr. Turin; though the one default over Elmer's Glue is that it does not last forever, and after a number of months the seam will no longer hold, so the actions must be repeated. Generally this does not matter—jungle fungus does creep in to all belongings rather quickly, and they rot quite away before they have a chance to wear out."

"Aha," the doctor said, and I had the satisfaction of smiling to myself, since he believed himself to have garnered some sort of information that he was looking for to add to his records. He really was a pathetic fallacy, this doctor, like a large spider with long sparsely haired arms.

But my little joke made me forget for a moment that I was not as free as he was. And it was brought to me of how difficult it is to dwell with dignity, to construct something of gracefulness and truthfulness. So it was that I began and ended with the skin that surrounded me, and my existence had nothing to do with the walls of the prison.

Who was I, after all, but a man small in stature, a man caught up in the incidents of time for which there is no control. A man who would have given up rawness for civilization, only because not to did not make any sense. A man who had seen large trees snapped off at the root, due to the thinness of the tropical soil and the swiftness of the tropical rains which easily wear away at the base of things and can carry off a man or a pig in its path. My mind hung heavy and hurt in its hole, yet I wanted so for it to burn clearly; this in the end was my lot.

"Is that all, Doctor?" I said, and he let me go back to my room.

So I lay on my bed, carefully blowing my scrambled dreams at the ceiling in chalky clouds of cigarette smoke. I had had to bear witness to things I could not understand: all right, then, this was how it was meant to be. But I would not stop.

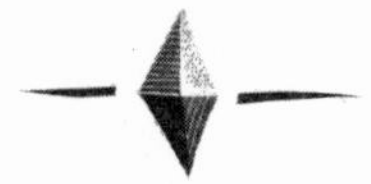

ACKNOWLEDGMENTS

The situations photographed in this book are dramatic re-enactments portrayed by actors who in no way represent the actual people in the original dilemma.

With thanks and gratitude to those who made this book possible, in particular Michael Zilkha, Girard Basquiat, Paige Powell, Betty Prashker, David Groff, Jim Davis, Susan Magrino, Amanda Urban, Wilfredo Rosado, Tony Wright, and everyone else who so generously participated.

—Introduction thanks to *Desultoria, The Recovered Mss of an Eccentric,* Baker and Scribner, 1850 (anon. author)

Design and art by Tony Wright

1. Anon.
2. Courtesy Fantasy Photo File, Inc.
3. Encyclopaedia of Vegetation, 1899.
4. Phyllis and Tama Janowitz photographed by Isadore Janowitz.
5. Photo by George Dubose.
6. With thanks to John Deyab.
7. Girard Basquiat and Paige Powell photographed by G. Dubose. Cannibal, styling—Patricia Cresswell. Miss Powell's hair and makeup—Gad Cohen for Gad Studios. Safari outfit courtesy Banana Republic. Stylist—Wilfredo Rosado.
8. Nora Fitzpatrick and Girard Basquiat photographed by G. Dubose.
9. Anon.
10. Album cover designed and modeled by Stephen Sprouse. Photograph and straitjacket—G. Dubose.
11. Anon.
12. Stephen Sprouse photographed by Patrick McMullan. Hair by Christiaan.
13. Brigid Berlin photographed by Paige Powell at Gianni's Restaurant, NYC. Styling by Wilfredo Rosado.
14. Common table altar, NYC, 1986.
15. Andy Warhol photographed by David LaChapelle in Frederick Hughes' office at Warhol Studios. Hat, jacket, shirt, scarf, courtesy Giorgio Armani. Pants by Stephen Sprouse. Styling—Wilfredo Rosado.
16. Jim Swindell, Paul D. Colliton, and John Rhodes photographed by G. Dubose.
17. Vito Bruno photographed by G. Dubose at Stromboli's Pizza.
18. Girard Basquiat photographed by G. Dubose.
19. Wedding scene photographed by David LaChapelle in the courtyard at

Tavern on the Green. Members of the Wedding—Girard Basquiat, Paige Powell, Vito Bruno, G. Dubose, Kevin Jarre, Nicole Miller, Stuart Pivar, Christopher O'Reilly, Robert Buxton, Steven Greenberg, Christiaan, Jeffrey Slonim, Edit DeAk, Stephen Sprouse, Randall Tang, Benjamin Liu, and several innocent bystanders. Miss DeAk's dress courtesy IF Boutique, NYC. Miss Powell's makeup—Randall Tang. Hair by Christiaan. Wedding outfit—Stephen Sprouse. Jewelry—Billyboy.* Cake and coffee thanks to Tavern on the Green. Flowers and floral hairpiece courtesy Salou. Furs by Ferguson.

20. Photograph by G. Dubose.
21. Photograph by G. Dubose.
22. Girard Basquiat photographed by G. Dubose.
23. Girard Basquiat photographed by G. Dubose.
24. Photograph by G. Dubose.
25. Courtesy Fantasy Photo File, Inc.
26. Photograph of Michael Schnayerson, Luca Bonetti, Jim Swindell, and Phil Quarterero by G. Dubose.
27. Courtesy Fantasy Photo File, Inc.
28. Photograph of Girard Basquiat by G. Dubose.
29. Photograph of Paige Powell by Marc Balet. Dress by Karen Beatty. Earrings—Jennifer Chaitman.
30. Photograph of Vito Bruno and a woman who wishes to remain anonymous by G. Dubose.
    Backdrop by Charles Broderson and Cynthia Altoriso.
31. Courtesy Fantasy Photo File, Inc.

Photo-fiction concept thanks to Michael Zilkha.

A Note on the Type

The initial letter of each chapter of this book was set in Wrightoni. In its structure Wrightoni displays the dark and morbid qualities of a master craftsman whose spirit is heavy with longing and pathos. The Wrightoni face has come to stand for the qualities that letters assume of grace under duress. Wrightoni died at the age of twenty-nine from high blood pressure brought on by the stress of daily existence in Italy in the sixteenth century, and too much pasta. Like his letters, Wrightoni was overweight. But it is this very brooding, weighty quality that accounts for the artistic success of the typeface.

PLATE 34

NEW BURNT NORTON

N
W
E
S
NEW GUINEA 582
Kickory Key
Gowa n Batama
Copra Factory
Methodis
Missi
Ancestral territory
of the Greater Pimbas
Crabb Cliff
JARANEKTA.pop6,895
River Ijaay
Igor
Limly Fork
Dry Salvages Rain Forest
Battery Park
Nationa
Grabmetz Peninsula
Delta of Nlfa
Terriac Island
Oscar Fishburn
lost here in 1961
AUSTRALIA 1,220
Mgu

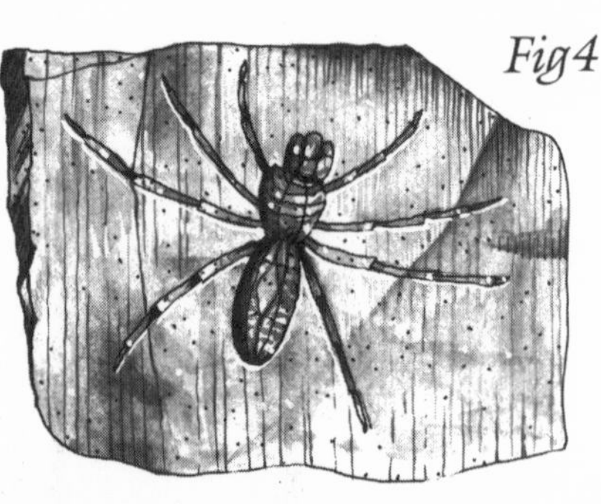
Fig4

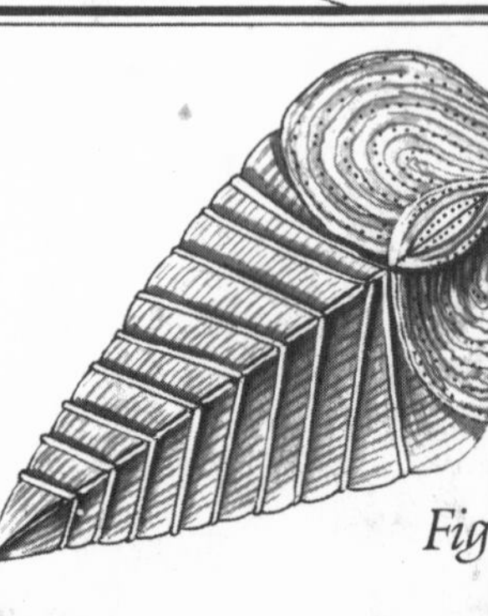
Fig